DISTRUST

LISA JACKSON

ZEBRA BOOKS
KENSINGTON PUBLISHING CORP.
www.kensingtonbooks.com

ZEBRA BOOKS are published by

Kensington Publishing Corp.
119 West 40th Street
New York, NY 10018

Compilation copyright © 2021 by Kensington Publishing Corp.
Renegade Son © 1987 by Lisa Jackson
Midnight Sun © 1985 by Lisa Jackson

Both titles comprising *Distrust* were originally published by Silhouette Books
by arrangement with Harlequin Books S.A.

All Kensington titles, imprints, and distributed lines are available at special quantity discounts for bulk purchases for sales promotion, premiums, fund-raising, educational, or institutional use.

Special book excerpts or customized printings can also be created to fit specific needs. For details, write or phone the office of the Kensington Sales Manager: Attn.: Sales Department. Kensington Publishing Corp., 119 West 40th Street, New York, NY 10018. Phone: 1-800-221-2647.

Zebra and the Z logo Reg. U.S. Pat. & TM Off.

First Zebra Books Mass-Market Paperback Printing: March 2021
ISBN-13: 978-1-4201-5243-2
ISBN-10: 1-4201-5243-2

ISBN-13: 978-1-4201-5244-9 (eBook)
ISBN-10: 1-4201-5244-0 (eBook)

10 9 8 7 6 5 4 3 2 1

Printed in the United States of America

Contents

Renegade Son

Prologue

Boise, Idaho
April 18, 1985

Chase McEnroe stared down at the cashier's check, greatly annoyed. Distrust darkened his clear blue eyes. Two-hundred-thousand dollars. More money than he'd made in all of his thirty-two years and it was being handed to him on a silver platter. *Or with strings attached.*

"So what's the catch?" he asked cautiously as he dropped the slip of paper onto his letter strewn desk. Ironically the check settled on a stack of invoices that were already sixty days past due.

"No catch," Caleb Johnson replied with a satisfied smile. "We've been over all this before, and everything's spelled out in the contract." The older man grinned encouragingly and thumped the partnership agreement with his fingers. "I trust you had your attorney go over it."

Chase stared straight at Caleb's ruddy face and nodded, but still he frowned and his chiseled features didn't relax. His tanned skin was drawn tight over angular cheekbones, square jaw and hollow cheeks.

"Let's just say that I don't trust strangers bearing gifts."

"It's not a gift. I own fifty percent of your company if you take the money."

Ah, there it was: the trap!

Rubbing a hand wearily over his beard-roughened jaw, Chase stood and walked over to the window of his small office, which was little more than a used construction trailer. He poured a cup of coffee from the glass pot sitting on a hot plate beneath the window.

"I don't like partners," Chase said almost to himself as he glared through the dusty glass to the empty parking lot. Sagebrush and grass were growing through the cracks of the splitting asphalt, as if to remind him how much he needed Caleb Johnson's money.

"The way I understand it, you could use a partner right now."

"How's that?"

"Didn't most of your staff walk off the job five weeks ago?"

Chase didn't answer. Instead he frowned into his chipped coffee cup. But Caleb's point had struck home; the unconscious tightening of Chase's jaw gave his anger away.

"And aren't they planning to start a rival company in Twin Falls with a man named Eric Conway as president?" Johnson added.

"There's a rumor to that effect," Chase replied tightly.

"So they've got the expertise, the money to back their project, the manpower to work efficiently and all the contracts that you worked ten years to develop. Right?"

"Maybe." Chase felt his muscles bunch with tension. The deceit of his best friend still felt like a ball of lead in his stomach. He'd trusted Eric Conway with his life, and the man had kicked him in the gut.

"So, the way I see it, you're just about out of options."

"Not quite." Chase took a long swallow from his coffee and set the cup on the windowsill. "I still like being the boss."

"You would be." Caleb smiled and shrugged his broad shoulders. "Think of me as a silent partner."

"So what's in it for you?"

"Your guarantee that when I'm ready with the resort—"

"Summer Ridge?"

"Right. I'll let you know, then you can come up to Martinville and make Grizzly Creek viable for trout. When the job's complete, I'll pay you by returning twenty-five percent of Relive, Inc., just the way it's outlined in the agreement." Satisfied that he'd taken care of everything, Caleb pointed a fleshy finger at the document.

"And what about the final twenty-five percent?" Chase asked, his blue eyes narrowing.

"Oh, that you'll have to buy back."

"For a substantial profit over what you paid," Chase guessed.

"Market value. Whatever that is."

"Sounds fair enough," Chase thought aloud. Not only had he looked for catches in the agreement, but he'd had his attorney poring over the documents for two weeks. Everything appeared legal. *And too good to be true.*

He returned to his chair, glanced again at the check on the thick pile of invoices and then studied the slightly heavyset man in front of him. He'd never laid eyes on Johnson before in his life, and suddenly the man was here, in his office, offering him a godsend.

"So why me?" Chase finally asked. "Why not go with Conway's outfit?"

The easy Montana smile widened across Caleb Johnson's face. "Two reasons I suppose—you've got a track record and, even though you're slightly overextended right now, you plow all of your money back into the operation of Relive. Unless Conway was the brains behind this operation, you're the best in the business."

"And the other reason?"

Caleb Johnson's eyes glittered a watery blue. "I knew your mother," he said with a reflective grin.

Something in the older man's voice brought Chase's head up. His gaze narrowed speculatively on the big man. "I never heard her speak of you," he drawled.

"It was a long time ago," Caleb replied. He tugged thoughtfully on his lower lip and gauged Chase's reaction. "Before you were born."

"And that was enough to convince you?"

"Any son of Ella Simpson had to be a scrapper."

"Her name was Ella McEnroe," Chase said slowly.

"Not when I knew her . . ."

The wistful ring in Caleb's voice rankled Chase. How had this slightly unsavory man been connected with his mother? The thought that she'd even known Caleb Johnson bothered Chase more than he'd like to admit.

In the distance the sound of a freight train whistle pierced the air as the boxcars clattered on ancient tracks. The noise broke the mounting tension in the room. Caleb glanced at his watch and then, shrugging off the memories of a distant past, stood abruptly. "Look, I've got a plane to catch. Do we have a deal?"

Chase glanced down at the check. Two hundred grand. Damn, but that money could make the difference between making it or not, especially with Conway intent on ruining him. With a nagging feeling that he was making the worst decision of his life, Chase clasped Caleb Johnson's outstretched hand.

"Deal," he said and then reached into the drawer of his desk for a pen and signed all four copies of the partnership agreement.

"You've made the right decision."

Chase doubted it but tried not to second-guess himself.

Caleb stuffed his copies of the paperwork into the pocket of his expensive, Western-style jacket and smiled in satisfaction. "Oh, there's one other thing," he said, walking to the door.

Here it comes, Chase thought, bracing himself for the elusive catch in the agreement. "What's that?"

"One of my neighbors is fighting me about developing Summer Ridge."

"Just one?"

"So far . . . oh, well, it'll all be cleared up by the time you come to Martinville. There's always a way to get people to come 'round to your way of thinking, y'know."

Yeah, like two-hundred-thousand dollars, Chase thought cynically.

Caleb waved a big hand and opened the door of the

trailer before walking down the three worn steps to the parking lot. Chase watched the big man from Montana drive off in a rented white Cadillac and tried to ignore the absurd feeling that he had just sold his soul to the devil; the same devil who had known his mother all those years ago.

Chapter One

The sun blazed hot in the summer sky. Dry grass crackled and grasshoppers flew from the path of the buckskin gelding and its rider as the horse headed toward the clear stream slicing through the arid field.

Sweat beaded on Dani's forehead and slid down her spine. She lifted the rifle to her shoulder and cocked it, her eyes squinting through the sight at the target: a tall, blond man with broad shoulders, a tanned, muscular torso, slim hips and the nerve to trespass on her property by wading in Grizzly Creek. No doubt this stranger was another one of Caleb Johnson's men.

The element of surprise was on her side and definitely to her advantage. The stranger's back was to her, his sweat-glistened muscles rippling as he waded in the mountain stream, his eyes scouring the clear ice-cold water. It didn't appear that he had heard the warning click of the hammer of her Winchester or seen the horse and rider approach.

Dani's elegant jaw hardened with determination and her lips tightened though her hands shook as she took aim. "Move it, mister!" she shouted.

The target looked up and visibly started, the muscles of his naked back bunching as he spun around to face her. Water sprayed upward from his sudden movement.

"Get the hell off my property!"

The stranger just stood in the middle of the creek as if dumbstruck, his eyes narrowing against the bright Montana sun and his body poised as if to run. But there was nowhere to hide. Aside from a few scraggly oaks, the fields of brittle sun-dried grass offered no cover. The gently sloping land was barren and dry as a bone.

Dani softly kicked the buckskin and advanced on the object of her outrage. When she was near enough to see the man clearly, she smiled at the mixture of indignation, horror and fury in his sky-blue eyes.

"I said, move it," she repeated, stopping the gelding a few feet from the creek and cocking her head in the direction of the bank where a pile of his belongings—shirt, fishing reel and worn boots—lay on the grass.

His square jaw was thrust forward, his tanned skin nearly white over his face as he slowly waded out of Grizzly Creek. He kept his gaze on the barrel of the rifle as she moved forward. The steel glinted a threatening blue in the afternoon sun. Dani kept the Winchester trained on the stranger's every move as he bent down, picked up a plaid work shirt and angrily stuffed his sinewy arms through the sleeves.

She placed the rifle across her thighs. "Why don't

you tell me what you're doing on my land?" she suggested, breathing once again when she realized that this man was complying with her orders. Some of Caleb Johnson's thugs hadn't been so easily buffaloed.

The intruder didn't flinch, but slowly buttoned his shirt. His lips were tight over his teeth, making his mouth seem little more than an angry line. "I was told this land belonged to Daniel Summers."

"*Danielle* Summers," she corrected.

"And you're she," he deduced.

"That's right." Dani almost grinned at his reaction. "Now, suppose you tell me just who you are and what you think you're doing on my property?"

"Why not?" he asked rhetorically and then muttered an angry oath under his breath.

"I'm waiting."

He shook his head and looked up at the cloudless sky. "How do I get myself into these things?" he muttered with a grimace before letting out a long, angry sigh and dropping his gaze from the heavens to horse and rider. "Okay, if you want to play out the bad B Western scenario, I'll state my name and business."

"Good." She stared down at him without a smile, her eyes glued to his chiseled features. She guessed him to be around thirty-five, give or take a couple of years. From the looks of him, the poor bastard had probably been on Caleb Johnson's payroll less than a week. Otherwise he wouldn't appear so clean-cut or have been so stupid as to wander blatantly over the property line in broad daylight.

"The name's McEnroe."

"Like the tennis player?"

He snorted at the inference, as if he'd heard it a million times. He probably had. "No relation. I'm Chase McEnroe."

"And you work for Caleb Johnson," she said, leaning over the saddle horn and pinning him with her wide gray-green eyes. Her braid of sun-streaked hair fell forward over one shoulder to settle over the swell of her breast and she forced a cold smile. "Well, let me tell you, Mr. Chase not-related to-the-tennis-star McEnroe, this is my land and I don't like anyone, especially one of Caleb Johnson's hands, snooping around. So you can take a message to your boss and tell him the next time he sends one of his flunkies around here, I'll call the sheriff."

McEnroe's blue eyes sparked and his square jaw slid to the side as he stared at her. "I think the line you're looking for is: 'Tell your double-crossing boss that the next time one of his low-life ranch hands steps one foot on my property, I'll shoot first and ask questions later.'"

Dani fought the urge to smile and arched an elegant dark brow at the man. "You're an arrogant S.O.B., aren't you?" *Not like the usual scum Caleb Johnson hired. Too smart. McEnroe wouldn't last long with Johnson.* Oddly, Dani felt relieved.

His brilliant blue eyes narrowed and his lips twisted cynically as he glanced again at the rifle. "Look, I'd like to sit around and trade insults with you, but I've got work to do."

"Work? Like trespassing?"

"I was just looking at the stream."

"On *my* side of the fence."

"I know."

"*That's* your job?" With a disbelieving sigh, she sat back in the saddle, balanced the rifle on her thighs and crossed her arms under her chest. "Surely you can come up with a better excuse than that."

Lifting a shoulder as if he didn't really care what she thought, he stuffed the tail of his shirt beneath the waistband of his jeans and tightened his belt buckle.

"So why are you here? I've already told Johnson that I'm not going to sell my land to him. *Ever.* He can build his resort right up to the property line if he wants to, but the only way he'll get this land from me is over my dead body."

"Look, lady," McEnroe said, his face relaxing slightly as he yanked off his hip waders, poured the water out of them and stepped into his scruffy boots. "I don't really give a damn one way or the other what you do. Johnson just asked me to check out the stream, and I did. Since it runs through your property, I climbed through the fence and took a look."

"Why?"

"I don't really know if it's any of your business."

"You're on my land aren't you?"

"A mistake I intend to rectify immediately," he said, grabbing his waders and creel before walking toward the sagging fence. He slipped through the slack barbed wires while keeping his eyes focused on the Winchester.

"You can tell Johnson one more thing," she said as he turned toward the Jeep parked in the middle of the field next to hers.

Chase faced her again, impatience evident on his angular features. "What's that?"

"Tell Johnson that I've hired a lawyer and if he tries any of his underhanded stunts again, I'll sue him."

"Tell him yourself," McEnroe replied furiously. "I'm out of this mess—whatever the hell it is."

With his final remark, he shook his head angrily, strode to the Jeep, climbed in and forced the vehicle into gear before starting it. The Jeep roared through the parched field, leaving a plume of dust in its wake as it disappeared through a stand of pine.

"I will," Dani decided, once she was sure Chase McEnroe, whoever the devil he was, had left and wasn't returning. "And that's not all I'll tell Johnson!" With the reins curled through the fingers of one hand, she turned the gelding toward the house and leaned forward in the saddle while gripping the unloaded rifle in her other hand.

Traitor got the message and eagerly sprinted up the slight incline toward the house. The wind whipped over Dani's face, cooling her hot skin as the quarter horse sped toward the barn, moving effortlessly over the cracked earth.

"I won't let them beat us," Dani said, as if Traitor could understand her. "Not while there's an ounce of life in my body. Caleb Johnson can hire all the new hands he wants, I won't sell! This land belongs to me and some day it's gonna be Cody's!"

She thought back to the man wading in the stream. He was different from the rest of Johnson's crew, less rough around the edges. "Just give him time," Dani muttered, reining Traitor to a stop near the weathered barn before dismounting.

After just two weeks of working for Caleb Johnson, Chase McEnroe would forget to shave, learn to spit tobacco juice in a stream between his teeth and drink himself into a drunken stupor every Friday night at the local bar in Martinville.

"What a waste," Dani said, shaking her head sadly as she thought about the furious man. She tied the reins of the gelding's bridle around a fence post near the barn, removed the saddle and started brushing Traitor's tawny coat, but thoughts of Chase kept nagging at her. She remembered his cool, blue eyes, his hard, tanned muscles, the thick thatch of dark blond hair that glinted like gold in the late summer sun and the leashed fury in his rigid stance.

"It just doesn't make any sense," she thought aloud, removing the bridle and giving Traitor a quick slap on the rump. With a snort, the horse took off to join the rest of the herd. Why would a man like Chase McEnroe hook up with the likes of Caleb Johnson?

Chase ground the Jeep to a halt in front of the two-storied farmhouse. Swearing loudly, he stormed into the building without bothering to knock. The sharp thud of his boots echoing on the polished hardwood floor announced to the entire household that he was back . . . and he was furious.

"Okay, Johnson," Chase said, every nerve ending screaming with outrage as he pushed open the door of Johnson's office and forced his way into the room. "Just what the hell have you gotten me into?"

Caleb Johnson had the audacity to smile. He didn't look much different than he had the day that Chase had met him two and a half years ago. Johnson was still a robust man who had grown up in Montana, been prominent in local politics and acquired land around Butte for less than fifty dollars an acre. At seventy, his eyes were still an intense shade of blue, his tanned skin was nearly wrinkle-free and only the slight paunch around his middle gave any indication of his age.

"What do you mean?" Caleb was already pouring bourbon into a shot glass. He set the drink on the corner of the desk, silently offering it to Chase, and then poured another stiff shot for himself.

Chase ignored the drink and crossed his arms over his chest, pulling the fabric of his shirt tight across his rigid shoulders. "That *woman! Danielle* Summers. She's got one helluva bone to pick with you and I'm not about to get into the middle of it!"

Caleb seemed almost pleased. He fingered his string tie and settled into the oxblood cushions of the leather couch. "You met her, did you?"

Chase's eyes darkened. "Met her? She almost used my butt for target practice, for crying out loud. Look, Johnson, getting myself shot was not part of the deal!"

"She wouldn't shoot you."

"Easy for you to say!"

"She doesn't like violence . . . Caleb sipped his drink and smiled.

"Like hell!"

"Dani Summers wouldn't harm a flea."

"Then what the hell is she doin' out riding her property like some goddamned sentry!" Chase shook his head and pushed his sweaty hair out of his face. He saw the untouched drink on the desk, decided he needed something to calm him down, reached for the glass of bourbon and drank a long swallow. "I don't like being threatened, Caleb."

" Don't worry about Dani."

"Don't worry about her!" Chase was flabbergasted by the older man's calm. He took another swallow of bourbon.

"Okay, you're right. I won't worry about her, because I won't deal with her or anyone else who points a rifle in my gut! Let's just forget the whole deal, okay?"

"No dice," Caleb said, "this is important."

"So is my life."

" I told you; the woman detests violence. She just wants to be left alone."

"So why was I walking on her property today?" Chase demanded, his jaw tight.

"Because it won't be hers for long."

Chase circled the scarred oak desk and leaned one hip against the windowsill. Rubbing his chin, he surveyed his partner and the place Caleb Johnson called home with new eyes. Braided rugs covered hardwood floors, pine walls were little more than a display case for weapons and tools of the Old West, a stone fireplace filled one wall and the furniture within the room was heavy, masculine and slightly worn. "She gave me a message for you. Words to the effect that you'd better leave her alone or she'd call a lawyer."

"She can't."

"Why not?"

"Hasn't got the money." Caleb downed his drink casually and lifted his feet to place them on the magazine strewn coffee table.

Chase's gut twisted and he experienced the same feeling

he had felt on the day when he'd reluctantly accepted two-hundred-thousand dollars from Johnson; the feeling that he was just a marionette and that Johnson was pulling the strings. "How do you know how much money she's got?"

"Common knowledge." Caleb smiled smugly and balanced his drink between his hands. "Her husband left her and her kid about six or seven years ago. The guy just vanished. Word has it that he took off with a hotel clerk from Missoula, but that's just gossip. Anyway, all Dani Summers had left is a nine-year-old kid and a dust bowl of a piece of property that she tries to scratch a living from."

"So why doesn't she irrigate and make the land more productive?"

"Irrigation costs money."

"Which she doesn't have."

"Right."

"But surely a bank would loan her the money, unless she's mortgaged to the hilt."

"Who knows?" Caleb took a swallow and lifted his shoulders. "Maybe she's a bad credit risk."

"You wouldn't happen to be on the board of the local bank?" Chase asked, suddenly sick with premonition.

Caleb's smile widened.

"You are a miserable son of a bitch!"

"Just a practical businessman."

"And you want her land," Chase said with a renewed feeling of disgust. "Dani Summers is the same neighbor that wouldn't sell to you two years ago, isn't she?"

Caleb grinned and a satisfied gleam lighted his eyes. "Her two hundred and forty acres sit right smack in the middle of my property. I can't very well develop the entire piece into a resort without it."

"If the land is so useless, why doesn't she sell?"

Frowning into his drink, Caleb shrugged. "Who knows? Just some damned fool notion. You know women."

Not women like Dani Summers, Chase thought with a sarcastic frown. She was the kind of woman who spelled trouble and Chase prided himself in avoiding any woman with problems. The way he figured it, he had enough of his own. Now it looked like he was right in the middle of the proverbial hornet's nest.

"Can't you build Summer Ridge without her property?"

Caleb's scowl deepened. "No."

"Why not?"

Caleb hesitated and studied Chase's intense features. The kid had so much to learn about business. It was about time he started. Caleb gambled with the truth. "Her place, the Hawthorne place, goes up to the foothills. And the hot springs are right there, at the base of the mountains."

Chase eyed his partner with new respect. "The Hawthorne place?"

Caleb swatted in the air as if at a bothersome insect. "Yeah, the Hawthorne homestead. She was a Hawthorne before she married Summers."

"So Dani Hawthorne Summers's land isn't as worthless as you'd like her to believe."

"Don't get me wrong," the older man said testily. "I've offered her . . . a reasonable price for that pathetic farm."

"But she won't sell and you've come up against the first person you've ever met who wouldn't bend."

"I wouldn't get so lofty, if I were you. Remember, I bought you a couple of years ago."

Chase didn't bother to hide his cynicism. "I remember."

"Good. Then as long as we understand each other, why don't you find a way to get Dani Summers to sell her land to me?"

"That wasn't part of the bargain. I said I'd check out the streams and do the work to make sure that the trout will run again, but I'm not dealing with *that* woman. No way." Chase finished his drink and placed his empty glass on the windowsill.

"What if I said that I'm willing to sell you back my part of your company if you can get her to sign on the dotted line?"

Chase tensed. He'd wanted to get rid of the yoke of Caleb Johnson's partnership for nearly as long as he'd agreed to it in the first place. Coming to Caleb's ranch had been the first step and now Caleb was dangling the final carrot in front of Chase's nose; the remaining twenty-five percent of the company would be his again, *if* he could convince Dani to sell her land. In all conscience, Chase could hardly afford to turn the offer down, yet he regretfully answered, "Can't do it."

"Why not?"

"The lady doesn't want to sell. She does have that right."

"Persuade her."

"Ha!" His gaze centered on Caleb's calm face. "She doesn't look like the type who's easily convinced."

Caleb smiled again. "Well, it's up to you, McEnroe. Either you want your company back, or you don't."

"I just don't like all the strings attached."

"Think of it this way, without Dani Summers's land, you won't be able to make Grizzly Creek viable for restocking of the trout, will you? The stream cuts right across her property. One way or the other, you've got to convince Dani Summers she has to sell her land to me."

Chase felt his back stiffen. "And how do you expect me to do that?"

"That's your problem." Caleb winked wickedly. "Use your imagination. She's been without a husband for over six years. Almost alone all that time." He took a long satisfied swallow of his bourbon. "Women have needs, y'know."

Chase laughed aloud at the arrogance of the man. "You expect me to try to seduce her?"

"Why not? Pleasant enough business, I'd say. Good lookin' woman."

"You've got to be out of your mind! That lady wanted to kill me today!"

"What can I say? She's passionate. I bet she'd be a regular she-cat in bed."

"And you're a ruthless bastard, you know that, don't you? I can't believe we're having this conversation!" Chase moved off of the sill and looked through the window at the well-maintained buildings comprising the center of the Johnson property. He tried to ignore the unwelcome sensation stirring inside him at the thought of making love to Dani Summers. In his mind's eye he could envision her supple, tanned body, her rich, honey-brown hair streaked by the sun, her small firm breasts . . . God, it had been a long time since he'd been with a woman. . . .

Caleb smiled to himself at Chase's reaction. "I didn't get where I am today by letting opportunities slip by me."

"And I'll wager that you've made a few of your own."

The older man smiled. "When I had to."

Chase stood and shook his head. "This time you're completely on your own. I don't bed women for business."

"Your mistake."

"Look, I've already told you that I'm out of this problem between you and Dani Summers." Chase walked to the door, placed his hand on the knob and jerked open the door. When he turned to face Caleb again, the fire in his eyes had died. "Why don't you just leave her alone? From what you've said tonight, I think the lady needs a friend rather than another enemy."

"Precisely my point," Caleb agreed with a crooked smile as Chase walked out of the room. "Precisely my point."

"Did we get any mail today?" Cody asked as Dani came into the house. The boy was sitting at the kitchen table, drinking a glass of milk. Sweat was curling and darkening his hair and dripping from his flushed face. A dusty basketball was tucked under one of his arms and Runt, a small Border collie, was lying on the floor beneath the table.

Silently cursing her ex-husband, Dani shook her head and offered her son an encouraging smile. "I don't know. I haven't been to the box."

"I'll get it." Cody finished his glass of milk, dropped the basketball and ran out of the room with the dog on his heels.

"Damn you, Blake Summers," Dani said. "Damn you for getting Cody's hopes up." She stood at the kitchen window, leaned against the counter and watched her son run the quarter mile down the dusty, rutted lane to the mailbox. In cut-off jeans and a faded T-shirt, the black dog at his heels, Cody sprinted along the fence.

Dani's heart bled for her son each time the boy brought up the subject of his father. Maybe she should have told him all of the painful truth—that Blake had never wanted the boy, that he'd had one affair after another, that he'd only married Dani because she'd inherited this piece of land, the Hawthorne property, from her folks, that the property Blake had owned, the Summers' place, he'd sold to Caleb Johnson and then gambled the money away. . . .

She squinted against the late afternoon sun and watched as Cody, his slim shoulders slumped, his tanned legs slowing, walked back to the house. Maybe It was time she talked to him about his father. At nine, Cody was nearly five feet and was just starting to show signs of pre-adolescence. Perhaps he was mature enough to know the truth.

She met her son on the porch.

"Nothin' much," Cody said, handing her a stack of bills and shrugging as if the missing letter didn't mean a thing to him.

"You got your fishing magazine," she said, trying to hand him back a small piece of the mail. He didn't lift his eyes as he pushed open the screen door.

"Cody—"

The boy turned to face her. "Yeah?"

"I know you were expecting something from your father."

Her son went rigid. His brown eyes looked into hers and Dani knew in that moment that she couldn't talk against Blake—not yet. "What about it?"

"He didn't say when he'd visit or write again," Dani pointed out.

"But it's already been three months."

"I know. Maybe he's been busy."

"And maybe he just doesn't care. Not about me. Not about you!" Cody's lower lip trembled but he managed not to cry.

"Don't think about it," Dani said, trying to comfort him.

"Don't think about my dad?" he repeated angrily. His small fist balled against the worn screen. "Don't *you* think about him?"

"Sometimes," she admitted. *Like now, when I know you're hurting.*

"You should be waitin' for him to come home!"

Dani pushed the hair that had escaped from her ponytail off her face. "I waited a long time, Cody."

"And then you divorced him," the boy accused.

Dani forced a sad but patient smile. "I know it's hard for you to understand but I can't . . . *we* can't live in the past."

"But he wrote me!" Cody said, his voice cracking. "He wrote me a letter and said he was comin' home!"

Dani leaned a shoulder against the side of the house. "I know he did, sweetheart—"

"Don't call me that! It's for babies."

"And you're not a baby anymore, are you?" She

reached forward to push his hair out of his eyes, but he jerked away.

"Aw, Mom. Give me a break!" Cody walked into the kitchen and the screen door groaned before slamming shut with a bang.

Dani looked down at the crisp white envelopes in her hand; no letter from Blake. She didn't know whether it was a blessing or a curse. Cody was getting harder to handle each day.

With a sigh Dani walked through the house to the back porch and sat for a minute on the rail to stare at the property her great-great-grandfather had homesteaded nearly a hundred years before. The sprawling acres of the farm stretched before her. A few stands of oak, pine and cottonwood spotted the acreage that descended to Grizzly Creek before slowly rising to the foothills of the hazy Rocky Mountains. Waves of intense heat distorted the image of the cattle trying to graze in the dry pastures.

Thank God the creek was still running! And the snow-pack on the mountains was still visible. So this year, at least, she wouldn't run out of water.

So what was Chase McEnroe doing in the stream? A new fear paralyzed her as she thought about the rugged-looking stranger and the fact that he worked for Caleb Johnson. Surely Caleb wouldn't stoop to sabotaging her only source of water for the cattle, would he? He'd tried a lot of underhanded methods to force her to move, but he wouldn't . . . *couldn't* cut off her water!

"I think it's about time to pay my neighbor a visit," she muttered to herself as she straightened. *Maybe tomorrow.* Right now she had to deal with Cody, so Caleb Johnson and Chase McEnroe would have to wait.

* * *

Just being on Caleb Johnson's land made Dani's skin crawl. The man was poison and she could feel it as she parked the pickup and walked up the brick path to the imposing two-storied farm house. Built of sturdy white clapboard with black shutters at the windows and a broad front porch running its width, the house was as imposing and cold as Johnson himself.

Dani pounded on the front door and waited impatiently for someone to answer.

Someone did, but not Caleb Johnson. Instead of being able to vent her wrath on Johnson as she had hoped, Dani was standing face to face with Chase McEnroe for the second time in two days.

At the sight of her, Chase's eyes narrowed and his jaw tightened. "If it isn't Calamity Jane," he drawled, moving out of the doorway as if to let her pass. "What can I do for you?"

"Nothing," she replied stiffly. A nervous sweat dampened her palms. It was one thing to come across this man when she had the advantage of being on her own property, astride a large gelding and holding a rifle. Standing toe to toe with him on Caleb Johnson's front porch was another matter entirely. Bracing her slim shoulders, she stated her business. "I'm looking for Caleb."

He lifted a skeptical eyebrow. "He's not here right now."

"Where is he?"

"In town."

"When will he be back?"

"I don't know." Chase offered her a humbling grin. "I'm

just the help." His smile became hard. "You remember—the arrogant S.O.B. and flunky you caught on your land."

"I remember," she replied, returning his stare without flinching. Pride lifted her chin and kept her gaze cool. "I just hope you gave Johnson my message."

"Loud and clear."

"Then I guess we won't have a problem anymore, will we?"

"Not as long as you keep that rifle locked in a gun closet and throw away the key."

"I don't think so, Mr. McEnroe. Not until I'm sure you'll stay off my property." She saw the tightening of his jaw and decided to make herself crystal clear. "And that includes staying away from any water running through my land. I have water rights and I intend to protect them."

"With a shotgun."

"Rifle," she corrected, realizing he was baiting her. "And whatever else it takes to get the message through your boss's thick skull: My property is not for sale or lease. He can build a city the size of New York around my land and I won't change my mind."

Chase leaned against the doorjamb and crossed his arms over his chest. Some of the harshness left his features "Tell me, Mrs. Summers," he suggested, noting that Dani bristled when he mentioned her marital status. "Are you always so tough?"

"Always," she lied. "Especially when I'm dealing with Caleb Johnson *or* his hands."

Chase's lips curved into an amused smile and his brilliant blue eyes softened to the point that Dani noticed how handsome his angular features could be. "I'll tell him you dropped by."

"And you'll let him know it wasn't a social call?"

"My guess is that you haven't dropped over here with an apple pie or for a leisurely chat in years," he mocked.

"Just give him the message."

"Are you expecting a response?"

"No." She placed her hands on her slim, jean-clad hips. "As long as you and the rest of Johnson's employees stay on this side of the fence, I'm satisfied. If not, I'll contact my attorney."

"And what's the attorney's name?"

Dani forced a smile though her stomach was churning. The man had just called her bluff. "Let's try and keep him out of it," she replied. "I don't think Caleb wants to get into a legal battle any more than I do."

"He claims you don't have an attorney; that you're bringing up this potential lawsuit as an empty threat."

"Try me," Dani said, hoping that she wasn't provoking McEnroe into following her suggestion. "I just hope it doesn't come to a costly legal battle. Neither Caleb nor I want the adverse publicity or the expense."

"I don't know," Chase thought aloud, walking to the post supporting the porch roof and leaning against the painted wood. "Caleb seems to have his mind set. He's already spent a fortune on architects, engineers, surveyors, lawyers and politicians. I don't think one more stumbling block is gonna deter him."

"We'll see," she said grimly, anger coloring her face.

"I'm afraid we will, lady," he agreed, seeing for the first time the trace of fear in her large gray-green eyes.

"Just tell him why I came by."

Dani turned on her heel and tried to ignore the dread stealing into her heart. So Johnson was going to play hardball. She walked down the brick path and ignored the urge to run. She could feel McEnroe's eyes on her back as she climbed into the pickup and shoved it into gear. As she cranked the wheel and turned the ancient rig around, she slid a glance through the window toward McEnroe. He was still where she'd left him, on the porch, leaning casually against the post and watching her intently. She could feel the burn of his eyes against her skin.

Oh, God, she thought desperately. *Johnson won't be satisfied until he takes it all*. Then, forcing her fatalistic thought aside, she muttered, "Pull yourself together, Dani. Dammit, Johnson can try to take your land, but if he does he'll find that he and McEnroe and anyone else who's involved with him will be in for the fight of their worthless lives!"

Chapter Two

For three days Dani watched Chase.

From her vantage point at the house, she had a view of the surrounding property from all angles. To the east toward the county road, there were only two small fields that were filled with livestock. Hereford cattle and a few horses mingled and grazed in the dry fields. To the west, behind the cabin, the larger acreage dipped down before slowly rising at the base of the mountains. Grizzly Creek, running south from Caleb Johnson's land, cut through the westerly side of her property in a clear blue ribbon and offered the only respite, save her hand-dug well, for the parched land.

Dani gave credit where credit was due and Chase McEnroe was the most persistent man she'd ever met. Though he'd stuck to his part of the bargain and stayed on Caleb Johnson's property, he'd pushed the boundaries to the limit, often walking along beside the fence posts and surveying the water rushing through her land.

She observed him wading in the creek, sometimes with another man, but usually alone. Though she never really understood why, she watched him from a distance.

One day, while she had been bucking hay, Dani had seen Chase fly fishing in the stream. Later, after she and Cody had stacked the bales in the barn, she'd observed Chase digging in the streambed. Dani had never caught him on her side of the fence, although he strayed near the property line, staring over the barbed wire to her land and the life-giving water slicing through the dry fields.

"I wonder what Johnson's got up his sleeve," she muttered to herself as she hoed a row of potatoes in the small garden near the backyard. An uneasy sensation had been with her ever since she'd spoken with Chase at the Johnson farmhouse. There had been something in his eyes, something close to pity, that had made her back stiffen in pride and had caused a stab of dread to pierce her heart. "That man knows something," she decided, straightening and leaning on her hoe to ease the tight muscles of her lower back. "And if I were smart, I'd try to find out what it is."

It was nearly dusk and McEnroe was still near the creek, shading his eyes against a lowering sun as he studied the rippling water. It crossed Dani's mind that he might wait until it was dark and then trespass on her land. By why? And what would he find in the darkness?

"And who cares?" she said aloud, grabbing her hoe and walking angrily back to the house. Sweat was dripping down her dust-smudged face as she shoved the hoe into the shed near the back porch and went inside.

Cody was propped on the worn sofa in front of the television and Runt was parked on the floor in front of him. At her entrance, Runt lifted his black head and thumped his tail on the floor; Cody hadn't noticed that his mother had come into the house.

Dani looked around the room and frowned. The dinner dishes were still on the table and Runt's dish was empty. "Cody?"

He slid a glance in her direction but didn't move. "Yeah?"

"I thought you were going to clear the table."

"I will . . . I will."

Dani sat on the arm of the overstuffed couch and smiled at her son. "I was hoping it would be sometime this century."

"Aw, Mom," Cody grumbled, his face crumpling into a frown as he tried to concentrate on the television.

"I mean it."

"I said I'd do it, didn't I?"

Sighing, Dani leaned against the back of the couch. "Look, we had a deal. You feed Runt, do the afternoon chores and clear the table, right?"

"Right."

"I think it's only fair that you do them the minute they need to be done."

He looked at her blankly. "Why?"

"Because the cattle, horses and dog need to be fed on time. As for the dishes, I'd like to clean them up and put them away before midnight, okay?"

Cody, wearing his most put-upon expression, sighed loudly. "Things wouldn't be like this if Dad was home," the boy said, glancing out of the corner of his eyes for her reaction.

"You don't know that."

"You wouldn't have to work so hard and . . . and . . . neither would I!"

Dani tried to hold onto her patience. "Cody, you have to understand that things never would have worked out between your father and me even if he had stayed on the farm."

Cody remained silent, staring at the television. As Dani rose from the couch, he muttered, "You never gave him a chance." And then, seeing his mother stiffen, he said a little louder, "The kids at school say he ran off with another woman. Is that true?"

"Where did you hear that?" she asked. "School's been out for a couple of months."

"Is it true?"

Dani's shoulders slumped and she rubbed her temples. She was too tired to start this kind of conversation with Cody, but saw no way to avoid it. "I think so," she admitted.

"Why?" Cody turned his accusing brown eyes on her.

"I don't know."

"I heard the kids talkin' at school on the day that I got the letter from Dad."

"You took it to school?"

"Yeah." He chewed on his lower lip. "Maybe it wasn't such a good idea, huh?"

"What do you think?"

"Isabelle Reece told me that her pa says Dad left because you weren't woman enough to hold him."

Dani felt her throat tighten but managed a smile. "That's the way Isabelle's father *would* say it. I wouldn't put much stock in Bill Reece's opinion . . ." She took hold of Cody's hand and squeezed his fingers before letting go. "Things aren't always quite that simple."

"Dad hurt you, didn't he?" Cody deduced.

"A little."

"Do you still love him?"

Dani paused. It was a question she'd asked herself

often in the past six and a half years. "No." She saw her son cringe. "Oh, I did love him. Once. A long time ago."

"But what happened?"

"A lot of things, I guess," she admitted. Dani felt the sting of tears behind her eyes but refused to give in to the urge to cry over Blake Summers. What they had shared was long over. "We got older, grew in different directions. Your dad wanted to sell the farm and move to Duluth."

"Minnesota?"

"Yep."

"Why didn't you?"

Dani hesitated. "It was hard for me to leave the farm."

"Why?"

She lifted a shoulder. "The same reason it would be hard to leave now. This place means a lot to me and I'm not talking about money. It's been in the family for so many years."

"So?"

"So I love it."

"More than you loved Dad."

Dani smiled sadly. "I don't like to think so. I know it's hard for you to understand but when your dad left me, my mother-your grandmother-was still alive. She lived here, with us. The farm was really hers, you know. I couldn't ask her to sell it. Her great-grandfather had homesteaded this piece."

"Big deal!"

"It was a big deal. Still is. Anyway, I told your dad I would move with him, but he claimed that he needed the extra cash from the sale of the property to get settled in Duluth.

"When he finally left, grandma was sick and you were

very young. It was the middle of winter and he said he'd
send me some money in the spring so that I . . . we—you
and I—could join him."

"But he never sent the money."

"Right."

"And he found another . . . woman?"

"I guess so," Dani said quietly, seeing no reason to
bring up the fact that Blake's interest in other women had
started long before he'd left Montana.

Cody sat still for a minute before turning large hope-
filled eyes toward his mother. "So maybe he's changed
his mind and wants to come back. Maybe now he'll come
home."

"He didn't say that in his letter, did he?"

"He kind'a did. Remember. He said, 'See ya soon.
Love, Dad.'"

*And it had been nearly three months since the damned
letter had arrived.*

"And he said that he'd write again," Cody added. "So
maybe he is coming home. Maybe he's on his way back
here right now! Wouldn't that be great!"

Hating to dampen Cody's spirits, she offered him a
small smile. "I don't think he'll be back. At least not for
a while."

"But when he gets here?" Cody asked hopefully.

"*If* he gets here," she said with a sad smile, "we'll just
have to cross that bridge when we come to it, won't we?"
She cocked her head in the direction of the kitchen. "Now,
I'm going upstairs to shower, Why don't you tackle the
dishes?" She slapped him fondly on the knee. "Deal?"

"Deal," he replied, rolling off the couch and nearly

falling on top of Runt, who growled at having to move from his favorite position near the fireplace.

Dani climbed the stairs and heard the sound of plates rattling as Cody cleared the table. *He's a good boy*, she thought to herself. *You've just got to take the time to talk with him and quit avoiding the truth about his father.*

Forty-five minutes and a relaxing shower later Dani came down the stairs to find Cody back in front of the television, a huge bowl of popcorn in his lap. The table had been cleared and the dishes had been placed in the dishwasher. The mess from making the popcorn still littered the kitchen, but Dani decided not to mention it.

"You've been busy, haven't you?" she asked.

"Yeah. I decided you were right about the chores."

"Aren't I always?" she teased.

"Oh, Mom, give me a break!" But Cody laughed and offered Runt a piece of popped corn, which the anxious dog swallowed as if he had been starved for days.

One glance at the dog's bowl near the back door indicated to Dani that Runt had been fed recently. As she straightened the kitchen, cleaning the counters that Cody had missed, Dani called over her shoulder, "I think it's about time you went to bed, don't you?"

"It's still light out!"

Dani glanced out the window over the sink. The only illumination over the land was from the silvery half moon. "It's not light and it's nearly ten," she pointed out as she finished wiping the counters.

"Just a little longer," the boy begged.

"All right. When the show's over, then you can read in

bed for a while, but I think you'd better hit the hay soon; my friend. Big day tomorrow."

"Doing what?"

"Guess."

Cody groaned. "Hauling hay again."

"You got it."

"So why are you all dressed up? Is someone coming over?" the boy asked with a frown as he stared at his mother.

"Hardly. It's too late for company." Dani laughed and shook her head. The damp strands of her long hair brushed the back of her blouse. "And, for your information, I'm not dressed up. You're just used to seeing me in my work clothes."

Cody eyed her clean jeans and crisp cotton blouse. "So why didn't you put on your pajamas?"

"Too hot and I thought I'd drink some lemonade on the back porch." She turned to face her son, an affectionate grin spreading across her tanned face when she recognized the concern in his eyes. "Hey, just because I changed from dirty work clothes doesn't mean you have to give me the third degree. But thanks for the compliment."

A few minutes later, Runt pricked up his black ears and growled just as the sound of an approaching engine caught Dani's attention.

"Hey, Mom. I think somebody's here," Cody said, looking over his shoulder and silently accusing her of lying. "You said you weren't expecting anyone!"

"I wasn't . . . I mean, I'm not." Dani was drying her hands on a dishtowel just as there was a knock on the door.

She glanced through the window and recognized Chase McEnroe, who was standing on the porch. *Now what*, she wondered, inwardly bracing herself for another confrontation with Caleb Johnson's most recent acquisition.

Opening the door, she pursed her lips and stared into his eyes. "Obviously you don't know how to take a hint, Mr. McEnroe."

"I was in the neighborhood," he commented dryly.

"Hey, Mom. Who is it?" Cody asked, dragging himself off the couch and sauntering to the door.

"This is Mr. McEnroe—"

"Chase," he corrected, smiling at the boy and offering his hand.

"And this is my son, Cody," Dani said, introducing the boy as Cody took Chase's hand and looked at the man suspiciously.

"Chase works for Caleb Johnson," Dani continued, and Cody immediately withdrew his hand. "I think maybe you should go upstairs to bed," Dani said. "Obviously Mr. McEnroe has business to discuss with me."

"You sure?" Cody asked.

"Positive." Dani's eyes left her son's to stare into Chase's enigmatic blue gaze.

"Okay." Cody went to the bottom of the stairs, looked over his shoulder, whistled to Runt, and then ran up the stairs, the black dog following eagerly. A few seconds later Dani heard the door to Cody's room close.

Crossing her arms under her breasts, she leaned a hip against an antique sideboard near the door. "What do you want?"

"To talk with you."

"So talk."

"This may take a while."

Sighing, Dani gestured toward the living room. "Okay. Come in."

Chase sauntered into the room, eyeing the contents of the cabin. Rustic pieces of furniture, well worn but comfortable, were placed between family antiques and heirlooms. A hand-knit afghan was draped over the back of the couch and pieces of embroidery and appliqué adorned the wooden walls. It was small, but homey and comfortable. *The house fits her*, Chase thought as he took a seat on the hearth of the stone fireplace and leaned forward, hands over his knees, *just as Caleb's meticulous but cold farmhouse fits him.*

Deciding that beating around the bush wouldn't accomplish anything, Dani walked into the living room, snapped off the TV, sat on the arm of the couch and faced him. "So, what do you want? Why are you here?"

Chase smiled. A brilliant, white-toothed grin slashed his tanned face and made his blue eyes sparkle. "You can drop the tough lady act with me."

"It's not an act."

"That's not what Caleb says."

Dani's lips tightened and a challenge flashed in her eyes. "Caleb doesn't know me very well. Otherwise he wouldn't keep trying to force me into selling my place to him."

"By offering you a reasonable price for it?"

Dani wasn't about to confide in one of Johnson's men; whether he was interesting or not. "Reasonable?" she repeated, rolling her eyes. "Look, Mr. McEnroe, obviously you came here for a reason, so why don't you get to the point and tell me what it is?"

"All business, right?"

"Right. Shoot," she encouraged and Chase laughed out loud. It was a deep rumbling sound that bounced off the rafters and dared to touch a secret part of Dani's heart.

"Bad choice of words," he said.

"Okay." She smiled in spite of herself. "So why are you here?"

"I want answers."

"From me?"

"To start with." He stood up and stretched before reaching upward to the rifle mounted over the mantel.

Dani bristled. "What do you think you're doing?" she demanded, leaping up and stepping forward.

He ignored her outcry and opened the chamber of the weapon. It was empty. "Just checking," he said, almost to himself.

"On what?"

"To see which one of you is lying. You or Caleb Johnson." He replaced the Winchester and looked over his shoulder at her. "So far the score is zero/zero for the truth."

"I think you'd better leave," she said, angry with herself for allowing him to enter her house in the first place.

"Not yet."

"If you don't—"

"Yeah. I know, I know." He walked around the room, staring at the woven baskets, brass pots, worn furniture and scratched wooden floor. "If I don't leave, you'll call the sheriff or that fictitious attorney of yours."

Shaking with anger, Dani stifled an urge to scream at him, and planted her hands firmly on her hips. "Just what is it you want, Mr. McEnroe?"

"How many times do I have to tell you to call me Chase?"

"And how many times do I have to tell you to get off my property?"

"I'll go, I'll go," he agreed amiably, though his jaw was hard. "I just want some answers."

Her temper snapped. "Well, so do I! Just who are you and why are you here?"

"I told you who I was, the other day, when you so graciously pointed the barrel of your rifle at me. As to what I do, I own a small business, the headquarters of which are located in Boise," he said, focusing his sky-blue eyes on her. "I rehabilitate streams, like Grizzly Creek, to make them viable for trout."

"Come again?"

He smiled slightly. "A lot of streams and rivers have become too dirty for the fish to spawn."

Dani shook her head and held up her palm to quiet him. "I don't believe you."

"Why would I make it up?"

"Heaven only knows. Probably because Caleb Johnson asked you to."

Pushing his hands into the pockets of his jeans he leaned against the fireplace, his broad shoulders resting on the mantel. "Contrary to your opinion, I don't do everything Johnson asks me to."

"Then you'll be fired soon," she said flatly.

"I don't think so. Caleb Johnson and I are partners."

"Partners!" Dani repeated, the word strangling her throat. *Good Lord, that was worse!* "In what?"

"A few years ago, I needed capital. For my business."

He looked at the pictures on the mantel and fingered one of Dani and Cody sitting astride the buckskin. In the snapshot Dani was laughing, her arms securely around a grinning four-year-old Cody. Chase stared at the picture a long time, taking it from its resting place on the mantel.

"You were saying," she prodded, feeling his presence filling the small cabin. Just the fact that he was in her home made her uneasy; more aware of him as a man, and less threatened. She had to remind herself that he was the enemy.

He returned the photograph to its spot. "I was telling you that just when my business needed funds for advertising and expansion, Caleb Johnson walked into my life."

"Convenient," she said dryly.

He frowned at the distasteful memory, remembering the unlikely events and odd set of circumstances that led Caleb Johnson to his door. "Maybe too convenient," he agreed, bothered again by Caleb's association with his mother. Stepping away from the fireplace, Chase looked out the back window, toward Grizzly Creek. "Anyway, Caleb offered me two-hundred-thousand dollars to become partners with me, and I took his money because I thought Relive needed a shot in the arm."

"Relive?"

"My company."

"Oh. And so Johnson provided it."

"Right."

"Money." Dani sank onto the couch. "Of course. That's all a man like Johnson can understand." She looked at Chase thoughtfully.

Chase was mesmerized by her stare. Her gray-green eyes seemed to look past the surface and search for the inner man. "Let me guess," Dani said. "There's a catch to this 'partnership.'"

His dark brows rose appreciatively. "A small one. Johnson has agreed to sell a quarter of the company back to me if I can rehabilitate Grizzly Creek. But I can't do that without your cooperation."

Here it comes, she thought. "What kind of cooperation?"

"If you won't sell or lease your land to Caleb—"

"I won't. You know that."

"Why not?"

Because Caleb wants it all and this farm is all I have; this land and my son. "Johnson's a snake. I don't like him and I don't trust him."

"What's the difference? His money is green."

Her eyes flashed. "Money isn't the issue."

"What is?"

"My right to live here, on this land, without *having* to sell. It's not that I'm really against the resort; I'm just against the resort on *my* land."

"Isn't that a little proprietary?"

"Damn right. The way I look at it, I am the proprietor. And maybe I would have changed my mind if Johnson would have played by the rules."

"He didn't?"

"What do you think?"

"I don't know."

Dani's muscles ached with tension. "Believe me, he's tried everything he could to get rid of me and it sticks in my throat."

"So you try to thwart him."

"I see it as exercising my rights," she pointed out, her voice rising.

Chase thought for a moment. He really didn't blame Dani. Didn't he have some of the same reservations about Caleb himself? Some of the things Caleb had told him just didn't quite seem to hold water. He tried a new tack. "Then I want your permission to work in the water on your land."

"Forget it." She shook her head and the glow from the dim lights in the room caught in her hair. "I told you: I don't trust that man and I don't trust you."

"So what has Caleb Johnson done to make you so suspicious?"

Dani laughed bitterly and looked at her hands. "Everything short of planting explosives in my house," she said, and then realizing that Chase might have come for the express purpose of prying information from her to take to his "partner," she became quiet.

She heard him approach, but didn't expect the touch of his fingers to warm her shoulder. Surprised, she raised her head, her startled gaze meeting his.

"You can trust me," he said, his voice deep and slightly husky. "I'll be straight with you."

Dani stared at the sincerity of his features, the honest lines of his rugged face, the depths of his deep blue eyes. If there were any one she could trust, she felt that Chase McEnroe might just be the man.

He started to bend over her, and for a moment Dani had the absurd impression that he might kiss her, but he drew away and she shook her head at her own stupidity. If men like Blake and Caleb Johnson had taught her anything, it was never to trust a man who had an ulterior motive.

"I think you'd better go," she whispered, shifting so that his fingers no longer touched her. "And don't come back."

"You think I'm your enemy."

"You are."

"Me and the rest of the world?" he asked. "Or just men in general?"

Stung and seething, Dani stood and faced him. "You, Caleb Johnson and anyone else, man or woman, who tries to steal my land from me."

"Steal?" His eyes narrowed thoughtfully. "Caleb Johnson tried to *rob* you of this land?" He seemed genuinely surprised and more than a little dubious.

Dani's lips twisted at the irony of it all "Go ask Johnson about it," she said. *As if you don't know already.* For all Dani knew about him, Chase could be a consummate actor playing a well-rehearsed role or a simple con man lying through his beautiful Colgate-white teeth.

"I will," he promised, heading for the door.

"Good!"

When he got to the door, he hesitated and his broad shoulders slumped as he turned around. "Dani?"

She didn't answer, but inclined her head.

"For what it's worth. Whatever this . . . problem is between you and Johnson, I'm not part of it. I told Johnson as much."

"But you *are* his partner."

Chase ground his back teeth together. "That's right," he admitted.

"And you did come here to get me to either sell, lease, rent or let you use my land."

He looked at her silently and the tension in the air seemed to crackle with the fire in her eyes.

"Then you have to understand, Mr. McEnroe, you can stand in front of that door until hell freezes over and I won't believe a word you say."

A muscle worked in the corner of his jaw and his blue eyes blazed angrily. "Okay, lady, have it your way. I just thought I could help you. Sorry if I wasted your time!"

Chase strode angrily out of the room, letting the door slam shut behind him. The hot night air did little to cool his seething temper as he strode to his Jeep, climbed inside and roared down the long lane leading back to the country road and eventually to Caleb Johnson's property.

Just a couple of months, he thought with an inward groan, a*nd then I'll be out of it. I'll be able to leave Dani Summers, her suspicious kid, and Caleb Johnson. Then they can all go for each other's throats for all I care!*

He slowed as the Jeep reached the main road. When the vehicle had come to a complete stop, Chase cranked the wheel of the Jeep hard to the right. Right now he couldn't face Caleb Johnson's smug face or the smell of the old man's money. Seeing the way Dani Summers lived soured Chase's stomach. In the distance, the lights of Martinville brightened the night sky. The town wasn't much more than a grocery store, post office, gas station and a couple of churches, but it did have a bar. Chase decided that the smoky atmosphere of Yukon Jack's had to be more comforting than the cold intenor of Caleb Johnson's house. Anything did.

Unreasonably he thought about Dani again and he experienced a tightening in his gut. She was beautiful, no doubt about it. With wavy sun-streaked hair that fell almost to her waist, high, flushed cheekbones and wide sensual lips, she was the most attractive woman he'd met in a long while.

The fact that her eyes could look right through him only added to her appeal and innate sexuality. She was trim and lean, probably strong and obviously intelligent; attributes Chase didn't normally look for in a woman. However, he sensed that Dani was different than the women he'd seen over the past few years and it worried him. It worried him a lot.

"Don't forget the chip she's got on her shoulder," he warned himself, trying to discourage his fantasies of the spitfire of a woman. "And the rifle-loaded or un-loaded. A dangerous lady any way you cut it."

So why then did he think about the photograph on the mantel? A snapshot of a laughing woman and happy child astride a rangy horse in the bright Montana sun. The image lingered in his mind even as he parked the truck, stepped across the concrete sidewalk and strode into the noisy smoke-filled interior of Yukon Jack's.

Chapter Three

"That's the last of it," Dani said, wiping the sweat from her eyes.

"Thank God," Jake responded with a groan. The lanky boy was one of the two brothers Dani had hired to help her haul the baled hay into her barn.

It was late in the season for cutting hay, but with the unexpected breakdown of her equipment earlier in the summer, she'd been forced to rent a baler from a neighboring rancher after he'd finished with his own fields. Though she couldn't prove it, she suspected that her machinery had been tampered with—by someone from Caleb Johnson's place—just as she suspected other problems at the farm had been instigated by Johnson or one of his hands. The stolen gasoline, sick cattle and broken hay baler were just a few of the worries she'd faced in the past year. Maybe they were coincidence. But the fact that the problems had increased since she'd refused to sell all of her farm to Johnson made her uneasy. Very uneasy.

She slid an angry glance toward the neighboring acres and frowned. "You're imagining things," she muttered as she put the tractor into gear. "Just because you couldn't get a part to fix the old baler." With a roar the tractor started moving again.

Cody, Jake and Jonathon climbed onto the top of the bales stacked carefully on the trailer as Dani drove slowly toward the barn through the straw stubble in the field.

It was nearly twilight, but she had opted to work late rather than face another day painstakingly driving the tractor through the fields and lifting hundred-pound bales of dry hay onto the flatbed trailer. Dani hadn't wanted to gamble that her cut hay might get ruined in the rain. She looked at the purple sky and noticed the clouds silently gathering overhead. If the weather forecast were to be believed, there was a good chance of thundershowers later.

The old tractor chugged up the slight incline to the barn and Dani carefully backed the trailer into the open door. The boys, though tired and dusty, put on their gloves and began placing the bales on the elevator and stacking them in the loft.

Dani cut the engine of the tractor and hopped to the ground. Climbing into the hayloft, she began to help Cody and Jake stack the bales while Jonathon loaded the elevator. The interior of the weathered barn was dark and musty, but the scent of freshly mown hay mingled with the dust.

"That about does it," Dani said with a tired grin as Jake shouldered the last bale into place. After climbing down the ladder, she tossed her gloves onto an old barrel and pushed the hair from her face. "Now, who wants a Coke?"

"Make mine a double," Jake teased, offering Dani a cocky sixteen-year-old grin as he jumped down from the loft.

"Mine, too," his younger brother agreed.

"Cody?"

"Yep," her son said with a smile.

"You got it," she laughed. "And Cody, you're off duty tonight; I'll do the chores and clear the table. You've worked hard enough for one day."

Cody beamed, scratched Runt behind the ears and walked with the other boys to the back porch. Dani went inside the house, pulled the Cokes out of the refrigerator and opened the chilled bottles before returning to the back porch and passing them around. Jake held the cold bottle to his hot forehead before tossing back his sweaty head, placing the bottle to his lips and swallowing the contents of the bottle in one long drink.

"I get the message," Dani said, returning to the house and grabbing three more Cokes. She took them to the back porch and was relieved that the boys' thirst had apparently slackened. Cody, Jake and Jonathon were content to sip from their bottles.

"I'm gonna get the mail," Cody said, while the two older boys sat on the rail finishing their drinks.

Dani felt her heart twist in pain. Cody never gave up thinking that his dad would write him again. "All right."

Cody whistled to Runt and ran around the corner of the house. Dani's shoulders slumped in defeat and she took a long swallow of the cold cola. Every day this summer Cody had run to the mailbox expecting a letter from his father and it had never come. Dani didn't think this day would be any different. Nor would the days that followed. If only Blake hadn't written the one friendly letter and buoyed Cody's spirits.

If I ever get my hands on him, I'll strangle him, she thought angrily, her fingers tightening around her bottle.

While the two brothers talked, Dani leaned against a post supporting the roof of the porch and stared across the fence to Caleb Johnson's property and Grizzly Creek. Things had changed in the past week.

The day after Chase had come to her house, heavy equipment had rolled over Johnson's land. Not only had there been dredging in the creek, but several loads of gravel had been carefully spread in the water, and a few fallen fir trees had been strategically placed along the banks of the stream.

While Dani had been bucking hay, she'd observed Chase, stripped to his jeans, as he supervised the operation. He was always at the creek at sunrise, carefully studying and working in the clear water. He supervised the placement of the gravel and boulders as well as the digging of deeper pools in the channel of the stream.

She couldn't help but notice the rippling strength of his muscles as he'd helped pull a log into position, or the way his shoulders would bunch when things weren't going just as he'd planned. The bright sun had begun to bleach his blond hair and his skin had darkened with each day. From her position driving the tractor, Dani had been able to observe him covertly and she'd begun to recognize his gestures; the way he would rake his fingers through his hair in disgust, his habit of chewing on his thumbnail when he was tense, or the manner in which he would set his palms on his hips when he was angry.

Several times she'd found him looking her way, and each time that he'd caught her eye, he'd offered a lazy, mocking grin. One time he'd even had the nerve to wave to her, and Dani, her cheeks burning unexpectedly, had responded by quickly stepping on the throttle of the tractor and turning her full attention to the task of getting the hay into the barn.

"What's goin' on over there?" Jake asked when he noticed Dani staring at the heavy machinery on the adjoining property. "I think Johnson's hired someone to clean up the creek—make it more livable for trout." Actually she knew it for a fact. Just to make sure that Chase had been straight with her, she'd called the Better Business Bureau in Boise and found out that Relive Incorporated was, indeed, a business owned by Chase McEnroe and Caleb Johnson.

"So he's cleaning up Grizzly Creek for that resort, Summer Ridge or whatever it's called, right?"

"Right." Dani's back stiffened slightly.

"Is it named after you?"

Dani smiled at the irony of the question and shook her head. "No. I'm really a Hawthorne," she explained. "This land is Hawthorne land and the piece next to it, the land where the equipment is parked, used to belong to the Summers family."

"But not you?"

"No . . . it was owned by my husband's family," she said, feeling rankled again when she thought about Blake and how he had sold his family's homestead only to gamble away the money.

"My pa can't wait for the resort," Jake said. "He says it will put Martinville on the map."

"No doubt about it," Dani replied with a frown.

"Pa says that his business is bound to double over the next year or two, with all the workers Johnson will have to hire. And then, once the resort is open, Pa expects to make a bundle!"

"Nobody's *ever* made a bundle selling groceries," Jake's younger brother, Jonathon, commented with all the knowledge of a fifteen-year-old.

"Just you wait!"

"Mom! Hey, Mom!" Cody screamed at the top of his lungs as he raced around the corner of the house. His boyish face was flushed with excitement and he was nearly out of breath.

Dani's heart constricted.

"He wrote again! Look! There's a letter from Dad!" Cody was jumping up and down with his exhilaration and Runt was barking wildly at the boy's heels.

Dani nearly fell through the weathered boards of the porch. *Damn you, Blake!* She managed to force a tender smile for her son. "What did he say?"

"That he's comin' home!" Cody looked from one of the Anders brothers to the other. "You hear that, *my* pa is comin' home!"

"Home? Here?" Dani asked.

"Yep! To see us and Uncle Bob!" Cody was holding the letter triumphantly and Dani guessed from the way that Cody was acting that Jake and Jonathon were two of the kids who had given him trouble about his absentee father. The brothers had the decency to look sheepish and Dani had to bite her tongue in order to refrain from giving the boys a lecture on the cruelty of gossip. At nine years of age, Cody would have to fight most of his own battles. And this time, at least for the moment, he'd won.

"I think we'd better be goin'," Jake said, handing Dani his empty bottle.

"Just a minute and I'll pay you." She took the bottles, placed them in the case by the back door and went into the house to the old desk in a corner of the kitchen. Once there she withdrew the checkbook from the top drawer, sighed when she saw the balance, and paid the Anders brothers their wages.

"Here you go," she said, giving each boy a check when she returned to the porch. "And thanks a lot."

"You're welcome, and you'll give us a call if you have any more work to do?" Jake asked.

"Sure thing," Dani said.

Jake sighed in relief. "Hey, Cody, good news about your dad," the cocky sixteen-year-old said.

"Yeah," Jonathon added, following his brother around the corner of the house. A few seconds later the rumbling sound of Jake's pickup could be heard as they drove off.

"I told you he'd come back!" Cody said, his brown eyes bright with pleasure.

"You sure did," Dani replied, feeling the corners of her mouth pinch. "Why don't you let me read what he said?"

"Sure." Cody handed the letter to her and Dani skimmed the hastily scrawled note. It was less than a page but there was the promise that Blake would return to Martinville "sometime this fall." She looked at the postmark. It read Molalla, Oregon; a town Dani had never heard of.

The letter was vague enough not to pin Blake down but with enough promise to keep Cody's hopes up. Dani felt all the rage of seven long years sear through her heart.

"When do you think he'll get here?" Cody asked.

"I don't know," Dani replied honestly.

"Before school starts?"

"I . . . I wouldn't count on it. . . ."

Cody flinched. "Yeah, I know *you* wouldn't. But *I* do! Dad says he's comin' home and he is!" He started to walk into the kitchen but stopped, a sudden uncomfortable thought crossing his mind. "When Dad gets here, he will stay with us, won't he?"

"No, Cody," Dani said, taking a firm stand.

"Why not?"

"Because your father and I aren't married. He can't stay here. It wouldn't be right."

"But he's my dad and he lived here before!"

"I know, but Blake will probably want to be in town with his brother, Bob. He won't want to stay here."

"You don't know that! He's coming back for me and *you!* So you'd better let him stay here because if he has to live with Uncle Bob, then I'm going to live with him!" Cody said, taking the letter from her hand and marching through the door.

Why now? Dani wondered, fighting the tears behind her eyes. *Why did Blake have to come back—or promise to—right now, when Cody was the most trouble he'd ever been and Caleb Johnson was hell-bent to take her land from her?*

"Don't borrow trouble," she whispered staunchly to herself. Blake hadn't returned in seven years; there was little chance he'd show up at all. *Either way, Cody would be brokenhearted all over again.*

"Just stay in Oregon, Blake," she muttered, looking past the equipment on the Johnson property. It was nearly dark and the field was empty of the workers that had been there during the day. Even Chase seemed to have disappeared. *Probably plotting with his partner*, she thought bitterly, but couldn't really make herself believe that Chase was quite that treacherous. "And neither is a rattlesnake," she muttered as she looked at the troublesome sky.

Thunderclouds, heavy with the promise of rain, roiled over the peaks of the Rockies to darken the evening sky.

A cool summer shower. That was what she needed, Dani thought sadly. The summer had been unbearably hot this year and all of the tension with Cody as well as Caleb Johnson and Chase McEnroe was getting to her. The thought of rain pelting against the windowpanes and settling the dust was comforting. Maybe the rain would wash away some of the strain . . . but not if Blake were really coming back.

With a sigh Dani walked into the house and deduced from the muted sound of rock hits coming from a radio that Cody was in his room. She wanted to go to her son, try to reason with him about his father, but decided it would be better to wait until they had both cooled off.

Wearily climbing the stairs, she stopped suddenly as the thought struck her that Blake might be returning to Martinville with the express purpose of taking Cody away from her. "Not in a million years!" she thought aloud, her fingers clenching the banister. As quickly as the horrible thought came, it disappeared. Blake hadn't wanted Cody in the first place; he'd even gone so far as to suggest that Dani have an abortion in the early months of her pregnancy. So why would he want a nine-year-old boy now?

Refusing to be trapped in the bitter memories of her stormy marriage to Blake, Dani stripped out of her dirty sweat-soaked clothes, brushed the dust from her hair and twisted it to the top of her head before settling gratefully into a hot bath.

The warm water eased the tension from her stiff muscles and lulled her into a sense of security. If Blake had the audacity to try and claim Cody now, he'd have the surprise of his life. Long ago Dani had shed her mousy personality in favor of that of a new independent woman. No one, not even Blake Summers, would take her son away from her; just as she wouldn't allow anyone to steal her land. And whether Chase McEnroe knew it or not, that's exactly what Caleb Johnson had tried to do over the past few years. He'd offered to buy her out far below the market value and then he'd tried to say that *she'd* swindled him on the sale of the Summers' place. Yep, Caleb Johnson was as crooked as a dog's hind leg, and he wanted her land; the land her grandparents had worked to save in the Depression, the land her ancestors had cleared and farmed with the strength of their backs and the sweat of their brow.

And maybe you're being a fool, she thought as she squeezed the rag over her shoulders and let the hot water drip down her back. *Maybe you should just sell the place and live comfortably for the rest of your life.*

"Never," she whispered to herself. "At least not to Johnson."

She smiled to herself with renewed determination and settled lower in the tub.

Chase stared at the lights in the cabin windows long after he'd seen Dani go inside. The first heavy drops of rain had begun to fall and he was still deciding whether or not to confront her again. It had been nearly a week since she'd thrown him out of her home. For six days he'd respected her wishes and kept away from her, but watching her work in the fields, her lithe body handling machinery and heavy bales of hay that would have strained the muscles of a man twice her size, gave him second thoughts.

"You're a fool," he chastised, but ignored his own warning and slipped through the barbed wires before climbing the short hill toward the cluster of buildings on the small rise.

The rain had begun in earnest. Large drops slid down his face as thunder rumbled in the mountains. He picked up his pace and ran the last hundred yards to the shelter of the barn before shaking the water from his hair and striding to the back porch.

Dani was already there, sitting in an old rocker near the door and wearing only her bathrobe.

"Dani?" Chase called, hoping not to startle her.

She nearly jumped out of her skin at the sight of him. "What're you doing here?" she asked, recognizing his voice before being able to discern his craggy features.

"Escaping the storm."

Leaning back in the rocker, she narrowed her eyes as she studied him. "So why didn't you escape to Caleb Johnson's house?"

"Too far away." He walked up the two steps to the porch and rested one hip against the rail as he looked at her. "Besides, I wanted to talk to you again."

"I thought we settled everything last time."

"Not really." He leaned against the post supporting the roof of the porch, folded his arms over his chest and stared down at her with shaded eyes. The rain had turned his blond hair brown and dampened the shoulders and back of his shirt. "I've been doing a lot of thinking lately. The last time I was here you insinuated that Caleb tried to steal your land."

"It wasn't an insinuation."

"Fact?"

Dani hedged. "Not exactly . . ."

"Then what happened?"

A simple question. And one of public record. Then why did she hesitate to tell him? "Why don't you ask Johnson?"

"He put me off, just like you. Right now he's out of town."

"For how long?"

"A few more days."

Dani's teeth clamped together. She still hadn't had it out with Caleb.

"Look, I'd just like to know what's going on between the two of you because, whether I like it or not, I've been put right smack dab in the middle of your . . . disagreement."

"Disagreement?" she repeated, smiling at the understatement.

"For lack of a better word."

Drumming her fingers on the edge of the rocker, she looked across the sloping land and listened to the heavy raindrops pound against the roof and run in the gutters. "It's no secret really," she said, turning to face him again. "About two years ago, Caleb Johnson tried to take me to court. He insisted that the land my great-great-grandfather had homesteaded—this place—wasn't staked out properly, and according to his survey, I was actually living on what is now his property."

"That should have been easy enough to prove."

"You'd have thought so," she whispered.

"So?"

"Well, Johnson's land is more than just his. Part of it used to belong to my ex-husband, Blake. He sold it to Caleb Johnson years ago, when we were first married. My property, which is known as the Hawthorne place, bordered Blake's family's acreage. Once Blake sold out to Johnson, Caleb became my neighbor."

"And the Summers' place doesn't exist any longer."

"Right. It's all part of Johnson's spread, although he made one minor concession to Blake's family and decided to name his resort Summer Ridge."

"What does that have to do with property lines?"

"Johnson claimed that when Blake sold him the land, he'd meant to include the strip of my property on the ridge of the mountains." She pointed westerly, toward the Rockies. "I don't farm the entire acreage; part of the land rises into the foothills."

"And has hot springs on it."

Surprised, she stiffened in the chair. "That's why Johnson wants the land so badly, I suppose."

Chase shifted and rubbed his hand around the back of his neck. "I suppose. So what happened?"

"Nothing."

"Nothing?"

"The judge threw the case out of court. It cost me several thousand dollars in legal fees, but the land is mine."

"How did Caleb take the news?"

"Not particularly well. It's common knowledge that he owns several of the judges in this part of the state. I'm willing to bet that some have even invested in Summer

Ridge. Fortunately I ended up with a judge who didn't happen to be in Johnson's back pocket."

"What do you mean?"

"Just that Johnson has powerful friends." Her small jaw was thrust forward and her eyes were guarded. "And I don't trust any of them, including you."

"I didn't say I was his friend."

"Partner. That's good enough." Standing, she cinched the belt of her robe more tightly around her waist. "Though Caleb Johnson didn't end up with my land, he still put a noose around my neck. I had to go into debt to pay off my lawyer and mortgage this land. I got behind on my taxes and it took me two years to get back to even again." Her blood boiled at the injustice of it all and her voice trembled slightly. "I offered to sell him part of the farm once. It wasn't enough for him. He tried to wheel and deal and swindle me on that piece as well as the rest of the farm! So I'm through dealing with him. As far as I'm concerned, I wouldn't give him the satisfaction of buying one square inch of this property!"

"No matter what?"

"No matter what! So, if you're entertaining any ideas of persuading me to sell, you'd better forget them."

"That's not why I'm here."

She lifted a delicate dark brow and cocked her head to the side. "What then?"

He shrugged. "I don't know. I guess I just wanted to see you again."

Brace yourself, Dani, don't fall for his line. You don't know a thing about this McEnroe character, she told herself. She took a step backward, toward the door. "Why?"

"I only wish I knew," he said shaking his head. "You're a very beautiful woman. Intriguing."

"A challenge, Mr. McEnroe?"

A crooked smile slid over his face. "Maybe—"

"Then forget it. I don't like dealing with anyone associated with Caleb Johnson. I don't know why you got roped into being his business partner . . . oh, yeah, it was something about giving your business a shot in the arm financially, wasn't it? Well that doesn't wash with me. There are lots of ways to raise capital. You don't have to go crawling to the likes of Johnson!"

"He came to me."

"Why?"

"A good question," Chase remarked thoughtfully. How many times had he asked himself why Caleb had traveled all the way to Boise? It just didn't make a whole lot of sense. And the answers Caleb had given him were vague, as if he were hiding something from Chase. The situation made Chase uneasy and restless.

"You were right about one thing," Chase said, straightening from the rail and advancing upon her.

Dani stood her ground. "Just one?"

"Everything has a price," he whispered. "And believe me, I'm paying for my partnership."

As Chase slowly walked the few steps separating them; Dani felt her pulse begin to race. "I feel sorry for anyone who gets involved with Johnson," she said.

"I don't want your pity." Chase stood inches from her and Dani was wedged between the screen door and the wall of Chase's body. He sent her a sizzling look that seared through all facades to cut into the woman within.

"Then what is it that you want?" she asked, wincing at the breathless quality in her voice.

He placed one hand against the wood frame of the door near her head. "I just want to get to know you better," he whispered, his head lowering and his lips brushing across hers.

Dani's heart began to hammer in her chest. The feel of his warm lips against hers was enticing. Little sparks of excitement tingled beneath her skin. *This is madness*, her conscience screamed as the kiss deepened, but she didn't draw away from him.

He placed his free hand on the other side of her head, trapping her, but he didn't touch her except for the fragile link of his lips against hers. She smelled the rain in his hair, tasted the hint of salt on his lips. . . .

Dani should have felt trapped and she knew it, but she didn't. Instead she felt the wondrous joy of being wanted and desired—more a woman than she'd felt in years.

"I—I think you should go," she said, clearing her throat when he finally lifted his head to gaze into her eyes.

"Why?"

"It's late."

"Not that late."

"Chase—" Her voice caught on his name. "Look, I think it would be better if we weren't involved."

"Too late."

The man was maddening! "I . . . look, I just can't. I don't have time—"

"Sure you do." His lips captured hers again and this time he wrapped the strength of his arms around her body. She felt small and weak and helpless, emotions she usually loathed but now loved.

"Chase— Please—" she whispered, but her words sounded more like a plea than a denial.

His tongue slid easily through her parted lips and her hands, pressed against his chest, were little resistance to his strength. She felt the corded power of bunched muscles beneath his wet shirt and the exhilaration of his tongue tasting hers.

Moaning as his hands pulled her closer still, she didn't realize that her robe had gaped open and that the swell of her breasts and the pulse at her throat were visible in the darkness. She was conscious only of the strong fingers holding her tight, the muscular thighs pressed against hers and the pounding of her heart as it pumped blood furiously through her veins.

When he lifted her head to gaze at her, his gaze had become slumberous, smoldering with a passion so violent he could barely keep his head.

Dani felt the rapid rise and fall of her breasts in tempo with her labored breathing.

Gently he kissed her cheeks and her neck before his mouth settled on the ripe swell of her breast Dani gasped. His lips and tongue felt hot and wanton.

"Dani," he choked out, his voice rough, his breath warm against the cleft between her breasts.

She tried to think, tried to push him away, but couldn't find the strength or desire to let him go. Crazy as it was, she wanted to be with him, to get to know him, to lie with him. He was like no man she had ever met and he sparked something in her that she had thought was long dead.

"Oh, God," he whispered when he gently tugged on her

robe, baring her breast. The dark tip pointed proudly into the night.

"Please, don't," she whispered, summoning all of her strength and pulling on her robe.

All of his muscles slackened and he leaned against her. "I can't apologize for what's happening, Dani," he said, his breath ruffling her hair. "I've tried to fight my attraction to you and I've failed." He sighed loudly before staring into her eyes and softly tracing her jaw with a long, rough finger. "I didn't want any of this to happen, y'know."

Swallowing, she placed her arms over her chest and stepped away from him. "Neither did I."

"But it's there."

"Not if we don't let it be," she said, her head clearing a little. "Look, I really can't get involved with anyone now. Especially not you."

"Why not?"

"You're Caleb Johnson's partner, for God's sake!"

"So you can't trust me?"

"Would you?" she demanded, her eyes bright.

Tortured by the bewitching gleam in Dani's gaze, the thick strands of her vibrant hair, the proud lift of her chin, Chase had to look away. "Maybe not."

"Then we understand each other."

"Not quite." He turned to face her again and this time frustration contorted the shadowed contours of his rugged face. He balled a fist and slowly uncurled it, as if in so doing he could release the sizzling tension that twisted his insides and made him burn with lust. "What I don't understand is why I can't keep away from you, why I can't quit thinking about you, why I lie awake in bed with thoughts of you. I don't want any of this, lady, and God knows I didn't ask for it, but it's there. I can't get you out of my mind and, unless I miss my guess, you feel the same way about me."

He reached for her and when she tried to pull away, he jerked her roughly to him. "You can't deny that you want me just as much as I want you."

"I don't want you!"

"Liar!"

"Chase, don't!" Dani felt like slapping him but when his lips came crashing back to hers, she kissed him hungrily and the fire in her blood raged wildly in her veins. An ache, deep and primal, awakened within her body and her fingers caught in the rain-dampened strands of his hair.

"Don't what?" he rasped, once his plundering kiss was over.

"Don't make me fall for you," she whispered, surprised at her own honesty.

He let out a sigh and tried to control his ragged breathing, his thudding heart. He noticed the worry in her eyes and attempted a smile that failed miserably. "All right," he finally agreed, wiping an unsteady hand over his brow. "I'll leave you alone, if that's what you want."

"It's what I want," she lied.

"Because you don't trust me," he said flatly.

"Because I *can't*, dammit!"

Chase looked up at the pouring rain before glancing back at Dani. "Just remember that you're the one who set down the rules," he said. "I can't promise that I'll stick to them, but I'll try." He gave her a scorching glare that touched the forbidden corners of her heart before he slowly walked away from the porch and into the pelting rain.

Dani clutched at the lapels of her robe, feeling more alone and desolate than she had in years as she watched Chase disappear into the darkness.

Chapter Four

All through the night, Dani listened to the sound of the rain running through the gutters and wondered what had happened to Chase. More to the point, she wondered what she was going to do about him. No matter which way she thought about it, Chase McEnroe was Caleb Johnson's partner. Even though he was attractive, her reaction to him was all wrong and much too powerful to ignore.

"Of all the men in the world, why him?" she asked herself as she tossed on the bed and flung off the covers in disgust. Sitting upright, her hair tangled and messed, she stared out the rain-streaked window and thought about the way she'd melted inside when he'd kissed her.

Even in the darkness she could feel her cheeks burn in embarrassment as she remembered how her heart and breasts had responded to the warmth and tenderness of his touch. "Oh, Dani," she sighed, flopping back on the pillows and trying to slow her racing pulse, "what have you gotten yourself into?"

* * *

Cody, hair still dripping from a quick shower, bounded down the stairs and took a seat at the kitchen table.

Hoping that the strain of the night didn't show on her face, Dani looked up and smiled at her son. "Good morning," she said as she placed a platter of pancakes in front of him.

"Mornin'." He poured syrup on his pancakes before lifting his eyes to stare at his mother. "What was that guy doin' here last night?"

Dani felt her back stiffen, but managed to pour a cup of coffee with steady hands, blow across the hot liquid, and meet her son's curious gaze. "Chase?"

"If he's that new guy who works for Caleb Johnson."

"One and the same," Dani admitted pensively. Thinking back to her intimate conversation with Chase on the back porch, Dani blushed and took a sip from her mug. "I didn't know you were awake."

"I couldn't sleep. My window was open and I heard him talkin' to you. What'd he want?"

Dani lifted her brows. "Didn't you hear that, too?"

"I couldn't hear what you said. Too much noise because of the rain. I just heard voices."

Thank God.

"But I knew he was here." He looked away from Dani and concentrated on the thick stack of pancakes and a bowl of peaches Dani had set on the ancient table.

"How?"

"Recognized his voice."

Her feelings in an emotional tangle, Dani sat across from her son and toyed with her breakfast. She knew that she couldn't trust Chase, but there was something about the man, something earthy and seductive, that she couldn't forget. She glanced out the window toward the creek where Chase and at least one other man were working, and wondered again why he'd come up to her house in the middle of the rainshower.

"Mom?"

"What?" Dani turned her attention back to her son and realized he was waiting for an explanation. His dark eyes were round with concern. "Don't worry about Chase," she said, hoping to put Cody's worries to rest. "He stopped by last night because he wants my permission to work on the creek where it cuts through our property."

"Why?"

Dani lifted a shoulder. "Beats me . . . Caleb probably asked him to, I suppose."

Cody made a sound of disgust and finished his pancakes. He took a long swallow of his milk, watched his mother over his glass and wiped his mouth with the back of his hand.

"More?"

"Naw."

"Next time, use your napkin," she said automatically. She studied her son as Cody scraped his chair back from the table and carried his dishes to the sink.

How like his father Cody looked; the same curly dark brown hair and deep brown eyes. Except for the lack of cynicism twisting the corners of his mouth and the honest warmth of his smile, Cody was growing up to be the spitting image of Blake.

"Why're you hanging out with one of Caleb Johnson's men?"

"Hanging out with him?" Dani repeated with a laugh. "I'm not."

Hopping up on the counter and swinging his legs, Cody looked at his mother and frowned. "But you don't hate him—not the way you hate the rest of Johnson's men."

"I don't *hate* anyone. Not even Caleb Johnson. As for Chase, I don't even know him."

"Doesn't matter. You like him."

Dani smiled and finished her coffee.

"You do like him, don't you?"

"It's not a question of liking him; I just don't know him."

"You didn't throw him off the place last night or the other night, either," Cody pointed out. He picked up a fork from the counter and began twirling it nervously between his fingers.

"That's not as easy as it sounds."

"It's your land."

"Well, yes, it is. And it means a great deal to me. Maybe more than it should."

"Why?"

She hesitated a moment. Could Cody possibly understand her love and obligation to the family farm? Probably not. "I'm attached to this place for sentimental reasons. Lots of them. For quite a few generations someone from my family—your family, too, y'know, has lived here and worked hard to keep the land in the family. Even when times were hard; a lot harder than they are now. It just seems a shame to give it all up so that Caleb Johnson can build his resort."

Still sitting on the counter, Cody dropped the fork into the sink. "Would a resort be all that bad?"

"I don't know." She stood and placed her cup and saucer in the sink. Bracing herself against the edge of the counter and looking up at her son, she tried to think calmly about the resort she found so threatening. But it wasn't the resort itself; it was Johnson and his methods that made her blood boil. "Not really, I guess. A resort would benefit a lot of people and change the complexion of the town."

"That would be good."

"Maybe. Maybe not. I'm not really sure. It certainly would mean more money and economic development for the town. But with that would come people, tourists, new zoning, new roads and construction. Sleepy little Martinville would grow up. Fast."

"Good!"

Dani smiled sadly and bit into her lower lip. "Maybe it's selfish of me to want to keep the land." She looked through the open window to the dry fields, across the silvery creek. past the few scrubby oak trees to the gently rising land near the mountains. In the distance the proud Rockies cut through the blue morning sky to be rimmed by a few scattered clouds.

"So why don't you sell?"

"I was going to once," she admitted, thinking back to how foolish she'd been to trust Caleb Johnson. "Right after Grandma died; you weren't even in school yet. Johnson and I'd agreed on the price for the back fifty acres. However, when it got down to signing on the dotted line, Caleb pulled a fast one and said he'd decided he needed all my land. All or nothing. I just couldn't sign away *all* of Grandma and Grandpa's land. So it was nothing. Caleb's been fuming ever since."

"And causing trouble?"

"Which I can't prove."

"I think he's behind everything that's gone wrong around here," Cody proclaimed.

"Not everything," Dani replied. "Sometimes it was just fate or mistakes that I made."

Cody shook his head firmly. "I think he poisoned the cows when they got sick and I'll bet he stole our gas!"

"We don't know that."

"Who else?"

Dani's brows drew together in concentration. How many times had she asked herself the same question? How many nights had she lost sleep wondering if Caleb were really as bad as she thought he was? "Good question."

"What I don't get," Cody said with a look far wiser than his years, "is why he wants *all* of this land?"

"Another good question." She rumpled his dark hair affectionately. "I wish I had the answers."

Cody looked up at the ceiling and shifted uneasily, avoiding Dani's gaze. "Isabelle Reece said her pa thinks you're a fool."

Dani laughed. *A fool!* Well, maybe she was. Judging from her reaction to Chase, she certainly felt the part. "So when did Isabelle Reece's dad become an authority?" Dani teased.

Cody looked down at her and grinned. "On being a fool?" he repeated. "Oh, I get it: it takes one to know one?"

"Something like that." Dani laughed and tapped him on the knee. "Now, if I've answered all of your questions,

Detective Summers, why don't you hop down and feed the livestock while I tackle the dishes?"

"But I wanted to go fishin'."

"Later, sport. I'll be out in a minute to help."

Cody swung his legs and jumped down from the counter. "Mom?"

She turned on the water. "Yeah?"

"So where does this Chase guy fit in?"

"I wish I knew," she admitted, squirting liquid dish soap into the sink. She'd wondered the same thing all night long. Her feelings for Chase were hard to define but the tangled web of her emotions was frightening, very frightening. For seven years she'd known exactly what she wanted from life and in just two weeks, he'd upset everything she'd been so sure of.

"Well, I wouldn't trust him," Cody said with authority. "Anyone working for Caleb Johnson is trouble."

"Is that what Isabelle Reece's pa says?" she asked, looking over her shoulder at her son.

Cody grinned at his mother. "I guess I'll have to ask."

"Don't bother," Dani said, slinging her arm around the boy and giving him a hug. "Somehow I have the feeling that once school starts, Isabelle will let you know."

"Yeah. She probably will."

Cody was laughing as he walked out the back door and called to Runt. The black dog stretched his legs and then followed Cody outside.

Once she was done with the dishes and the kitchen was straightened, Dani took off her apron and grabbed her gloves as she shouldered open the back door. As she walked toward the barn, she glanced across the fence to the spot where Chase and his men were working. Chase was easy to pick out. Taller than the other two men, he was shirtless and bare headed, his blond hair shining with sweat in the summer sun. He was leaning against the side of a dirty dump truck, ignoring the work going on around him and watching her every move.

Dani's heart leaped unexpectedly and vivid memories of the night before flashed in her mind. She could still smell the rain, taste Chase's lips, feel his hands sliding between the lapels of her robe. . . .

"Mom?"

Dani nearly jumped out of her skin. She hadn't realized that she'd stopped walking toward the barn. "Oh, what?"

Cody was sitting on the fence post. He cocked his head in the direction of the barn. "If ya don't mind?" Hopping to the ground he reminded her, "You're the one who wants the animals fed early."

"So what have you been doing?"

"Waiting for you."

"Cody—"

"It's hard for me alone," he said, looking suddenly contrite.

The boy was only nine. "Sorry," she apologized quickly. The she jerked on her gloves and walked into the darkened interior of the barn.

The cattle were already inside, lowing loudly and shuffling for position at the manger.

"Why were you staring at Johnson's land?" Cody asked.

"I was just thinking."

"I know that much." Cody frowned as he climbed the ladder to the loft and began dropping some of last year's hay bales to the main floor below. "I saw." He looked down at her from the loft above and his brows were drawn together in frustration. "You were looking at that guy again."

She cut the strings on the bales with her pocketknife and began breaking up the hay before tossing it into the manger. "I just can't figure him out."

"If I were you, I wouldn't try." Cody leaped down from the loft, his boots crunching on some spilled grain as he landed on the dusty floorboards.

Dani shook her head. "Next time, use the ladder—"

"Aw, Mom."

"I just don't want you to break your neck. Especially in front of me," she added, trying to lighten the mood.

"I'm not a little kid anymore," Cody said firmly.

Dani's smile was bittersweet "That's what worries me." She watched her son as he rationed out the grain for the cattle. His body was changing; he was growing up faster than she wanted him to. "I'll check the water and you can sweep the floor, okay?"

"Okay," Cody grumbled.

Dani walked from the barn and into the bright morning sunlight. Stuffing her gloves into the back pocket of her jeans, she began filling each of the troughs near the barn with fresh water. As she waited for the troughs to fill, listening to the cool sound of rushing water pounding against the old metal tubs, she chanced looking at Chase again.

He wasn't leaning on the dump truck any longer. Instead he was shoveling mud from the bottom of the creek and supervising the planting of several trees near the deep hole he was creating. The morning sun caught in his blond hair and gleamed on the sweat of his back. His back and shoulder muscles, tanned and glistening in the sun, stretched fluidly as he worked.

"Hey, Mom, watch what you're doing!" Cody yelled as he walked out of the barn.

Shocked out of her wandering thoughts, Dani noticed that the trough was overflowing; precious water was swirling in the tub before running down the hillside in a wild stream.

"For crying out loud," she chastised herself as she turned off the water and looked over her shoulder to the other trough where Cody was furiously twisting the handle of the spigot.

Frowning, he wiped his hands on his jeans as he approached. "You've got the hots for that guy, don't you?"

"Cody!"

He shrugged and pouted. "Well, don't say I didn't warn you about him."

"I wouldn't dream of it," Dani remarked. "Hey . . . wait a minute. *You're* warning *me?* What do you know about 'the hots'?"

Knowing he'd managed to goad his mother, Cody looked slyly over his shoulder before saying, "Isabelle Reece says her pa—"

"I'm not sure I'm ready to hear this—"

"Just kidding, Mom," he said, a grin growing from one side of his boyish face to the other before he sobered again. "But . . ."

"But what?"

"You haven't forgotten about Dad, have you? He *is* coming home."

Not wanting to cause her son any further pain or confusion, Dani had trouble finding the courage to tell him the truth and burst his bubble of hope. "When your dad gets here, we'll talk. All of us."

Cody visibly brightened.

"But you have to understand that we don't love each other anymore; not the way a man and wife love each other."

Doubts filled his eyes. "But you were married!"

"Unfortunately people change."

"Or give up," he accused, his small jaw tight, his dark brows pulled together and his eyes bright with challenge.

"Or give up," she agreed. "I'm not saying I was right—"

"You weren't! You should have stayed married to him!"

"Believe me, I tried."

"Not hard enough!"

"Cody—"

Tears filled his eyes and he tried to swallow them back. "Can I go fishin'?"

"Now?"

"Yeah."

"I think we should talk about this."

"What good will that do?" he threw back at her. "Nothin's gonna change. I still don't have a pa. Just like the kids say!"

"That's not true!"

His defiance eased a bit. "I just want to go fishin', okay?" Pain twisting her heart, guilt washing over her in hot waves, Dani nodded tightly. "The sooner, the better," she said before her anger subsided. "Just be back by noon, okay?"

"Sure."

He started to turn, but she stopped him by touching his arm. He jerked it away. "Where are you going fishing?"

"Probably the hole near the south fork."

"Okay. Do you want to take something to eat?"

Forcing a smile, he fished in his pocket and pulled out three candy bars. "I'm all set."

"For nutritional suicide."

Cody swiped at his tears and Dani pretended not to notice. Turning his back to her, he went to the back porch, grabbed his fishing pole and stained vest and whistled for Runt. Then he was off, running through the fields toward the foothills with the dog racing ahead, frightening grasshoppers, birds and rabbits in the stubble of the pasture.

With a tired sigh, Dani walked up to the porch, reached for her hoe and leaned on it while watching her son until Cody was out of sight. What had she done to the boy? Should she have stayed married to a man she didn't love, a man who had done everything in his power to hurt and embarrass her for the sake of her son?

Without any answers to her questions, she looked across the fence to the Johnson field. Chase was there, standing with his muscled back to her and staring at Cody's retreating figure as the boy crawled under the fence separating one of her fields from another before disappearing through the brush at the far end of the pasture.

Chase watched the boy and dog sprint through the dry fields and, for a moment, he remembered his own youth and the warm Idaho summers.

The boy ducked under the fence and disappeared into a thicket of blackberries and brush, the lop-eared dog on his heels. Chase couldn't help but smile. Cody and his beautiful mother made him feel dangerously younger than his thirty-four years.

For the first time in what seemed forever, a woman had

gotten under Chase McEnroe's skin. It had been only hours since he'd left Dani but, despite his promise to the contrary, he was already restless to be with her again. The fact that she was near enough to see only made it worse.

He jabbed his shovel into the soft ground near the bank and cursed quietly to himself. The memory of touching her had made the rest of the night excruciating. He'd lain awake for hours, twisting and turning on sweat-dampened sheets and feeling a gentle but insistent throb in his loins. A throb that reminded him of her willing, warm body, softly parted lips and perfectly rounded breasts. Hell, he'd felt like a horny kid all over again. Just because of one damned woman!

Dissatisfied with life in general, Chase continued to dig, throwing the power from his tense shoulders and arms into each jab. The ground around the creekbed gave way under the thrust of his shovel. Swirling muddy water filled the hole.

Still he couldn't get Dani out of his mind and it sure wasn't for lack of trying. Telling himself that he had to avoid her at all possible costs, he plunged into his work with a vengeance, thrusting his shoulders and mind into the task of working the creek and getting the hell out of Montana as soon as he could.

All morning he'd made impossible demands on the men and himself, trying to exorcise Dani's image from his mind.

But each time he looked up from his work, she was there. Whether she was standing at the kitchen window, working with the cattle, or as she was now, hoeing that miserable patch of ground she considered her garden, she was there; only several hundred yards away.

The effect was devastating for Chase. *Torture*, he thought angrily to himself, working so close to her was sheer torture. "She's just a woman," he grumbled to himself, "just one woman!"

"Hey, Chase! Over here!" Ben Marx, one of his employees, shouted, dragging him out of his fantasies about Dani.

"What?"

"I don't know," Ben said. He was a young, bearded man who had been with Chase for nearly two years, ever since Eric Conway had walked out on Relive to start a rival company. Ben's hat was pushed back on his head, sweaty strands of sandy hair were protruding under the brim and the man himself was staring at a large ten-gallon metal drum that he'd pulled from the creek. Rotating the drum on the ground, he gave out a long, low whistle just as Chase approached.

"Looks like an old barrel of some kind of herbicide," Ben said.

"Herbicide?" Chase repeated, bending to examine the can. "Wait a minute. There it is. Dioxin."

"And you found it in the creek?"

Ben glanced up at Chase. "Buried in the creekbed."

"How deep?"

Ben shrugged his shoulders. "Hard to tell. We've been working here for quite a while, so I can't be sure, but probably four, maybe six inches. And look here," he pointed to what would have been the lid of the barrel. "It's been punctured."

"Intentionally?"

"I don't think a woodpecker made those holes, do you?"

"Son of a bitch!" Chase jerked his gloves from his back pocket and rotated the metal drum again. The label was scratched and muddy, but some of the letters were still visible. The lid of the drum had a few barely visible holes in it. "No wonder there's no fish in the creek . . ." His eyes narrowed on the empty can.

"You reckon it wasn't empty when it was buried?" Ben asked, reaching into his breast pocket and pulling out a crumpled pack of cigarettes.

"Hard to tell."

"Who would bury a drum so close to the creek?" He lit the cigarette and inhaled deeply.

Chase's mouth pinched. "I can't hazard a guess," he said sarcastically. "Show me exactly where you found this."

After wrapping the drum in oilcloth and placing it in the back of his Jeep, he followed Ben back into the water and stared at the hole Ben had been digging when he'd unearthed the barrel of poisonous herbicide, if that's what it was.

"I was just smoothing the bottom of the creek out, makin' it ready for more gravel when I decided to deepen it near the bank. My shovel struck metal, so I worked to find out what it was."

"Don't touch anything," Chase commanded. "I want to take some samples of the water and the soil." He returned to his Jeep for his hip waders and sterile vials and set about collecting the samples, careful to label each specimen. Then, muttering under his breath, he crawled through the rusted wires of the barbed fence and began taking soil and water samples a few feet inside Dani's boundaries.

"Tell the men to take the rest of the day off," Chase said. "And I don't want any of them in the creek without waders."

Ben nodded.

"As for drinking from the creek—"

"No one does."

"Let's keep it that way. And don't say anything about this," Chase warned, looking at the man on Johnson's side of the fence.

Ben took a final drag on his cigarette before flipping it onto the muddy bank of the creek where it smoldered and died. "You can count on me. I've heard tales about that one," he said, nodding in the direction of Dani's house. "If she finds out you've been on her land again, there'll be hell to pay."

Despite the cold dread stealing through him, Chase forced a sly smile. "No reason to disturb the lady, right?"

"Right." Ben chuckled, took off his gloves and grinned lazily. "Leastwise, not by steppin' on her land." He looked at Dani's house again and his gaze grew distant. "But there are other ways I'd like to bother her."

A muscle tightened in Chase's jaw and his blue eyes turned stone cold. "Not a good idea, friend," Chase said.

"No?"

Chase was spoiling for a fight and he knew it. But having it out with Ben Marx was just plain stupid. He ground his back teeth together and said, "Considering how she feels about Caleb, I think it'd be best if you left her alone. Don't you?"

Ben read the message in Chase's glare. His lazy smile

dissolved under the intensity of Chase's cold eyes and he reached for another cigarette. "Whatever you say; you're the boss."

"Then it's understood that Dani Summers is off-limits to anyone working for me." Chase could hardly believe what he was doing; acting like some fool male dog staking out his territory. With his own men, no less! And yet he couldn't stop himself or the feeling of possession that ripped through him any time another man said Dani's name.

"Sure, sure," Ben said hastily. He'd been on the receiving end of Chase's wrath enough times to know that he didn't want to cross McEnroe. Especially about a woman. Chase was a fair employer but if pushed hard enough, he had a temper that wouldn't quit. In Ben's opinion it didn't make much sense to get him mad.

"Good. Make sure the rest of the men get the word. And don't tell anyone about the drum of dioxin or whatever the hell it is. I want to check it out first." *And then there'll be trouble. Big trouble.*

Ben lit his cigarette, shoved his hat over his brow and nodded mutely.

Chase glanced uneasily up the hill to where Dani was working in the garden, but, as usual, she seemed disinterested, as if she weren't paying any attention to what was happening on the property adjoining hers. He hoped to God that it wasn't an act and waded farther downstream to the middle of Dani's land before taking more samples.

Dani pursed her lips in frustration as she watched Chase slip through the fence. Seeing him out of the corner of her eye, she leaned on her hoe, wiped the sweat from her forehead and wondered if she really wanted to make a scene in front of his crew. Not that she wanted to, but damn the man, he was forcing the issue! She watched him walk backward, downstream, farther onto her property.

And just last night he'd promised to stay away. Now he was breaking his word, pushing her to the limit in full view of his workers. After her argument with Cody, she was in no mood to get into another fight. But she really didn't have much of a choice.

With a sigh she put the hoe on the porch, wiped her palms on her jeans and started through the gate and down the sloping field to the creek.

Chase was there, just as he had been the first time she'd come across him, except for the fact that he was about a hundred yards away from Caleb's land and right in the middle of hers. He was digging on the bank and taking samples of the water. *Her water.*

She felt her pulse begin to race but assured herself that it was because she was furious with him as well as Caleb Johnson.

"I thought you understood that I didn't want you here," she said as she approached the bank.

"I did." He looked up, smiled, and then went about his business.

Infuriated, Dani planted her hands on her hips. "I wasn't kidding about calling the sheriff."

"Go ahead—call him."

"Chase—"

He looked up again, his piercing sky-blue eyes causing her stupid heart to flutter. "At least this time you didn't bring that damned rifle."

"I hoped that I didn't need it."

"You don't." He offered her a brilliant smile that was meant to dazzle away her worries. It softened her heart, but didn't quite convince her head that he was on the up-and-up.

"What're you doing?"

"Taking samples."

"I can see that, but *why*?"

"I just want to check the creek. Remember, I did ask for permission."

"And I didn't grant it."

"Right."

"So you just barged right over here anyway." She crossed her arms under her breasts and didn't bother to hide her exasperation.

He grinned again and muttered, "Actually I tried to sneak."

"In broad daylight? When I was up in the garden?" She smiled despite the headache beginning to pound at the base of her skull. "I'll admit that I don't know you very well, but I doubt that you were trying to sneak. You did a much better impersonation of a cat burglar last night."

The corners of his lips were drawn down and deep furrows lined his tanned brow. "Maybe we'd better not talk about last night."

Dani couldn't agree more. "I don't want to talk about anything. I just want to know why you're defying me."

"I don't like edicts."

"But this is my land—"

"So I've heard. About a hundred times. From you." He sighed and placed another small vial into his fishing creel before wading downstream deeper into her property.

"I know why you're here."

"Sure you do. I told you, I'm taking samples."

"That's not the only reason. You're proving to those men—" she made a sweeping gesture to Johnson's land where Ben Marx was pretending not to see the ensuing argument "—that I can't tell you what to do."

"They have nothing to do with this."

"Like hell!"

His face went taut, his chin tight with determination. "For once, just trust me."

"Chase—"

But he was backing up again, watching the water as it rushed into a thicket of brush and trees at the corner of the field. The stand of cottonwood and pine offered the only seclusion and shade in the entire field. Beneath the leafy trees, hidden in the brush, Chase was out of view.

Dani had to walk into the thicket to carry on the conversation. She had to bend to avoid the low branches that caught on her blouse. Chase had stopped between the scraggly cottonwoods clinging to the banks of the stream. Ignoring her, he began once again to take samples of the water.

Furious, Dani stood on a large boulder near the water's edge. "I thought you understood." She glanced upstream, but couldn't see if Chase's men were watching. The branches offered both shade and privacy as a slight breeze whispered through the canopy of leaves above the creek.

"I do. But this was something I had to do, okay?"

"And leave it at that?"

"For now."

"No, Chase. No, it's not okay. Look, I thought you were

different from the rest of Caleb's hands. I thought you would keep to your part of the bargain."

His muscles tensed and he replied flatly. "My bargain's with Johnson."

"I see," Dani said, her stomach tightening with disappointment. Despite his arguments otherwise, Chase was solidly in Caleb Johnson's corner. He was the enemy. "Then I think you'd better move it and get out of here because I really am going to call Tim Bennett."

Chase raised a skeptical brow but continued to work. "He's the sheriff," Dani clarified.

"I *know* who he is. I just don't give a damn."

"You've certainly got a lot of nerve! More nerve than brains."

His shoulders slumping slightly, Chase dropped the final vial into his creel and stared up at her. Even enraged, she was beautiful.

Standing on the bank, with the warm morning sunlight drifting through the shimmering leaves of the cottonwood, her arms crossed angrily under her breasts, her chin held high, Dani looked almost regal. She hadn't bothered to tie her long hair back and it billowed away from her flushed face in the heavy-scented summer breeze. "And you're gorgeous," Chase replied, studying the pucker of her lips and the fire in her hazel eyes.

"I don't want to hear it."

"Sure you do."

"Calling attention to my looks right now in the middle of this argument is a typical male trick to change the subject!"

"It's no trick," he said calmly, wiping his wet hands on his jeans while he stared at her.

Dani's eyes followed the movement and she had to tear them away from his flat abdomen and the tight faded jeans that rested on his hips.

She licked her dry lips and he smiled; that same lazy, seductive grin that made her heart flutter expectantly. "Just get out of here," she said, hating the breathless tone of her voice.

"Dani—"

"What?"

"Why don't you ask me to stay?" He stuffed his gloves in his back pocket and began slowly walking through the knee-deep water and toward the shore.

Her defenses melted and she leaned against the white bark of a cottonwood for support. "Are you always going to fight me?" she asked.

"Only when I have to." He waded out of the stream and stood next to her, kicking off his boots.

She tried not to notice the way the sweat ran down his throat, or the way his hair curled at his neck, or the fluid movement of his shoulder muscles when he leaned back against one of the lower branches of a scrub oak. "And when is that?" she asked, her throat suddenly tight. "When Caleb tells you to?"

His jaw hardened and he stretched out an arm along the branch to break off a small twig and rotate it between his fingers. "Contrary to what you think, I don't do everything Caleb suggests."

"You could have fooled me."

His eyes stared deep into hers and her chest seemed suddenly tight. Breathing was nearly impossible. "Why do you hate him so much?"

She smiled despite the tension charging the summer

air. "Hate's too strong a word," she said, remembering that Cody had accused her of hating her neighbor earlier in the morning.

"What would you call it?"

"I don't trust him."

"So I gathered." He cocked his head to the side. "But you never really said why."

"He's done a few things that, though I can't prove . . . I'm convinced— Wait a minute. Why should I tell you?"

"Because I asked. Look, Dani, I'm not against you."

"That's hard to believe."

"Is it?"

She stared into the honesty of his clear blue eyes and wanted to trust him with all of her heart. Instead she shrugged. "I thought I already explained all that."

"Not really. Why are you so dead-set against Summer Ridge?"

"I'm not against the resort, not really. I'm against the fact that come hell or high water, Caleb Johnson thinks he can manipulate me into selling my property. It might sound corny, but this land means a lot to me."

"Meaning that you want a higher price."

She ran her fingers through her hair and sat near the edge of the stream. Linking her arms around her knees, she stared at the rushing water. "You'd better watch out, McEnroe. You're starting to sound like him."

Picking a blade of dry grass and chewing on it, he sat next to her with his bare feet sticking out in front of him, his thighs nearly brushing hers. "So if it's not money, what's the problem?"

Dani glanced into his concerned eyes. "Did Caleb tell you I was willing to sell some of the acreage to him?"

"No."

"About two years ago, I think," she said remembering the meeting at Caleb's house. "He'd even agreed to the sale. But then he changed his mind, he wasn't satisfied; he wanted the whole farm."

"And you didn't want to sell."

"Not all of it. My great-great-grandparents home-steaded here and I wanted to keep it in the family." She picked up a handful of dirt and let it slip between her fingers. "This land is all my folks ever had and they worked until they dropped to keep it."

"So you've been preserving the heritage—for what, your son?"

"If he wants it."

"And what if he doesn't?"

Dani frowned and clasped her hands together. "I've thought about that, and I suppose if Cody inherits it and wants to sell, he has that right." She pushed the hair out of her eyes and smiled. "It certainly won't matter to me then."

"So you don't trust Caleb because he tried to buy all of your farm."

She avoided his eyes. "There were other reasons."

"Name one."

"I can't," she admitted. "It's just a feeling that I have; nothing I can prove."

"Prove?" When she didn't respond , he reached over and touched her cheek with his index finger. "Prove what?"

"Nothing," she said quickly.

"Dani," he whispered, pulling her chin so that she was forced to stare into his eyes, "you can trust me."

"Aren't you the man who just said he had a bargain with Johnson—not with me?"

His gaze slid to her mouth. "What do you think Caleb has done to you?"

Gambling, she said, "I think he's done everything he could think of to discredit me, make me sell my land to him and ruin me financially."

Chase dropped his finger and whistled softly. "Heavy charges."

"Like I said, there's nothing I can prove." She tossed a rock into the creek. "At least not yet. So, how come you're involved with him?"

"Good question."

"You went to him when you needed financing."

"Actually, I'd never laid eyes on him before. But he knew all about me and my company."

"Isn't that odd since your company is located in Boise?"

"I don't know," Chase admitted, his blue eyes clouding as he pondered the question that had been nagging at him for over two years. "There wasn't much competition in the business at the time. Relive Inc. had a corner on the stream-rebuilding market and Johnson claimed to have known my mother, before she was married."

"She's never mentioned him?"

Chase shook his head. "She's dead."

"Oh . . . I'm sorry."

Shrugging off the uncomfortable feeling that settled on him each time he thought about his mother knowing

Caleb, Chase placed his hands behind his head and leaned against the trunk of a cottonwood. "So why don't you tell me what, specifically, Caleb's done to make you so damned mad?"

"I don't think that would be wise."

"Why?"

"Probably for the same reason you won't tell me why you decided to ignore my edict, as you called it, and crossed the fence."

A slow smile spread across his rugged features and his eyes warmed as he looked at her. "Maybe I just wanted to see you again."

"So you waded in a frigid creek with all those bottles of yours? No way."

Seductive blue eyes delved into hers. "It worked, didn't it?" he asked, brushing a golden strand of hair from her cheek and letting his fingers linger at her nape.

Dani's breath caught somewhere in her throat. "Don't you have work to do?"

"Probably." He inched his head closer to hers until the warmth of his breath fanned her face and his arms surrounded her shoulders. With eyes fixed on hers, he leaned closer still, and his lips brushed slowly over hers in an agonizing bittersweet promise that destroyed all her defenses.

I can't let this happen again, Dani thought, but didn't stop him. His fingers caressed her arms as he drew her closer, tighter against his chest and she could hear her thundering heartbeat echoing his. When he pressed his mouth over hers and kissed her, she felt the raging passion that had been destroying his nights and driving him insane during the day. Its fire ignited her own blood and it coursed in wild, hot tandem through her trembling body.

His tongue sought and danced with hers and she didn't protest, but linked her arms around his neck, moaning his name as he unbuttoned her blouse and caressed her breast in slow, sensuous circles that awakened dangerous fires deep within her soul. His hands were warm and comforting against her skin and a fine tremor in his touch told her just how easily his control could slip.

He kissed the top of her breast, letting his tongue wet the lacy edge of her bra and the warm skin peeking through the sheer fabric.

"Please, Chase," she whispered brokenly, knowing she should break off the embrace but unable to find the strength to do anything but surrender to his lovemaking.

Looking up, he saw the doubt in her eyes. He groaned and rolled away, closing his eyes and mind to the thundering desire.

Dani felt suddenly cold and very much alone.

"Oh, Dani," he whispered hoarsely, lying on his stomach and willing the swelling in his jeans to subside. "If you only knew what you do to me." Though his eyes were still closed, he rubbed them with his thumb and finger and massaged the bridge of his nose. "I don't know how much more of this I can take."

She swallowed the lump in her throat along with her pride. "Why are you trying to confuse me?" she asked, her voice raspy as she buttoned her blouse.

"I'm not."

"Then why don't you make up your mind?"

"I don't understand."

"Neither do I, Chase. But it sure looks like you're playing both ends against the middle."

"Meaning?"

"That one minute you're telling me that your only allegiance is to Caleb Johnson, a man who's tried everything he can think of to ruin me, and the next minute you're . . . you're . . . *acting* like you care for me!"

"It's not an act," he admitted. "I do care for you. Too much, I think."

She smiled sadly. "I wish I could believe you."

"Just trust me—"

The same old words! Trust me! Sadness sizzled into anger. Anger at her twisted emotions and anger at him for confusing her. "*Trust you?* How can I? I don't believe in blind trust, Chase." *Not since Blake left me.* "You promised that you'd stay off my land and leave me alone. The minute my back was turned you were here again, digging in the mud and taking water from the creek."

"Dani—"

"I'm not through!"

"Just wait a minute! Listen to you! Why do you care if I'm on your land? I'm not hurting a damned thing!"

She was trembling with passion and rage, confusing the two, wishing that she'd never laid eyes on the enigma that was Chase McEnroe. "Not hurting anything?" she repeated. "Well, maybe not yet! But you're working for Johnson and God only knows what he's got up his sleeve!"

She started to get up but he grabbed her wrist, pulling her close to him. "You know, you act like you've got something to hide."

"Me!" She laughed at the absurdity of the situation but couldn't help being mesmerized by his gaze. "Why don't you go track down your boss? Ask him about my dead cattle. Ask him about the time I was going to sell off part of the property to him. Ask him about my hay baler! And ask him about the time he tried to siphon off all the water in Grizzly Creek for his private lake!"

She wrenched her arm free and stood staring down at him. She was shaking with rage. "For all I know, you're just part of one of Caleb's schemes. I wouldn't put it past him. He probably asked you to come over here and try to work your way into my confidence by any means possible!"

Chase's square jaw tightened and his clear eyes clouded when he remembered Caleb's suggestion that he bed Dani. He tried not to let his thoughts show, but his very silence was incriminating.

"Oh my God, Caleb is behind this, isn't he?" she guessed, feeling suddenly sick. She could read the evidence in Chase's eyes. Bitterly she turned away in disgust and self-loathing overwhelmed her. "And it's laughable what easy prey I am!"

"What happened between us has nothing to do with Johnson," Chase said, rising to his feet.

"Like hell!" She backed into a tree and stood looking at him. Her face was pale, her expression stricken. "Just get off my property and don't ever come back!"

"Dani—"

"You're a bastard," she said. "A first-class A-1 bastard, and I never . . . *never* want you to set foot on this place again!"

"You're making a mistake," he said slowly. A muscle worked in his jaw and the skin over his forearms tightened.

"Not nearly as bad as the one I almost made."

He pushed his hands into the back pockets of his jeans and looked upstream through the leafy overhanging branches of the trees to the fence and beyond, where his men and machinery were still in position on Johnson's property. When he turned to her again, he was able to control some of his rage. "I didn't want any of this to happen."

"Good. Then we can both forget that it did."

"I want to help you," he admitted, and the torture in his voice almost convinced her. But not quite.

"I don't want to hear any more of your lies. Now just get the hell off my property!" Reaching down, she scooped up his fishing creel. "And take all of this with you!" She threw it at him, but the toss went wild. Chase scrambled to catch it, but the creel fell on the rocks near the bank. The glass within the wicker basket tinkled and shattered. Mud and water started trickling through the woven bottom of the creel.

"No!" Chase was horrified. He picked up the creel and opened the lid, eyeing the shattered vials, oblivious to the water running through the wicker and down his jeans. "Do you realize what you've done?" he accused, fire returning to his eyes as he looked up at her. "Every vial is ruined!"

"I don't really give a damn!"

He let the creel fall to the ground and advanced upon her. "What was in those jars might just have been the evidence you need!"

"Evidence?"

"That Caleb isn't on the up-and-up!"

"What? How can water samples—" Shaking her head as if to clear it, she focused sharp hazel eyes on him. "If you expect me to believe that you were trying to prove that Caleb Johnson is a crook, you've got another guess coming! You're his partner," she reminded him, her voice rising. "You owe him a ton of money as well as your entire business!"

Chase was standing over her, looking down at her with judicious blue eyes. His nostrils were flared, his chiseled mouth tight. "Go ahead and believe what you want to, lady, but I'm going to get to the bottom of this feud between you and Johnson with or without your help."

"Be my guest," she threw back at him, "as long as it's not on *my* property!"

He looked like he wanted to kill her. The frustration and anger in his look bore deep into her soul. Dani's heart froze and her lips parted in surprise when he grabbed her, jerked her body against his and forced his head downward so that his lips crushed hers and stole the breath from her lungs.

Struggling, she managed to pull one of her hands free and she swung it upward, intending to land it full force on his cheek. But he was faster than she would have guessed and he grabbed her wrist, pinned her hand behind her and continued kissing her, forcing his tongue through her teeth, moving his body sensually against hers until, to her mortification, she felt her body responding. Her breasts peaked, her heartbeat accelerated and she felt like dying a thousand deaths.

When he lifted his head from hers, he slowly released her, dropping her hands. How he was coming to loathe himself. "Oh, God, Dani," he whispered, pushing the hair out of his eyes with shaking fingers. "I'm sorry."

She swallowed and let out a shuddering sigh. "So am I."

"You are, without exception, the most beautiful, intriguing and frustrating woman I've ever met."

"And you're the most arrogant, self-serving bastard I know," she said, holding the back of her hand against her swollen lips.

He stepped toward her, but she held up a trembling palm, "Just leave," she whispered. "Go away. Get away from me! Why don't you find the next train to Boise and jump on it! I can handle Caleb Johnson by myself!"

"Can you?"

"Yes!"

His jaw thrust forward, his eyes glinting a silver-blue, Chase reached down, jerked on his waders, picked up his creel and strode along the bank.

Dani watched him leave, positioning herself outside of the thicket so that she could follow his movements as he walked through the trees and into the sunshine, across the field and through the parted strands of barbed wire. Tears stood in her large eyes and she wondered why she couldn't find the strength to hate him.

Chapter Five

Early in the afternoon, wearing a proud smile and waterlogged jeans, Cody returned with two small trout in his possession. Runt scampered up the two steps of the porch and flopped in the shade to pant near Dani's chair.

She was sitting in her favorite rocker, mending some of his clothes and hoping that a few pairs of the pants would still fit him for the coming school year.

"Congratulations," she said when Cody proudly displayed his catch. "Looks like we have fish for dinner."

Cody made a face. "I *hate* fish."

"Then you should have thrown them back," she said, smothering a laugh.

Sitting down on the top step, he glanced up at her. "What were you doin' at the creek with that guy?" he asked.

Taken by surprise, Dani looked up from her mending and then slowly set the torn shirt aside. "You were there?"

"Yeah. Well, no, not really. I was just comin' back and I'd planned on fishin' in the hole below the fork in the creek. You know, by the cottonwood trees."

Dani nodded, hoping that her cheeks weren't as warm as they felt. She'd never thought about Cody surprising her and Chase. But then, she hadn't expected to find Chase in the creek . . . on her side of the fence.

"I saw that Chase What's-his-face—"

"McEnroe," Dani supplied, meeting her son's curious stare.

"Yeah. I saw him walking back to Johnson's property. He looked madder than a wet hen. You were standing down there." He gestured toward the cottonwood stand, "And you were watching him leave and looking real sad."

Dani folded her hands on her laps. "So you saw that, did ya?"

Cody nodded. "Was he bothering you?"

"A little," she hedged. "I caught him trying to take water samples," she explained. "We had a rather unfriendly . . . discussion."

"You mean a fight."

"I mean a battle royal."

"What does he want with our water?"

"Beats me," Dani admitted, wondering for the thousandth time exactly why Chase was so anxious to get water from her side of the fence. And what did it have to do with "evidence?" Damn Chase McEnroe; he held all the cards. And he knew it. "I suppose he wants the water because Caleb probably told him to get it."

"And he got mad when you told him to leave."

The understatement of the century. "Very."

"I thought you told him not to come back here." Cody began playing in the dust with a stick and avoided Dani's eyes.

"I did."

"Well?"

"I don't know why he keeps comin' back," she admitted,

gazing across the dry fields. "I guess maybe it's just part of his job."

"Or maybe he likes you." Cody glanced over his shoulder again, pinning his mother with his dark brown eyes.

"Why would you say that?" Dani asked, worried that she and Cody were about to argue again.

"Because you always do. When some girl gives me trouble at school, you always say it's because she likes me."

Dani laughed and wiped the sweat from her forehead. "I do, don't I? And you never believe me."

"Maybe you're right."

"That's a big concession coming from you."

Cody's solemn face split with a smile. "I figure you've got to be right part of the time—"

"Get out of here," she teased, her eyes sparkling. Standing, he winked at his mom. "How about a Coke?"

She eyed him and nodded. "You go get cleaned up and I'll get us each one. Then I think you'd better brush up on your schoolwork."

"Why?"

She stood, wrapped both arms around the post supporting the roof and stared across the creek. "Summer's almost over, Cody," she said reluctantly, her fingers scratching the peeling paint from the post. Soon Chase and all the problems he brought into her life would be gone. And those problems would be replaced with new ones from Caleb Johnson. "Go on. Scoot," she said to her son.

"Aw, Mom—" He let out an exaggerated sigh. "I'll start tomorrow night. Okay?"

"Is that a promise?"

Cody nodded but bit at his lower lip.

"I m going to hold you to it."

"I know, I know," he mumbled as he slipped through the creaking screen door and hurried up the stairs.

A few minutes later Dani heard the sound of water running in the pipes. She folded her mending and glanced down the hill to Johnson's side of the fence. All the equipment was still in position, but no one was in sight. They'd probably all gone up to the house for lunch.

"And good riddance," she murmured, but the ache in her heart wouldn't subside.

Water was still dripping from Cody's dark hair when he bounded down the stairs half an hour later. He grinned at his mother when he saw the two glasses of Coke on the table.

"I saved you from a fate worse than death," Dani remarked, shooting him an indulgent look. She was standing at the stove and frying Cody's trout. Both small fish sizzled as they browned in the pan.

"How's that?" he asked.

"We're eating the fish you caught for lunch."

"Wait a minute—"

Careful not to spill the grease, Dani scooped the fish from the pan and set them on a platter lined with paper towels. "That way you don't have to have them for dinner tonight."

"Mom—" he began to protest, but she placed the platter on the table between her plate and his.

"Eat, son, and I promise not to give you any lectures on starving children in the rest of the world," Dani said as she sat at the table, took a fish and wedge of lemon and began squeezing lemon juice on the tender white meat.

With a grimace, Cody speared the remaining fish and placed it onto his place as he sat down. Drinking plenty of Coke between each bite, he mumbled and grumbled to himself.

"Great trout," Dani teased, her eyes sparkling.

"Don't rub it in." But Cody returned her smile. "Have you got the mail today?"

Dani nodded.

"Was there, uh, anything for me?" he asked, staring down at his plate.

Dani forced a smile she didn't feel and the piece of trout she was chewing stuck in her throat. "Not today."

"Oh." Her son slowly speared another piece of fish and Dani's heart twisted.

The phone rang and Cody raced to get it. After a short conversation, he hung up and returned to the table. "That was Shane. He wants me to spend the night."

"Tonight?"

"Uh-huh. I told him it was okay. It is, isn't it?"

Dani shrugged. "Sure. But next time maybe you'd better ask first, don't ya think?"

"I guess so. He said I could come over about four."

"Good. I've got to run into town for some groceries anyway. I'll drop you off then. Okay?"

"Great!" With that, Cody was up the stairs, packing a change of clothes and his treasures into his bag. Dani watched him take off with a trace of sadness. He was growing up so fast and slipping away from her.

With a philosophical frown, she got up and cleared the table. Little boys grow up and if their mothers are smart, they let them, she told herself. Wondering why it had to hurt so much, she set the pans on the counter and turned on the hot water. As the sink filled, Dani glanced through the steam and out the window. Work had picked up on the Johnson place again. Men were digging and heavy machinery was placing logs and boulders in strategic positions along the creek.

Two men she didn't recognize were planting saplings along the bank, but nowhere did she see Chase. *No big loss*, she told herself, but felt that same dull pain in her heart. "You're a fool," she muttered. "A first-class fool." Then she attacked the dishes as if her life depended upon it.

Chase didn't stop fuming all the way to Johnson's house. He'd spent the last four hours with the manager of an independent chemical laboratory and his blood was boiling. As he'd suspected, the drum that Ben had found in the creek had held dioxin. There were still traces of the herbicide in the empty can. Although more tests were to be run and eventually the county agriculture agent would have to be notified, Chase was convinced that someone had intentionally put the drum of dioxin in the creek to poison the water. But why? To kill the fish? Ruin the plant life? Get rid of the illegal toxin? Not likely.

No doubt, Caleb Johnson would know.

Though he ached to have it out with Caleb, for the time being Chase had to sit tight. Or as tight as his temper would let him.

Parking his Jeep near the barn, he cut the engine and hopped out of the cab. Trying to control his anger, he strode through the front door of Caleb's home. Aside from

Caleb's housekeeper, who was humming and rattling around in the kitchen, the house seemed to be deserted.

Chase hesitated only a second before walking into Caleb's study, pulling out the files and finding the documents he wanted. His jaw working in agitation, he read the appraisal reports, geographic studies, mortgage information and every other scrap of paper dealing with Dani's farm. When he'd finished with the file he replaced it and the anger in his blood had heated all over again.

"You miserable son of a bitch," he muttered as he slammed the file drawer shut and walked down the short hallway to the back of the house and the kitchen where Jenna was working and humming to herself.

"Hasn't Johnson shown up?" Chase asked the elderly woman as he grabbed a bottle of beer from the refrigerator.

"He came in 'bout twelve-thirty," Jenna replied as she continued rolling out pie dough.

Chase could barely control himself. "He didn't bother showing up at the creek."

"Oh, no, he's too busy working with some new quarter horses."

"At the stables?"

Jenna shook her gray head and wiped her hands on her flour-dusted apron. "I'm not sure. He took off for the stables but he said something about taking the horses over to the track."

Chase started for the door but paused and took a long swallow of his beer. "You've known him for a long time, haven't you?"

"Since we were kids," Jenna replied.

Leaning against the door, Chase looked directly at the plump woman with the unlined face and pink cheeks.

Jenna Peterson was the only person on the whole damned Johnson spread that Chase felt he could trust. "And would you say he's trustworthy?"

She seemed surprised and turned quickly from the marble counter. "Oh, yes," she said. "When he was younger, while we were in school, he was straight as an arrow, don't you know?" She smiled as she stared out the kitchen window. "But that was years ago."

"What about now?"

"Still the same man . . . but—"

"But?"

"Oh, well, nothin' really. He's different, of course. But we all grew up. After school, I lost track of him, got married myself and had the kids. I didn't think much about Caleb, only what I heard from the town gossip mill. It wasn't much. But several years later, after his folks had passed away, I heard that he was marrying some girl from another town."

Chase's eyes grew sharp. "I didn't know he had a wife."

"Oh, he didn't. Seems this woman wouldn't marry him for some reason or another; no one really knows for sure. He came back here and threw himself into this farm, hell-bent on expanding it and making it the best in the state. Worked at it for years."

"So why the resort? Why is it so important to him?"

Jenna glanced at him with kind blue eyes. "You have to remember that Caleb hasn't got a family. No sons or grandsons to carry on his name. He needs something to be remembered by."

"So that's the purpose—immortality?"

"Maybe a little. Besides, a man has to do something to keep busy. Just 'cause you reach a certain age is no reason to curl up and die."

"I suppose not," Chase thought aloud, taking a long swallow of beer. "But, tell me, do you think that he would do anything . . . underhanded to get the resort going?"

"Illegal, you mean?"

Chase didn't answer.

"I doubt it."

"Not even bend a few rules?"

Jenna's countenance became stern. "You don't like him much, do you?"

Chase's brows drew together thoughtfully. "I don't think it's so much a question of liking the man; I'm just not sure I can trust him."

Jenna sighed and shook her head as she placed the top crust over the sugared apples in the pie pan. "All I know is that he's been a fair employer. And—" she paused in her work to look Chase straight in the eye "—you're special to him."

"I don't think so—"

Jenna waved off his thoughts. "I've seen him with a lot of men. He treats you different."

"Different? How?"

Jenna thought for a moment, trying to find just the right words. "Like you was kin," she finally said, nodding as if in agreement with her thoughts. "That's it. He treats you like he would a son, if he had one."

Chase experienced a strange tightening in his gut and he forced a smile. "Fortunately, I already had a father. He died a few years back, but I certainly don't need Johnson to fill his shoes."

"I don't think Caleb would want to try."

"And I don't think Caleb thinks of me as anything but

a business partner," Chase said, taking another swallow of his beer and sauntering out the back door.

Flies and wasps were trapped in the hot back porch. They buzzed in frustration against the old screens as Chase passed through. He stopped to adjust the brim of his Stetson and walked out into the late afternoon sun.

Caleb was leaning over the top rail of a fence, staring out at the dry pasture where his herd of horses was grazing on the sun-parched grass.

Chase felt the anger ticking inside him like a time bomb. How much of Dani's story was true—that Caleb had done everything he could to run her off her land? And how much was just her imagination running wild? Did Caleb know about the drum of dioxin poisoning the water? Just how far would the old man go to achieve his ends? Stomach tight from reining in his anger, his jaw clenching rigidly, Chase approached the older man.

"We sure could use some more of that rain we got the other night," Caleb observed, spotting Chase.

Rain. The other night. Dani. "Weather service predicts another shower in the next couple of days."

"Good."

"How was the trip?"

"'Bout what I expected."

Chase put his foot on the bottom rail of the fence and tried to appear congenial. An actor he wasn't, but he could remain calm if he had to. And right now, he had to. Dani's future was on the line. *If he believed her.* Things just weren't black and white anymore and gray never had been Chase's favorite color. "Sounds good," he remarked.

"Could've been better."

"Or worse."

"I s'pose." Caleb swatted at a fly and swore under his breath. "Damn things. Used to be able to get rid of them."

"But not anymore?"

Caleb grimaced. "It's a helluva lot tougher now."

"So what do you use to keep the insects and the foliage in control around here?" Chase asked, his eyes skimming the fields to watch the scampering foals kicking up their heels around their sedate dams. The mares stood in pairs, head to buttocks, flicking at flies with their tails and ears.

"Whatever is available." Caleb leaned back and eyed the younger man. "And whatever the government allows us to use. They're getting stickier all the time."

"No doubt about it. Used to be a time when you could use DDT or dioxin and no one cared," Chase said evenly, his gaze flicking from the grazing mares to Caleb and back again.

"Made ranchin' a helluva lot easier," Caleb agreed with a lazy smile.

"Ever use the stuff?" Chase asked.

"Sure. A lot. When it was legal. But that was a long time ago. Had to get rid of all of it."

"How'd you do that? Bury it?" Chase felt the tension in his muscles, but forced a calm expression, as if he were just making idle conversation.

Caleb's watery eyes narrowed but he shook his head. "Hell, no. Couldn't. Afraid it might seep out into the ground; get into the grass and then the food chain. Nope. I turned all mine in to the agriculture department. And let me tell you, it's been hell to keep the blackberries and tansy under control ever since." He slapped the rail and straightened, changing the course of the conversation.

"So, tell me, how's it been goin' around here? Everything on schedule?"

"We're a little behind," Chase admitted, "but not much. Another couple of weeks and it'll be over."

"So you got through to Dani Summers?"

Chase grimaced. "No. I doubt if anyone can."

Laughing lewdly, Caleb agreed. "A regular spitfire, that woman." His eyes gleamed. "Come on, boy, don't tell me you haven't noticed."

"I noticed. She was the lady with the gun aimed at my gut, remember."

"Just a little scare tactic."

"Well, it worked. She scared the hell right out of me!" Chase took a swallow of his beer and tried to appear anything but involved with Dani Summers. It was hard not to think of her sparkling green-gray eyes and her tawny sun-streaked hair falling to her waist.

"Bah! You wouldn't be a man if you weren't interested in a piece like that."

Rage flooded Chase's veins, and his blue eyes, when he turned them on Caleb, became ice cold. "Not my type."

"Not her husband's, either, I'd guess," Caleb drawled, noticing the muscle jump in Chase's jaw. The kid was a cool one, Caleb thought as he watched Chase standing in front of him, leaning over the fence, nursing a bottle of beer, looking as if he couldn't give one good goddamn about the conversation and yet listening to every detail. Caleb smiled to himself. Things were beginning to look up.

"Why don't you tell me about her old man," Chase suggested.

"Not much to tell. A bastard, the way I hear it. He sold his land to me and took off with the money and another woman, leaving Dani with a little kid and a sick mother." Caleb ran his rough fingers along the top rail. "Like I said, that woman's a helluva scrapper." He paused. "Reminds me of your ma, when she was a girl."

Chase ignored the remark. He didn't want to think about his mother and Caleb. Not now. "So you tried to get Dani Summers's husband to talk her into selling her farm to you."

Caleb shrugged his wide shoulders. "Business is business. And she would've been better off selling. She could've bought a little house in town, put some money in the bank and been able to take care of her kid proper-like."

"She's doing a good job with the kid."

"You met him?"

Chase's jaw thrust forward. "Once."

"A good kid?"

"Yeah. I'd say so."

"Hard for a single woman to handle a boy that age."

"Like I said, she seems to be doin' fine." Chase finished his beer and straightened. "She also told me that she was ready to sell off a parcel to you once, but you reneged."

"Wasn't enough land."

"But you'd agreed to it," Chase pointed out.

"Changed my mind," Caleb said defensively. "Just like I intend to change hers."

"By any means possible?"

"Within the law, boy," Caleb said. "Any means within the law." He eyed the empty brown bottle in Chase's hand. "Now, how about you comin' into the study and we'll have ourselves a real drink while you tell me how Grizzly Creek is comin' along? I plan to start building just as soon as all of the permits are approved and I want that creek stocked and proved viable by the time the brochures go into print next summer."

"I said I'd be done within the month."

Caleb slapped him on the shoulder. "I know, I know. But I want to be sure that the trout survive and spawn, y'see. *And* we're not done until Dani Summers comes around. You'll have to work on her side of the fence as well."

"It won't happen," Chase said.

"Sure it will. It just takes a little time." Caleb had begun walking to the house. He was a big, lumbering figure who strode with the authority of one who knew that his commands would be obeyed without question.

Chase gritted his teeth and followed, remembering the information he'd found in Caleb's study. He hesitated but then took off after the old man. For the time being, at least, he'd have to listen to all of Caleb's demands and pretend to follow them to a T. But just until he found out what made Caleb Johnson and Dani Summers tick.

Dani shoved the pickup into gear and waved at Cody, but he didn't even notice. He and Shane were already playing catch with a basketball as they walked to the park to meet a few other friends for an impromptu game.

"You'll roast in this heat," Dani had warned, but Cody had smiled and waved off her fears.

"Better than playing in the snow and ice," he'd said, laughing as he'd tossed the ball to Shane.

"Okay. I'll pick you up in the morning," she'd said, but Shane's mother had insisted that she would bring Cody home the following day.

"So it looks like it's just me and you, right?" Dani scratched Runt behind his ears as she drove away from the Donahue's house.

Runt whined and stuck his head out the window.

"Benedict Arnold," Dani said with a laugh as she scratched the dog's back and drove through town to pick up groceries and supplies.

Once the pickup was loaded, she drove out of town, intending to return home. But at the corner of her property she hesitated, and rather than turning toward her house, she stopped and let Runt out. Once the dog had run up the lane, she drove north to the next tree-lined road, the long gravel drive leading to Caleb Johnson's farm house. She had business to settle with Johnson and there was no time like the present to take care of it.

Her heart hammering nervously in her chest, she drove through the stately oaks and pines and parked her pickup between the barn and the house. With more determination than courage, she hopped out of the cab and strode around the house to pound on the front door.

Within minutes the door swung inward and Jenna Peterson, Caleb's cook and housekeeper, was standing in the expansive entry. She smiled at the sight of Dani.

"Dani! This *is* a surprise."

"Hi, Jenna," Dani greeted, trying to calm herself and be polite. "How've you been?"

"Can't complain. And yourself?"

"Good," Dani said automatically.

"And that boy of yours," Jenna said, stepping away from the door. "He's growin' like a weed. The spittin' image of his dad."

"You've seen Cody?"

DISTRUST

115

"School pictures, last year. My youngest grandson is in the same class. Come in, come in. Can I get you something? Iced tea?"

Dani smiled at the older woman's hospitality and felt a little foolish. "No, thanks. I'd just like to see Caleb for a couple of minutes. Is he in?"

"You lucked out," Jenna said with a grin. Dani doubted it. "Caleb's in the study with Mr. McEnroe."

Dani's stomach tightened, but she managed to hide her case of nerves. "Good. I may as well kill two birds with one stone."

"Pardon?"

"It's nothing," Dani said with a smile. "I'd just like to talk to Mr. McEnroe as well."

"Wonderful!" Jenna walked to the double doors off the foyer and knocked softly before entering and telling the men that Dani had arrived.

"Always ready to have a neighborly chat," Caleb said loudly. Dani inwardly cringed. "Send her in."

As Jenna opened the door, Dani walked through. She looked around the room and saw Chase standing near the window, a drink in his hand, his shoulder leaned against the frame. "Afternoon," he drawled.

"Chase," she said. Her heart leaped at the sight of him, but her face was set with determination. Gritting her teeth but managing a slight nod in his direction, she finally turned her attention to Caleb.

The older man was seated behind the desk, his glasses perched on the end of his nose, his eyes assessing her every move. He'd half-stood when she'd entered the room but now was sitting again.

"Well, Mrs. Summers," he said, leaning back in his chair

and observing her over the rim of his glasses. "Can I get you a drink?"

"No thanks."

Caleb grinned. "I see. Business as usual. That's what I admire about you, Dani, the way you always come straight to the point. Now, to what do we owe the honor?"

Dani stood directly before Caleb's desk. She couldn't see Chase, but she could feel his eyes boring into her back. Without flinching, she held the older man's gaze. "I just came to tell you that I don't want any of your hands on my land. And that includes Mr. McEnroe."

"Has there been a problem?" Caleb asked, feigning concern.

"On more than one occasion."

Caleb turned to Chase. "Nothing I heard about."

"You can cut the bull, Caleb. You know I was on Dani's land," Chase said before finishing his drink and setting it on the windowsill.

"I hadn't heard that she objected."

"Sure you did," Chase said calmly.

Dani took an uncertain step toward the desk, glanced at Chase, who seemed to be watching her with amusement, and poked a finger onto the polished wood. "Then let me make myself perfectly clear. I don't want *any* of your associates near my land. As I told Mr. McEnroe, I'm willing to call the police, the FBI or the President—anyone I can to keep you off my place!" She was shaking with rage, but her eyes remained calm and fixed on Caleb Johnson.

Caleb spread his hands over the desk and lifted his shoulders. "Don't you think you're being a little melodramatic, Dani? After all, we are neighbors. Just calm down and I'll pour you a drink or a cup of tea. Jenna's baked a fresh apple pie and if I do say so myself, it's the best in the county."

"No thanks." She turned on her heel, caught Chase's eye and strode toward the door.

"Dani—" Caleb's voice accosted her.

She turned slowly to face him.

"Let's not act like enemies, all right? You never know when you might need my help."

"Is that a threat?" she asked.

"Of course not. Just some neighborly advice. And, as for your land, it might be simpler for all of us if you just sold out to me."

Chase straightened. "For how much, Caleb?" he asked cynically, eyeing the older man.

"That's between Dani and me."

"Is it?" Chase walked over to a filing cabinet, withdrew a file and tossed an appraisal of Dani's land onto the desk. "Is that the figure you're talking about?"

Caleb's countenance changed. His face whitened. "Not quite that much—"

"I didn't think so," Chase muttered.

"Just who the hell do you think you are, going through my files?"

"Your partner," Chase said flatly as he walked out of the room, taking hold of Dani's arm and pulling her with him.

"What was that all about?" she asked.

"I did some digging today," he said. "And I'm not talking about the creek. Seems that Caleb might just be interested in your land for more than the resort."

"What do you mean?"

"I'll tell you later," Chase said, looking over his shoulder to see Caleb, still red-faced, sitting at his desk. "Now

I think you've made your point; you'd better leave before all hell breaks loose."

"I'm not afraid of Johnson," she said.

"Then maybe you'd better be." With a look of cold determination, Chase let go of her arm and inclined his head to her pickup. "Leave Johnson to me," he suggested.

"This isn't your fight—"

"Oh, but it is," Chase disagreed with a cynical smile. "More than you can guess."

Chase's enigmatic words were still echoing in Dani's ears when she finally got home. What was he doing, putting himself between Caleb and her? A thousand questions flitted through her mind as she put the groceries away and managed stacking the sack of grain in a corner of the barn. By the time she was done, she still had no answers but felt hot and gritty and in desperate need of a shower. She wiped the sweat from her forehead with her hand and felt the dirt streak her skin.

"This is certainly no life for a prima donna," she said to Runt as she headed inside.

The sun seemed hotter than it had been before the other night's rainshower. Though it was late in the afternoon, shimmering waves of heat distorted Dani's view of her acreage. She shaded her eyes and looked northwest, over the fence, to the banks of the creek on Caleb's side. There was no activity. All of the men seemed to have taken off early.

So what was Chase doing? she thought idly and then frowned when she remembered the confrontation with Caleb. She went inside and stayed under the cool shower longer than she needed. After washing her hair and wrapping it in a threadbare towel, she slipped into a cool summer sundress and went downstairs to make a pitcher of lemonade.

"It's too bad Cody isn't here to share this with me," she said to the dog who perked up his ears, cocked his head and resumed whining at the door. "For Pete's sake, Runt, stop moping will ya? You're giving me a case of the blues."

After making the lemonade and watching the slices of lemon swirl in the glass pitcher, Dani poured herself a tall glass, pressed it against her forehead and closed her eyes. Already she was beginning to sweat.

She combed her hair and sat on the back porch sipping the cool liquid and thinking of Chase. She couldn't forget nearly making love to him at the creek, or the way he'd come to her defense at Caleb's house. But he'd said he was Johnson's partner, not hers. His loyalty was with Caleb Johnson—or was it? And what had he hoped to accomplish by taking soil and water samples from her land? *Evidence*, he'd said. But evidence against whom?

"Stop it," she said when the questions got too confusing. With a sigh, she tried to concentrate on a mystery novel she'd been reading long before Chase had stormed into her life, but the pages didn't hold her interest and it was hard to see in the gathering twilight.

Disgusted with herself, she tossed the book aside, continued rocking in the chair and watched a vibrant sunset as the sun settled behind the Rocky Mountains and the sky turned from vivid magenta to dark purple.

She wiped the perspiration from her neck and throat with a handkerchief and turned, gazing over the darkened fields to the north, to Caleb Johnson's property, to Chase. . .

Chapter Six

Chase walked briskly around the stable yard, as if with each stride he could shake the rage that burned in his gut. He felt as if he were on a tightwire and that no matter which way he turned, he was going to fall off into the black abyss of the future.

With an explicit oath, he headed back to the house—to face his partner. *Partner.* The word stuck in his throat. He'd been a fool to accept Caleb's money in the first place and now he wondered just what his partner's intentions were.

Walking through the open door and into Caleb's study, he wasn't surprised to find the old man still sitting behind his desk, his face ruddy with alcohol, his blue eyes small and hard. A near empty bottle of Scotch sat on the corner of his desk and the glass he sipped from was full.

"Looks like I can't trust anything you say," Caleb growled in disgust. He took a long swallow of Scotch. Some of his anger had cooled, but his fertile mind was working fast. His fingers twitched nervously around his glass. "Just what the hell right do you have to snoop in my files?"

"As much right as you have to try and swindle Dani out of her land."

"Swindle?" Caleb sneered. "I just wanted a fair price."

"Do you call a hundred thousand under market fair?"

"That land's worthless."

"Not to you—or her." Chase's eyes cut through Caleb's anger. "She seems to think you've tried to sabotage her."

Caleb had the audacity to grin, as if Chase's anger amused him. "Sabotage? Don't tell me you believe her."

"I don't know what to believe."

"Sabotage," Caleb snorted again, his lips twisting sarcastically. "Sounds like somethin' she'd say. I know she's had a run of bad luck, but I don't see how she can blame me."

Chase ran his fingers through his hair, stretched his tense shoulders and sighed. "I'd just like to know where you get off trying to buy off everyone who gets in your way!"

"Business is business," Caleb retorted, refilling his glass. "Maybe someday you'll learn." He pointed a condemning finger at the younger man. "And you'd better hope it's soon, before a traitor like Eric Conway tries to steal all of your business again. He almost did it once before and I might not be around to bail you out again."

Chase didn't flinch even though the thought of Eric Conway's betrayal still bothered him. "I didn't ask for your help."

"But you certainly took it, didn't you? And now you've got to help me get the Hawthorne place."

"I don't see how that's possible."

"Convince Dani. There must be a way to get to her."

"Forget it." Chase reached onto the windowsill and

grabbed his hat. With a grimace, he forced the old felt Stetson onto his head.

Caleb snorted when he saw the determined set of Chase's jaw. "Going somewhere?" he mocked.

"Out." Chase reached for the door but the old man's voice stopped him.

"To find Dani Summers?"

Chase hesitated. "Weren't you the one who suggested I get to know her better—use my imagination?"

Caleb's eyes became slits. "She really got to you, didn't she? So much in fact that you're willing to hack off your nose to spite your face."

Chase lifted his chin a fraction and regarded Caleb with cold eyes. "Don't wait up."

Taking a sip from the drink he was cradling in his hands, Caleb said, "I wasn't planning on it. I was waiting to hear just how you think you can handle Dani Summers."

"Handle her?" Chase repeated, his back stiffening. "Look, not that it's your business, but as far as I'm concerned I'm not dealing with Dani about her land. Not anymore. Face it, Johnson, the lady doesn't want to sell. Not you, or me, or anyone else on God's green earth can get her to change her mind!"

With the intention of letting Caleb stew in his own juices, Chase stormed to the door of the study.

Instead of ranting and raving as Chase had expected, Caleb just smiled smugly to himself and said in a voice loud enough so that Chase would hear, "Well, we'll just have to see about that, won't we?"

Chase walked out of the house and slammed the door behind him. God, he'd had enough of Caleb Johnson to last him a lifetime, he thought as he jumped into his Jeep.

Through the open window, Caleb watched as Chase ground the gears of his sorry-looking vehicle and roared down the tree-lined lane. Then Caleb put on his reading glasses and searched for a telephone number he'd written on a scrap of paper only two days before. Finding the hastily scratched note, he reached for the phone and dialed, looking distractedly at the cloud of dust Chase was leaving behind him.

Angry with Chase, but knowing be still held the trump card, Caleb balanced the receiver between his ear and shoulder, poured himself another stiff shot and waited impatiently as the long-distance call connected.

Caleb's ominous threat hung in the hot summer air and nagged Chase as he drove away from Johnson's spread. What had the old man meant? His mouth compressed tightly and he squinted through the dust and grime on the windshield and wondered what the devil Caleb was up to. The sun had already set and lavender shadows had begun to stretch over the farmland, but Chase was oblivious to the beauty of the surrounding countryside. His fingers were coiled tightly around the steering wheel and his shoulder muscles were bunched, as if he were spoiling for a fight.

"Relax," he told himself as he switched on the lights and radio and tried to think of anything but Johnson's greed or Dani's precarious position. "Caleb couldn't have anything to hold over Dani." But he couldn't forget the glint of satisfaction in Caleb's pale eyes or the older man's knowing smile. " Don't let him get to you," he told himself.

He drove recklessly toward Martinville and the noisy raucous anonymity of Yukon Jack's. All he needed was a couple of beers, some loud music and the smoky oblivion that the bar offered so that he could forget about Caleb Johnson, Summer Ridge and Dani Summers.

However, forgetting about Dani wasn't all that easy. As some of his anger dissipated and he eased up on the throttle, his thoughts swirled back to her. Now that Chase knew that Caleb had tried to buy the Hawthorne place for much less than it was worth, he was furious.

And so was Caleb. Chase knew that the old man had wanted to tear him apart after the confrontation with Dani in Johnson's study. Caleb had been just sly enough to rein in his temper and that worried Chase—a lot. Because whether he liked the fact or not, his concern wasn't for himself, or his company. Not any longer. Right now, he was worried sick about Dani.

Dani.

Just at the thought of her, unwelcome emotions surfaced and the image of making love to her burned in his brain. In his mind's eye he saw her skein of honey-brown hair, loose and wild in carefree sun-kissed curls, her face flushed with desire, her green-gray eyes warm with excitement and longing. "Get a hold of yourself," he said, stepping on the gas again and heading into town. "Forget her."

He drove straight to the bar, parked the Jeep, stuffed his keys into his pocket and walked into the dimly lit room where he took a table in the corner and ordered a beer. He sat alone, ignoring speculative glances from some of the women patrons, and nursed his beer while pretending interest in a dull game of pool.

The conversation around him didn't spark his interest until he overheard one brawny, bearded man—one of the two men shooting pool—trying to convince his friend that Caleb Johnson's Summer Ridge was the best thing that had happened to Martinville in years.

Chase heard only snatches of the conversation over the clink of bottles, click of billiard balls and spurts of laughter.

"Yep. Think of the value of your old man's farm," the bearded man was saying. ". . . double in price within the year. Same with the price of mine. A few years ago, I couldn't give that rock pile away. Now, thanks to Johnson, it's worth a fortune!" He grinned, showing off a gap in his teeth, while he chalked his cue. "No more cleaning barns and fixin' fence for me, no-siree-boy. I plan on spendin' my time in the Bahamas countin' my money!"

His friend laughed and offered a quiet reply that Chase couldn't hear.

"Oh, she'll sell, all right," the brawny man insisted, signaling to the barkeep for another beer and finally getting off his shot. "Six ball in the corner pocket." He waited until the ball had rolled across the green felt into the appropriate hole. "The way I see it, Dani hasn't got much of a choice . . ."

Chase's every muscle tensed, but he continued to lean back in his chair and eye the two men from beneath the brim of his hat.

". . . no one's yet managed to stop Johnson. Remember Red Haines? He fought Johnson, too, and look what happened. One minute Red's all set to fight the zoning commission and what-have-you, insisting that Johnson's a crook and the next thing ya know, he's changed his tune.

If ya ask me, Red was just holdin' out for more money— same as Dani Summers . . . nine ball in the side—"

Chase scraped his chair back just as the ball banked away from the pocket.

"Damn!"

"So you think Dani's just waitin' for a better price," the skinny friend prodded as he eyed his shot.

"'Course she will. She always was a smart one, y'know. She'll come around to Johnson's way of thinking, you wait and see. And then watch out!"

His teeth clenched, Chase left some change on the bar and walked outside, taking in the clear night air. As he walked back to his Jeep he uncurled his fists and relaxed the muscles that had tightened while he had listened to the conversation at Yukon Jack's.

"You're losing your grip, old boy," he told himself as he drove out of town. When he reached the rutted lane leading to Dani's house, he slowed the Jeep and with a curse at himself, yanked on the wheel at the last minute. The wheels slid a little on the sparse gravel, but Chase held the Jeep steady up the rutted lane to Dani's house.

Dani was still sitting on the back porch when the sound of an engine cut through the night, disturbing the gentle drone of insects. Her heart started to pound expectantly when she realized the engine probably belonged to Chase's rig and that he was driving up the lane toward the house. She took the final swallow from her glass just as she heard the engine die.

Please, Chase, go away, she prayed, though her pulse raced with excitement. She heard him knock loudly on the front door of the cabin. Steadying herself, she stood and walked around to the front of the house.

He was standing under the porch light. His face was taut, his lean features harsh under the soft glow from the solitary lamp. His shirt sleeves were rolled up his arms and he held his hat in one hand.

"You don't have to wake the neighbors," she said, climbing the two steps to the porch.

"Neighbors?" His gaze cut across the ghostly fields. In the distance, lights winked from houses positioned across the main highway. Somewhat closer, the lights from Caleb Johnson's large house burned in the darkness. Chase's lips drew together in a thin, determined line. "Impossible."

"Maybe," she agreed, leaning one shoulder against the house.

"And if you're talking about Caleb, I don't really give a damn if I wake him or not. Besides, he'll probably drink himself to death before the night is over."

"I don't suppose he's too happy with what happened this afternoon," Dani observed.

"I'd say he'd like to kill me," Chase said. "He seems to think I owe him my life."

"Maybe you do," she said gently. "Two-hundred-thousand dollars is nothing to sniff at."

One corner of his mouth lifted sardonically. "I know you probably won't believe this, but I can't be bought."

"Does Caleb know it?"

"Not yet."

Dani sighed and ran her fingers through her long hair. "Don't let him know it. Otherwise, you'll find yourself in a world of hurt."

"Like you?"

"I do okay."

He chuckled and as he gazed into her eyes he felt as if he'd finally come home after a long hard-fought battle. "Yep," he agreed. "I suppose you do."

"And you?"

"I can handle myself."

"Even with Caleb?"

"Especially with Caleb."

"I hope so," she said, glancing anxiously away.

He offered her a lazy smile. "Do you?"

Dani lifted a shoulder and the strap of her sundress slipped. "I don't want anyone to get caught in Caleb Johnson's trap."

"Including me?"

"Yes. Including you," she admitted honestly.

"Then we're friends?"

"Of a sort, I suppose. I don't really know . . . but . . ."

"But what?"

"But sometimes I'd like to think so," she admitted, adjusting the wayward piece of fabric.

Chase reached forward and helped her place the strap back on her shoulder. His fingers lingered against her neck and Dani shivered unexpectedly.

"What about now?" he asked. His expression became less cynical and his eyes darkened as he stared at her. "Are we friends now?"

Nervously she lifted a brow and then swallowed. "You mean, because of this afternoon, when you came rushing to my defense against Caleb?" She paused and bit her lower lip pensively. "Well, yes, I guess I'd have to say that *tonight* we're definitely friends."

His gaze softened and he offered her his most engaging smile. "Then why aren't you inviting me inside?"

"Good question. And one that I don't have a good answer for," she admitted, taking a step backward. "Probably because I'm not sure it would be such a good idea to be alone with you."

"Why not?"

"I thought we settled 'why not' at the creek . . . and again, in Caleb's house."

Chase let out a sigh and rolled his eyes heavenward. "And just two hours ago, I thought I'd never darken your doorstep again. But here I am."

"Why?"

"Maybe to apologize," he said thoughtfully, his voice as low and seductive as the cool breeze blowing from the west.

"And maybe to try and wear me down so that I'll sell my land to Caleb."

"Do you really believe that? After this afternoon in Johnson's study? If you don't remember who was on that white charger—"

She shook her head and laughed. The lamplight caught in the long, silken strands of her hair, turning the soft brown to gold. "Like I said, I really don't know what to believe. Not anymore. But I've got to hand it to you, McEnroe, you don't give up easily."

"Not when something is important." He lifted his hand to touch the bottom of her chin, forcing her gaze to meet his.

She swallowed against the dryness settling in her throat. "And this is?" she asked. "Is it that important to get your company back?"

His finger slid sensually down her neck to rest on her shoulder, near the strap of her sundress. "It was," he admitted, his eyes following the path of his finger. "But I'm afraid it's gone further than that."

"Oh?"

"Much further."

"What's that supposed to mean?"

His eyes centered on her lips. "This whole mess is driving me out of my mind. And it isn't just my business anymore. Hell, I'm not sure I really even give a damn about it, not after all the trouble I've had with Johnson. But you. You're something else again. What was important to me is all confused and the damnedest thing is that all I can think about is you. And me. Together."

She licked her lips and waited, her heart hammering so loudly it drowned the other sounds of the night.

"*You're* what's important to me. *You*, Dani."

Hating herself for asking, she took a step backward to break the intimacy of the moment and whispered, "Why, Chase?" Her voice was raspy with emotion. "*Why* am I important? So that you can get your company back? So that you can get your job with Caleb completed and go back to Idaho?" She inched backward until she felt the rough siding of the house.

"If only things were so simple." He ran one hand over his face and leaned his back against the screen door as he stared into the night. Shoving his hands into the front pockets of his jeans, he rotated his head between tense shoulders. "Everything was so cut and dried a few weeks ago. Black and white. No gray. Now everything's a mess." He looked at her and saw the skepticism in her gaze. "I just know that nothing's been the same since I met you."

"Better or worse?"

His smile was easy, lazily stretching over his tanned skin. "A little of both maybe."

"It couldn't be all that bad because you're still here, when I told Caleb I didn't want any of his men on my land."

Chase ran a tired hand over his chin. "I'm not one of 'his men.' If I were, I wouldn't have saved your neck today."

Dani's chin jutted forward a bit. "Saved my neck?" she repeated. "I was doing fine—"

"You were losing control." Chase moved and sat on the railing of the porch, while his gaze cut across the fields to the hill on which the Johnson house stood. "Caleb had you just where he wanted you and—"

"And?" she asked, defiance sparking in her eyes.

He glanced back at her. "—and you've got a gorgeous neck."

"You're changing the subject."

"No, I'm not."

"Then you're being an arrogant, chauvinistic male." But she couldn't help but grin, exposing the hint of a dimple.

"I'm being honest. And that kind of insult went out in the seventies."

"You are, without exception, the most frustrating man I've ever met."

"I hope so, lady," he whispered, his eyes lingering on her mouth. Reaching forward, he placed his hands on either side of her waist and drew her nearer so that she stood facing him, close enough to feel the heat from his body, smell the liquor on his breath, see the shadows in his eyes.

She had to swallow and lick her suddenly dry lips. "So, why are you here?"

He shrugged, but his gaze never left her face. "I thought maybe I'd take you and Cody to dinner. You know, as sort of a peace offering for trespassing on your land earlier in the day."

"Cody's at a friend's for the night."

"Too bad." But his grin widened.

"I can see you're heartbroken," she mocked.

"Don't get me wrong, I like your son . . . but I can't knock the chance to be alone with you. Since Cody's already gone, how about just you and me?" He reached up and brushed a wayward strand of hair from her cheek. "Maybe it's time we got to know a little more about each other."

"I thought you said that you were partners with Caleb."

Chase frowned. "I still am. Whether I want to be or not. Does that brand me?"

She wanted to smile but couldn't. "In more ways than one, I'm afraid."

"How about what happened at Caleb's house this afternoon?"

She tried to pull away from him, but his fingers closed tightly over her waist "I'm not sure I understand what happened."

"I found out that Caleb tried to cheat you."

"Is that the evidence you were talking about at the creek," she said and then stopped. "No, it was the water samples. What do they have to do with Caleb trying to buy out my property?"

"I wish I knew," he admitted. trying to put together the pieces of the strange puzzle. "Maybe Caleb is just playing games."

"With my water?"

Chase's eyes grew cold. "Believe me, what's happening with your water isn't a game," he said. The lines around his mouth deepened into sharp grooves. *Unless it was a deadly game and if it was, Caleb would have more than Summer Ridge to worry about. . . .*

"Chase . . ." Dani's brow was puckered, her eyes concerned. "What is it? There's something you're not telling me . . ."

Deciding that worrying her needlessly would cause more harm than good, Chase tried to forget his suspicions, at least for the night. He offered Dani a lopsided grin and touched his nose to hers. "There's a lot I haven't told you," he said. "And a lot you haven't told me. Let's discuss everything over dinner."

"I don't know—"

"Afraid to fraternize with the enemy?"

She lifted a shoulder and grinned. "Something like that"

"Just once," he said slowly, his eyes delving into hers, "I want you to let all your defenses down. Okay? Forget that I have anything to do with Caleb Johnson or that Johnson even exists."

"That's a pretty tall order."

"Come on, Dani. Just take me at face value."

She looked at the lines of honesty creasing his skin near the corners of his eyes and mouth. She studied the hard but clean angles of his face. And she stared into his eyes. Dear God, those vivid blue eyes would be her downfall; they seemed to cut clear to her soul. On looks alone, she couldn't doubt him, and for the first time since she'd met him, she didn't try.

"All right," she whispered. "I'll give it a shot."

He laughed, a warm sound that echoed through the still night.

"Bad choice of words," she admitted, her eyes crinkling at the corners and her lips lifting into a graceful smile that Chase found irresistible.

"I'll forgive you," he said, brushing his lips against hers with a tenderness that made her heart ache. She felt his fingers grip her waist, warming her skin through the light fabric of her dress, leaving soft impressions on her flesh.

"You'll forgive me," she retorted, trying to sound and feel offended when all she could concentrate on was the warmth of his lips against hers, the feel of his hands as they circled her and pressed against her naked back, the sound of her heart thundering in her chest.

"If you beg me—"

"Chase McEnroe!" she said, lifting her head. But any further arguments were quickly stilled by the sweet pressure of his mouth on hers and the wet feel of his tongue touching hers, darting into and stroking the inside of her mouth and destroying any thoughts of breaking the embrace. It had been so long since she'd been wanted by a man, so long since she'd wanted to be with one. And this man, damn him, was so very special.

She felt the strap of her dress fall again and then the heat of Chase's lips as he touched her neck and shoulders, kissing her exposed skin and the top of her breast. Legs trembling, she leaned back against the post, lost in his seductive power. One of his hands splayed against the firm muscles of her back and the other came forward, reaching up to claim one breast and touch the smooth skin rounding softly over the top of her dress.

Groaning, he slid lower. His tongue was rough and warm, leaving dewy impressions on her dress as he knelt and kissed her cotton-draped torso, burying his face in the smell and feel of her. Caught in the folds of her skirt, he captured the rounded swell of her buttocks and pulled her urgently forward.

His breath was warm and it fanned the wanton fires of desire in her blood. He held her close, her abdomen positioned near his face. Her hair fell down to her hips, brushing against the back of his hand. She struggled, but not to break away from him, only from her own heated fantasies of making love to him all night long.

"I want you," he whispered into the dress, his breath permeating the soft cloth and burning against her flesh, turning her insides liquid. "And you want me—you can't deny it—"

"Wanting isn't enough," she whispered.

Standing, but still holding her close, he shifted against her, pressing her against the post, letting her feel the hard need rising within him while the weathered wood cooled her back. His eyes were dark and glazed, his fingers twining in the golden strands of her hair.

"I wish I'd never met you," he admitted, hating himself for his need to bare his soul. "Because you've been driving me out of my mind. I've never wanted a woman, any woman, the way I want you. I know this is crazy, but I can't fight it any longer."

She tried to reply, but couldn't find her voice. The thick night air grew tense.

"Tell me no," he whispered, kissing her lips and letting his hand tug on the strap of her dress, pulling the ribbon of fabric still lower until her breast was free and the soft white mound with the dark nipple protruded forward, eager for his touch.

She reached up, covering herself with one hand and he placed his larger hand over hers, gently kneading the soft, warm flesh. A warm glow started burning deep within her as he clasped her wrist and forced the hand away, baring her skin to the moonlit night. "You can't hide from me," he said, tracing the point of her nipple with the finger of his free hand. "And you don't want to."

"It's just that I . . . I don't know what I want." Deep within her, an ache had begun to throb, destroying her rational thought.

"Let me love you."

"Oh, Chase— Oh, God," she whispered as he bent forward and kissed the point of her breast, teasing it lightly with his lips, wetting it and letting it cool in the still night air.

Dani was dizzy with desire, her knees threatened to collapse beneath her, but she managed to claim one last doubt. "I . . . I just can't forget about Caleb."

Chase stiffened, his eyes sparkling as they delved into hers. "Caleb has nothing to do with this."

"But . . . but today, by the creek. I saw your reaction. I know that Caleb suggested that you . . ."

"The hell with Caleb Johnson," he swore, his eyes blazing. "If you believe anything on this earth, Dani, you've got to believe that what's happening between you and me had nothing, *nothing* to do with Johnson or his damned resort. I didn't want to fall in love with you, God knows I hate myself for it, but I can't deny it either."

Before she could protest, he captured her parted lips with his mouth, his arms surrounding her possessively, his tongue searching her mouth for its mate. Without thinking, she molded herself against him, felt the heat of his body surround her and knew that tonight she was his and his alone!

He picked her up and carried her inside the dark house, letting the screen door slam shut behind him.

Dani couldn't stop returning the fever of his kisses. Even when he laid her on the worn rug near the fireplace, she clung to him, almost desperate for the comfort and warmth of his body next to hers. She didn't cry out when he found the zipper of her sundress and slowly slid the dress off her body, easing the soft cotton fabric over her breasts, hips and down her legs. Pale light from a crescent moon and a few winking stars filtered through the open windows. It was just enough illumination to allow her to see the shadowed contours of his face, to read the passion in his slumberous eyes.

She was cool for a moment, the sultry summer air drying the perspiration clinging to her skin. But as Chase slipped the dress past her ankles and began kissing her bare legs, moving upward with his lips, caressing the smooth skin of her hips and abdomen as he gently, pulled her tighter against him, the yearning within her ignited to sparks of desire, long dead but now white hot.

When she was lying beside him, pressed hard against his body, he struggled out of his shirt and cast it aside and then kicked off his jeans. He began rubbing the length of his sinewy body over hers, letting her feel the strength of his corded muscles, the power of his raw masculinity, the smooth texture of his flesh against hers.

She touched him hesitantly at first, but when he moaned against her hair, she couldn't stop herself from tracing the firm line of his muscles with her fingers, and she felt him suck in his breath when she circled his flat hardened nipple.

"You have no idea what you do to me," he groaned as he rolled atop of her, holding her face between his hands as he slowly parted her legs and moved gently, watching as he embraced her, dipping his head to touch his mouth to hers as he found her.

She felt the softness of his lips on hers, the gentle warmth of his fingers molding her breasts and the heart-stopping ecstasy of union when he entered her. Her heart was hammering expectantly, her breath shallow and tight as he moved, slowly at first and then more quickly when she responded, holding him close, her fingers digging into the hard muscles of his back, her voice whispering his name over and over as her blood ran in hot rivulets through her veins.

She felt warm and loved and whole and the joy in her heart increased with the tempo of his lovemaking until she felt she couldn't breathe, couldn't speak, couldn't do anything but quiver in the warmth and desire controlling her mind and body.

She closed her eyes in that final moment when both their bodies released the tension that had built between them for weeks. She cried his name and quaked with an inner, rocking explosion that caused a thousand shooting stars to burst inside her head. Tears of joy and relief filled her eyes when the weight of his body fell against her, his flat chest crushing her breasts, his belabored breathing whispering against her ears and the pounding of his heart echoing the rapid thunder of hers.

"Oh, God, Dani," he murmured at length, gazing into her eyes and cradling her small face in his large, rough hands. "What are we going to do?"

"I don't know." She brushed his golden hair off his brow, smoothing the deep furrow lining his forehead. Slowly, through the haze of afterglow, her mind began to clear. "We'll have to go on as we have, I suppose."

"I can't." He saw the tears standing in her eyes and kissed them as he rolled onto the shabby carpet and wrapped his arms lovingly around her.

"We don't have a choice."

"There are always choices," he whispered.

"Chase—"

"Shh." He placed a finger to her lips. "For just this once, don't argue with me."

His gaze slid down her body, and he noted the sheen of perspiration on her skin, the soft bend of her waist, her rounded hips and slim legs. "You're an incredibly beautiful woman."

Balancing on one elbow, she laughed, brushing aside her remaining tears and tossing her hair away from her face. Even in the darkness, the silken strands shimmered gold. Chase reached forward and touched a wayward curl that fell across Dani's shoulder and brushed across the tip of her nipple.

"Lady Godiva," he whispered, and Dani laughed again.

"I don't think so. Besides, she was more than a little notorious."

"So are you."

"Me?" She shook her head and Chase was mesmerized

by the tousled honey-gold curls sweeping over her breasts. "You ve got the wrong lady."

"Do I?" His teeth flashed in the darkness and he traced the round edge of her nipple with his finger, watching as the dark peak stiffened. "I hope not. I hope to God not."

Then he bent forward and circled her nipple with his tongue and Dani felt shivers of delight dart up her spine. "Chase . . . please . . . I don't think—"

"Don't think." He kissed her again; gently at first and then harder and with a hungry, burning passion that surprised even him. It was as if he couldn't get enough of her, as if he had to claim her as his own, brand her with his mark.

Deftly he lifted her to her feet and then into the air, carrying her up the stairs, holding her body against his and pausing only slightly at Cody's room before walking down the hall to her bedroom and placing her on the old four-poster. The springs squeaked, the mattress sagged and the old hand-pieced quilt her grandmother had made for her slid off the bed. But Dani didn't notice. She was concerned only with Chase and giving and receiving the warm comfort he offered.

He rolled over her and parted her legs with his and she welcomed him again, offering herself eagerly and never once thinking that their lovemaking was for only one night.

Dani woke with the dawn. Sunlight was streaming through the open window, birds were chirping merrily and the cattle were already bawling for breakfast.

Chase was still asleep. Sprawled over three-quarters of

the bed, with one tanned arm draped possessively across Dani's breasts, he snored against the pillow.

She watched him quietly, noticing the way his blond hair fell across his forehead, how his dark lashes rested over his angular cheeks and how his relaxed back and shoulder muscles rose and fell with his steady breathing.

Her heart swelled at the sight of him and she had to tell herself that what had happened only hours before could never be repeated. No matter how right making love to Chase had felt, she still couldn't trust him. One foolish night could be forgiven, another would be suicidal because the closer she got to Chase, the closer she wanted to get.

"It would be so easy to love you," she whispered, kissing him on the forehead before lifting his arm and slowly sliding out of the bed. "Too easy. Too convenient." *And Caleb Johnson was probably banking on the fact that Dani would fall for Chase.*

Determination clenching her jaw, she pulled clean clothes from her bureau, glanced in the mirror to assure herself that Chase was still sleeping soundly, and after tying her hair back, slipped into jeans and a T-shirt.

Then, before her wayward mind could convince her to crawl back into bed with Chase, she hurried out of the room and down the stairs. She'd just about made it to the kitchen when she saw the pile of discarded clothes lying on the floor. Her sundress and Chase's jeans were wrinkled and piled negligently together.

"Oh, Dani, how could you have been such a fool?" she wondered aloud, rolling her eyes to the ceiling and the room overhead where Chase was sleeping peacefully. "You can't fall in love with him, you just can't!" She picked up the clothes and folded them, frowning at the wrinkles in her sundress and remembering all too vividly how the soft material had been crushed.

She hurried outside. It was early. The air was still crisp and cool and she went through her morning chores by rote, her thoughts not on feeding the cattle and horses or watering the garden, or even on petting Runt, though she managed to do all those things and more. Her mind was with the man in her room, the man she'd spent the night with: Caleb Johnson's partner.

Daylight made things so much clearer. "You're doing everything imaginable to get hurt," she chastised herself once she was inside the barn and the scent of dust and hay filled her nostrils. Her eyes adjusted to the dim interior and she looked around it lovingly. Old bridles, saddles and blankets were hung on the wall or sat on sawhorses in the corner. Huge bins of wheat and corn were still nearly overflowing, and the cattle and horses were shifting restlessly on the other side of the manger, chewing noisily, or indignantly stomping their feet or flicking their ears at the ever-present flies.

"God, I love this place," Dani whispered. "How can I ever give it up?" Slumping onto a broken bale of hay, she took off her gloves and set them on an old barrel where she kept her oats.

"Regrets?" Chase's voice was clear and loud.

Dani nearly jumped out of her skin. Heart pounding, she looked up and saw Chase lounging against the barn door, his arms folded over his chest, the bright morning sunlight at his back. His blue eyes looked deep into hers.

"A few, I guess," she admitted, standing nervously and dusting her hands together.

"I thought we got over that hurdle last night."

"Last night . . ." To her embarrassment she blushed. "Look, Chase, I—I'm not a prude, not really. But neither am I the type of woman who sleeps with men I barely know."

"You know me."

"That's the problem; I don't. I don't know a damned thing about you! Oh, sure, I know that you own a company and you're Caleb Johnson's partner and you owe him a bundle of money, and he knew your mother way-back-when, but that's about it." All her insecurities came right to the surface. "I don't know anything else. You could be married with a wife and six kids."

"I'm not married and I don't have any children." He pushed his hair out of his eyes and shook his head. "But you knew that, didn't you? Certainly you know enough about me to realize that I wouldn't be here if I had a family."

"What I know is that you're here and you're Caleb's partner."

He let out a long, tired sigh.

"Actually," she said, leaning over the top of the manger and scratching a two-year-old heifer between the eyes. The cow jerked her head upward and Dani took her hand away, leaning on it instead. "You're here *because* you're in business with Caleb."

Anger pinched the corners of his mouth. "I'm in Martinville because of Caleb, yes. And I want to work the creek because of him." He started advancing upon her. "But being here, with you, has nothing to do with Johnson. I'm here because I want to be with you; because for a reason I don't understand, I'm compelled to be here."

He didn't stop until he'd reached her and once there he placed his arms around her waist. Dani knew that she had to break free or she'd be lost to him, but when she tried to struggle, his arms tightened and he had the audacity to smile. "Tell me you didn't want last night to happen."

"I didn't."

He kissed her slowly, lazily. "Tell me you regret it."

Warmth began to spread throughout her body. "I—I regret it," she whispered.

Chase's eyes centered on her racing pulse, visible in the hollow of her throat. "Tell me it will never happen again."

"It won't . . . oh, Chase . . . please, don't," she said, but couldn't help sighing against him when his hands slid under her T-shirt and splayed familiarly against the muscles of her back. She trembled at his touch and her mouth parted expectantly as he kissed her.

"Tell me you don't love me," he prodded.

"I don't even know you."

The hands tightened. "Say it then."

"I don't . . . I don't love you."

"And you're a liar." His fingers began to move sensually against her skin and he lifted his head to stare into the uncertainty in her eyes.

"Chase—" She tried to push against his chest but his next words stopped her cold.

"I love you, Dani. It's as simple as that. I love you and I don't know what the hell to do about it. My instincts tell me I should run, just like yours tell you to, but I can't."

She swallowed and tried to stop the thundering of her heart and her rapidly racing pulse.

"Dani, I want you to marry me."

Chapter Seven

Dani bit back the easy answer because she knew that marrying Chase would be a mistake, possibly the biggest mistake of her life.

"This isn't the eighteen hundreds, you know," she said quietly. "You don't have to make an honest woman of me just because of last night."

His lips thinned as he stepped nearer and touched her shoulders. "I want you to marry me," he repeated, stroking her cheek. "I don't have any ulterior motives and this has nothing to do with Caleb, your creek or guilt about last night." His sky-blue gaze caressed her face. "I'm thirty-four years old and I want you for my wife. Is that so hard to believe?"

"In light of the circumstances—"

"The hell with the circumstances! Marry me, Dani."

Her heart was beating rapidly in her chest and all of her irrational female emotions were screaming inside her head, *Yes, yes, I'll marry you.* "I—I'd like to," she whispered. "But there's so much to consider."

"Such as?"

"Oh, Chase—"

"Such as?"

Her lips compressing, she pushed her hair out of her eyes. "Such as Cody, for one thing."

"I'll adopt him."

"Just like that?"

Chase muttered to himself and then shook his head. "Of course not. It will take time. He doesn't much trust me yet."

"I wonder why," she taunted. "It couldn't be because you're Johnson's partner, or that you keep trespassing on my land or that you always seem to be getting into fights with me, could it?"

Chase pinched the bridge of his nose. "I'll work things out with Cody. Now, give me another reason."

Her hazel eyes narrowed. "Okay. What about the fact that you live in Idaho and my life is here, on this farm?"

"For as long as you own it, you mean."

"Okay, there's another point. And a big one. *Caleb. And Summer Ridge.* The creek. It's the whole damned mess, the reason you're here in the first place. You're Caleb's partner. You can't get out of that, not until you convince me to sell my property to him, right?"

He lifted a shoulder. "Essentially."

"Then I'd say we have some pretty hard bridges to cross before we even talk about marriage."

He didn't seem convinced, but rammed his fists into his pockets. His thick brows pulled into an angry scowl. "Okay, Dani, we'll play it your way for now. But just answer one question."

"If I can," she agreed.

"Do you love me?"

The question hung in the air. She swallowed back the

thick knot in her throat. "I don't know," she whispered, thinking back to the love she'd shared with Blake and how fragile it had been. Her feelings were strong for Chase, very strong, but to label them love? "I—I think it would be very easy to love you . . ."

"But you won't let yourself," he said flatly.

"I can't. Not yet." She cleared her throat and held up her hand, as if she could make him understand. "If things were different; if Caleb weren't trying to manipulate me, if you weren't his partner and if Cody . . . were more secure in his relationship with his father, I think I would fall in love with you very easily."

"A lot of ifs and none of them can be changed." He kicked at a bale of hay and then dropped onto it as he reached for a piece of straw and twirled it between his fingers. "You know what I think?"

"I'm not sure I want to."

"I think you're afraid, Dani. Afraid to fall in love, afraid to trust, afraid to feel." He studied the dry piece of straw before looking up at her. "l think your husband hurt you deeper than you want to admit and so you avoid any relationship with strings attached."

Her eyes clouded. "Then I would never have let you into my house last night," she whispered. "'Cause I've never met a man with more strings tied around him than you've got!"

Chase's head snapped upward but before he could reply, she marched out of the barn and up the short rise to the house. Kicking off her boots, she strode into the kitchen and poured herself a strong cup of coffee. Sitting at the table, she was angrily looking through the window and across the fields when she heard Chase enter.

"There's coffee in the pot," she said, glancing at him before looking out the window again.

"Thanks." He poured a cup, took a long swallow, turned a chair around and straddled it while his eyes were focused on Dani. "I'm sorry," he said gently.

"Don't be."

"I said some things I shouldn't have."

"No . . . it's all right," she said, thinking how close he'd come to the truth. She had been running from men, avoiding them, afraid of being hurt again. Blake's betrayal had cut deep. In some ways both she and Cody were still bleeding.

"You want to talk about it?"

She lifted her shoulder and blew across the hot coffee. "I don't think so."

"Maybe I can help." He reached across the table and took her hand in his. The tears she'd fought all morning formed in her eyes. "I do care about you," he whispered. "More than I want to. Dani, just believe me: I love you."

"If only it were that simple," she said, her voice catching. Brushing aside her tears, she slowly withdrew her hand from his. "How about some breakfast?" she asked, hoping to lighten the thickening atmosphere in the room. "Ham and eggs?"

"Sounds great." He leaned across the back of the chair and smiled at her, a warm, lazy grin that stretched across his face and stole into her heart. "And I still owe you dinner. How about tonight?"

"Tonight? Cody will be home."

"He's welcome, too."

"I'll think about it," Dani said. Finishing her coffee, she got up from the table, took a few things from the refrigerator and pulled a cast-iron skillet from the cupboards. She cut thick slices of ham and slipped them into the fry pan. As she made breakfast, she was aware that Chase was silently sipping his coffee and watching her.

"The newspaper's in the box," she offered.

"Later. Right now I'm enjoying the view."

"That sounds like a line, cowboy," she remarked, looking over her shoulder but laughing nonetheless.

"It was."

"At least you're honest—" she said and dropped the egg she was cracking onto the floor. "Damn!"

"I've got it." Chase got out of his chair, grabbed a wet dishrag and began mopping up the mess. Dani bent down to swipe at the floor with a couple of paper towels. "I try to be, y'know," Chase said, when most of the broken egg had been placed in Runt's bowl and the floor was clean again.

"Try to be?"

"Honest."

"Oh." Dani avoided his eyes and concentrated on the hash browns and ham and eggs that were still cooking on the stove. How desperately she wanted to believe him. Feeling his arms wrap around her waist and the warmth of his breath brush against her hair, she closed her eyes for a blissful second before opening them again and concentrating on the sizzling eggs.

"Careful," she admonished gently. "I'd hate to spill this hot grease—"

"Dani . . ."

"What?" She turned in his arms and his lips caught hers, kissing her with a hunger that stole the breath from her lungs and left her weak with longing.

"You can't deny what we feel for each other."

"I haven't. I'm just not sure I want to label passion as love."

His thick brows lifted. "How much passion have you felt for other men?"

"I haven't . . . not since Blake."

"Then why do you have so much trouble admitting that you love me—because of him?"

"Maybe a little," she conceded, turning again and busying herself with the meal.

"You can trust me, y'know," he whispered, kissing the back of her neck gently. "I won't hurt you."

Please don't, she thought but said nothing as she slipped the fried eggs, ham and hash browns onto a platter. Chase let go of her and was seated at the table by the time she'd finished buttering the toast and had placed silverware, plates and jam on the red-and-white checkered cloth.

"Looks great," he mumbled.

"Especially when you're starved," she teased.

He took a bite and winked at her. "Especially when you're on the other side of the table."

"Don't—"

"Don't what?" His amused eyes sparkled a crystal blue as he continued eating and watching her.

"Don't be charming. Okay? I just can't handle it this morning."

"Why not?"

She spread raspberry jam on her toast and avoided his gaze. "You wouldn't understand."

"Try me."

After several seconds of trying to eat breakfast and avoiding the subject, she pushed her plate aside in disgust.

"It's just that I've got too much to think about right now. Cody's trying to grow up too fast, he's waiting on pins and needles for a father who won't show up, the farm's barely surviving, half the equipment is broken down, Caleb's trying everything he can to convince me to sell and—"

"And some guy you barely know who works with your worst enemy has just asked you to marry him."

"Yes! Yes!" she said, nodding. "It's just too much right now. Understand?"

"Nope. You were right. I don't understand. Because you could make your life so much simpler if you just learned to trust a little."

She glared at him across the table, picked up her plate and carried it to the sink. "So you have all the answers, don't you?"

"Not all of them," he admitted, finishing breakfast and bringing his plate to her.

"Name one question you don't have an answer for," she baited.

He poured himself another cup of coffee and lounged against the doorframe as he thought. "I don't know what happened to your cattle last year. Didn't you say something about them getting sick?"

"My cattle?" She looked up sharply and then shrugged. "It was a mix-up, I guess. They got into some old pesticide we had around here. A couple died. Two cows and a calf had to be killed, but the rest survived."

"A pesticide?" Chase's countenance grew hard.

"No, that's wrong. It was really a herbicide—an old can of dioxin got spilled in the barn, though it beats me how it happened. I didn't even know we still had any of the stuff around."

"You said you blamed Caleb."

"I said I'd like to blame him."

"But you can't?"

"I didn't catch him snooping around my barn, if that's what you mean. He's been careful to stay on his side of the fence—until you came along."

"And broke all the rules."

She grinned at the pile of suds in the sink. "Maybe not all of them, but more than your share."

He finished his coffee and set his empty cup on the counter. "I've got to run," he said. "Can't keep Caleb waiting too long."

Dani grimaced but didn't argue. She needed time to think. Alone. Before Cody returned. Chase had upset her life more than she would have ever thought possible.

She watched from the porch as he drove away, his Jeep leaving a plume of dust in its wake. Wrapping her arms around the post supporting the porch roof and leaning against it wearily, she closed her eyes to the obvious fact that she loved him with all of her heart.

"Loving Chase is crazy," she told herself. "He'll only cause you heartache because no matter what he says, he still works for Caleb Johnson."

The Jeep turned left at the end of the drive and Dani watched sadly as it climbed the hill leading to Caleb Johnson's rolling acres of Montana farmland.

She felt like crying but instead clenched her teeth with renewed determination. No matter how much it hurt, she would never let Chase know how she felt about him. Their lovemaking of the night before would never be repeated!

* * *

Cody returned from Shane's five dollars richer.

"Let me get this straight," Dani said, trying to remain calm and watching her son smooth the crumpled dollar bills on the kitchen table. "You were gambling for baskets?"

"Yeah, and Shane and I beat these two other guys."

"Who were they?"

Cody shrugged. "Beats me, just a couple of kids that Shane knew. Don and Mark, I think."

"Slow down, will you?" she begged. "How could you bet? I didn't think you had any money on you."

"Fifty cents."

"And you bet it and came out with five dollars?" Dani asked, astounded.

Cody opened the refrigerator and pulled out the pitcher of lemonade. "Don't you understand about betting, Mom? Shane and I were ahead and the other guys kept pressing their bets."

"What does that mean?"

"Double or nothing." He poured himself a tall glass of lemonade and polished it off in three long swallows.

"What if you would have lost?"

He shrugged and poured another glass. "I would have owed the other guys."

The headache Dani had been fighting all morning began to throb. "How would you have paid them back?"

"From my allowance for the chores."

"But that's for college."

"Not all of it." Cody scowled at his mother.

"I just don't like you gambling."

"Aw, Mom, lighten up. Okay? It was just a bet on a ball game, not the end of the world!" He walked into the living room, switched on the television, kicked off his shoes and flopped onto the couch.

"I think we need to talk about attitude."

"Again?"

She walked into the room and sat on the arm of the couch. "Cody—"

"Geez, Mom, lay off, will ya? I'm sorry I brought up the lousy game. I thought you would be thrilled." He turned his attention toward the TV, drank his lemonade and effectively ignored his mother.

After counting to ten, Dani said, "I'm glad you had a good time with Shane. I'm also happy that you enjoyed your game and that you won, *but* I'm just not that crazy about the gambling."

"Why not?"

"Usually, when people gamble, somebody loses money they can't afford."

"Then they shouldn't bet," Cody said philosophically.

"Precisely."

Cody slid her a knowing glance. "You're just mad because of Dad, aren't you?"

"What do you mean?"

"I heard you say that Dad gambled all of his money away. Somethin' about the cash he got from Caleb Johnson for his land. He went to Las Vegas or somethin'. Right?"

"Reno," she replied woodenly. "But how did you know—"

"I heard you say a couple of things and then some of the kids at school. . . ." He shrugged one shoulder as if the subject were of total disinterest to him.

"Let me guess: Isabelle Reece."

Cody grinned and finished his drink. "Yeah. Not too hard to figure, huh?"

Dani pursed her lips together. "Seems that Isabelle's father knows more about our family than he does his own."

"Maybe his own family is boring."

"I'd be glad to take a little of that boredom right about now," she whispered, slapping Cody's knee affectionately. "Listen, Diamond Jim, just try not to get into any high-stakes poker games, okay?"

Cody laughed and nodded as he handed his mother his empty glass. "Okay, Mom. It's a deal."

It had better be, she told herself as she walked back to the kitchen and tried not to compare her son with his father.

The moonlight created a silvery ribbon that danced and fluttered on the rippling water. Chase waded carefully under the fence while darting glances up the hill toward Dani's house. Nervous sweat ran down his neck and between his shoulder blades. If Dani caught him now. . . .

Silently cursing himself for his duplicity, he carefully took the water and soil samples he needed, quickly labeling each one with the aid of a flashlight and waterproof pen.

"Damn you, Johnson," he muttered, moving down-stream and working as quietly as possible. His waders slid on the rocky bottom of the creek, but he managed to stay on his feet and slip the vials into his creel.

The sound of the rushing water filled his ears, but still he strained to listen for any noise disturbing the night and hoped against hope that Dani was safely tucked in bed and sleeping soundly. He heard the distant sound of a dog barking and Runt's sharp answer.

Go back to sleep, Chase thought. *Whatever you do, dog, don't wake the house!* But Dani's cabin remained dark, no lights flickered on.

By this time Chase had made his way to the cottonwood stand and he had to bend to avoid the overhanging branches of the scrub oaks and cottonwood trees. It was darker in the thicket, more private, but he couldn't help feeling that he was betraying Dani even as he tried to help her.

You're just trying to get to the bottom of this, he told himself for the thousandth time. *And you can't tell her what you've found until you're sure.*

Runt barked again and this time the sound was much closer. Chase froze. *Damn!* He squinted through the branches but could see nothing but the dark shapes of the cattle slowly moving in the adjoining fields.

Letting out a relieved breath, he placed the final sample in his creel and decided to get out while the getting was good.

"What're you doin' here?" a boy's voice demanded.

Chase turned and found Cody standing on the bank of the creek.

Great. Just what I need. "I wanted some soil and water samples."

"From our land?" Cody asked. The boy's dark hair was askew and he was wearing only hastily donned cutoffs.

"Yes." Chase waded to the edge of the creek.

"I don't think you should be here, Mr. McEnroe—"

"Chase."

Cody crossed his arms over his bare chest and his jaw jutted out angrily. "Does Mom know about this?"

"Not yet."

"She won't like it."

Chase looked at the sky and then shook his head. "Maybe not at first, but I'll explain why I needed them."

"Then why don't you do it right now," Dani suggested as she approached. Unable to sleep herself, she'd heard Runt bark, Cody go downstairs and out the back door. After flinging on her robe, she'd followed her son and hadn't caught up with him until now, when he was confronting Chase, who was standing, predictably, she supposed, in the creek. "I thought I told you to stay off my property," Dani said and then ran her fingers through her tangled tresses. "But then I forgot, you don't pay any attention to what I say."

"Mom?" Cody asked.

"You go back to the house," she said. "You know better than to get up in the middle of the night."

"But I heard Runt—"

"Take him with you."

Cody looked at his mother and then back to Chase. "Maybe I should stay."

"I can handle this," Dani said angrily. "Go back, to the house. If I don't come up in half an hour, call the sheriff and tell him that one of Caleb Johnson's men is trespassing!"

Cody's eyes rounded in the darkness, but he did as his mother had commanded. With a short, sharp whistle at the dog, he was gone.

"You don't have to get melodramatic," Chase said angrily, wading out of the creek. "I get the message."

"About time."

"Dani, look. I only want these samples to prove that Caleb's trying to force you off your land."

"How?"

"I'm not sure, yet. But I will be soon. Can you trust me for a few more days?"

"You're pushing it, Chase. Why didn't you tell me you needed some more samples?"

"I thought that was pretty obvious since you ruined the last ones. And I thought you knew I needed these—"

"So you had to come trooping out here in the middle of the night?" she mocked, pursing her lips together. "You could have told me—last night or this morning. Or didn't it occur to you?"

"I wanted to wait until I was sure."

"Sure?" she repeated, her fury causing her to shake. "Of what? That I'd fall for you?"

Chase swore angrily. "Didn't I stand up for you yesterday?"

"Yes," she said tightly, trying to hang on to her rage. But seeing Chase in the moonlight, his shirt fluttering open, his straw-blond hair mussed in the night breeze did strange things to her.

"Didn't last night mean anything?" he asked softly.

She had to remind herself that she was outraged. "I don't know. You tell me."

"Nothing's changed."

"Except that you snuck over here again, without my knowledge, and started digging in my creek. It's not that I really care if you're on my land anymore," she admitted, "it's all this sneaking around and mystery that I don't understand. From the first time I saw you, you haven't been straight with me."

"I have."

"Then what the hell are you doing here?"

"Looking for proof."

"Of what?"

He stared straight into her eyes. "That Caleb knowingly contaminated your water."

"What!"

"Look, Dani. Just go home and go to bed. I'll contact you when I know more," he promised, as he climbed the short rise of the bank to stand next to her.

"But . . . wait a minute. What are you saying? Caleb contaminated my water."

"The creek."

"With what?"

"Dioxin."

"Dioxin?" she repeated, incredulous. "Is . . . is that why you were asking me about herbicides earlier today?"

"Yes."

"You thought I'd done it?"

"No, I just wanted to be sure."

The weight of what he'd said to her made her lean against the trunk of a tree. "But . . . how?"

"The other day—the day you destroyed my first samples—I found an old five-gallon drum of something buried in the creekbed, just on the other side of the fence. I had it checked. It was dioxin, but what I don't know yet is why the drum was buried, who buried it, and whether it was done for malicious intent."

"But you think so," she whispered, shivering with dread.

"Didn't you say some of your cattle died last year?"

"Yes, but—"

"Did they drink from the creek?"

"Of course."

"And the rest of the herd?"

"Wasn't affected. A few got sick, but they recovered. You know, I had this feeling, I guess you'd call it, that Johnson was behind the poisoning, but I wasn't sure. Oh, God," she whispered, not really wanting to believe that Caleb Johnson was so desperate he would stoop to killing her livestock.

"I'm still not sure that Caleb was involved. But I'm working on it."

She stared up at him and noticed his blue eyes had darkened to the color of midnight as he walked over to her. "You know, I really want to believe you, to trust that you're on my side."

"But you don't?"

"I didn't say that," she whispered. He jerked off his gloves and touched the underside of her jaw. In the moonlight her hazel eyes looked silver. "It's . . . it's just that I don't really know what to think. Ever since you've come here, nothing has made a lot of sense."

"Just trust me."

"Oh, God, Chase, I want to!" she said, her throat tight as his cool lips touched hers. Willingly, she wound her arms around his neck and sighed when he parted her robe to touch her breast. Her thick hair streamed down her back in soft waves of brown and gold.

"I love you, Dani," Chase admitted against her neck. "Just remember that I love you—"

"Mom!" Cody's voice, distant but worried, cut through the night.

"Oh, Lord, I told him to call the sheriff, didn't I?" Pushing Chase aside, she clutched the lapels of her robe in one hand. "I'm coming," she called before turning back to Chase. "Just don't lie to me," she whispered. "For God's sake, Chase, don't lie to me."

And then she was off, running through the rough field and up to the house. She glanced back once. Chase had walked out of the trees and was standing, feet wide apart, shirt billowing in the breeze, and watching her. Her heart squeezed painfully at the sight of him and though she stumbled once, she continued to the house.

By the time she reached the back porch, she was out of breath and shaken.

"Are you okay?" Cody asked, his eyes round with worry.

"Of course I am, sport," she said, hugging the boy. "I can take care of myself."

"But that guy works for Johnson."

"I know, but I think he's different than most of Johnson's men—hey, you didn't call the sheriff, did you?"

"Not yet."

"Good." She sighed and hugged her son, but Cody's expression was puzzled.

"How can you be sure? That he's different, I mean?"

"I don't know. Maybe intuition." She planted a kiss on the top of Cody's head. "Now you go upstairs and go to bed, okay?"

"Okay," Cody said begrudgingly as they walked through the screen door.

Dani lingered at the door for a minute, staring down toward the creek and squinting into the darkness as a cloud passed over the moon.

Chase was gone, or at least she couldn't see him. Involuntarily she placed her fingers to her still-swollen lips and wondered if trusting Chase would only cause her heartache.

She didn't hear from him for the rest of the week. Deciding that he'd probably come to his senses and had just given her some cock-and-bull story about the drum of dioxin, she tried to ignore the pain in her heart and told herself that it was all for the best that she hadn't seen him again.

"So why have you thought about him day in and day out for the past week?" she grumbled, driving back from Martinville with a load of seed grain for the October planting of winter wheat.

The pickup bounced as she tried to avoid the most severe potholes in the rutted lane. Before the weather changed, she'd have to buy several yards of gravel and spread it over the rough road.

"Just one more expense," she told herself. *One of a hundred that she couldn't afford.*

Chase's Jeep was parked near the house. Dani's pulse jumped at the sight of the dusty vehicle. Why was he here? Did he know that she'd be gone?

She got out of the pickup warily and heard the sound of voices near the barn. Following the noise, she rounded the corner of the house and saw Chase and Cody playing one-on-one basketball on the far side of the barn where Cody had hung a hoop two years earlier. The netting had all but rotted off the metal rim, but Cody still used the basket for practice. Both Chase and Cody were into the game, to the point that neither one had heard or seen her arrive. In the shade of an ancient apple tree that stood near the back porch, Dani watched as Chase played with Cody, gave the boy pointers, and in the end, let him win.

"Good match," he said, his low voice drifting up to the house as he clapped Cody on the boy's bare back.

"Aw, you let me win."

"You think so?"

"Didn't ya?" Cody asked, his brown eyes crinkling at the corners, his sweaty, heat-reddened face beaming up at the tall man.

Chase was wiping the sweat from his face with his T-shirt and his taut muscles rippled in the hot summer sun. His blond hair hung limply over his forehead in dark, wet strands. "How about a drink?" he asked the boy.

"Sure, Mom's got some lemonade and maybe a couple bottles of Coke." Cody started sprinting toward the house before he noticed his mother. "Hey . . . when did you get here?"

"Just a couple of minutes ago." Dani cocked her head in Chase's direction. "What about him?"

"Oh, I don't know. A while."

"I'm surprised you let him stay."

"Why not? You do," Cody said, before dashing to the house.

Dani was still watching Cody's vanishing act and wondering what to do about it when Chase approached. He saw the vexed expression clouding her clear eyes. "Don't worry about him," Chase suggested, cocking his head in the direction of the house as Cody sprinted up the steps and ran inside. "He's a good kid." Sweat was still trickling down his neck.

"But he's growing up."

"They all have a habit of doing that."

"I know," she whispered. "But sometimes it just seems to come too fast."

Chase draped a familiar arm around her shoulders. "I don't know a parent who would disagree with you."

"How did you convince him to let you stay?"

"That wasn't so easy," Chase drawled, offering her a lazy smile. "He wasn't too keen on me showing up."

"I'll bet not."

"But I told him I was a friend of yours."

"Oh, great."

"Yeah, that wasn't the smartest thing I'd done. But I noticed he was packing around a basketball and I offered to show him how the game was played."

"And?"

"He didn't think he needed a teacher."

Dani laughed. How many times had she seen Cody's stubborn streak surface?

"But I wasn't about to take no for an answer. I wanted to wait for you. So I offered to play him one-on-one for the privilege of staying."

"And he agreed?" Dani was surprised.

"Not exactly."

"Well?"

Chase's grin broadened. "He wanted to play for a dollar a game."

"Oh, God," she groaned.

Chase squeezed her shoulders and wrapped his T-shirt around his neck. "Don't worry. He didn't take the shirt off my back. See, I've still got it." He grinned and his eyes sparkled with the afternoon sunlight. "And don't bother with a lecture, I gather he already had one."

"Apparently it didn't work." She pursed her lips and started for the house.

Chase's fingers tightened around her arm. "Don't say anything to him."

"Why not?"

"'Cause part of the deal was that I wasn't supposed to let you know anything about it. And," he smiled to himself, "I think he learned his lesson."

"Oh, no," Dani whispered. "How much does he owe you?"

"You don't want to know."

"Yes, I do! He's my son and—"

"And I think his gambling days are over. Let it lie."

Dani let out a sigh of frustration. "All right. This time. But if he ever so much as—"

"He won't."

"You sound so sure of yourself."

"I am. It's a lesson my pa taught me when I was just a little older than Cody. We were playing cards with a neighbor and Dad let me bet against him. I kept pressing my bets and I lost to the point that I owed the guy over two hundred dollars. I spent that whole summer working off my debt doing yard work for the neighbor."

"And regretting every minute of the card game."

"You got it."

"So how is Cody going to pay you back?"

"He doesn't have to. I let him off the hook this time. But I doubt if you'll ever have trouble with him gambling over his head again."

"I hope you're right."

Cody returned with three glasses of lemonade, downed his and after asking permission, took off on his bike to visit the Anders brothers.

"Don't bother them if they're working," Dani said as the boy hopped on his ten-speed.

"I won't! I already called. Jonathon wants me to go fishin' with him." Then he pedaled out of sight with Runt galloping behind the back wheel.

Chase leaned against the fence under the shade of the apple tree. "He's a good boy," he observed, finishing his drink. "You worry about him too much."

Dani swirled her ice cubes in her glass and stared across the fields to the creek. "Something I just can't help."

She felt Chase's hand on her shoulder, his fingers gentle as they forced her to turn and face him.

"Have you wondered why I stayed away this past week?" he asked.

"I thought you'd changed your mind."

"Nope. First, I didn't want Caleb to get too suspicious. If he gets wind of the fact that I found that drum of dioxin, he'll cover his tracks."

"So that wasn't just a story."

"What? The herbicide?"

She nodded.

"No. But I'm still doing some checking with the agriculture department and the extension office. I want to make sure I know where I stand before I confront Caleb."

"I see."

He studied the doubts in her eyes and then let out a long breath of air. "Besides, I had to stay away because I wanted to give you some time to think things through, to realize that I was sincere. I thought you'd come to the same conclusion that I have; that we love each other and should be together."

"Like some fairy-tale romance," she countered.

He grimaced and leaned over the fence. "Like two sensible people would. You can't tell me you haven't thought about it."

"To tell you the truth, I haven't thought about much else," she admitted.

"And?"

She sighed and lifted a shoulder. "I think we should just give it a little time, that's all. I—I want to be sure this time."

"I thought you realized that I'm not like your ex-husband," he said softly.

She flinched and bit her lower lip. "And I won't hurt you or Cody."

She forced a trembling smile and looked into his eyes. They were a clear ocean-blue that seemed to see into the shadowed corners of her soul. "I'd like to marry you," she admitted huskily. "But I can't. Not yet. I just need a little time to think things through."

"I'll be here about two more weeks," he said.

"And then?"

He raked his fingers through his hair. "Then it will be near the first of September. I have another job to go to."

"In Idaho?"

Shaking his head, he stared across the fields and watched the grazing cattle. "Central Oregon. Then I'm back in Boise."

She ran her fingers along the top rail of the fence and shivered despite the heat. "And what about Caleb Johnson?"

"I don't know."

"You told me part of your deal with him was to get me to sell off my land."

"He'd like that. For the final twenty-five percent."

"And . . . and do you think that by marrying me you could convince me to sell my land and move to Boise with you?"

His brow creased and impatiently he ran a hand over his tight jaw. "You still don't trust me, do you?"

"I want to."

"But it's impossible?" he said, his temper flaring.

"I'm just trying to be cautious."

Closing his eyes, he tried to count to ten. He got lost at three. "Son of a bitch!" he whispered through clenched teeth and began pacing along the fence line. "You don't trust Caleb and with good reason, and I'm convinced that he'd do just about anything to get you to move off this land, but for crying out loud, Dani, I am not asking you to marry me because of Caleb Johnson! Or my company! As far as I'm concerned, he can keep the final twenty-five percent of the company. He's in a minority position and will have no authority! I can do as I goddamn please!"

He walked up to her and with his face twisted in anger, took hold of her shoulders. "And what I want, lady, is you! I've waited and been patient and asked you nicely to marry me, and you've pussy-footed around the issue, as if I've got some dark ulterior motive. Now I realize that you have your reasons to doubt me, but dammit, I love you!"

His lips came down on hers hungrily and his strong arms wrapped around her so tightly and possessively that she was barely able to breathe. He moaned into her mouth and his broad hands covered her back, pulling her close to him, against the hard wall of his chest and between the muscular lengths of his legs.

"Dear God, Dani," he whispered into her hair, his breath ragged and torn, his heart thundering in his chest. "Just say yes."

She swallowed hard, looking into his deep blue eyes and, with a trembling smile, nodded. "Yes, Chase," she said irrationally. "I'll . . . I'll marry you."

"Thank God." A weary grin stretched from one side of his face to the other and he kissed her again, softly this time. "I've spent the last week lying awake at night and wondering what I'd do if you turned me down."

"And what did you decide?"

His smile turned wicked. "It was simple. I was going to ask Jenna Peterson to watch Cody and then I was going to kidnap you and take you to a mountain cabin and hold you hostage until you agreed to become my wife."

Dani laughed and winked at him. "Maybe I should have held out," she said. "Sounds like I missed out on a lot of fun."

Chase pulled her close and traced the angle of her jaw with his finger. "I'll make it up to you, I promise." His lips captured hers in a bittersweet kiss filled with the promise of the future.

"And what will Caleb say about this?" she asked.

"Let's not worry about Caleb," he said. "We've got better things to do."

"Such as?"

He released her slightly and let his arms rest on her shoulders. "Well, I can think of a lot of things . . ." His eyes slid suggestively down her neck to the fluttering pulse at the base of her throat. "But they can wait . . . for a little while. How about a picnic?"

"A picnic—now?" She was surprised.

"Sure. Sort of a celebration. You could show me around this place." He straightened. "I'll shower and you can throw some things into a basket."

Dani laughed. "You're starting to sound like a husband already."

He arched a thick brow. "On second thought, you could shower with me . . ."

"Then we'd never leave."

"That would be okay."

He leaned closer, but she pushed against his shoulders with her flat hands. "Later, cowboy. Right now, you hit the showers, and I'll pack and leave a note for Cody."

They walked into the house, arms linked, and Dani felt as if she were on top of the world.

The only trouble with being on the top, she told herself cynically when she heard the sound of the shower running and had begun making sandwiches, was that there was only one way to go.

Chapter Eight

The easiest way to get to the site of the original homestead house was on horseback, so while Dani fixed a lunch that could be carried in saddlebags, Chase saddled and bridled the horses. The ride across the creek, through a series of fields and finally into the wooded area surrounding the old buildings, took about twenty minutes.

Dani pulled Traitor up short and the rangy buckskin, his ears flicking backward, responded with a toss of his head. Chase rode Whistlestop, a heavy-boned bay mare. At the top of a small knoll he held his restless horse in check beside Dani.

"So this is where it all started," he said.

"At least for the Hawthornes," she replied. Indicating the surrounding hills with a sweeping gesture, Dani looked lovingly over the sprawling acres of farmland and pockets of timber. "This—" she pointed to what had once been a large two-story farm house "—was the spot my great-great-grandparents chose to homestead." Dropping the reins over Traitor's head, Dani heard the bridle jingle as the horse grazed on the dry grass and weeds.

Chase still sat astride Whistlestop, leaned forward and squinted into the late afternoon sun. With a backdrop of virgin-growth timber and the craggy Rocky Mountains reaching up to the Montana sky, the ancient house looked pitifully neglected; a skeleton of what had once been a grand old farm house now surrounded by thistles and brush.

The main timbers sagged, all of the windowpanes had long been broken, and the roof had collapsed on the second story, exposing the interior to the rugged elements of the harsh Montana winters. Blackberry vines, now laden with heavy fruit, had crawled over what had been a broad front porch and clung tenaciously around the doorway.

Some of the wallpaper, bleached and stained, was still visible where part of the second story walls had been torn away by the wind.

"It was beautiful once," Dani said, eyeing the sad, dilapidated structure.

"I can see that." Chase got off the mare and let the horse graze. Pushing his hands into the back pockets of his jeans, he continued to study the old house while he walked toward Dani. He placed an arm around her shoulders and some of the poignant desolation that had crept over her disappeared.

"The hot springs are over there." She pointed to the stream seeping through the earth near the back of the house. "And since there wasn't hot and cold running water when the house was built, the spring was a real luxury. Hot water could be carried into the house."

"So what happened?" he asked. "Why wasn't the house kept up?"

"Money," Dani said with a frown. "When my grand-parents were young, sometime in the thirties or forties, I think, they built the cabin that Cody and I live in because it was so much closer to the road. It was cheaper to build and make modern with gas and electricity and running water than to rebuild this place. And they always thought that if they got enough money together, they'd restore the old house."

"But it didn't work out."

"No." She walked up to the porch, touched one of the rotting timbers at the corner of the house and sighed. "It's a shame, though. I've seen old pictures of it. This front porch ran the whole length. It really was very grand . . ."

"Let's look inside."

"I don't think it's safe."

"I'll make sure it is before we step on any rotted out boards."

"But the berry vines; the door is nearly blocked off—"

"Come on. Where's your sense of adventure?" He took her hand in his and gently pulled her forward. With his free hand he managed to push the undergrowth aside and break a path to the front door. Bees buzzed in the berry vines overhead and the thorns caught in Dani's hair and blouse, but Chase, bending over slightly to protect himself, was finally able to lead her through the open doorway.

It had been a long time since she'd been inside the house and the years and weather had taken their toll on the place. The wooden floors were scarred and dulled by a thick covering of dirt. Though the stairs were still intact, the banister had long since fallen away and lay in scattered pieces in the entry hall. Cobwebs hung in dark corners and broken glass littered the floor.

Chase reached down and picked up one of the hand-carved balusters, cleaning off the dust to stare at the once beautiful spoke that had helped support the railing. "How old is this house?" he asked, looking around. On either side of the main hall were two large rooms, each with a blackened fireplace on the outside walls.

"I don't know exactly. Over a hundred years."

"At least." Walking into what must have been a dining room, Chase stopped at the fireplace. "It looks like the mason knew what he was doing." He placed a hand on the ancient bricks and noted the few places where the mortar had begun to crumble. With a frown, he went through an open archway.

Following, Dani walked through the big dining room and down one step into the kitchen. It was a lean-to room, only one story, with a fireplace all its own. There was a huge black pot still hanging from a hook over the hearth. The hinge groaned when Chase tried to wipe the cobwebs from the ancient kettle.

"I'd love to rebuild this house," Dani thought aloud. Chase looked up at the sagging ceilings and broken walls.

"You'd have to start from the ground up."

"I know. It's just a pipe dream, I suppose."

Chase took hold of her hand. "Don't ever give up your dreams, Dani."

She laughed and shook her head. "But I'd never be able to afford to restore this place."

"If you think that way, you've lost the battle before it's even begun." He kissed her on the forehead and wrapped his arm protectively around her shoulders. She leaned her head against his chest as they walked through the splintered back door and into the bright afternoon sunlight.

"You do see why I love this land, don't you?" she asked suddenly, biting her lip and staring at the stark mountains jutting up against the brilliant blue sky. "My family has been here for generations . . . I just can't stand the thought of these beautiful hills covered with asphalt, burger stands, condominiums and hotels. Is that selfish?"

"I don't know," Chase admitted. "Seems like there should be a way to compromise."

She nodded and walked over to Traitor to get the lunch from the saddlebags. Chase grabbed the rolled blanket from his horse and spread it on the ground under a rough-barked pear tree.

After sitting down, Dani placed the sandwiches, apples and oatmeal cookies on the old quilt and then poured Chase a cup of iced tea. "Maybe I should just sell out to Caleb Johnson," she said distantly, but then shook her head. "Maybe if it were anyone else—but it's just Caleb's damned take-it-all attitude that drives me out of my skull. The man is poison."

"I'd like to disagree with you," Chase said as he took the cup Dani offered. He leaned on one elbow, unwrapped a sandwich and started to eat as Dani poured another cup of tea for herself.

"But you can't argue the point, can you?"

"Not unless he had nothing to do with the drum of dioxin."

"Have you asked him about it?"

"Not yet But I'll have to soon," he answered, finishing his sandwich.

"What are you waiting for?"

"The right time, I suppose. When I've got all the information I need to back me up."

"Such as?"

He shrugged and reached for an apple, polishing it on the tail of his shirt. "Such as knowing for sure that the dioxin belonged to him and that he had it placed in the creek himself; that it wasn't the accident of a careless hand who worked for him. There's still a chance that Caleb told one of his hands to get rid of the herbicide and the guy thought the best place to store it would be to bury it in the creekbed."

"You don't believe that."

"Nope. I think it's pretty obvious Johnson isn't on the up-and-up. I just don't know why he dragged me in to it."

They ate in silence and slowly the black cloud that had settled over Dani disappeared. The late afternoon sun was warm as it filtered through the branches of the pear tree to dapple the ground in bright splotches of light. The late summer air was fresh and clean and a few leaves had already turned yellow with the promise of autumn.

Finished with his lunch, Chase stretched out on his back and clasped his hands under his head to stare through the leafy branches to the sky. "Come here," he suggested.

"I am here."

"No, over here," he said, patting the blanket beside him. "I want you right here."

"Any particular reason?"

"Quite a few, actually. But the most important is that I'm going to be gone for a few days."

"Gone?" she repeated, her head jerking up. The thought that he wouldn't be near hit her full force.

"I'll be back. Promise. There's just a couple of loose ends I have to tie up back in Boise."

"No one else can handle them?"

He sighed and shook his head. "Apparently not."

"Don't you have a supervisor or vice-president or something."

"Nope. I tried that once. A man by the name of Eric Conway worked with me." Chase scowled at the thought of Eric's betrayal. Personally and professionally Eric had managed to cut him to the bone. "We were best friends until he decided to form his own company, take all my staff and techniques and hightail it."

"Oh."

"Since then I haven't trusted anyone to do some of the work. So, I've got to go home for a couple of days."

"Just as long as you come back," she whispered, hiding the disappointment that tugged at her heart. She put the remains of the lunch into the saddlebags and sat next to him, her hands folded over her knees, her eyes mere slits as she squinted west toward the mountains. Tendrils of hair escaped unnoticed from the braid she wore down her back.

Chase reached upward and brushed one of the locks of honey-brown hair away from her face. The caress of his fingers against her cheek made her tremble.

"Until I met you, I'd never wanted a woman to spend the rest of my life with me."

"Have you changed your mind?" She looked down at him, saw the twinkle in his eye and felt his fingers against her back as he tried to unwrap the band that held the single plait of hair in place.

"Nope."

"How can you be so sure of yourself?" she asked.

"Maybe because I haven't experienced a bad marriage." He pulled the band from her hair and watched in fascination as the tight braid loosened.

"Toss your head," he said.

"Oh, Chase, honestly—"

"Come on."

She laughed and shook her hair free. In glinting, sun-brightened highlights, it fell past her shoulders to her waist in soft tangled waves.

"That's better," he said with a crooked, charming grin, his hand sliding down her back.

"I think you're just trying to change the subject."

"Wouldn't dream of it. What do you want to know?"

Smiling sadly, she pushed the hair from his eyes. "You said you haven't been married."

"That's right."

"But surely there have been other women . . ."

"A few."

"And no bad memories?" she asked skeptically.

"None that I care to remember," he said, thinking for a minute about the one woman he'd trusted; his secretary and lover, Tracy Monteith, the woman who'd run off with Eric Conway when Eric had started a rival company. Later Chase had learned that Tracy had only used him to gain information for Eric. Tracy and Eric had been married just about as long as Eric's company had been in operation.

"What is it?" Dani asked; seeing the painful play of emotions on Chase's rugged face.

"Nothing important," he said, pushing himself up on one elbow and wrapping his other arm securely around her waist.

"So you can just forget any of the bad relationships you've had?"

"I try to. No reason to dwell on them."

She couldn't find fault with his logic.

"But then I don't have a kid who reminds me of what happened."

Dani forced her sad thoughts out of her mind and smiled at Chase. "I wouldn't trade Cody for the world," she said. "Sure, sometimes he reminds me of Blake, but that's okay. I mean, Blake is Cody's father and no matter how painful the marriage eventually became, I did end up with my son and managed to hold onto the farm. Some women aren't so lucky."

"Do you still love him?" Chase asked, his eyes delving into hers.

"Cody asked me the same thing," she whispered.

"Well?"

"No. I did once. When I was very young, before Cody was born and when my folks were still alive. But that was a long time ago. . ." She avoided Chase's eyes and slid away from him. "I don't know why I'm feeling so melancholy. It's silly really. Probably because of the old house. It looks so sad and lonely up here, falling apart and—"

Chase had taken hold of her arm and pulled her against him with such force that she was left breathless as she half lay across his chest, her golden hair streaming over them both. "All I want to do is make you happy," he said slowly. "And I promise that I'll never hurt you."

She swallowed against the thick lump forming in her throat as he placed a hand behind her head and drew her face to his. "I love you, Dani," he said slowly as he kissed her. "And I don't want you to ever forget it."

"I won't." She breathed softly into his mouth and he groaned, pulling her on top of him and kissing her face, her neck, her hair.

She felt the buttons of her blouse give way and her breasts spilled forward against his chest.

Groaning, Chase tugged at their clothes until they were both naked on the blanket, her white skin touching his tanned muscles, her beautiful dark-tipped breasts supple and ready for the feel of his fingers and mouth, her long hair streaming down to brush and tickle his skin erotically.

Taking her nipple between his lips, he felt her quiver and moan his name while her fingers worked their magic on his skin. He held her as close as he could, pressing urgently against her, feeling the need to protect her. For even as he began making love to her, he felt a quiet desperation deep in his soul, as if forces outside his control would drive her away. Closing his eyes against the ugly thought, he moved against her until he was spent and then, cradling her head against his chest, whispered words of love in the shade of the tree, oblivious to the humming insects or the sweet scent of the honeysuckle and lilacs that filled the air around them.

The first warning that things weren't going smoothly came just two days later. Dani hadn't heard from Chase, but wasn't particularly worried as she knew that he was back in Boise. She was still thinking about his proposal and the consequences of marrying him when she drove into Martinville for a week's worth of groceries on Friday morning.

Cody was with her and not particularly pleased about

it. Pouting, he'd propped himself against the passenger side of the pickup. Runt was standing on top of Cody, his black nose poked through the partially open window that allowed some fresh air inside the stuffy cab of the truck.

"I don't want to go shopping," Cody grumbled as Dani pulled into the parking lot.

"But you need some new school clothes and shoes," she pointed out.

"Not today! School's still a few days off."

"And all the sales have just started."

"Aw, Mom," he grumbled, getting out of the pickup when Dani had parked between the faded lines tn the dusty asphalt. "Give me a break, will ya?" Angrily, he slammed the door of the pickup, nearly clipping Runt's nose in the bargain.

"Be careful," Dani reprimanded.

"Oh, sure."

The dog paced and whined, sticking his head out the open window.

"We'll only be a couple of minutes," Dani said, patting Runt's head and glancing pointedly at her son. Then, thinking the dog would be too hot inside the cab, she let Runt out and had him sit in the back of the truck. "Just don't bark your fool head off, okay?"

The temperature seemed to soar as Dani walked across the hot parking lot to the store. Things were no better inside Anders' Super Market. The air conditioning had gone out and one of the coolers had broken down.

"Land o' mercy," Marcella Anders said to Dani as she carefully repacked the meats into the remaining, still-cold display case. "And every repairman in town working overtime. I hope to heaven this meat doesn't spoil." She was a

large woman, big boned and heavyset. She wore her graying hair piled high on her head and a starched white apron
over her clothes. For nearly as long as Dani could remember, Marcella had worked in the meat department of her
husband's store.

"It's been incredibly hot this year."

"Don't I know it?" Marcella grumbled. "Brings out the
worst in people, ya know. Just yesterday, Jenna Peterson
came in here fit to be tied."

"That doesn't sound like her," Dani remarked, thinking
of Caleb Johnson's kindly housekeeper as she eyed the
packages of frozen fish.

"No, indeed, it don't. But she was in a regular tizzy, let
me tell you. Something about one of Caleb's men . . . a
new man he'd hired. Jenna seemed to think that this man
was no good, just on Caleb's payroll to cause trouble."

Dani felt her face go pale. "Did . . . did she tell you the
man's name?" she asked, looking Marcella square in
the eyes.

"Nope. I think she wanted to tell me more, but she
thought better of it, ya know. Jenna needs her job; she prac-
tically supports her daughter and grandson and she never
was one to gossip much."

"Loose lips sink ships," Dani said to herself, thinking
about Chase and finding him in the creek in the middle
of the night. And now he was gone. . .

"Pardon?"

"Nothing," Dani said, and forced a smile. "You were
right, it was probably just the weather."

Marcella's face pulled together in a thoughtful frown.
"I hope so," she said aloud. "I wouldn't want to think that
any of Caleb's men are dishonest. The people of this town,

we're all countin' on that resort of his. My husband thinks it'll triple business in the next year. He's already had the plans drawn up to expand, put in a delicatessen and a garden department." Marcella chuckled to herself as she placed the last package of meat into the full display case. "This is his big chance, he thinks. Just like most of the rest of the folks in this town."

"Except Mom," Cody said.

Marcella nodded curtly. "Well, we're all entitled to our own opinion, aren't we?" she said, still smiling as she wiped her hands on her apron. "It's a free country."

"Yes," Dani said, pushing her cart forward.

"See ya around," Marcella said, and moved down the meat counter to help another customer.

Dani pushed her cart down the crowded aisles and tried to concentrate on shopping, but found it nearly impossible. She came out of the store with only half the items she'd planned to pick up.

"You think Mrs. Anders was talking about Chase, don't you?" Cody said once they'd climbed back into the pickup with Runt.

"I don't know."

"I can tell it's what you think."

She eased the truck into the sparse traffic of the main street of the small town and pushed the hair from her eyes at the one stoplight near the gas station. "I didn't say that."

"You didn't have to."

Dani sighed and looked at her son. "How about getting those school clothes now? We can drop Runt and the groceries off and run into Butte, maybe eat dinner in the park."

"If you really want to," Cody replied.

"I really want to."

"Okay," Cody said without much enthusiasm.

Later, once they'd managed to finish the necessities, Dani and Cody sat on the grass in the park and watched as children ran and played on the various pieces of equipment.

The bustle of the city was in sharp contrast to the sleepy little town of Martinville. In Dani's estimation, Butte was a major metropolis. She laughed to herself when she thought what people from New York or Los Angeles would think of her perception.

"Somethin' funny?" Cody picked a blade of grass and tore it into small pieces.

"Not really," Dani said with a smile for her son. "But what about you? Is something bothering you?" Dani asked. "Looks like you've got something on your mind."

The boy shrugged. "I guess," he said, looking away from her.

"What is it?"

"Chase McEnroe."

Dani let out a long sigh. *Here it comes*, she thought. "What about him?"

"You're serious about him aren't you?"

Dani thought for a moment and decided her son was entitled to the truth. "Yes, I am."

Cody hesitated a minute. "You gonna marry him?"

"I don't know. Maybe."

"And what about Dad?"

Dani leaned back on her elbows, watching as the late afternoon shadows darkened the grass. "I don't really know, I guess. I haven't thought it all through yet."

"He's comin' home, ya know."

"Oh, Cody," she said on a long, wistful sigh. "Just because you got a couple of letters—"

"It's more than that, Mom," Cody cut in angrily, confusion clouding his brown eyes.

"Cody—"

"He called."

"What!" Dani's world seemed to stop spinning. For a minute she couldn't speak. *"When?"*

"When I got back from the Anders' house the other day. You and Chase were on that picnic at the homestead house . . ."

Catching her breath, she nodded to her son. "Go on."

"I'd only been home a little while. The phone rang and it was Dad. He said he was on his way."

Dani was stupefied. "He can't come home, not now," she whispered.

"Why not? He is my dad."

Sitting upright, she let her head fall into her open palms and tried, for Cody's sake, to pull herself together. "But why . . . why now?" she wondered. "And why didn't you tell me when I got home?"

"Chase was there. I didn't think it would be a good idea."

"But that was two days ago!"

Cody looked away. "I know. But I didn't want you to get mad at me."

"I'm not mad at you, honey. I just wish you would have told me about this sooner." And then seeing the wounded look in his eyes, she touched his hand and offered him an apologetic smile. "Look, honey, I'm sorry I overreacted. Okay? It's just such a shock."

"But he wrote. Twice. I told you he'd come back."

"That you did," she said with a sigh.

"You didn't believe it, did you?"

"No, not really. Not after this long," she admitted, bracing herself and managing a worried grin. "But it looks like I was wrong. When will he get to Martinville?"

"He didn't know."

"So what's he going to do when he gets into town?"

Cody bit at his lower lip and dropped the shredded blade of grass. "He said he'd call."

"Good."

"You will let me see him, won't you?"

Dani let out a long breath and fought the worry in her heart. "Of course I will," she said, trying to keep all of her worst fears at bay. "He's your father."

Cody's face split into a wide grin and impulsively he hugged his mother. "It's gonna work out," he said, his brown eyes sparkling. "And we'll be a family again. Just you wait and see!"

Three days later, Dani was up to her elbows in blackberry juice.

She finished cleaning the spatters of juice from the kitchen counters and then tossed the stained rag into the sink and glanced out the window at the freshly turned earth stretching from the house to the road in a dark swath. Rubbing her tired muscles, she wondered what had possessed her to plow the front field because now she was faced with the prospect of harrowing it and getting it ready for the October planting of wheat. The ground had been nearly rock hard and it had taken hours to turn the sod.

Her back and shoulders ached and the tip of her nose

was sunburned. "This is no life for a princess," she scolded herself, and laughed as she finished sealing the small jars of blackberry jelly she'd made earlier in the morning.

After washing her hands, she walked onto the back porch and noticed that there was no activity on Caleb's side of the fence. Some of the heavy equipment was still parked near the stream, but it was much farther upstream and Dani couldn't see any men working in the creek.

"Chase is probably just about done," she murmured. And then what was she going to do? Marry him? Sell the farm to Caleb? Pull Cody out of school and move to Idaho or stay where she was? And what about the rumor in the grocery store that Caleb's new man was trouble?

Shaking her head as if she could dislodge the doubts from her mind, she frowned to herself and wondered when Chase would return and if he'd been able to confront Caleb about the herbicide.

"Stop it," she told herself, jerking off her apron and tossing it over the back of a chair. She walked down the two steps of the porch and leaned over the top rail of the fence, watching the horses trying to graze or find a shady spot in the open fields.

"We sure need rain," she murmured to herself, looking upward at the clear blue sky.

Her thoughts were disturbed by the sound of a truck rolling up the drive.

Thinking Chase might have returned, Dani, her brow furrowed, walked around the outside of the house and frowned when she didn't recognize the battered pickup slowing in the front yard.

But by the time the driver had cut the engine and stepped from the cab, Dani realized that her life had just changed forever and the meeting she had been dreading for the better part of seven years was about to take place. She was staring face to face with Cody's father!

He didn't look much different than the day he'd left all those years ago. Tall and rangy, with dark hair turning silver at the temples, Blake Summers was still a handsome, rugged looking man. With flashing dark eyes, a gaunt, weather-toughened face softened by a sheepish grin, he sauntered toward the house.

"Dani." He stopped a few feet from her.

Knowing the blood had drained from her face, she managed to meet his wary gaze. "What are you doing here, Blake?" she demanded.

"'Bout time I came back, don't ya think?"

"I think it's probably too late."

"Still an optimist I see," he said, with a knowing smile.

"Don't bait me," she snapped, as the years seemed to slip away. She could still remember the day he had slammed the door in her face, leaving her crying for him to return to her and her young son. Shaking, she swallowed hard. "Why now—why'd you come back?"

Ignoring her question, he took a seat on the top step of the porch and mopped his sweaty brow with a handkerchief. "God, this heat is miserable," he said, and then chuckled as he gestured toward his old pickup. "The air conditionin' is out." Fishing a cigarette from his shirt pocket, he lit up and blew a long stream of smoke into the clear air. Squinting against the smoke, he looked around the place. "Been plowin' I see."

"I asked you a question, Blake," she said calmly, although her insides were churning with emotions she'd hoped were long dead.

"Didn't Cody get my letters?"

"Yes—"

"I said I was comin' to see him." Blake settled against the porch column and smiled engagingly. "And he told you I called?"

"Just the other day." She leaned against the hot fender of his truck for support, oblivious to the dirt and oil brushing against her jeans.

"Well, like I said, I think it's about time I got to know the boy, don't you?"

"I'm not sure it's such a good idea," she said honestly, fear squeezing her heart at the thought that Blake would take Cody away from her.

Blake didn't even blink. "Geez, you're a suspicious thing."

Cocking a golden brow, she explained, "It's been a long time—nearly seven years. Cody doesn't remember you, not really. Now, all of a sudden, you're interested in becoming a father. I'd just like to know what made you change your mind."

"Nothin' special," he said. "Maybe I just got tired of driftin'." He took another drag from his cigarette.

"So you drifted back here." Dani's eyes narrowed a bit. "I don't know if I can believe that."

Blake shrugged. "Can't blame you, I guess. But, in time, everyone grows up. Includin' yours truly. God, Dani, I'm thirty-five years old."

"So you came all the way from . . . wherever you were in Oregon just to see your son?"

"That's about the size of it." He tossed his cigarette into the dirt, grinding it out with the heel of his boot. "That and the fact that the job in Molalla gave out. I thought maybe I'd try my luck here, in Martinville."

Dani's heart sank. Blake. *Here.* Wanting to be with Cody. "The talk is that there will be a lot of work soon as Caleb gets goin' on Summer Ridge."

"So I've heard," she said wryly, trying to disguise her fear. She refused to show any weakness to the man who had stripped her soul bare and left her to fend for herself.

Blake pressed his lips together and looked over the hazy fields. Standing and stretching, he came up to Dani and grinned. "So where is he?"

"Cody?"

"Yep."

"At a friend's," Dani replied, an uncomfortable tightening in her stomach warning her not to trust Blake.

"When will he be back?"

"I'm supposed to pick him up before supper."

"I'll do it," Blake decided, with a sharp nod of his head. "May as well jump in with both feet."

Dani's heart dropped through the floor. Whatever Blake's game was, he intended to play out his hand to the end. "It's hard for me to believe that you really want to see him," she said furiously, "since you wanted me to have an abortion when I turned up pregnant and then walked out on us barely three years later!"

"I know. I know," he cajoled, lifting his hands in the same patronizing manner he'd used when she'd been his wife. "But can't you believe that I've had a change of heart?"

"It's hard."

"Let me go get my boy, Dani," he begged.

Dani wavered, but only for a minute. "I . . . I think it would be better if I picked him up," she said cautiously. "You can see him here when he gets home."

Blake ran a hand over his chin and smiled lazily, his dark eyes regarding Dani with practiced seduction. "Is that an invitation to dinner?"

Clenching her teeth against her impulsive response, Dani studied the man who had once been her husband. He'd aged in the past seven years. Features that had once been boyishly charming were now gaunt and grizzled. "I think it would be okay if you ate here tonight. Cody's been anxious for you to return."

"What about you, Dani?" he asked, stepping closer to her.

"I think it probably would have been better if you'd stayed away."

He reached up to touch her hair, but Dani, still holding her ground pushed his hand aside. "Haven't you missed me?"

"Not for a long time," she stated.

"Ya know, there's still a chance that we could work things out," he suggested, his brown eyes saddening a little. "I could make it up to you."

"Never."

"You're sure of that?"

"More sure than I've been of anything in a long while," she said, her hazel eyes focusing on his face, her jaw jutting with renewed determination. "And since you're Cody's father and he wants to see you, I won't get in the way. But I'm telling you this straight out, Blake: Don't try to make trouble. Not for me. Or Cody. We're happy here and we don't need you."

"A boy needs a father," he contradicted.

Dani bit back the fury on her tongue. "Maybe that's true. But he needs a father he can depend on, a man who will stick by him no matter what, not someone who abandoned him when he was barely two years old then plans to waltz back into his life when he's half grown. Think about it, Blake. And before you entertain any thoughts of ruining what Cody and I have together, think how it will affect your son!"

"I never said I wanted to make trouble."

"Good. Then I'll try to remember that."

"You'd do that much for me?"

"No. For Cody." Her lips tightened. "I'm not giving you back your son; you threw away that right a long time ago when you took off without a backward glance. But I won't deny Cody the right to know his father *unless* you do something I don't approve of."

Blake's smile twisted appreciatively. "That almost sounds like a threat, Dani."

"It is."

He shook his head as if in utter amazement. "You sure have changed."

"You made me change. I learned to depend on myself."

"And I respect ya for it."

"Don't try to flatter me, Blake. It won't work. If you want to see Cody, come back here at six-thirty. Otherwise get out of my life."

He took one step closer, looked deep into her eyes and saw the sparks of ready-fire in their depths. "I'm stayin' at Bob's place, but I'll be back," he said softly, touching her on the underside of her chin.

She jerked away from him. "Fine," she retorted and watched as he climbed back into his pickup and drove away.

Chapter Nine

"Hey, Mom, somethin' wrong?" Cody asked on the way home from his friend's house.

"Not really," Dani lied, her fingers sweaty around the steering wheel, her teeth sinking into her lip as she drove the pickup out of Martinville.

Cody shrugged and stuck out his lower lip thoughtfully. "You looked kind'a worried."

"Don't I always?" she teased, but the joke fell flat. She tried to lighten the mood by ruffling his hair, but Cody moved his head to avoid contact.

"Come on. Somethin's buggin' you. I can tell." He slid down in the seat and propped his knees against the dash of the pickup while glancing at his mother. "Caleb Johnson did something again didn't he?"

"Not that I know of," she said with a sigh. "Okay, Cody, I guess I'll have to level with you."

"'Bout time."

Bracing herself for an emotional reaction from her son, she said, "I was going to wait until we were home, but you may as well hear it now: Your dad is back in town."

Cody didn't move a muscle, just stared at her with round brown eyes. "You saw him? When?"

"Earlier. He stopped by the house looking for you. He'll be back for dinner."

"Tonight?"

"Tonight."

Letting out a piercing whoop that any coyote would envy, Cody pounded his fist against the seat of the truck and grinned from ear to ear. "I told ya, didn't I? I told ya that he was comin' home."

"That you did," Dani admitted, turning the old truck into the drive. The pickup bounced its way up the lane. "You never lost faith."

"This is great!" Cody said, beaming and hardly able to sit still.

When Dani parked the old truck near the side of the house, Cody reached for the door handle and climbed down, but Dani took hold of his arm. "Cody—"

"Yeah?" He swiveled his head around, his bright teeth and dark eyes flashing eagerly.

She had trouble finding the right words, but her face was lined with concern. "Look, I don't want to burst your bubble, but I just don't want you to be disappointed. Don't expect too much of your father."

Cody jerked his arm away from her and gestured dismissively. "He's back, Mom. That's all that matters. And if you weren't so hung up on Chase McEnroe, you'd be happy, too."

"Chase has nothing to do with this."

"Like hell!"

"Cody!" But the boy was off, dashing across the gravel and beating a path to the back door.

Dani lifted the two sacks of groceries she'd bought before she'd picked up Cody and walked inside the house. Setting the bags on the counter, she listened to the sound of the shower running and Cody's off-tune singing.

"I hope I'm up to this," she thought aloud, placing the meat and vegetables in the refrigerator. Feeling that the dinner with Blake was sure to be a disaster, she put the rest of the groceries away and started preparing the meal. The first step was lighting the barbecue on the back porch. After seeing that the charcoal was burning, she came back inside, noted that the shower had quit running and started cutting greens for a salad.

Cody, wet hair gleaming, was back downstairs in fifteen minutes. He was wearing some of the new clothes they'd purchased in Butte and a smile as wide as his face. "What can I do to help?" he asked.

"Here, why don't you slice the loaf of French bread?" She took a deep breath and added, "Look, I wasn't too crazy about what you said to me earlier."

"What?"

"You know what. Just try to control your temper, okay?"

"Okay," the boy agreed sullenly, looking out the window before grabbing a knife and slicing the loaf.

Dani pursed her lips and gazed fondly at her son. "Don't you like Chase?"

Cody shrugged. "He's okay."

"I thought you were getting along—"

"I said he's okay, didn't I? It's just that he's not Dad, if ya know what I mean."

"I guess I do," she said, feeling a dull pain deep in her heart. Cody would never accept Chase as a father or even a stepfather while Blake was around. And, regretfully, Cody had that right, she supposed.

"When did he say he'd be here?"

"Six-thirty."

"It's almost that time already." Cody looked out the window and his brows drew together in vexation. "You're sure you said six-thirty?"

"I'm sure. Now, don't worry; he said he'd come," she replied, slicing a ripe tomato from the garden and trying to ignore her own doubts about the evening.

"Aren't you going to change clothes or something?" Cody asked as he fidgeted between the front door and the kitchen.

"No." She started buttering the bread.

"But you could put on one of those dresses—you know the ones you always wear when Chase comes over."

Dani whirled to face her son. She saw the expectation in his eyes and had to bite her tongue to keep from telling Cody exactly how she felt about his father. Instead she put her hands behind her and gripped the counter tightly. "Look, Cody, I don't 'dress' for Chase or anyone for that matter. I realize this is probably hard for you to understand and I don't really know what you think is going to happen tonight, but you may as well know that there's no chance your dad and I will get back together."

"You don't know that—"

"I do," Dani said firmly.

"But maybe he's staying!"

Dani couldn't stand the pain written all over Cody's eager face. Looking out the window, she saw Blake's pickup turning into the drive. With a sinking feeling, she said, "Your father said something about staying at Uncle

Bob's, looking for a job around town, but that doesn't mean it will work out. It also doesn't mean that he and I will ever get back together again. And I already told you that Blake couldn't stay here in the house with us." She turned to Cody, her eyes honest and kind. "You have to face the fact that it's over between your dad and me."

"But you won't even give him a chance—" Cody heard the sound of Blake's pickup and froze. He went to the window and watched as his father slid out of the truck, stretched, and with hat in hand, sauntered up to the front porch.

As soon as Blake knocked, Cody opened the door. Blake Summers and his son stared at each other for a minute before Blake opened his arms and the boy ran to him and hugged his father fiercely. "Dad," Cody choked out and Dani's heart nearly broke.

"Well, look at you," Blake said, clapping Cody on the back and then holding him at arm's length. "Ain't you grown up?"

"Not quite," Cody muttered.

"Oh, I don't know 'bout that." He walked into the kitchen and watched as Dani, balancing a platter of raw steaks, stepped outside to broil the meat.

Through the screen door, she could hear Blake and Cody talking, slowly at first and then more rapidly. *Like long lost buddies*, she thought, trying not to worry. Cody had the right to know his father; she couldn't deny him.

"How about gettin' your old man a beer?" Blake asked, and soon the sound of a can popping open reached Dani's ears.

Oh, God, Blake, please don't drink. From firsthand experience, Dani knew that Blake Summers and alcohol didn't mix. Never one able to hold his alcohol, Blake became at first friendly, then belligerent, and eventually violent when he drank. It was only one beer, she reminded herself, and maybe he'd changed.

Nonetheless, she couldn't get the steaks turned and broiled fast enough.

When she returned to the kitchen she found that Blake and Cody were in the living room involved in a heavy discussion about the NBA draft. Safe enough, Dani thought with relief and tossed the salad.

"Time to eat," she called over her shoulder, and Blake got up and stretched. He took the spot that used to be his at the table.

"That's where Cody usually eats," she said.

"It's okay," the boy insisted. "Dad can sit wherever he wants to."

"Thanks, son. And how about another beer?"

"Sure." Cody nearly tripped over himself to get to the refrigerator to serve his father.

Inwardly cringing, Dani served the meal, and smiled politely at Blake's compliments.

It took some effort, but she slowly began to relax as the conversation flowed easily and stayed clear of sensitive subjects. Blake seemed to take a genuine interest in Cody, and though Dani still didn't trust the man's motives, she was pleased to see how Cody responded to his father. Soon the meal was finished and Dani served dessert.

"Apple crisp," Cody said appreciatively as she set the pie plate on the table. "My favorite."

"Mine, too," Blake agreed with a slow grin.

News to Dani; Blake had never been one for sweets.

"You know," Blake said, his near-black eyes moving from his son to his ex-wife. "Your mom is one of the best

cooks I've ever met. That was a fine meal, Dani. Fine."
He leaned back and patted his belly to show his appreci-
ation.

Dani felt her jaw tightening, but forced a thin smile.
"Thanks."

"Always did say you were a helluva cook."

She let that one slip by; no reason to get into an argument in front of Cody. Her son wasn't old enough to understand that Dani wanted to be more to her husband than
a cook and a maid. "How about coffee?" she asked, her
nerves raw. Soon, she hoped, Blake would tire of their
company and leave. Blake shook his head. "Too early for
me." He reached for his beer and realized the can was
empty. "I could stand another one of these, though."

"I think we're about out—"

"No, Mom. There's one more can in the fridge and
another six-pack on the back porch."

"But it's warm," she protested.

Blake held up his hand and waved in the air before
smiling at Cody. "No matter. Why don't you get me the
last cold one and put the rest in the cooler, boy?" Then,
ignoring the challenge in Dani's eyes, he settled back in
his chair and lit a cigarette.

Cody got up to do as he was asked, but Blake put a
hand around the boy's wrist and winked at him. "After
that, you can go out in the pickup and reach under the seat.
I got you a surprise."

"I don't think—" Dani started to say, but held her
tongue.

"Great!" Cody's eyes lit up. As quickly as possible he
served Blake the beer and hurried out the front door.

Once the boy had gone outside, Blake smiled to himself and nodded in satisfaction. Popping the tab on the aluminum can and watching the frothy beer roll down the side, Blake squinted thoughtfully through the smoke from his cigarette and offered Dani a seductive grin. "You've done a helluva job with him, Dani. He's a good kid."

"Can't argue with that." She began to clear the table and put the dishes in the sink.

"Thank God for small favors," Blake said.

"What's that supposed to mean?"

"Just that you've been on my case since I got here, spoiling for a fight."

"I just don't think I'm ready to have you back in town," she admitted. "Cody and I were getting along just fine without you."

Blake leaned back in the chair, propping his boots on Cody's vacated chair, his eyes becoming slits as he watched her work. "I can see that. It couldn't have been easy doing it all by yourself."

She lifted a shoulder. "It wasn't so bad. We've made out all right. Like you said, he's a good boy."

Stroking his chin and rocking the chair back on its two hind legs, he said, "I can see that. But then, he's had a good mother." Blake's voice was soft and warm, almost tender, but it didn't touch Dani the way it once had. In fact, Blake's attempts to close the gap between them only increased the distance. He stubbed his cigarette out in the ashtray.

"You don't need to compliment me, Blake, but what I would like to know is why you want anything to do with Cody." She stacked the dishes near the sink and turned to face him and all the old anger that she'd tried to repress for her son's sake rushed to the surface. "It's been seven years, for crying out loud. *Seven years!*"

"Maybe it's not just Cody I want," he said.

That did it! What little patience she'd held onto was instantly replaced by anger and resentment. "I don't want to hear any of this, Blake. You had plenty of chances to come home, way back when we both wanted and needed you, but we don't; not anymore—"

He stood and walked over to her and wrapped one big hand around her waist. "Just relax, Dani, and remember how good it was between us."

"I remember, all right. I remember that I was never enough woman for you—wasn't that how you phrased it?—that you never slept at home, that you didn't want Cody, that you tried to get me to sell my land, when my mother was ill, to pay your damned gambling debts! If you think for one minute that you can con me into believing that you've changed, you've got another thing coming!"

She stepped away from him and though he reached for her, the ice in her eyes and proud lift of her chin convinced him that she meant every word she said.

"I'm only putting up with you because I think Cody has the right to know his father!"

An excited scream came from outside and Cody ran into the house carrying a brand new .22. "Hey, Mom, look. Dad bought me a gun!"

"What!" she said, horrified.

"It's just a little .22," Blake said.

The anger she'd felt earlier was nothing in comparison with the rage that consumed her now. "You can't keep a .22," she said, shaking as she looked first to Cody and then past her son to Blake. "What's the matter with you?"

she demanded. "You can't give a nine-year-old boy a rifle!"

"It's not a rifle; just a .22. I had one when I was his age." Cody's grin fell and to his embarrassment, tears started to form in his eyes. Hastily he swiped them away. "Come on, Mom, lots of kids have 'em."

"And you're not 'lots of kids.' You know how I feel about guns. They're a big responsibility."

"He can handle it." Blake said.

"How would you know? You've been gone most of his life! How can you tell after just an hour that he can handle a .22 for God's sake!"

"Dani—"

But she couldn't think straight. All she knew was that Blake, whether intentional or not, was ruining her relationship with her son. "I think you'd better leave, Blake. It's late."

"Mom, no!" Cody wailed, looking frantically from one parent to the other. "It's barely eight o'clock. Dad, please, stay—" Eyes red-rimmed, Cody stared at his mother, silently pleading with her to change her mind.

Dani felt like dying on the spot, but though her insides were shaking, she ignored the desperation in Cody's eyes and said softly, "And when you go, take this damned thing with you." She took the gun from Cody and shoved it into Blake's hands.

"You can't—" Cody said, tears now streaming down his face.

"Maybe when you're older," she said, touching her son's shoulder. He recoiled as if she'd bitten him.

Blake's face turned granite hard. "Maybe I judged you

too quickly, Dani," he said furiously. "Looks like you're not such a perfect mother after all."

"Just leave, Blake," she said through clenched teeth. "Before we say something we'll both regret and our son can't possibly be able to understand."

"I think you've already taken care of that!" he replied, his dark eyes blazing as he took the gun, offered a few words of comfort to his boy and walked out into the night. Cody stood at the screen door, crying and sobbing bitterly.

"Cody, I'm sorry that—"

"No, you're not!" the boy said, turning and screaming at her. "You're glad he's gone! You chased him away! *Again!* You didn't want him here, didn't think he'd come back and now that he did, you sent him away!" Sniffing and wiping his hand under his nose, Cody glared at his mother. "I hate you!" he said angrily. "I wish I lived with Dad!" He stomped up the stairs and slammed his door so hard that the windowpanes rattled.

"Oh, dear God," Dani whispered, supporting herself by holding onto the railing of the stairs. Cody's shot had hit its mark and Dani felt her heart crumble into a thousand pieces. The one thing in the world she'd hoped to avoid, she'd managed to do. Inadvertently she'd pushed Cody away from her. Walking up the stairs she stopped at Cody's room and quietly tapped on his door.

"Go 'way."

"I think we need to talk."

"No!"

She cracked open the door. Cody was lying on the bed in the semidarkness. His back was turned to her. "Son—"

"Leave me alone!"

"Okay, I will," she said, fighting her own tears. "But

we'll talk in the morning and I want you to know one thing."

No response. He didn't move except for the rise and fall of his shoulders and back as he breathed.

"I love you, Cody, and everything I do is because I want to protect you and help you grow up to be a responsible person. Believe me, not letting you have something is really harder than giving in."

"Sure. You just didn't want me to have something my dad, *my dad*, gave me!"

"No, Cody—"

He sat up suddenly and turned his red face to her. "You said you'd leave me alone!"

Quietly she closed his door and walked down the stairs to the living room. She saw the empty beer cans on the hearth, noticed the still dirty pots and pans in the sink and realized that her life would never be the same. Blake was back in Martinville and for some reason known only to him, he wanted to make amends with his son. Maybe she was too suspicious; maybe she should take Blake at face value, believe that he'd finally grown up and wanted to share the responsibilities of a son. . . .

Cold dread settled between her shoulder blades. It was already starting, she realized in wild desperation. Blake was back and was trying his damnedest to increase the rift between Cody and her.

"I can't let it happen," she told herself as she picked up the beer cans and tossed them into the plastic sack on the back porch. "No one is going to stand between me and my child!"

She tried to clear her mind and found it impossible. Her thoughts were swimming, her entire world off balance.

"If only they'd leave us alone," she thought, thinking about Blake and Caleb.

Walking down the two steps to the backyard, she looked up the hill to the Johnson farm and her thoughts turned to Chase. Where was he and when would he be back? If he were here, things would be better so much better.

The next morning Dani had already watered the garden, fed the cattle and horses, showered, dressed in clean clothes and started breakfast before she finally heard Cody rustling around upstairs. He came down the stairs a few minutes later. Barefoot, tucking his shirt into his pants and eyeing his mother cautiously, he walked into the kitchen.

"Feeling any better?" Dani asked.

Cody didn't respond. Taking a chair at the table, he didn't even bother to look up when Dani placed a stack of waffles and two strips of bacon on a plate and set the hot breakfast in front of him.

"I think we should talk," she said.

"Don't want to," he grumbled, spreading jam on his waffles before attacking them hungrily.

Her stomach in nervous knots, Dani sat down at the table across from her son and cradled a hot cup of coffee in her hands. She studied the anxious lines of his young face and wished she could make growing up easier on him. "Just because I don't let you have everything you want doesn't mean that I don't love you," she said. When Cody didn't respond, she sat back in her chair and blew across her coffee. "You hurt me very badly with the things you said last night."

He ignored her and kept eating in sullen silence.

"I had trouble sleeping."

"That makes two of us," he admitted.

"Believe it or not, I don't want to stand between you and your father—"

"Then why wouldn't you let me keep the .22?" Cody demanded, dropping his fork and piercing her with furious dark eyes. "You just didn't want Dad to give me something."

"No . . . I didn't want your dad to give you something you weren't ready for. A .22 is still a gun, Cody. A weapon. It's dangerous."

"I'd only use it on rabbits and birds—"

"Is that what you want to do? Go hunting?"

"Why not?"

"You've never shown any interest in it before."

Cody's lips pressed together. "Maybe that's because you've always treated me like a baby."

"And having a .22 makes you a man?"

"I just don't like being treated like a little kid."

"You're not. You have responsibilities around here, and you get paid for them. I think you're a very grown-up nine-year-old."

"Then—"

"But guns are for adults. Period."

Cody's chin stuck out and he crossed his arms over his chest. "Don't you think my father has any say in it?"

"Not when he's been gone for seven years." Dani forced a sad smile at her son. "I'm not trying to stop you from growing up, you know, I just want to make sure that you do it one step at a time."

When Cody realized she wasn't about to change her mind, he bravely fought off another round of embarrassing tears.

"I know you've missed your dad, and I hope that the two of you can make up for lost time," she said, wondering if she really believed her own words. "But you're my responsibility and I have to do what I think is best for you."

"Even if Dad disagrees."

"Yes."

He studied his remaining waffles and pushed them aside. "Would you let me live with Dad?" he asked suddenly.

Dani's stomach dropped, but she tried not to show it. Though she couldn't imagine her life without Cody, she managed to meet his inquiring gaze with steady eyes. "I don't think so," she said honestly. "Oh, I suppose if you were really unhappy with me and I thought Blake would do a better job of being a parent, then maybe I'd agree that you should live with him. But I think it's a little too early to make that kind of decision, don't you?"

"I don't know." He couldn't keep the anger out of his voice.

"Well, there's one thing you'd better think about."

"What's that?"

"I won't be threatened. And I won't let you play me against your father."

"What do you mean?"

"Exactly what I said. As long as you're with me, which I hope is for a very long time, we do things my way."

"And I don't have any say in it."

She shook her head and laughed. "You know that I always listen to you, don't you?"

He shrugged his shoulders.

"Sure you do. And neither of us wants to argue anymore. So, let's put it aside for now. I fed and watered the animals for you this morning. I figured you might want this last day off to do whatever you want. Tomorrow's a school day."

"Don't remind me," he groaned, but picked up his plate and carried it to the sink.

"If you want, you can have Shane over or maybe one of your other friends."

"Thanks, Mom," he said, as if understanding she was trying to mend fences. "But I don't think so. Dad said he'd come by. Maybe we can go fishin' or somethin'."

"Maybe," Dani agreed, silently telling herself it was the boy's right to be with his father.

"You won't get mad?"

"Not unless he tries to give you the gun again."

"Good." Cody went outside and Dani finished her coffee. A few minutes later, she was hanging clothes on the line when she heard the sound of an engine coming down the drive. Bracing herself for another confrontation with Blake, she hurriedly snapped a clothespin on the last corner of the sheet just as there was a knock on the front door. She glanced out the window and recognized Chase's Jeep.

Thank God!

Heart beating wildly at the sight of him, she threw open the screen door and fell into his arms. "Thank God you're back," she whispered, clinging to him, drinking in the smell and feel of him as his arms surrounded her.

A lazy grin slid easily over Chase's face. "I sure didn't expect this kind of reception, lady." But his arms closed securely around her waist and he rested his head on the top of hers. "It's been a helluva week and I'm glad I'm back." He placed an index finger under her chin and tilted her face so that he could look into her troubled eyes. "What's wrong?"

"Wrong?" she repeated.

"Yes—something happened." His jaw hardened and his eyes narrowed suspiciously. "What's Caleb done now?"

"Nothing . . . it's nothing to do with him," she said, breaking out of his embrace and rubbing her arms as if suddenly chilled.

"That's hard to believe."

"Cody's father came back yesterday."

"What!?"

"My reaction, too," she whispered.

Chase went stock-still. "And?" he prodded.

Dani let out a long, worried sigh. "And he had dinner with us last night"

Chase's face became hard, his eyes slits as he walked over to the fireplace, leaned against the mantel and watched her. "Just like that—all of a sudden?"

"No. There were some letters and then Cody got a call from him . . . I just can't believe he's here."

"Neither can I," Chase muttered. " Strange, don't you think?"

"What do you mean?"

"He's been gone for—what, six years?"

"Seven."

"And now, just when things are coming to a boil with Johnson, when I'm out of town, he shows up." Chase paced in front of the fireplace, rubbing the back of his neck and his suspicions gelled. "Son of a bitch," he muttered under his breath, his fists balling.

"He said something about a job giving out; that he wanted to get to know Cody—"

Chase cranked his head to stare at her. "You believe him?"

Dani sighed and dropped onto an arm of the couch. "I don't know what to believe. All I know is that I don't want him here and Cody does. So—I let him come over, just last night. Things were going along just fine until after dinner when Blake tried to give Cody a gun—a .22—and I objected. We argued and I ended up asking Blake to leave with the gun."

"And Cody didn't like it."

"No." She shuddered. "He screamed and yelled at me, told me he hated me, said he wanted to live with his father . . ."

Her voice cracked and she had to take a deep breath to control herself. "I . . . I stood my ground, but—"

"You're afraid you're losing him," Chase guessed, coming up behind her and placing his hands on her shoulders. She was turned away from him, but the tender warmth of his fingers soothed some of her fears. He nuzzled the back of her neck and the strength flowing from his body to hers helped ease her fears.

"I just wish Blake had never come back," she said bitterly, balling her fist and pressing it to her lips.

"Maybe it's better that he did," Chase said, trying to stamp down his own insane feelings of jealousy. "Cody needed to meet him; see what kind of a man his father is."

"If I just hadn't gotten so . . . angry."

"Shh. Don't blame yourself for doing what you think was right." Chase rotated her and folded her body neatly to his. "He's not going to come between you and Cody or us."

She heard the beating of his heart, felt the security of his hard, strong body against hers. Her arms wrapped around Chase's neck and she sighed in contentment when he kissed the top of her head. "I'm just glad you're back," she whispered.

"Mom?" Cody stepped through the screen door and stopped dead in his tracks when he saw his mother and Chase. "Oh, no," he whispered, starting to back out of the room and staring at Dani with accusing eyes.

Dani extracted herself from Chase's embrace and followed her son to the porch. "What did you want?"

"Never mind," he grumbled.

"Cody—"

"He's the reason you don't want Dad around, isn't he?" he said, jerking his head in the direction of the house just as Chase came outside.

"Of course not—"

"Why don't you just go away, mister," Cody said, squinting up at Chase. "Instead of trying to be friends with me and coming on to my mom, why don't you just go back to Caleb Johnson's place where you belong? Or better yet, go to Idaho or wherever it is you come from!"

"Cody!"

But Cody didn't bother listening. Instead he jumped on his ten-speed and rode the bike around the corner of the house and down the lane as fast as he could.

Dani started after him and got as far as the side of the house where her pickup was parked before Chase grabbed her arm and restrained her from running after the boy. "Let him go."

"I can't!"

"He needs to blow off some steam, work things out in his own mind," he said. "Let him cool off. He'll be back."

Knowing in her heart that Chase was right, Dani looked despairingly down the drive to the rapidly disappearing image of her son. "It's just so damned hard to let go."

"I know." Chase tugged at her arm. "Come on. Let's go inside. I'll buy you a cup of coffee."

"I don't think I could eat or drink anything," she said.

"Try. For me."

Once in the kitchen, Chase poured them each a cup of coffee and then, as Dani carried the cups outside, he followed with the red enamel pot.

They sat together in the quiet shade of the apple tree and watched the sheets billowing in the slight morning breeze.

"Feeling better?" Chase asked.

"A little," she said, and then amended the statement. "Make that a lot."

"I thought so. At least I hoped."

The crown of her head was warm from the morning sun. A slight breeze cooled her skin and Chase's presence gave Dani a sense of peace and contentment she'd been lacking in the past few days. If only Cody were here to share this blissful serenity, life would be perfect.

"He'll be back," Chase whispered.

"You're sure?" Her smooth brow puckered with worry.

"I promise." He touched the side of her face, caressed her cheek, and let his fingers tangle in the soft honey-colored strands of her hair.

"I could almost believe anything you told me," she said with a dimpled smile.

"That's encouraging. Listen." Over the hum of insects and the whisper of the wind in the leaves overhead, the sound of a pickup as it turned into the drive caught Chase's attention. "I'll bet Cody ran into a friend who gave him a lift home."

"I hope you're right," Dani said, standing and running to the front of the house only to have her soaring expectations dashed to the ground.

Blake.

"Oh, God," she whispered, her throat tight. Cody's bike was in the back of the pickup and Cody was sitting in the cab of his father's truck as Blake maneuvered the pickup up the twin ruts of the lane.

"I take it Cody's with his father." Chase grabbed his hat and put it on.

"You take it right."

"Do you want me to leave?" Chase asked, though he had no intention of doing anything of the kind.

"No . . . it's all right."

"Good." Chase's chiseled mouth was set firmly and his arms were folded over his broad chest as he crossed his ankles and leaned against one of the fence posts.

"Mornin'," Blake said as he got out of the cab of his truck. Chase touched the brim of his Stetson in reply. The hat shaded his eyes and gave him an opportunity to watch Blake Summers. He felt immediate dislike for the man but didn't say anything because of the boy. Instead he held his tongue for a later time, when Cody wasn't present. The effort made his muscles ache with tension.

"I—I didn't expect you back so soon," Dani said, looking nervously from Blake to Chase and back again.

"Found my son hightailin' it into town. Thought I'd better find out why."

A muscle jumped in Chase's jaw, but still he leaned on the fence post, as if content to stay out of a family argument.

"We had a little misunderstanding."

"A big one, the way I hear it."

"It was just a disagreement, Blake." She turned concerned eyes on her son. "Cody, are you okay?"

The boy lifted a shoulder and stared at her with total disrespect. "I guess so."

"You know I don't like to fight with you."

"Then why's he still here?" Cody asked, pointing at Chase. Chase shifted, pushed up the brim of his hat and straightened. Walking over to Dani and standing near her, he introduced himself to Blake and was offered a tight-lipped nod in return.

"Chase is here because I want him here," Dani said, feeling color burn her cheeks.

"Just like Dad's here 'cause I want him here," Cody retorted. He took a step closer to Blake and continued to glare at Chase.

"The boy and I plan to go fishin'," Blake said. "He claims he's got himself a right good hole above the south fork." Blake glanced at Chase and his lips twisted downward before he looked back at Dani. "So if ya don't mind."

"I don't mind, as long as you stay on the place."

Cody took hold of Blake's arm and eagerly started leading him to the back of the property. "Come on, Dad, you're gonna love it!"

"I'm sure I will," Blake said as they passed Dani and he darted her a quick, assessing glance. He was wearing a smile that didn't seem quite natural and his skin was taut over the angles of his face. He hadn't shaved and there were bags below his reddened eyes.

Dani's stomach curled. She'd seen Blake in the same shape before; hungover and surly after a long night's binge.

"Why did he come back here?" she asked herself once Blake and Cody were out of earshot.

"Your guess is as good as mine," Chase said, rubbing his jaw thoughtfully as he watched Cody and Blake walk past the barn. "Maybe he's feeling mortal; needs the security of knowing his son."

"And maybe he's up to no good," Dani thought aloud.

"Time will tell."

"That's what I'm afraid of," Dani said. "I just hope that he doesn't hurt Cody."

"So you honestly don't think that Blake is just here because he loves his son?"

"I don't think Blake Summers is capable of love," she said firmly, as Blake, Cody and Runt waded across the creek and walked through the final field before disappearing into the thicket of brush and pine trees in the foothills.

Chapter Ten

Chase noticed the lines of worry etching across Dani's forehead and the way she chewed on her lower lip long after Cody and Blake had left. "Maybe you'd better tell me if you want me to stick around," he suggested.

"What's that supposed to mean?" she asked, turning her attention to him.

He was standing in the shade of the apple tree. Reaching upward, he picked an apple that was beginning to stripe red over green and tossed it in the air, catching it deftly. "Just that I don't want to interfere—cause any more problems between you and Cody."

"You aren't."

"I heard what he said."

"I know, but he was angry with me, not you. He can't seem to understand that what Blake and I shared is over. He thinks we should be able to resurrect it somehow."

Chase shoved his hands deep into his pockets. "And what do you think?"

"Honestly?"

He nodded, his firm mouth turning down at the corners. "Honestly."

"I wish he'd never come back. That he'd just leave us alone."

Chase's thick brows arched. "Well, once the newness of having his dad around wears off, maybe Cody won't be so quick to champion Blake's cause. Right now Blake's come back for the boy and that makes him a hero in Cody's eyes. But you've always been here for him. Cody's a smart boy. He'll come around."

"I doubt it," she said with a sigh as she walked back toward the house. "But I don't suppose there's any point in brooding. Blake's back and that's that. I'll just have to learn how to deal with him."

Chase grinned. "That's the spirit." He tossed the apple to her and she caught it. Smiling, she took a bite of the tart Gravenstein and then made a face. "I think you rushed this one," she said, opening the screen door and waiting until Chase had walked inside.

"Meaning the apple?" he asked.

"I don't know; I get a feeling you rush everything. Jump in feet first."

"Sometimes."

She straightened the afghan on the back of the couch before going into the kitchen. "Can I get you something? Coffee? Tea? Or—" she opened the refrigerator and peeked inside "—uh, we still have some orange juice, half a pitcher of lemonade and a few cans of beer that Blake hasn't found."

"Coffee's fine." He walked to the kitchen and leaned one shoulder against the arch separating the rooms as he watched her nervously pour the hot liquid into heavy ceramic mugs. "Try to relax."

"Easier said than done," she admitted.

"Great. Then I don't suppose you want to hear what I found out while I was gone."

Looking over her shoulder and seeing his grim countenance, she braced herself for the worst. "More bad news?"

"I'm afraid so."

"I may as well hear it," she said with a sigh and then forced a feeble grin. "Give it to me straight." Handing him a cup of coffee, she took a sip from her mug and sat at the table.

"It looks as if Caleb put the drum of dioxin in the creek on purpose."

"He admitted it?" she asked dubiously.

"No, but I managed to talk to the hand that actually did the dirty work, a guy by the name of Larry Cross. Shortly after Johnson asked Cross to puncture the lid and bury the drum in the creekbed, Caleb gave the guy his walking papers . . . along with quite a substantial amount of money to keep quiet."

"So why did he talk to you?"

"Johnson's money didn't last long. And the man wasn't opposed to making a few extra dollars on the deal."

"So you bribed him?"

"Paid him for information."

"Same thing." She dropped her chin into her hand and fought off the waves of depression that threatened to wash over her. "When it rains it pours," she said, drinking thoughtfully from her cup. "And they say trouble comes in threes."

"They might be wrong."

"I don't know. First Blake wanting to be with Cody, then proof that Caleb would stoop to just about any lengths to get me to sell my farm and then—" She stopped midsentence, as if in not speaking the thought would make it go away.

"Then what?" Chase asked, crossing the room, turning a chair around and straddling the seat.

"Well, it's nothing really," she said, her hands beginning to sweat.

"Something's wrong."

"Maybe—"

"Why don't you tell me about it?"

Why not? No time like the present to get things out in the open. "Cody and I were in the grocery store the other day and I heard a rumor about one of Caleb's hands."

"That doesn't surprise me," Chase said, noticing the band of freckles across her nose. "What about him?"

"I'm not really sure. But Jenna Peterson is pretty upset with him. The way I heard it she doesn't trust him."

"What's his name?"

"I . . . don't know. She didn't say. But it's some new guy who works with Caleb."

"Maybe he hired someone when I was gone," Chase said thoughtfully. "But even if he did, that doesn't sound like Jenna. She's usually a rock. The only person on the whole damned spread I can trust."

"That's what makes it so worrisome," Dani admitted, her hazel eyes staring at Chase's rugged face. It was a handsome face, hard around the edges, but softened by a sensual dimple when he smiled. The self-effacing glint in his clear blue eyes balanced the determination in the set of his jaw and the pride in his bearing. Chase was a con-tradictory man of so many emotions and passions and Dani loved him so much it hurt.

"Wait a minute!" he said, holding his cup, his blue eyes

becoming hard. "You heard a rumor and you thought it had something to do with me, didn't you?"

"I don't know who it was about—I just want to know if there's any truth in it. It would take a lot to upset Jenna Peterson. She's worked with and trusted Caleb Johnson for years."

"Dani," Chase said, his lips whitening at the corners as he tried to stay calm, "I've done everything I can to be straight with you!" Scraping his chair back, he stood, rammed his hands, palms out, in the back pockets of his jeans and began pacing. "I don't know what more I can do or say to let you know I'm on your side." His boots clicked on the cracked linoleum with each of his long, impatient strides. "I've found evidence you need against Caleb, I stood up for you when you came ranting and raving into his house, and I've done everything short of throwing my contract into his face." Spinning on his heel, he impaled her with his furious gaze. "Lord, woman," he said through clenched teeth, "I've even asked you to marry me and you still can't trust me! What the devil do you want from me?"

"Just honest answers, that's all," Dani said, feeling a little contrite but still angry. All the frustrations of the past weeks burned inside her. "I feel manipulated by the whole lot of you—Caleb, Blake and you!"

Chase came over to the table and placed his hands flat on the polished maple. Pushing his face to within inches of hers, he stared straight into her eyes. She could see his rage in the flare of his nostrils, the way his skin tightened over his tense jaw and the flecks of blue anger in his eyes. He was trying to hold his temper in check, but failing miserably. Rapping the table with his index finger, he growled, "I don't like being put in the same corral as Caleb and Blake, lady. All I've ever done is try to help you—whether you believe it or not. Now, if you don't want my help, fine. All you have to do is say the word and I'm outta here."

Her throat was dry, her emotions raw, but she tossed her head back and glared at him. "I trust *you*, Chase. As a person."

"What the hell is that supposed to mean?"

"It's just that this whole damned situation has gotten to me. Not only is Blake back, maybe with the intention of taking my son from me, but now we know for sure that Caleb will do anything, *anything* to get me off my land. If that isn't bad enough, you're partners with the man, for God's sake!"

"So we're back to that, are we?"

"I don't think we ever got past it."

"And *I* don't know why I have to keep proving myself to you." His eyes narrowed and his hand reached forward to clasp her wrist. "I think we'd better settle this right now! Come on!"

"Wait a minute—"

He jerked her out of the chair, grabbed his hat and shoved it onto his head as he walked out of the door with Dani, still in tow, continuing to protest loudly.

The day had turned hazy and dark clouds had begun to surround the mountain peaks. "Where do you think you're taking me?"

"Away."

She looked back at her house in confusion. "But I just can't leave. Cody—"

"Cody's with his dad!" Chase snapped. "Do you think Blake will hurt him?"

"No, but-—"

"Then come on! We'll be back by the time that Cody gets home!"

"But I should leave him a note!"

"Yeah, maybe you should. But you don't have time." Chase jerked open the door on the passenger side of the Jeep and waited for her to climb in.

"It will just take a minute to scribble a note," she said, the wind picking up and whipping her hair around her face, "Be sensible, Chase."

"I have been! Now it's time we did things my way!"

Dani stood her ground and didn't get into the Jeep. "Where are we going?"

"To Johnson's."

"What the devil—"

"I'll explain later," he said, eyeing the darkening sky and releasing her. "Go on, write your damned note. But be quick about it."

Anger radiating from her body, she marched back to the house, wrote a quick message to her son and strode outside. Chase was where she'd left him, leaning insolently against the side of the dusty Jeep, the door of his vehicle still swung open and waiting.

"Has anyone ever told you you're an arrogant bastard?" she asked as she climbed into the Jeep.

"You! Several times." He slammed the door shut, ran around the front of the vehicle, climbed in the driver's side and then did a quick U-turn in the driveway, spinning gravel from under the tires as the Jeep bounced down the long lane leading to the main highway.

Dani sat with her arms crossed over her chest, staring straight ahead. "Do you mind telling me what you've got up your sleeve?"

"You'll see," Chase said grimly, shifting down and barely slowing as he turned off the highway and into Caleb's tree-lined lane. The Jeep roared up the gravel drive and Dani's stomach twisted nervously at the thought of confronting Caleb again on his property. After all, she'd never caught Caleb himself on her land and none of what he'd done to her could be proven—until now.

"Get out," Chase ordered once he'd parked the Jeep.

"Wait a minute—"

"You wait a minute! You're the one who's been itching to have it out with Johnson. Okay, here's your big chance. Let's go."

"But what if Larry Cross lied? It's just his word against Johnson's."

"Except that I've got the evidence, remember?"

"Which is?"

"The drum of dioxin—the drum that Caleb purchased."

Without any further words, he jumped out of his side of the Jeep, slammed the door shut and waited, his jaw set in anger, as Dani climbed out of the rig and fought the urge to run away. She was seeing a side of Chase she hadn't seen since the first day she'd watched him wading in the creek. But then she'd had the advantage; she'd been on her property and in the right. Now she wasn't sure whose side he was on and even where the battle lines were drawn.

Trust him, she told herself as she stood next to him.

Chase scanned the stable yard, his eyes going over every inch of the clean white buildings and fence surrounding the parking lot behind the large farmhouse. Then, seeing the object of his wrath, he took Dani's hand in his and started walking quickly to the track where Caleb was watching his latest acquisition sprint at breakneck speed for a quarter of a mile.

"Here we go," Dani muttered under her breath as they approached Caleb and the old man turned toward them.

Frowning slightly at the sight of Dani, Caleb leaned one elbow over the top rail of the fence and straightened the string tie at his neck.

"Mrs. Summers," he said congenially. "How're you?"

"Well as can be expected," she replied, glancing nervously at Chase and wishing she'd refused to come with him. Beneath the facade of neighborliness, she could see Caleb's hostility, feel his hatred.

Caleb glanced at the threatening sky. "Looks like we'll be gettin' that rain we need tonight. Weather service says that we'll have a few storms in the next few days . . ." Pleasantries aside, Caleb got down to business. "Now, what brings you here this afternoon?" he asked, looking pointedly at Chase. "I don't s'pose it's to see my new colt run, now, is it?"

"No," Chase said, leaning his back on the fence and eyeing the horse as the stocky colt, done with his sprint, was being walked around the track. The horse's dark muscles gleamed with sweat and he was blowing hard. Chase eyed Caleb.

Dani watched Caleb's reaction.

The older man's mouth twitched nervously and his blue eyes were filled with impatience and subdued anger.

"Actually Dani didn't want to come up here. It was my idea."

"Oh?" Caleb's jaw slid to the side but he refused to be baited. Chase would get to the point. Eventually. And if given enough rope, the younger man would hang himself. Caleb made a mental note to give him all the rope he needed.

"Yep. Y'see, while I was in Idaho, I did some checkin' around."

"On that job in Spokane?"

"That, too," Chase said slowly. "But I was looking into something else; something that happened here last year. I managed to locate a man who used to work for you. A man by the name of Larry Cross. You remember him?"

Caleb nodded slowly and waved at the boy who'd ridden the colt during the workout. "Keep cooling him off and then put him back in his stall. Jim'll clean him up," he called to the hand before turning back to Chase. "Larry Cross? Sure, I remember him."

Dani felt the sweat run down her back, though the breeze whispering through the pine trees near the track was cool.

"I had to let him go," Caleb admitted. "Turned out he was stealing me blind, selling part of my feed to friends of his. I couldn't prove it, of course, but I think he was into cattle rustlin' as well. I'm surprised you bothered to look him up."

"Seems he had a few other tricks up his sleeve."

Caleb frowned. "Wouldn't surprise me."

"He placed a drum of dioxin in the creekbed last year. The poison got into the water and killed several of Dani's cattle."

"You're sure of that?" Caleb asked, rubbing his chin and glancing sideways at Dani.

Her heart beginning to pound, she nodded.

"I've got the empty drum," Chase remarked.

Caleb's bushy eyebrows raised and he drew his mouth into an exaggerated frown. "Sounds like something Cross would do."

"He claims you were behind it."

"'Course he does."

"He says you did it to give Dani a bad time; ruin her herd, force her to sell her property to you."

Caleb snorted, but beads of sweat had broken out over his brow. He mopped his forehead with a handkerchief he found in his pocket. "Well, what did you expect him to say—that he was behind it himself?"

"No. Because it doesn't make any sense that way. Why would he want to hurt Dani?"

Caleb stared at Dani with cold, cruel eyes. "Who knows? Maybe he was involved with her. She's been alone a long time till you came along—"

Chase took a step closer and curled his fingers over Caleb's arm. "Don't even suggest—"

"I never met anyone named Larry Cross!" Dani said angrily, color flushing her face. She tried to step forward but felt Chase's hand grip her forearm and restrain her as he backed a few steps away from Caleb.

Caleb shrugged. "I can only guess at his motives, but the man was bad news. I got rid of him as soon as I found out about him, but I didn't know about any drum of dioxin."

"What about the time you tried to siphon off all the water from Grizzly Creek for your own private lake?" Dani demanded, her fury getting the better of her tongue.

"Well," Caleb said, spreading his hands, "I'd like to blame

Cross for that one, but I'll have to own up to it. I thought I'd be able to deter a little water for the lake without interrupting the flow too badly. Looks like I misjudged."

"Looks like," Dani agreed, her eyes narrowing to slits.

"But I admitted it and as soon as I realized that you weren't getting enough water, I scrapped my idea for a lake."

"But you didn't know anything about a drum of dioxin?"

"Nope," Caleb said, shaking his head slowly. "First I've heard of it."

"Cross says different," Chase said.

"Cross would."

"He claims you paid him to keep quiet. To the tune of five thousand dollars."

Caleb laughed outright. "I'm not the kind of man who likes to throw money away," he said. "You know that. I gave Cross the boot and an extra week's pay and, as far as I'm concerned, he was lucky to get that." He smiled smugly. "Check the books if you don't believe me."

"I have."

"Well?"

"Nothing."

Caleb lifted his shoulders. "Cross is willing to testify."

"It's just his word against mine, McEnroe. Who do you think the judge would believe?" Smiling, he slapped the top rail of the fence. "Now, how about a drink—or some lunch?"

"No thanks," Dani said. "Cody's expecting me back."

"But I would like a chance to talk to Jenna," Chase said, propelling Dani toward the house.

"I don't think that's possible," the older man replied.

"Why not?"

"Didn't you know? Jenna left me high and dry. Yes, sir! Just two days ago. Took off and swore she wasn't comin' back."

Chase, his countenance grim, whirled on his boot heel to face the old man. "Why?"

Dread, cold as winter night, skittered down Dani's spine.

"She claimed she was moving . . . somewhere in Wyoming, I think. Has a sister near Laramie or Cheyenne or somewhere. Couldn't even give me a couple weeks notice, if ya can believe that."

"I believe it," Chase said through clenched teeth. "But I think you put her up to it."

"Now why would I do that? Best cook in the county. Jenna's been with me for nearly twenty years and just the other day, quick as a cat climbing a tree, she up and quits."

"So who's taking care of the house?" Chase asked.

Caleb seemed more relaxed. "Maria. Wife of one of the hands. She's got lunch on the table, I reckon. Sure you can't stay?"

"Positive," Dani cut in before Chase could say anything. They had been walking toward the house through the parking lot and Dani stopped at Chase's Jeep.

The wind caught on one of the shutters and it banged against the barn. "Looks like we're in for a nasty one," Caleb said.

Chase glanced up at the threatening sky. "I'll be back later."

"Good." Caleb clapped Chase on the back and then walked slowly toward his farmhouse.

"So what do you suppose prompted Jenna to quit?" Chase asked once they were back in the Jeep and heading toward Dani's farm. Big drops of rain began to pelt from the sky, hitting the windshield and running down the glass in grimy streaks. Chase snapped on the wipers and squinted as he turned off the main road.

"You don't believe him," she said flatly.

"Not for one minute. Do you?"

"No."

"I didn't think so;" Chase muttered, parking the Jeep by the house. "Maybe we'd better do some checking around."

"Now?"

"Before Jenna has a chance to leave town."

"I can't go," Dani said, eyeing Blake's pickup. "Not until I've touched base with Cody. They shouldn't be out in this storm. . . ." She hoped that Blake and Cody had enough sense to come back to the house.

Chase looked as if he were about to argue, but kept quiet. Instead he jumped down from the Jeep and held his jacket over Dani's head as they ran to the house. Once they were on the porch, Chase wiped the raindrops from his hair. "Caleb certainly is a cool one, isn't he?"

"As ice." Dani held the screen door open with her body to allow Chase to pass. "It's spooky."

"Spooky?" he repeated with a laugh.

"Laugh if you want, but that man gives me the creeps. I've never met anyone who can talk out of both sides of his mouth the way that Caleb can," she said while rubbing her arms before shaking her head at the impossibility of the situation. "I hate to admit it, you know, but I suppose I owe you an apology."

"Probably," Chase agreed. "But let's call it even."

"Fair enough." Dani flashed a quick smile and then walked to the window near the fireplace and stared across the fields and past the creek. "I wish I knew what Caleb was up to," she said, idly brushing the dust from the windowsill with her finger. "But then, I wish I knew what Blake wanted, too."

"And me?" Chase asked, standing beside her.

"Yes," she admitted with a thoughtful frown. "I'd like to know what you really want."

"It's simple," he said. "I just want out of the yoke of this mockery of a partnership with Caleb and I want you to come to Boise and marry me."

"You make it sound so easy." Sighing, she leaned against him, grateful for his strength.

"It could be, if you'd let it." He reached into his pocket and withdrew a small black jeweler's box. "Open it," he instructed as he wrapped her small hand around the velvet case. Dani felt tears in her eyes as she snapped open the case and viewed the dainty gold ring with a large pear-shaped diamond.

Her throat was so swollen, she couldn't speak.

"I was going to wait until tonight, when we were alone and Cody was in bed . . . but I hadn't counted on Blake showing up or all your suspicions about my being in-volved with Caleb."

"I don't know what to say," she whispered, eyes brim-ming with unshed tears.

"Just say yes."

Pausing only a moment, she extracted the ring from its case and slid it onto her finger. "Yes," she murmured, clos-ing her eyes and letting the tears drizzle down her cheeks.

Chase took her face in his hands and kissed the salty tracks on her skin. "I love you, Dani. And no matter what happens, we'll pull through this together." Kissing her gently on the lips, he silently promised her a future of togetherness and joy.

Dani slid her arms around his neck and listened to the comforting beat of his heart. Desperate for the security and love he offered, she returned his kiss and managed to forget, for a little while, all the problems still plaguing her.

Cody and Blake hadn't returned. Dani was worried, but Chase insisted that she calm down. "Every good fisherman knows that the best time to catch fish is just as the sun sets," he said.

"But it's after nine! And it's been raining off and on all afternoon. And the wind—" As if to add emphasis to her words, the wind picked up and banged a branch of the apple tree against the back porch. "Oh, God," she whispered, still pacing back and forth. "Something's wrong. I can feel it."

"Do you want me to go looking for them?"

"No— Yes— No, I don't know what to do," she moaned, running her fingers through her hair. "Damn!" Perching on the edge of a chair, she rested her chin on her hands and tried to ignore the worries nagging at her. "You know, before this all started, I used to be a competent woman—"

"I remember," he said, smiling and glancing at the empty rifle hanging over the fireplace. "Look. Cody knows the way home. He'll be back soon—"

Just then, they heard Runt's familiar bark. Dani leaped out of the chair and opened the door to allow a drenched dog into the house. He ran into the kitchen, shook his coat and checked his bowl for dinner scraps.

Dani walked out to the back porch and though it was dark, she saw Cody running up to the house. Blake was several yards behind the boy.

"Thank God," Dani whispered.

"Hey, Mom," Cody cried jubilantly, "we caught a million fish!"

"A million?" she repeated.

"Well, maybe twelve or thirteen," Cody corrected, pushing his hair out of his eyes and streaking his forehead with mud. Then he clomped onto the back porch and tried to knock the mud from his shoes. He set his pole and creel against the rail.

"I was worried about you," Dani said softly.

"Aw, Mom—"

"Why?" Blake asked, finally catching up to the boy.

"It's late and the storm—"

"Just a little rainshower, Dani. And it's not that late—only a little after nine—"

"Nearly ten," Dani corrected. "And Cody has school tomorrow."

"He'll make it, won't ya, boy?" Blake asked, kicking off his boots as if he intended to stay, and then seeing Chase in the doorway, changed his mind. Swearing to himself, he put the boots back on his feet "So ya still got company, huh?"

"That's right."

Blake ran a hand over his beard-roughened chin. "I thought maybe you'd let me stay the night—" Then, seeing the fury blazing in Chase's eyes and the way the man's shoulders bunched, as if he'd like nothing better than to whip the tar out of one Blake Summers, Blake added, "On the couch of course."

"Other plans?" Blake asked, eyeing Chase as he walked through the door and stood beside Dani.

"That's enough, Summers," Chase warned, his lips thinning menacingly.

Blake shivered and stood.

"Cody, I think you'd better go upstairs and get cleaned up and ready for bed," Dani suggested, smelling the fight that was brewing between the two men.

The boy stood his ground, though he chewed anxiously on his lip. "But. Mom—"

"Now."

Swallowing hard, Cody looked to his father, but Blake just slowly shook his head. "Listen to your ma, boy. It's time I was shovin' off anyway." He stood and scowled darkly at Chase as he brushed his hands on his jeans.

"You can stay," Cody blurted out, his boyish, confused eyes darting from one adult to another. "I have an extra bed in my room and—"

"Not tonight, son," Blake said after reading the warning in Dani's eyes and the set of determination in her jaw. "Another time, maybe."

"And maybe not," Dani said.

Smiling briefly at his son and then sending Dani a threatening glance, Blake walked off the back porch and around to the front of the house. A few seconds later Blake's pickup roared to life.

Cody, who'd stood stock-still throughout the argument, ran through the house to the front porch where he waved frantically at his father as the taillights of the pickup faded into the night.

Without another word, the boy dashed up the stairs and

into his room. A few seconds later he stomped to the bathroom and took a shower.

"Do you want me to talk to him?" Chase asked.

Dani shook her head. "No. I think this one is between Cody and his mother."

"Then maybe I should go." He took her into his arms and kissed her gently on the mouth.

Warmth invaded Dani's body, coloring her face. " You can stay," she whispered.

Groaning and hazarding a glance at the stairs, Chase shook his head. "You need time to sort things out with Cody, and besides, I still need to check on Jenna Peterson. I don't buy Caleb's story. My guess is that he fired her. Now the only question is why?"

"Not the only question," Dani said with a sigh.

"First things first," Chase said, releasing her. "You deal with Cody and I'll be back as soon as I can."

She watched him leave and slowly closed the door when his Jeep was out of sight. Then, ignoring the loneliness settling over her, and with renewed determination, she mounted the stairs to tell her son that she was going to marry Chase McEnroe.

Chapter Eleven

The next morning Dani still hadn't talked to her son. After Chase had left the night before, Dani had tried to talk to Cody, but he'd refused to speak to her. Now, nothing had changed, she thought ruefully as she swept the kitchen floor and waited for him to get up.

He waited until the last minute before dashing down the stairs and pausing at the table for breakfast. While she put the jug of milk on the table, he sat, avoiding her eyes, his fingers nervously drumming on the polished wood.

"Slow down a minute," Dani said with a warm smile. "I think we've got a few things we should discuss before you take off for school."

"But I'm already late—"

"I know. But I can drive you. I want to talk."

"'Bout what?" He poured milk on his cereal and started eating.

"Last night, for starters," she replied, leaning on the broom. "And then maybe just about us—you and me—and how we're going to handle dealing with your dad now that he's back in town."

Cody's eyes flashed. "*I* can handle dealing with him just fine."

"You think so?" she said gently, trying with difficulty not to sound like a dictator.

"You're the one with the problem, Mom."

"Believe it or not, Cody, I'm trying to be very open-minded about this and work it out so that we're all happy." After putting the broom back in the closet, she poured a cup of coffee and took a chair opposite him.

"Humph," Cody said stubbornly. "I suppose you think you're gonna try to tell me when I can be with him."

"No, but—"

"Sure you are!"

Dani held up her hands to ward off the battle, and Cody stared straight at her left hand, his mouth dropping open and his eyes reflecting an inner pain at the sight of her engagement ring. "Where'd you get that—from Chase? You're gonna marry that guy aren't you?" he said, balling a fist and pounding it on the table, his face flushing red and contorting in a battle against tears of outrage. "Dammit!"

"Cody!"

"Well, are you?" His brown eyes pierced hers and though she ached to soften the blow, she had to tell him the truth.

"Okay. Yes, Chase asked me to marry him and I agreed, but I was going to talk it over with you before we made any definite plans."

"It looks pretty definite to me!" he shouted, pointing at the ring angrily before pleading with her. "Mom, don't do this! Not now." And then a look of new horror spread over his face and his tears began in earnest. "Oh, I get it. You're doing this *because* of Dad, aren't you?"

"Your father has nothing to do with the fact that I want to marry Chase—"

"But Dad loves you! He told me so, just yesterday!" Cody cut in.

"He doesn't love me, Cody—"

"He does! I asked him and he told me he never stopped loving you or me! He wants to come back and you . . . you're marrying a man who works for Caleb Johnson just to keep Dad and me apart!" Livid, he pushed his chair back, grabbed his backpack from under the table and flung open the front door.

"Oh, Cody, I would never—"

"You would! You have!" he screamed. "You couldn't even give Dad a chance, could you?"

With that, he ran outside and raced down the hill to the bus stop.

"That does it!" Dani said, thinking about chasing him down and even following the bus to school if she had to. She'd reached for her keys and purse and taken a step toward the door before she thought better of her plan and sagged against the wall. Following Cody would only end up in another bitter argument that would probably embarrass them both in front of his friends and teachers. He would never forgive her.

Knowing that she had to give him time to cool off and think rationally, she hung her keys back on the hook in the kitchen and watched him anxiously through the window. The bus stopped at the end of the lane, honked and waited as Cody ran the final few yards and climbed aboard.

"When he gets home, we're having it out—all of it!" she promised herself angrily. "I've got to make him understand that I'm marrying Chase for both of us." *And no matter how much it hurts, I'll get used to the fact that Blake is back and Cody needs to spend time with him,* she added silently to herself.

When Cody didn't get off the bus after school, Dani tried not to panic. Several times in the past, Cody had gone to a friend's house without telling her. Though she'd made him promise never to go anywhere without calling her, she rationalized that he'd left in a huff in the morning and was probably childishly attempting to punish her by staying away from home.

And it was working. She glanced at the clock every two minutes and listened for his step on the back porch while folding clothes in the kitchen.

Where was he? She thought about calling Chase, but didn't. "Stop it, Dani," she told herself. "Don't depend on him too much. This is your problem. You can handle it." But deep down she yearned to pour her troubles out to him. Absently, she toyed with her new ring. "It'll all work out," she told herself and looked out the window, wondering where the devil Cody was.

After a half an hour of waiting, she couldn't stand the suspense and dread beginning to settle on her shoulders. She started calling all of Cody's friends, beginning with Shane Donahue. Twenty minutes later, she replaced the receiver slowly and felt her insides begin to quiver in fear. No one had seen her son.

"Blast it, Cody," she whispered. "Where are you?"

Her heart beating double time, she called the school

and was connected with Cody's teacher, who explained that Cody hadn't been in school all day.

Panic swept over her as she listened to Amanda Ross's apologies and worries. Hanging up the phone with shaking fingers, Dani closed her eyes against the very real fear that Blake had taken Cody away from her.

She could imagine the scene: Cody, still brooding from the fight with Dani had gone to Blake's brother's house, had found Blake and told him that his mother intended to marry another man and move far away, taking Cody away from his father. Blake's natural response would have been to comfort the child and take him away from the intolerable situation.

"Oh, no," she whispered. "Please God, no." Images of Blake and Cody rambling across the country in Blake's battered old pickup filled her mind before other, more terrifying thoughts struck her. Maybe Cody wasn't with his father. Maybe he'd taken off on his own, or started hitchhiking to God-only-knew-where.

Trying to think clearly, Dani called Blake's brother, who lived in Martinville, but no one answered. She slammed the receiver down and held it in place before scrounging in the desk for the phone book and looking up the number of the company where Blake's brother worked. No good. She was told politely by the receptionist that Bob Summers was out of town on a sales trip.

"What now?" she wondered. Then, trying to keep a level head, she hastily scrawled a note to Cody, hung it on the refrigerator and ran out the back door. "Come on," she said to Runt, who took his cue and followed her outside. When she opened the pickup door, the dog leaped into the cab. "Let's hope we can find him," she confided as she started the truck and put it in gear.

Dark clouds swept over the sky, shadowing the land. The wind, hot and dry, blew leaves and dust across the road. "Looks like we're in for a good one," Dani said to Runt while eyeing the purple, roiling sky and praying that Cody was safe. "Oh, son, use your head and come home!"

She tore out of the driveway like a madwoman, and though she tried to calm herself, she could feel her heart in her throat. beating at twice its normal rate. Sweat dampened her arms and back and her fingers were clenched around the steering wheel as she drove into the quiet school parking lot.

"You're sure he was never here, today?" Dani asked Cody's teacher once she'd dashed through the hallways to his room in the elementary school.

Amanda Ross was visibly distraught. "Yes, but I thought he was probably just ill. I had no idea—" Then, catching herself, she touched Dani on the arm. "I asked all the teachers; no one saw Cody—not even the duty teacher who supervises the playground in the morning before the final bell when the kids go into their class-rooms."

"But I saw him get on the bus—"

"I know. I called over to the bus barns and talked to the driver of the bus Cody rides. The driver remembers picking up Cody and bringing him to the school. So we know he got here, but from that point, no one's sure what happened. From what I can tell, Cody never came into the building or even stopped at the playground. With all of the students arriving by bus and car, he could very easily have walked off the grounds unnoticed."

Sick with worry, Dani sat on a corner of Cody's desk and swallowed back her tears as she looked at the empty chair. "So no one knows where he is?"

"I'm sorry," Amanda said. "Is there anything I can do?"

"I don't know."

The young teacher thought for a moment before broaching what she knew would be a sensitive subject for Cody's mother. "I heard that his father was back in town," she said gently.

"Yes, but not with me. And no one answers at his place."

"Do you think Cody's with him?"

"I don't know," Dani admitted, pressing a finger to her temple. "I hope this is just one of Cody's pranks to get back at me; we had an argument this morning." She pursed her lips together and stood. "I hope to God that Blake hasn't taken off with him."

"So Cody was pretty upset when he left the house?"

"Beside himself." Her heart twisting, she looked at Cody's teacher. "I—I was going to run after him, but I thought maybe we should both cool off before we got into another disagreement."

"I see." Amanda rubbed her arms and nodded. "He does have a stubborn streak."

"Like me."

"Have you gone to the police?"

"Not yet. I thought I'd get my facts straight first. Look, can I talk to the bus driver?"

"Sure. You can use the phone in the office to call over to the bus barns."

The phone conversation was short. Unfortunately the bus driver wasn't able to tell her anything other than the fact that Cody had definitely gotten to school. Dani hung up the receiver and felt her shoulders slump under the weight of not knowing what had happened to her son.

"Any luck?" Amanda said hopefully.

"None."

"Listen, why don't you call me in the morning?" Amanda suggested. "If Cody hasn't shown up, all of the teachers will ask their classes about him. Maybe one of the children will know where he is. And I'll call all the students in my class tonight, if that will help."

"Thank you," Dani murmured as she walked out of the building.

"Good luck."

Without much hope, Dani drove away from the school and after stopping at Blake's brother's house and finding no one home, she steered her pickup to the police station where she reported Cody missing, talked to the sergeant, filled out a missing person's report and gave the police one of the pictures of Cody she kept in her wallet. She repeated the procedure at the sheriffs office and finally, drained and exhausted, she returned to her dark, empty house.

Runt barked excitedly and whined at the door as Dani opened it, but she walked into the shadowed house with a heavy heart. Nothing had changed. Cody hadn't returned. The note she'd written him was still on the refrigerator, the ice box hadn't been raided, there was no loud music filtering down from his room, nor any dirty tennis shoes or books scattered in the living room.

The pain in her heart wouldn't go away. Nor would her wild imagination, filled with horrible scenarios of what had happened to her son, be still.

Once she'd had a steadying cup of coffee, she called everyone she could think of, including the Anders brothers and, much as it rankled, Caleb Johnson.

"Well, I'm sorry to hear that your boy's missin'," Caleb said, his insincerity drifting over the wires. "Anything I can do?"

"Just let me know if you see him," Dani replied.

"Will do. And I'll tell the hands."

"I appreciate it."

"Good."

"Caleb—" she said, hating herself for having to ask anything of the old man, but desperate to find her son.

"What?"

"Is Chase there?"

"Not now. Seems he had some business in town and then he went right down to the creek. But I'll tell him you called," Caleb said coldly. "Soon as I see him again."

"Thanks."

She managed to get through the evening chores alone, all the while listening and praying for the phone to ring. It took twice as long to feed the cattle and horses and by the time she was done, she was sweaty, dirty and despondent. Rain peppered the tin roof of the barn and gurgled in the gutters, and the wind, blowing with gale force, shrieked around the buildings.

"Let him be safe," she prayed quietly over the restless shifting of the cattle and the whistle of the wind. The facade she'd held in place all day began to slide away and tears slid down her cheeks.

Too tired to wipe them aside, she sat on a bale of hay and sobbed quietly to herself. "Oh, Cody," she whispered to the dark interior of the barn while listening to the rain, "where are you?"

Through the sheets of rain, Chase looked at the stream and silently congratulated himself on a job well done. The clear water swirled over deep pools and rippled over strategically placed rocks and logs as it ran its course through Johnson's land. Now, if Caleb kept to his word and didn't disturb the banks while constructing his resort, there was no reason Grizzly Creek wouldn't become one of the best trout fishing streams in western Montana.

He glanced at the sky and hunched his shoulders against the thick rain that was pouring from the heavens. Water ran past the collar of his jean jacket and slid down his back. *Miserable weather*, he thought in agitation, *and unusual. Hot and dry one minute, a downpour the next.*

"That about wraps it up," Ben Marx said with a satisfied smile as he lit a cigarette and pushed his shaggy wet hair out of his eyes.

"All that's left is to stock it."

"And then we're outta here, right?"

Chase nodded and wiped his hands on his jeans. "Right. You and the rest of the crew can leave tonight if you want; I'll finish up with some of Johnson's hands."

"Whatever you say!" Ben drew on his cigarette and let it dangle from the corner of his mouth. "Right now I'm going to get the hell out of this rain and head into town. Check the action at Yukon Jack's. I could use a beer and a change of scenery."

"Take Frank and Brent with you," Chase suggested, and watched as the bearded young man shouted to the rest of the men. They all climbed into a pickup, waved to Chase, and drove across the field to the gate in the corner and the dirt road leading to the center of Johnson's farm.

Chase waited until they were out of sight and then slipped through the fence and ran up the slight incline toward the back of Dani's house. He hadn't seen her all day. Throughout the afternoon, he'd experienced an uncanny sensation that something was wrong; he attributed his discomfiture to the trouble with Cody the night before and the fact that the boy obviously preferred his father's company to Chase's.

"Can't blame the kid," Chase told himself, wiping the rain from his face and hair before sauntering up the back steps. He rapped on the screen door with a knuckle and wondered why none of the interior lights had been turned on.

"Cody?" Dani called, jumping to her feet. She'd been sitting in a corner of the couch, her feet tucked beneath her, her fingers absently scratching Runt's ears.

"Nope. Sorry to—" Chase walked into the room and met her halfway. Immediately he saw the pain in her eyes. "—disappoint you. Dani?"

She couldn't help the small cry that caught in her throat as she ran to him and threw her arms around his neck. "Oh, God, I'm glad you're here," she whispered into his wet shirt. "Just hold me. Please."

He did just that. Resting his head on her crown, he tightened his grip and said softly, "Believe me, I have no intention of ever letting you go."

"Why didn't you come sooner?"

"I was working . . ." He held his head back and studied her tear-filled eyes. "Hey, wait a minute. Something is wrong. Really wrong. Maybe you'd better sit down." Guiding her to the couch, he scrutinized her while she slipped back onto the worn cushions and sniffed back her tears. "What's going on?"

"Didn't Caleb tell you?"

"I haven't seen him all day," Chase replied, every muscle in his body tensing. "What's he done?" He pulled a clean, slightly damp handkerchief from the pocket of his jeans and wiped the back of his neck.

"It's not Caleb," she said, shaking her head and sighing.

His jaw clenched. "That bastard of a husband of yours has something to do with this, doesn't he?"

"It's my fault," she breathed, gathering her courage. "All my fault."

"What is?"

"Cody," she choked out, pressing the back of her hand to her lips and looking up at Chase. "He's missing."

"Missing? What do you mean?"

"Just that. He got on the bus around seven-thirty this morning and no one's seen him since."

"You're sure?" Sitting on the arm of the sofa, his blue eyes scanning her white, pinched face, he placed his large hand on her shoulder and her fear infected him. Dani wasn't a woman who panicked easily. Usually strong, now she was scared to death.

"I've called everyone, looked everywhere," she said, standing, pacing and wringing her hands.

"Wait a minute. Slow down and back up," he insisted, taking hold of her and sitting her back on the couch. "Now why don't you start at the beginning. Cody got on the bus to go to school—then what happened?"

Slowly, in a slightly broken voice, she told him every last detail of the search for her son.

"You should have come to me."

"I—I couldn't. I didn't know where you were and . . . well, you know how it is with Caleb. I did call him and he said he'd get word to you."

"He didn't bother."

"Figures." Dani sniffed.

"You haven't heard from Blake?"

Dani shook her head and sighed. "Nothing."

Pacing the length of the house, Chase tried to unscramble his jumbled thoughts while his suspicion increased. Chase didn't trust coincidence and there were just too many coincidences in Dani's life right now. "I wonder if this has anything to do with Jenna Peterson taking off?"

"I don't see how. Jenna had an argument with Caleb and Cody . . . Cody's probably run off with his father. They could be in North Dakota by now, or Idaho . . . or Canada. I wouldn't put it past Blake to take him out of the country."

"But why, Dani?" Chase asked, his thick brows pulled over his eyes as he strode purposefully into the kitchen, rummaged in Dani's cupboards, found a dusty old bottle of Scotch and poured them each a stiff drink. He carried the glasses in one hand and the bottle in the other as he came back into the living room and snapped on one of the table lamps.

"Why did Blake take Cody?" she repeated. "To be with his son, of course."

"I don't think so." Chase handed Dani a glass. "Drink it." When she started to protest, he set the bottle on the table and wrapped her fingers around the glass. "Just this once, Dani, don't argue."

"But Cody's got to be with Blake—they're both missing."

"You think." Chase downed his drink in one swallow and poured himself another. His knuckles whitened around the glass as he frowned into the amber liquid. "Y'know . . . there are just too damned many twists of fate around here to suit me."

"I don't understand."

"Don't you think it's odd that Jenna Peterson, a woman who's worked for Caleb for years, took off about the same time that Blake blew into town?"

"But Blake's been writing Cody for months—"

"And don't you think it's just a damned sight too convenient that both Blake and the boy are missing—right after we confronted Caleb Johnson with the fact that we know he's done everything from poison your water to low-ball you on the land to get you to sell out to him."

Dani sipped from her drink and a chill ran down her spine. "You're trying to tell me that Caleb's behind Cody's disappearance."

"I'm saying that I don't trust him and that things are happening too fast to be just a matter of fate." He glanced out the window to the gathering storm. "You're the one who put the idea into my head, y'know. You said it yourself: You were tired of being manipulated. I think it's about time to set a few things straight with my 'partner.'" He finished his drink and set the glass on the table with a thud. "Get your coat. This time when we talk to Johnson, we're going to get some answers—straight answers!"

* * *

"You can't be serious!" Caleb said, shaking his great head and even managing a nervous laugh. "I don't know anything about your son's disappearance other than what you told me on the phone this afternoon."

He was standing near the fireplace in his living room and looking at Dani and Chase as if they were out of their minds.

"Why did Jenna leave?" Chase demanded.

"I told you, I have no idea."

"I talked to her daughter. She said that when Jenna left the woman was beside herself. Jenna apparently had an argument with you and something happened to make her leave. It had something to do with someone you've hired recently . . ."

Caleb's eyes grew cold. "We had words," Caleb admitted.

"About?"

The old man stepped forward, close enough that he could reach forward and touch Chase. Instead he rubbed the back of a leather couch and concentrated on the hard angles of Chase's face. The younger man was regarding him warily, silently accusing him with those damned indifferent eyes—eyes so much like his own.

Dani, her arms wrapped around her torso, felt suddenly cold; a premonition of what was to come. "I just want to find my son," she interjected, looking from the face of one angry man to the other. Tension radiated between them.

"Just as I wanted to find mine all those years ago," Caleb said evenly.

"Pardon?" Dani said. "*Your* son? But I didn't think—" She broke off midsentence and saw the unspoken message pass from Caleb to Chase.

Beneath his tan, Chase blanched, all of his muscles tightening in revulsion, his back teeth clamping together in denial. "What are you trying to say, Johnson?"

"It took me a long time to find you. Ella hid her tracks well," Caleb said.

"You're out of your mind!" Chase said angrily.

"Face it, boy: I'm your father!"

"What the hell is this, Johnson?" Chase demanded, getting hold of himself and eyeing the older man with a deadly calm that belied the raging torrent of emotions roiling deep inside. "This is just another ploy to avoid the subject—"

"It's something I've been meaning to bring up for some time."

"Like hell!" Chase's anger boiled to the surface. "I'm sick of your lies. Come on, Dani!"

He turned to go, but Caleb's words stopped him. "This is no lie, boy. Jenna guessed the truth and knew how you felt about me. Seems you'd had a discussion earlier. When I told her that I was going to spring the news on you, she had one helluva fit. Told me to leave well enough alone."

Chase's eyes narrowed to hard, glinting slits. His back and shoulder muscles bunched and it took all of his control to keep his hands off Caleb's throat. "You're wrong!"

"Why do you think I went to the trouble of finding you? There were a dozen other companies I could have contacted. Eric Conway underbid you by thirty-five-hundred dollars. You can check it yourself, in the study. It's all in the files. But I wasn't interested in the lowest bidder," he said with chilling clarity. "I wanted you, and don't flatter yourself thinking it was because you were the best!" Laughing at his own weakness, he said, "I had this stupid, mortal desire before I died to meet the only son that I'd sired."

Hatred and fury radiated from the younger man. Chase grabbed hold of Caleb's shirt, the clean, starched fabric wrinkling in his angry fists. "You're lying. This is just one more of your cheap tricks to blow smoke in my face!" His nose was pressed up to Caleb's, and his furious blue eyes burned into those of the older man. "Now why don't you tell us the real reason Jenna left. While you're at it, you can tell Dani how you're involved with her ex-husband and where the hell her son is."

"I don't know."

"You're pushing it," Chase warned through clenched teeth.

Caleb glanced nervously at Dani and then fixed on Chase. "Let go of me and I'll prove it."

Chase hesitated and his nostrils flared. "Go ahead." He unclenched his fist and Caleb smoothed his shirt.

Without a word Caleb walked out of the living room, crossed the foyer and walked into his study. He was gone several minutes. When he returned he carried a faded photograph in one hand and a stack of letters banded together in the other.

He dropped everything on the glass-covered table near the fireplace. Dani stared at the picture in disbelief. It was a grainy photo of a man and woman, their arms linked, a cocker spaniel pup at their feet. She didn't recognize the short, blond woman in the picture, but the man was Chase—or someone who looked enough like him to be his brother. *Or his father!* Shock waves rippled through her as she accepted what Chase couldn't.

"Isn't that your mother?" Caleb demanded, pointing at the woman.

"Looks like her," Chase admitted slowly. Stunned, Chase fought the truth that stared him straight in the face.

"And the dog—didn't you grow up with a black cocker pup?"

"It's not the same dog."

"Named Charlie."

Chase didn't move. His guts wrenched painfully as he stared at the picture.

"And what about the man?" Caleb asked. "Is that your pa?"

"No!"

Caleb snorted and shook his white head. "Give it up, son. That's me!" He tapped his finger on the slick picture. "And the first time I saw you, it was like lookin' into a mirror thirty years ago!"

Chase flinched and tried to hold on to his temper. "I don't believe you. I don't know how you manage to—"

"Then look at the letters. They're all addressed to me, in your ma's handwriting. Read what's inside," the old man demanded, pushing the stack of letters from the table and letting them scatter on the floor. "They're from your ma all right. And they even told me about you. But of course, that was when she'd already made plans to marry another man. She never told me his name and it took me nearly thirty years to track you down. By then she and her husband were both gone."

Chase picked up a letter, scanned the handwriting and then crumpled it in his fist. Anger and disbelief mingled into an ungodly rage that contorted his features and made his insides knot. "Go to hell!"

Dani took hold of his arm. "Let's go— Come on, we've got to find Cody. It's obvious he can't help us."

"And all this time you thought another man was your pa," Caleb taunted.

Chase coiled like a rattler ready to strike and his eyes sparked, but there was a trace of wariness in his voice. "If you knew all this when you first came to me, why didn't you tell me?"

"Would you have believed me?"

"I still don't."

Caleb shrugged his big shoulders. "Then it didn't really matter none, did it?"

Dani watched the argument with growing horror. Whether Chase believed it or not, it was evident to her that he was Caleb's son. Sick with the thought, she backed to the window, watching as the two men glared and argued with each other, their voices climbing with the fever pitch of emotion. Chase, ready to strike, ready to lash out at the cause of his pain, and Caleb, smug in his knowledge of the truth.

"You miserable son of a bitch," Chase said, his anger finally exploding as he crashed a fist into the wall. A painting slid to the floor with a thud, the expensive frame splintering apart. "Why did you drag me into all this? Why didn't you leave me the hell alone?"

"Because I didn't want to die without seeing you. Some day you might have children of your own. Then you'll understand," Caleb predicted.

"But all this plotting and sneaking around." Chase rubbed the bridge of his nose and tried to stave off another wave of fury. He wanted to crash his fist into Caleb's smirking face but realized that injuring a seventy-year-old man would prove nothing. He was shaking with rage, his voice low and firm as he pierced Caleb with eyes so like the old man's.

Dani shuddered and backed out of the room.

"Listen to me, Johnson, I don't want to talk about this . . . I don't want to *think* about it! I just want to find Dani's boy!"

"I have no idea where that kid is—"

"Let's go!" Chase said, grabbing Dani's arm and propelling her to the door.

Dani glanced at the letters on the floor, the photograph on the table and Caleb's ruddy face. "No," Dani said, holding up her hands and backing toward the door. "I think you should stay here and work this out. He's your father, Chase. Your own flesh and blood!"

Stunned and bewildered, she tried to make some sense of it all—deal with the emotional onslaught that twisted her into a thousand little pieces. Chase—Caleb's son? She was numb with shock and didn't think she could stand another. "I'll go home and wait for Cody—"

She raced for the door and ran outside, grateful for the cool air as it pushed her hair from her face. The wind was lashing furiously at the house and rain was peppering the ground in thick drops, settling the dust and splattering on the flagstone walk.

"Dani—" Chase called after her and followed her into the stormy night. He caught up with her at the pickup, his hands jerking on her shoulders and forcing her to face him. "Where are you going?"

"To look for my son!"

"I'll drive—"

"Don't you think you'd better stay here and work things

out with your *father*?" she said sarcastically. "How long have you known about this, Chase?" she demanded, knowing she was being irrational, but losing all control of her emotions. "First I thought you worked for Caleb, then I found out that you were his partner, but it's more than that, isn't it? *You're his son, Chase. His son!*"

He looked at her as if stricken, his blue eyes filled with shock and rage. "You think this was some kind of plot? That I was involved?"

"Oh, Chase," she moaned, rain drenching her hair and shoulders, drops streaming down her face. "I don't know what to think," she admitted, "but I can't worry about it. Not now. Not until I find Cody—"

The sound of an explosion ripped across the land, and Chase reached for Dani, pushing her hard against the pickup, protecting her body with the strength of his.

"Oh, God, what was that?" she whispered, clinging to the rough fabric of his denim jacket.

"No!" Chase let go of her suddenly and ran to the fence on the south end of the parking lot.

Her heart slamming in her chest, disbelief and horror wrenching her face, Dani followed him and looked down the hill to her property and saw a blaze of fireworks reaching up to the black heaven. Orange flames stretched upward like a hand from hell and scraped at the black, smoke-filled sky;

"Oh, God . . ."

"It's the storage shed . . . where you keep the tractor," Chase said, pulling her away from the terrifying spectacle. "Come on."

Caleb had come out and was standing on the back porch. "Call the fire department! Send them to the Hawthorne place," Chase commanded, yelling over the storm. "And find someone to take care of Dani!"

"You're not leaving me!" she shouted, her eyes round with horror. "I've got to go home."

"There's nothing you can do—"

"Let go of me!" she hissed, running to the pickup and wrenching open the driver's door. "Cody might be down there!" She jumped into the pickup and reached into her pocket for her keys.

His jaw tight with determination, Chase climbed in after her, ignoring her protests while he started the truck and drove down the rain-slickened drive toward Dani's house.

She stared at it with dull eyes, her heart filled with dread as she tried to cling to the hope that Cody was far away from the inferno.

The house was illuminated by the orange and red flames that licked up to the sky.

"We can't get any closer," Chase said, maneuvering the truck through the first open gate to a field several hundred yards from the house and keeping the lane free for the fire trucks.

"I'm going up there!"

"No way—"

"Cody might be there!"

"I'll go look for him! You stay here."

"Not on your life!" She shoved open the passenger door and Chase jerked her back into the cab, her hair flying into her face, her eyes wide with fear and anger. "Let me go! Chase, I have to—"

"Dammit all anyway!" With a curse, Chase drove up the rest of the driveway. The pickup bounced up her lane and before Chase stopped the vehicle, Dani jumped from the cab. Heavy black smoke filled the air while the rain still poured from the sky.

"Cody!" she screamed, swallowing back her fear and desperation. "Runt!" *God, where was the dog?* Shimmering heat radiated from the buildings behind the house; even the driving rain couldn't contain the blaze.

Chase was on her heels as she sprinted up the two steps and raced into the house. Shouting Cody's name at the top of her lungs, she ran through the rooms. She bounded up the stairs and flung open the door to Cody's room.

"Runt's missing," she screamed at Chase. "Cody must've come home— Oh God!" On the bed was the note she'd left on the refrigerator. Beside the note was his backpack, the same backpack he'd taken to school, and through the window ugly flames brightened the sky, coloring the room with flickering orange shadows and filling the air with acrid smoke.

"No!" Dani screamed. "Oh, God . . . Oh . . . God!" And then she fell, feeling Chase's strong arms arround her before she hit the floor.

Chapter Twelve

When Dani opened her eyes, she had trouble focusing. She felt a sensation of movement . . . and noise, lots of noise, sirens shrieking, men shouting, and stench . . . something burning. . . .

Blinking twice, she found herself in Chase's arms. He was carrying her down the driveway, away from the house. "No," she whispered, her throat dry. "Chase . . . let me down!"

"This time we're doing it my way, lady," he said through clenched teeth. His hair was slicked down with rainwater and his face was streaked with mud and soot.

"But Cody—"

"I'll find him." Trucks were rushing past them, and one paramedic stopped to talk to Chase.

"Is she all right?"

"I think so—"

"I'm fine," Dani insisted. "Please, put me down!" Once on her feet she stared in amazement at the scene in front of her. Fire trucks were pumping water from the creek and hosing it over the storage shed, and men, neighbors she supposed, were letting the animals out of the barn, into the farthest fields from the house. The cattle lowed and the horses raced.

"Where did everyone come from?" she asked.

"Caleb called the fire department and the neighbors heard the blast—you've been out of it for a little while."

Placing a hand on her head, she tried to think past the headache and her burning eyes. Finally her thoughts began to clear and crystallize with fear. "Wait a minute. Where is Cody? His backpack was on the bed, I saw his shoes and the note I'd written. He was home, Chase! In that house—" She pointed to the wet, dark home she'd shared with her son. "Dear God, where could he be?" Attempting to jerk free and climb back up the hill, she fought the strong arm around her.

"You can't do anything more," Chase said. "Let the fire department handle the fire."

At that moment the Anders' truck pulled into the lane. Marcella, her face a mask of horror, was at the wheel. "What the devil's goin' on?" she asked. "I was just on my way home from the store when I saw all the commotion—"

"The storage shed caught fire and the gas tank blew," Chase filled her in.

"Good Lord!" Marcella looked at all the frantic activity and her face became grim.

"Oh, no," Dani whispered, understanding the explosion. "But how . . ."

"Fortunately Dani didn't have much gas in the tank," Chase continued.

"Thank God," Dani murmured.

"You still lookin' for your boy?" Marcella asked.

"Yes." Dani's clouded eyes brightened. "Have you seen him?"

"'Fraid not. And the boys, they've been lookin'. Neither one of them has seen him anywhere in town."

"I only hope he's safe," Dani said, thinking about Cody's things in the house. "Let go of me," she said, starting for the house again.

"If you'll look after Dani, I'll check the barn," Chase said. "I want to talk to the fire chief and use his phone, if I can."

"I don't need to be taken care of! I'm coming with you."

"Whoa," Marcella said kindly. "The way I hear it, you've had yourself enough shocks for one day. Sit with me here in the truck till he gets back. I've got coffee and donuts I was bringing home."

"I couldn't eat a thing," Dani said, while Marcella opened the door of the truck and helped a protesting Dani inside.

"Well, the least you can do is share a cup of coffee and keep me company. Chase, he'll find your boy."

"God, I hope so," Dani whispered, cradling the top of the thermos in her fingers and staring through the rain-streaked windshield toward her house and the scarlet flames beyond.

Three hours later the fire was contained. Blackened pieces of the shed were still smoldering, but all in all, the fire had run its course, taking with it the tractor, plow, harrow, baler and trailer and leaving charred skeletons of what had once been Dani's equipment.

Dani had suffered through what seemed a thousand questions from the fire chief and the police, because the fire department suspected that the fire had been set intentionally.

"I was up at Caleb Johnson's when I heard the explosion," Dani said for the fifth time to yet another deputy from the sheriffs department. Bone weary and worried sick, she was tired of the questions and unspoken accusations. "You can ask him or Chase McEnroe. He was with me at the time."

"Where's he?"

"Looking for my boy."

"The boy you reported missing?"

"Yes." She'd gone over it a hundred times. "I could tell that Cody had been home; his shoes and backpack that he'd taken to school, along with a note I'd left him, were in his room."

"Do you mind if I take a look?"

"Please do," she agreed, closing her eyes and twisting her neck to relieve the strain of her shoulder muscles. "Just, please, find my son."

"You haven't seen him since the fire?"

"I haven't seen him since this morning!" Dani followed the young deputy into the house. It had been saved, but reeked of drenched soot. The walls were water stained from the efforts of the firemen to save the house and several windows had been broken from the water pressure of the gigantic hoses.

Fortunately, the Anders brothers and several of the neighbors had tended to the animals for the night and once the young deputy left, promising to return in the morning, Dani was left alone with Marcella to wait for news of Cody and Chase.

"Where do you think Chase is?" she asked, running her fingers through her hair.

"Like I said before, he's lookin' for the boy."

Restless, Dani paced the living room, ignoring the fact that the floor was still wet. "Why don't you go home now?" Dani asked, offering Marcella a smile as she looked around the rooms. "There's nothing anyone can do tonight and I'm fine. Really."

"Not until Chase gets back," Marcella said, plopping herself onto the sofa and picking up a magazine.

"It's nearly ten—"

"And everyone in my family is old enough to take care of himself! The boys know where I am if they need me." She read one headline in Cody's fishing magazine and then tossed the slick-covered periodical on the table. "How about if I make you a sandwich or a hot bowl of soup?"

"I don't think so; but if you're hungry—"

"Nonsense! You look like you haven't eaten for days. No wonder you fainted upstairs what with all the excitement around here!" Against Dani's wishes, Marcella made herself right at home in Dani's kitchen, donned an apron and rummaged around in Dani's cupboards until she finally found a pan and a can of soup. In less than ten minutes, she had Dani at the table, drinking warm broth, and was listening attentively while Dani explained everything that had happened over the last few weeks.

"My Lord!" Marcella exclaimed. "No wonder you're upset with Caleb. And now he turns out to be Chase's father!" She tapped her fingers on the rim of her coffee cup. "You know, if you would have told a few people around town, maybe we all wouldn't have been so gung-ho on this Summer Ridge project."

"I couldn't say anything," Dani said. "I really didn't have any proof until Chase found the drum of dioxin and located Larry Cross. Besides it all would have sounded like sour grapes." She looked at the clock again. Eleven-thirty. Still no sign of Chase or Cody.

"Why don't you go upstairs and get cleaned up?" Marcella suggested. "I'll tidy up the kitchen—"

"Please, don't bother."

"Go on. I can wait for Chase just as well as you can. And if the phone rings, I'll catch it. Now, go on, scoot!"

Dani was too tired to argue. She settled into the hot tub and listened to the sound of Marcella cleaning the dishes. Smiling sadly to herself she remembered years ago, when she'd been a teenager, how she'd liked to listen to the comforting sound of her mother rattling around in the kitchen . . . But that was long before Cody had been born. Now he was missing.

She washed her hair and scrubbed the grime from her body before wrapping her hair in a bath towel and slipping into her robe. Still rubbing her hair with the towel, she walked down the stairs and stopped midway when she heard Runt's familiar bark at the back door. Dani's heart leaped to her throat. "Cody!" she shouted.

Racing down the remaining stairs and to the back door, she let the dog inside and saw Cody and Chase trudging up the backyard. Without another thought, Dani flew down the steps, her long wet hair streaming behind her, tears of relief flowing from her eyes.

Cody threw himself into her arms and clung for dear life. "Mom," he choked out. "Please don't be mad at me!"

"Mad? For what?"

"For takin' off from school and hiding," he said.

"It's all right. Everything's all right now that you're safe," she choked out, clutching her boy in a death grip and turning tear-filled eyes up to Chase. "God, I was worried sick about you." Still clinging to her son, she noticed the tired lines of worry on Chase's face. She'd never been so glad to see anyone in her life! "Where did you find him?"

"At the homestead house."

"Thank you," she whispered, straightening and throwing her arms around his neck to kiss him full on the lips. "I was afraid I'd lost you both."

"Never, lady. You can't get rid of me that easy."

She sniffed back her tears.

"I think we'd better go inside," Chase said. "This boy here is starving and dead tired and there's a lot you need to know about what happened."

Marcella was standing in the doorway and tears filled her eyes. She dabbed at the corners of her eyes with the hem of Dani's apron. "Don't you worry about anytthing," she said. "I'll get Cody a good, hot meal while he goes upstairs and cleans up." With that she bustled into the house.

It was nearly two hours later when Marcella had gone home and Cody, exhausted from a long, harrowing day, fell asleep in Dani's arms. Finally, weary but content, Dani came down the stairs just as Chase hung up the phone.

"Okay, out with it," she said, leaning against the wall while Chase dropped onto the couch. "I know something's up, so you may as well level with me. Did Cody set the fire in the shed?"

"No," Chase said, rubbing his neck with his hands.

"Let me do that," she insisted, standing behind the couch and rubbing his tight shoulder muscles. "So who did?"

"Blake."

"Blake!" Dani was thunderstruck and angry. Her fingers worked furiously on his muscles. "But why? And how do you know?"

"Whoa, slow down, take it easy will ya?" he said, jerking away from her strong fingers.

"Oh, sorry."

"Cody saw his dad light the fire."

Dani didn't move. "Wait a minute. Back up. Cody was here when the fire started?"

"Right. Apparently, Cody walked home early in the night and intended to make up with you. But we were up at Caleb's place. Cody went upstairs and looked out the window and saw Blake in the shed, so he walked outside just as the shed caught fire and blew sky high."

"Oh my God," Dani whispered.

"Cody was scared out of his wits. He didn't know where you were and he was afraid that his father was hurt or killed. After doing a quick search for Blake, he ran to the old house to sort things out. When I got there, he was ready to come home."

"But why didn't he just stay here—on the property, or go to a neighbor's?"

"Because he was confused! You have to understand that he'd just suffered a major disappointment. The father he wanted so badly had shown his true colors and turned out to be a criminal. That's not easy for Cody, or any of us to understand."

"So where is Blake?"

"Who knows?"

"But why would he want to blow up my farm?"

"I don't think he wanted to— I think he was paid to," Chase said grimly.

"Oh, no. You're not back to that again, are you? You really think Caleb was behind it?"

"Positive."

"But how?"

"Come here."

She walked around the couch and he took hold of her wrist, pulling on it gently so that she fell on top of him. "You're getting me dirty," she protested with a smile.

"That's not the half of it." He drew her head to his, wound his fingers in her still damp hair and breathed deeply of the scent of her. "God, I've missed you." Kissing her softly, he groaned when her body molded easily to the hard contours of his.

He started kissing her face and pushing the robe off her shoulders, when she stopped him. "Wait a minute, hero," she said. "First things first. Tell me what else you know."

"Anyone ever tell you that you've got your priorities mixed up?"

She laughed. "Come on, out with it."

"Okay. I talked to Jenna Peterson earlier on the phone."

"When?"

"Just a few minutes ago, when you were upstairs with Cody."

"At this hour?"

"I decided that the sooner we figured this out, the better. Her sister had told me that she was due back tonight, so I gambled and called. It worked out."

"So what did she say?"

"Jenna left Caleb, not because of me, but because she knew that Caleb had put Blake Summers on his payroll."

"What?"

"That's right. When I couldn't convince you to sell, Caleb got hold of Blake."

"But why?"

"Because he knew that Cody had received a letter from him. The way I see it, Caleb figured Blake was his ace in the hole. If Blake showed up, either one of two things would happen: Blake would work his way back into your heart and convince you to sell—"

"No way!"

"—or scare you into wanting out of this town and away from him. What Johnson didn't count on was the fact that you weren't going to let Blake boss you around. Apparently Blake figured it out, too. My guess is that he has some sort of deal with Caleb—a deal like Larry Cross had and if he convinced you one way or the other to move, that he'd get a bundle of cash. Why else would he come back now, try to make amends with his son and then set fire to your shed?"

"If he did it."

"You don't think he did?"

She smiled into his eyes. "I don't know what to think. I just know that I'm glad you're here with me, that Cody's safe and that we can be together tonight. Tomorrow morning we'll deal with everything."

"Such as fire inspectors, insurance investigators, nosy neighbors—"

"Wet hay, frightened animals, Caleb, Blake and the

rest of the world," she murmured, placing her head against his neck. "But it really doesn't matter," she whispered, shuddering. "A few hours ago, when I thought Cody might be dead and I didn't know where you were, I realized that nothing, not even this land, is worth all this trouble—"

"Shh," he said, pulling the afghan over them both. "Sleep. Don't think about giving up the land tonight. If you do, Caleb's already won."

"I'm just tired of fighting . . ." she murmured, snuggling against him.

"So am I, Dani," he agreed, kissing her hair. "So am I. But I won't let Johnson win . . . even if it does turn out that he's my father."

With his arms wrapped around the woman he loved, Chase McEnroe stared at the ceiling long into the night and silently vowed that no matter what happened, he would never give up Dani or her son. With every ounce of strength he could find, he'd fight Caleb Johnson for Dani's right to own this land she loved with all of her heart.

Dani woke up with a crick in her neck. She moved her head from side to side and found herself staring into the most brilliant blue eyes she'd ever seen.

"Morning," Chase drawled, smiling down at her.

"Lord, what time is it?"

"After seven."

"Ooh," she groaned. "I've got to get up and feed the animals. And Cody'll miss the bus—"

"Let him."

"What?" Rubbing her eyes, she tried to clear the cobwebs from her mind.

"Give the kid a break—"

"But school barely started."

"I know, but this is a special day."

"Oh?" She pressed closer to him. "Tell me more—"

"We're going to talk to the minister of your choice and plan a wedding for next week."

"Oh, Chase, how can you even think about getting married so soon?" she said, laughing at the absurdity of the situation.

"I've had all night," he replied, dead serious. "And there's no way around it, lady. We're getting married next Saturday come hell or high water."

"Such a wonderful proposal," she mocked. "How could any woman refuse?" She stretched and pulled herself upright, ignoring the slumberous look of passion lurking in Chase's stare. "But I think I'd better talk to Cody."

"I did."

She'd started to stand and walk to the kitchen, but she whipped her head around, her long golden hair streaming behind her. "When?"

"Yesterday. When I found him at the homestead house. I told him how I felt about you and him and I told him I wouldn't get in the way of his relationship with his natural father even though I wanted to adopt him."

"And?"

"And he seemed to accept the idea. But then, he was pretty disappointed with his father."

"I can imagine . . ." She looked longingly up the stairs.

"You go on up," Chase suggested. "See what he has to say. I've got a few calls to make anyway."

Dani walked up the stairs and knocked softly on Cody's door.

"Huh?" she heard from within the room and then an excited yip from Runt.

"Can I come in?"

"Sure." Cody was lying in the bed with half the covers spread upon the floor. When Dani opened the door to his room, Runt ran out like a shot.

"How're ya feelin'?" she asked.

He frowned. "Okay, I guess. Mom, I'm real sorry I took off. It's probably my fault that Dad came back to the shed and . . . and . . . well, you know."

"Don't blame yourself," Dani said, sitting on the edge of the bed and pushing Cody's tousled hair out of his eyes. "I'm just glad that you're home and safe."

"But the equipment—"

"Can be replaced. You can't."

Cody swallowed hard and then sat up and hugged her with all the strength of his nine years. "I love ya, Mom," he said to his own embarrassment.

"Oh, honey, nothing could be better," she said, her eyes filling with tears.

"'Cept maybe marryin' Chase?" he asked.

"What do you think about it—would you be willing to give me away?"

"Huh?"

Dani laughed at his perplexed expression and then explained about a simple wedding ceremony. Though not jumping for joy, Cody seemed to accept the fact that she would marry Chase.

"Okay, I'll give you away," he said blushing. "As long as it's not for good."

"Silly!"

"Where would we live?"

"Good question," she said.

"Why don't you ask Chase? He thinks you deserve a day off from school."

"Great!"

"I'm not so sure about it—"

"Maybe having Chase as a stepdad wouldn't be so bad after all!" Cody said, leaping out of bed.

"I don't think so—but, look, you can't get out of doing your chores, okay?"

"Okay," he grumbled, reaching for his favorite pair of jeans.

Still smiling to herself, Dani went into her bedroom, combed the tangles from her hair, put on a little makeup and changed into a summer dress. By the time she was back downstairs, Cody had already talked to Chase and was in the barn feeding the animals.

Chase was seated at the kitchen table, his feet up on a free chair while he sipped coffee. He looked very proud of himself.

"You look like the cat who caught the canary," she observed as she poured a cup for herself.

"Not a canary, but the prettiest woman east of the Rockies."

"Give me a break." But she laughed despite his outlandish compliment. "What have you been up to?"

"More than you want to know."

"Try me."

"Okay." He held up one finger. "I called the police, they already have Blake in custody."

Shaking, she sat down and let her head fall into her hand. "No," she whispered.

"Yep. He turned himself in because he was scared to

death that he'd hurt or even killed Cody. Apparently, Blake hadn't thought anyone was home; then he saw Cody just before the gas tank blew and then he couldn't find the boy. He admitted to being in league with Caleb and the police are up at Johnson's house now. I told them about the dioxin and they're trying to get in contact with Larry Cross. You'll probably hear from the D.A. He'll want to know if you want to press charges."

"I see," she whispered. "So how does that affect you?"

"It doesn't. Blood or no blood, Caleb Johnson was never my father. But, I did call him; told him everything we knew and believe it or not he's agreed to lay off you."

"I'll believe that when I see it."

"Oh, it won't be that hard since he'll probably be in the penitentiary for the rest of his life."

"And you don't care?" she asked gently.

"He's never been a father to me. What happened between him and my mother was something that occurred before I was born." He took a long sip from his coffee. "But, I made another agreement with him."

"Now what?" she groaned.

"I'm moving my company to Martinville."

"That, I like."

He stood and came over to her chair, taking her hand and drawing her to her feet. "I thought you might. The next part is even better, I hope. I told Caleb that since he's bound and determined to build Summer Ridge, that we would deed over the rights to the hot springs to him."

"You what!"

"Just listen, okay? He'll have to divert the water down the hill, of course, through the trees, to the back of his resort."

"I don't know about this—"

"In return, he'll grant us the right to control the water flow. With the money we get from the sale of those water rights, we're going to restore the old homestead house and maybe add on a couple of extra rooms," he said.

"Oh, Chase," she said, happiness swelling in her chest. "That's wonderful, but it's a big house. Why more rooms?"

"Modern ones—such as bathrooms with plumbing and a nursery—"

"A nursery?" she said, laughing.

"At least one." He stood and took her into his arms. "Now, what do you say?"

"What took you so long to come into my life?" She looked up at him with bright hazel eyes, all the love in her heart reflected in her gaze.

"Then next Saturday is a good day for a wedding?"

"If we can't do it tomorrow—"

He swept her off her feet and grinned. "You know, I've just had a change of heart."

"Oh?"

"Yep. Maybe we should send Cody to school after all. Then we'd have the rest of the day together."

She smiled seductively. "Sounds like heaven, but you already made a promise that he could stay home."

"My mistake," he groaned and kissed her neck. "But just you wait, lady. Once Cody goes to sleep tonight . . ."

"Promises, promises," she quipped.

"That's right," he said. "Promises for the rest of your life." Then he kissed her gently, his mouth softly moving over hers, causing her heart to pound and her pulse to flutter.

"Forever?" she asked.

"Forever."

Midnight Sun

To the two and only,
Cousin Dave and Cousin Les

Chapter One

Holding her head proudly, Ashley walked into the room and gave no outward sign of her flagging confidence. Her elegant features were emotionless and the regal tilt of her chin didn't falter. The only signs of the emotional turmoil which stole her sleep were the deep blue smudges beneath her eyes.

She was reminded of vultures circling over carrion as she stepped into the law offices of McMichaels and Lee. Alan McMichaels held the chair for her, and as she took her seat between her cousin Claud and Aunt Beatrice, Ashley could feel the cool disdain in the pinched, white faces of the five people seated near the oiled oak desk.

Claud's rust-colored eyebrows had raised in mild surprise when she entered the room, but he said nothing. Aunt Beatrice nodded stiffly and then turned her pale gold eyes back on the attorney.

The family had never been particularly close. Or, at least, Ashley had never felt the kinship with her father's relatives that some families share.

Today was no exception. Her father's death hadn't brought the family together. If anything, the family, whose members each owned a small piece of Stephens Timber Corporation, seemed more fragmented than ever.

Though the room was spacious and decorated in opulent tones of cobalt blue and brown, the atmosphere within the brushed plaster walls was awkward and confining. Tension, like an invisible electric current, charged the air.

Alan McMichaels took a seat at the modern desk. Behind his chair, through a large, plate glass window, was an expansive view of the West Hills of Portland. The fir-laden slopes, still a rich forest green in winter, were covered with expensive, turn-of-the-century homes that overlooked the city. In the distance, spanning two high ridges, was the Vista Bridge. Its elegant gray arch was just visible in the gentle morning fog that had settled upon the city.

The lean attorney with the silver hair and black eyebrows cleared his throat and caught everyone's attention. "As you know, we're here for the reading of Lazarus Stephens's will. Please hold your comments until I've read the entire document. When I'm finished, I'll answer all of your questions."

McMichaels adjusted his reading glasses and picked up the neatly typed document. A claustrophobic feeling took hold of Ashley and wouldn't let go. The tears she had shed for her father were dry and the only thing she felt was a deep, inexplicable loneliness. She and her father had never been close, but she felt as if a part of her had died with him.

Despite the unspoken accusations of the other people in the room, Ashley met each questioning gaze with the cool serenity of her intelligent green eyes. Her blue-black hair was coiled neatly at the nape of her neck in a tight knot of ebony silk, and she was dressed expensively in a dark blue suit of understated elegance.

Ashley understood the condemning looks from her father's family. With very few exceptions the relatives of Lazarus Stephens didn't approve of Ashley and made no bones about it. Ashley imagined that they had all been secretly pleased when they had learned of the falling-out between Lazarus and his headstrong, spoiled daughter. Aunts, uncles and cousins alike treated her like an outsider.

Ignoring the surreptitious glances being cast in her direction, Ashley folded her hands in her lap and stared calmly at the silver-haired, bespectacled man sitting directly across the desk from her. Alan McMichaels was addressing everyone in the room, but Ashley was left with the distinct impression that he was singling her out.

"I, Lazarus J. Stephens of Portland, Oregon, do make, publish and declare my Last Will and Testament, revoking all previous Wills and Codicils. . . ." Ashley listened to her father's attorney, and her wide green eyes showed no sign of emotion as the reading of the will progressed. Though she remained outwardly calm, her stomach was tied into several painful knots while the small bequests were made to each of Lazarus Stephens's closest friends and relatives.

McMichaels had insisted that Ashley attend the reading of her father's will, although she didn't understand why. Unless, of course, it was her father's wish that she listen in humiliation while Lazarus publicly announced for the last time that he had disinherited his only child.

She paled at the memory of the violent scene that had resulted in the rift separating them. Vividly she could recall the rage that had colored his cheeks, the vicious accusations that had claimed she had "sold out" and betrayed him, and the look of utter disdain and disappointment in his faded blue eyes.

Over the years, the gap between father and daughter had narrowed, but never had that one, horrible scene been forgotten. Though Ashley had chosen to ignore the rumors about her father and his business practices, she hadn't been immune to the malicious gossip that seemed to spread like wildfire whenever his name was mentioned in private conversation.

Alan McMichaels cleared his throat and his dark eyes locked with Ashley's for an instant. ". . . my nephew Claud," McMichaels continued. In her peripheral vision Ashley saw Claud lean forward and noticed that his anxious fingers ran nervously along the edge of the polished desk as he stared expectantly at the attorney. ". . . I bequeath the sum of one hundred thousand dollars."

Claud's self-assured smile, hidden partially by a thick, rust-colored mustache, wavered slightly as McMichaels paused. Claud's nervous eyes darted from McMichaels to Ashley and back again.

"I give, devise and bequeath all of the residue of my estate unto my only child, Ashley Stephens Jennings, to be hers absolutely."

Ashley's heart dropped and her face drained of all color. She was forced to close her eyes for a second as she digested the intent of her father's will. *He had forgiven her.* But his stubborn pride hadn't allowed Lazarus to confront his daughter. Her fingers clenched together. Hot tears of grief burned in her eyes as she accepted her father's final forgiveness.

McMichaels had continued reading, but the words

were a muffled sound in Ashley's private world of grief. She couldn't look into the eyes of the startled family members.

"Wait a minute—" Claud started to interrupt, but a killing stare from Alan McMichaels forestalled any further comment from Ashley's cousin. Claud sent Ashley a stricken look bordering on hatred.

McMichaels's voice droned on for a few minutes until he finally tapped the neatly typed sheets of white paper on the tabletop and smiled. "That's it. If you have any questions—"

The voices around the table started to buzz, and Ashley felt the eyes of distant relatives bore into her. Pieces of the whispered conversation drifted to her ears.

"I never suspected . . ."

"Didn't Uncle Laz cut her off?"

"I thought so. Something about an affair with that Trevor Daniels, you know, the one running for the senatorial seat this fall."

"How could she? And with that man! He was accused of taking a bribe last summer sometime. The charges didn't stick, but if you ask me, he paid somebody off to save his neck! Trevor Daniels isn't a man to trust or get involved with!"

"Daniels swore he'd break Lazarus, you know. He always blamed Lazarus for his father's disappearance. If you ask me, Trevor Daniels's father . . . what was his name? Robert—that's right. I'll bet that Robert Daniels just took off with another woman. . . ."

Ashley lifted her chin fractionally and leveled cool green eyes on the members of her father's family. She was accustomed to the pain of gossip and she managed to let her poise lift her above the insulting speculation being whispered just loud enough for her to hear. Pushing her chair away from the desk, Ashley stood and started toward the door.

Claud was leaning over McMichaels's desk, his ruddy complexion redder than usual. Though he was whispering, Ashley was well aware of what he was threatening. Claud considered himself next in line for control of the Stephens timber empire. No doubt cousin Claud was already devising ways of contesting the will.

Alan McMichaels noticed that Ashley was leaving, and he broke off his conversation with Claud in order to talk to her. He held up his palm to get her attention. "Ms Jennings—please. If you could stay for a few more minutes. There are a few matters I'd like to discuss with you."

Managing a frail smile, Ashley nodded before smoothing her skirt and walking across the room to stand near the windows. She felt, rather than saw, the hateful glances cast at her back.

Though Ashley's gaze studied the view from the eighth floor of the building, she didn't notice the tall spire of a Gothic church steeple in the foreground or the fact that the fog had begun to lift, promising a cold, but clear, November day. Her thoughts rested on her father and the horrible fight that had torn them apart.

It had taken place in the spacious library of Lazarus's Tudor home on Palatine Hill. "How could you?" Lazarus had shouted, his shock and rage white-hot when he had discovered that the man Ashley had been seeing all summer was the son of Robert Daniels, the man who had been Lazarus's rival before his mysterious disappearance not two years earlier. Lazarus's faded blue eyes had sparked vengeful fire, and his shoulders had slumped in defeat. Nothing Ashley could have done would have wounded him more.

When she had tried to explain that she loved Trevor and planned to marry him, her father had laughed. "Marry a Daniels? Damn it, Ashley, I thought you had more brains than that!" Lazarus had shaken his graying head. "What do you think he wants from you? Love?" When Lazarus read the expectant light in her eyes, he had spit angrily into the fire. "He's using you, don't you see? He's after the timber company, for Christ's sake! He's on some personal vendetta against me. Wake up girl. Trevor Daniels doesn't care a damn about you."

When Ashley had staunchly refused to stop seeing Trevor, Lazarus had slapped his open palm on the table and threatened to disinherit her. Angrily, she had told him to do just that and had stomped out of the room, out of his house and out of her father's life. Determined that she was right, Ashley had been hell-bent to prove him wrong.

It had been an impossible task. Lazarus had been correct about Trevor and his motives all along. At the vividly painful memory, Ashley sighed and ran her fingers along the cool window ledge. Once again tears, bitter and deceitful, threatened to spill.

"Ashley, could I have a word with you? It will only take a few minutes."

She turned to face her father's attorney and noticed that the room was empty. "First, let me tell you I'm sorry about your father." She nodded, accepting his condolences and somehow holding on to her frail composure. "And that I hope you'll continue to retain the services of McMichaels and Lee for yourself as well as the business." Once again she nodded, encouraging him to get to the point.

"You must realize that, with your father's bequest, you own a large majority of the stock of Stephens Timber. It's within your power to run the company or hire someone else—"

"Mr. McMichaels," Ashley interrupted, finally able to collect her scattered thoughts. "Right now, I don't think I'm qualified to run the company myself."

"But your father thought you could. Don't you have a degree in business administration?"

"A master's—"

"And didn't you work for the corporation?"

"Years ago—during the summers between school terms. But the industry has changed a lot in the last eight years," she protested.

"Your father seemed to think that you had a real knack for handling the executive end of Stephens Timber."

"Did he?" Ashley shook her head in confusion. Why hadn't her father been able to tell her what McMichaels was repeating? "I think we should leave things just as they are for the time being. It was my understanding that Claud had been managing the day-to-day transactions for all practical purposes. My father was in semiretirement."

"That's right."

Ashley forced herself to think clearly. The strain of the past few days had been exhausting, but she couldn't ignore her responsibilities. "So, until I know a little more about the business, and until my teaching contract is fulfilled, I'll have to rely on Claud. The only thing I'll require for the present is an audit of the company books and monthly financial statements. I'll talk to Claud and ask him to continue to stay on as general manager of the corporation, at least temporarily."

McMichaels stuffed his hands into his pockets and appeared uneasy.

"Is there a problem with that?"

The attorney frowned, seemed about to say something and thought better of it. "No, I suppose not. You can do whatever you like."

"I know about the company's reputation," she assured the surprised lawyer. "I haven't lived my life with my head in the sand. I expect that Claud will see to it that anything Stephens Timber does is strictly legal. Advising him will be your job."

McMichaels smiled. Relief was evident on his tanned features. "Good."

Ashley managed a thin smile. It was the first since the news of her father's heart attack. "Whether I like it or not, I've got a teaching contract that doesn't expire until June fifteenth. I'll talk to the administration and explain the situation, and if the community college can find a substitute for next term, I'll consider moving back to Portland and working with Claud."

"I think that would be wise," McMichaels agreed. He touched her shoulder in a consoling gesture. "You're a very wealthy woman, now, Ashley. You'll have to be careful. People will be out to take advantage of you."

"Only if I give them the chance," she replied. Ashley spoke a few more minutes with her father's attorney and left his office with the disturbing feeling that something was on Alan McMichaels's mind. She shook off the uncomfortable sensation and reasoned that the lawyer wanted to give her a little more time to deal with her grief before hoisting any corporate problems onto her shoulders.

Once in the elevator, Ashley was alone. She closed her eyes and moved her head from side to side, hoping to relieve some of the tension in her shoulders.

Pushing through the glass doors of the building housing the firm of McMichaels and Lee, Ashley stepped into the subdued winter sunlight. A slight breeze caught in her hair and chilled her to the bone. She had just started down the short flight of steps to the street when Claud accosted her. Ashley braced herself for the confrontation that was sure to come. Ever since her falling out with her father, Claud had been groomed to inherit the presidency of Stephens Timber. No doubt his feathers were more than slightly ruffled.

"You knew about the change in the will, didn't you?" he charged, falling into step with her.

"Of course not."

"I don't understand it—"

"Neither do I. Not really, but the fact is that father left the company to me." When she reached her car, she turned to face her cousin. "Look, Claud, I know this must be a shock and disappointment to you. The thing of it is that I'd like you to continue to run the corporation just as you did for Dad, but you'll have to report to me. I've told Alan exactly what I expect from you."

Claud tugged uneasily on his mustache. His dark eyes bored into hers. "You won't interfere?"

"Of course I will—*if* I think you're doing an inadequate job. The next few days I'll be at the corporate offices, looking over your shoulder. We can get any of the more pressing problems ironed out then. I want to know every-thing that happens to Stephens Timber Corporation."

"Then you're moving to Portland?" Claud asked, shifting from one foot to the other. He pulled at the knotted silk tie and found it difficult to look Ashley in the eye.

"Maybe after spring break, if the school administration can replace me. I expect you to send me reports and call me if you have a problem."

"I think I will handle everything," Claud stated with his cocky self-assurance. "Your old man didn't bother to oversee what I was doing."

"Well I am," Ashley stated, her eyes glittering with determination. "Because now it's my reputation on the line."

"Don't tell me you believed all those rumors."

"Gossip is a cheap sort of entertainment for idle minds. What I believe happened in the past doesn't matter. But, from here on in, we keep our corporate nose clean. Stephens Timber can't afford any more bad press." She added emphasis to her words by tapping her fingers on the hood of her car.

Claud grinned broadly. He reassessed his first cousin and his eyes slid appreciatively down her slender body. Ashley Jennings was a woman with class. It was too damn bad she just happened to be Lazarus Stephens's daughter. "We do have one particular problem," Claud speculated aloud.

"What's that?" Ashley had pulled the keys from her purse and her hand was poised over the handle of the car door. She and Claud had never gotten along, but because of the situation, she was forced to trust him, if only temporarily.

"Trevor Daniels."

"Why is he a problem?" Ashley looked unperturbed and gave no indication of her suddenly racing pulse. After eight years of living with the truth, she was able to react calmly whenever Trevor's name was mentioned.

"If he gets the senatorial seat in the fall, he'll put us out of business."

"I don't see how that's possible, Claud." She turned to face her cousin. Her green eyes were still clear and hid the fact that her heart was pounding erratically.

"He's always been out to get the family. You, as well as anyone, should know that," Claud stated.

Ashley felt her body stiffen, but she promised herself not to let Claud's insensitive remarks affect her.

She straightened before crossing her arms over her chest and leaning on her sporty BMW. "Trevor's family, as well as ours, is involved in the timber business. We're competitors—that's all. There's no way he would be able to 'put us out of business.'"

Claud's hands were spread open at his sides. "But you know how he is—he's trying to get the government to make all the forests into designated wilderness areas. If he gets elected—"

"He'll try harder." Ashley's small hands pushed her away from the car. "But not to the point that it would destroy the timber industry. If he did that, Claud, he'd not only thwart his own family's business, but he'd also put a lot of his constituents back in the unemployment lines. He's too smart to do anything of the sort."

"I can't figure it out," Claud said, his eyes narrowing suspiciously.

"What?"

"Why the hell you still stick up for that bastard!"

Ashley raised an elegant eyebrow and smiled confidently. "What happened between Trevor and me has nothing to do with Stephens Timber."

"Like hell! When are you going to face the fact that the bastard used you, Ashley? And all for a chance at the timber company. He thought you would inherit it all, didn't he? And then, when your father cut you off, he split! Swell guy."

"There's no reason to discuss this any further," Ashley replied, her cheeks beginning to burn.

"Just remember that he's out to get Stephens Timber," Claud warned. "He still thinks Lazarus had something to do with his father's disappearance."

Ashley managed to smile sweetly despite the fact that her blood had turned cold. "And just remember who signs your paycheck."

"You need me," Claud reminded her.

"Of course I do, and I'd hate to lose your expertise at managing the company. But that's all I expect from you, and I don't need any lectures about my personal life." Her dark brows arched over determined green eyes.

At that moment Claud understood that tangling with his beautiful cousin would be more difficult than he had imagined. It looked as if, after all, Ashley had inherited more than the timber fortune; she also had received some of her father's resolve. Claud raised his hands in mock surrender. "All right. Just be careful, Ashley. It wouldn't surprise me a bit if Trevor Daniels suddenly started paying a lot of attention to you. You can't trust him."

"I think I can deal with Trevor," Ashley responded with more confidence than she felt. When Claud finally left her alone, she slid into the car, placed her hands on the steering wheel and let the bitter tears of pain slide down her face.

Trevor opened a weary eye. As he lifted his head the weight of the hangover hit him like a ton of bricks. He was still seated in the leather recliner by the fireplace, and his muscles were cramped from the awkward position and the cold morning air. A half-full glass of Scotch, now stale, sat on the small table near his chair next to the newspaper article that had been the impetus for his uncharacteristic binge. The bold headlines were still visible, but the rest of the article was smeared from the liquor that had slopped over the rim of the glass and spilled onto the newsprint.

Running a tired hand over the stubble on his chin, Trevor stretched and cursed himself for his own lack of control. How many drinks had he consumed while locked in memories of the past—four, five? He couldn't remember. The last time he had been so drunk was the night of Ashley's betrayal. . . .

Of their own accord, his vibrant blue eyes returned to the headline: TIMBER BARON DEAD AT 70. The paper was three days old.

"You bastard," Trevor murmured before wadding the newspaper and tossing it into the smoldering remains of the fire. The paper ignited and was instantly consumed by hungry flames.

The first gray light of dawn was already shadowing the spacious den with the promise of another cold November morning. With an effort, Trevor pulled himself out of the chair and ran his fingers through his thick chestnut hair. His mouth tasted rancid and he wondered if it was from too much liquor, too little sleep or the painful memories of Ashley. The article about the death of Ashley's father, Lazarus Stephens, had conjured up all the old pain again—the pain Trevor had promised to put behind him.

Maybe it was impossible. Perhaps Ashley's life and his were entwined irrevocably by the sins of their fathers. Whatever the reason, Trevor had difficulty dismissing the image of her shining black hair and intriguing sea-green eyes.

Trevor rubbed his temple as he walked to the window and let his eyes wander outside the house, past the landscaped lawns and through the denuded trees of the estate his father had purchased. He leaned against the windowsill and considered the unlikely course of events that would never allow him to be free of her.

The feud between the two timber families had been long, ruthless and bloody. Rumor had it that sometime before the Korean War, the partners, who owned a small Oregon logging firm, had become embroiled in such a vicious argument that they had parted ways, each vowing to destroy the other. The stories varied slightly but all seemed to agree that the cause of the dispute was graft. Robert Daniels had supposedly caught Lazarus Stephens skimming off company profits for personal use.

The result of the breakup was that Stephens Timber Corporation and Daniels Logging Company became bitter enemies within the Oregon timber industry.

Trevor didn't know how many of the rumors that had circulated scandalously over the past forty years were true and how many were fictitious. But he was certain of one thing: Lazarus Stephens had been involved in the disappearance of Trevor's father, Robert Daniels.

Ten years before, when Robert had disappeared, Trevor had sworn that not only would he avenge his father, but he would personally see to it that the people responsible for the crime would be punished. But he had been deterred by his feelings for Ashley.

What had happened to Robert Daniels, after he was last seen leaving the dinner meeting with a lobbyist from Washington, D.C., remained a mystery. And now Lazarus Stephens, Ashley's father, the one man who knew the answer, was dead.

Ashley. Just the thought of her innocent eyes and enigmatic smile touched a traitorous part of Trevor's soul. He squeezed his eyes tightly shut, as if he could physically deny the vivid image of her elegant face surrounded by glossy ebony curls.

Thinking of Ashley and her betrayal still made him clench his teeth together in frustration, and he silently cursed himself for caring. Hadn't she shown her true colors? Hadn't she tossed him out of her life and married another man?

Trevor had been blind to her faults and had let his feelings for her manipulate him. But now the tables had turned; if the senatorial race ended in his favor, he would personally see to it that all the suspicious dealings of Stephens Timber were investigated and halted.

His blue eyes narrowed as he stared past the leafless trees to the silvery waters of the Willamette River. A soft morning fog clung tenaciously to the shoreline.

What if Ashley inherited Lazarus's share of Stephens Timber Corporation? What if all those rumors that her father disinherited her were only idle speculation? What if Ashley was now the woman in charge of the corporation Trevor had vowed to destroy?

His headache began to pound furiously just as the telephone rang. Trevor Daniels was jerked back to the present and the most pressing problem of the day: winning the election in the fall.

Chapter Two

During the next few weeks, Ashley's impatience with her cousin mounted with the passing of each day, and her concern for Stephens Timber drew her attention away from Trevor and his candidacy in the May primary. Trevor's face was continually in the news and Ashley was glad for the distraction of the timber company. It helped her keep the memories of the love she had shared with him pushed into a dark corner of her mind.

Between studying the reports that Claud had grudgingly begun to send her and instructing her classes, Ashley barely had a moment to herself. When she was able to find a few minutes to relax, her thoughts would invariably return to Trevor and the few blissful months they had shared together nearly eight years ago.

Now she owned the lion's share of the company Trevor had vowed to destroy.

"Oh, stop it," she admonished as she sat at the cluttered kitchen table in her small apartment near the campus. "You're beginning to sound as paranoid as Claud." At the mention of her shifty cousin's name, Ashley frowned.

It didn't take a supersleuth to realize that Claud was up to something, but Ashley didn't know exactly what. The information he had been sending concerning the timber company was sketchy at best. Ashley had the uneasy feeling that Claud was deliberately trying to hide something from her.

The first report from Claud hadn't been as encompassing as Ashley had hoped, but when she had asked her cousin for a more lengthy audit of the books of Stephens Timber, Claud had been reluctant to send it to her.

"Don't worry yourself," he had soothed when she had called him and demanded more complete information. "You've got more than you can handle with your teaching job. Besides which, I've got everything under control up here."

"That's not the issue, Claud. I need the reports," Ashley had insisted.

"Then you'd better come up and look at them," Claud had growled, losing his veneer of civility. "I don't like sending out that kind of information. Right now we've got a shortage of personnel in the bookkeeping department, and I wouldn't want to trust the post office to get the reports to you, even if we were able to put them together."

"You're stalling, Claud," she had responded. "Get the reports together and send them in tomorrow's mail, or I just might take you up on your offer and come up to Portland to see for myself just how well you've 'got everything under control.'"

"Look, Ashley, I don't need a keeper!"

Ashley had begun to worry in earnest.

"And Claud?"

"What?"

"For God's sake, hire the help you need in accounting!"

Claud's reply had been a disgusted snort, indicating all too well what he thought about Ashley's interference in what he considered his domain.

Claud's reluctance had been all the reason she needed to talk to the school administration about getting out of her teaching contract. Within a week, the administration had found a suitable replacement to take over her classes for the rest of the school year. All she had to do was finish the term, and that task was nearly accomplished. Christmas vacation started next week.

At that thought, Ashley quit thinking about her cousin and let her gaze return to the untidy stack of papers sitting on the table. As she started grading the tests, she listened to a local news channel on the television.

She was frowning at a particularly bad answer to one of her questions and sipping coffee when news of an accident involving Trevor was announced by the even-featured anchorman.

Ashley almost spilled her coffee, her throat constricted in fear and her eyes snapped upward to stare at the small television situated on the kitchen counter. She had left it on for background noise, but at the sound of Trevor's name, all of her attention became riveted to the set.

". . . Trevor Daniels was rushed to Andrews Hospital in Salem when the car he was driving slid off the road, broke through the guardrail and rolled down an embankment. . . ." The screen flashed from the earnest reporter to the site of the accident and the twisted wreckage of Trevor's car.

Ashley's stomach knotted and nausea rose in her throat.

"Dear God," she whispered, placing her hand protectively over her heart. Her blood ran as cold as the clear December night. The pencil she had been holding over a stack of papers dropped unobserved onto the table as she concentrated on what the wavy-haired reporter was saying.

"Reports have varied as to the cause of the accident," the reporter, once again on the screen, told the viewing audience. "Police are investigating the site, but as yet have not confirmed the rumors of foul play. Mr. Daniels remains in serious, but stable condition."

"No," Ashley murmured, at the fleeting thoughts of Trevor and the love they had shared. Absently, she removed her reading glasses, rubbed her temples and stared at the screen. When she found the strength to move, she pushed her chair away from the table and some coffee spilled onto the tests. She didn't notice.

Without considering her motives, she dialed operator assistance and was given the number of Andrews Hospital. Her fingers were trembling when she punched out the number for the hospital in Salem. After several rings, a member of the staff answered and told her politely, but firmly, that Mr. Daniels was taking no calls and seeing no visitors.

Ashley replaced the receiver and slumped against the wall. What was happening? Within the course of three weeks her father had suffered a fatal heart attack, she had inherited the company and now, Trevor Daniels, the only man she had ever loved, had nearly been killed. The reporter had glossed over the mention of foul play; certainly no one would want to harm Trevor. . . .

Get a hold of yourself, she warned. *He doesn't care for you—never did. Nothing will ever change that.*

She continued to listen to the news program, hoping

that a later bulletin would give her an update on Trevor's condition. After wiping the table, she poured herself a fresh cup of coffee and tried to concentrate on the test papers she had been grading. The task was impossible.

Teasing thoughts of Trevor, provocative images of a younger, more carefree time, continued to assail her. She remembered the first time she had seen him more than eight years before. She had been immediately attracted by his flash of a rakish smile, and his lean, well-muscled body. But it was his eyes that had caught her attention and captured her heart. They were a brilliant shade of blue and challenged her silently. The hint of amusement in their clear depths had touched a very intimate part of her—and had never let go. Those damned blue eyes seemed to look through her sophisticated facade and bore into her soul and they had dared her to seduce him. . . .

With a start, she dragged herself back to the present. "Don't brood about what might have been," she told herself, though her stomach had knotted painfully.

If she could just get through the next few days, she would have time to herself and by that time she would know more about Trevor's accident.

"No one is allowed to visit Mr. Daniels," the rotund nurse insisted upon Ashley's inquiry. The large woman was standing behind the glass enclosure of the hospital reception area and had only looked up from her paperwork when Ashley had inquired about Trevor.

"But I'm a personal friend," Ashley stated with a patient

smile. She hadn't spent the last two hours in the car to be thwarted by hospital politics.

"It wouldn't matter if you were his mother," the strict nurse replied, glancing up from the chart she had been studying. In the past two days she had dismissed five reporters, seven photographers and about fifteen "personal friends" of the famous man lying in room 214. Security in the hospital had been increased due to the celebrity of Trevor Daniels. The sooner Mr. Daniels was out of the hospital, the better, for staff and patient alike.

The nurse, whose name tag indicated that she was Janelle Wilkes, smiled warmly. "I'm sorry, Ms.—"

"Jennings. Ashley Jennings," Ashley supplied.

"I'll tell Mr. Daniels that you were by."

"I'd appreciate it," Ashley retorted, sneaking a longing look down the corridors of the building. If she could only have a quick glimpse of Trevor—just enough to ease her mind, so that she would be convinced that he was indeed recuperating and on the road to recovery.

She left the hospital in frustration, after giving the nurse her name and telephone number.

Ashley didn't really expect Trevor to call, and she wasn't disappointed. In the next few days, while school was ending for the holidays, Ashley had been in and out of her apartment, but either Trevor hadn't called, or she had missed him. She suspected that the would-be senator had received her message and promptly tossed it in the trash.

She told herself that she would never try to contact him again.

* * *

His wound had healed to the point where he could take charge of his life again, and Trevor Daniels intended to start this morning. Ignoring the warnings from his concerned campaign manager, Trevor hoisted his suitcase from the closet and tossed it carelessly onto the bed.

He couldn't wait to break away from Portland. His plan was simple. All he needed was a few hours alone with Ashley.

Hiding a grimace of pain, Trevor withdrew a faded pair of jeans from the closet and stuffed them into the open canvas bag. Determination was evident in the knit of his thick, dark brows and the hard angle of his jaw.

Everett Woodward, wearing an expression of disapproval on his round face, walked into the room and silently observed Trevor's deliberate movements. He sipped his second drink patiently while he watched Trevor fill the bag with casual clothes. It was obvious that Trevor had a purpose in mind, a purpose he hadn't confided to his campaign manager. Everett took a chair near the window in the master suite of Trevor's home. The would-be senator had noticed his entrance, but chose to ignore it. Everett frowned into his drink, silently plotting his line of reasoning to deter Trevor from making the worst political decision of his life. The damned thing of it was that Trevor had never thought rationally whenever Ashley Stephens was involved. And this time, Ashley was involved. Everett knew it.

"You know that I think you're making a big mistake," Everett ventured, stealing a quick glance through the window at the threatening sky. The chill of December seeped through the panes. There was the promise of snow in the air.

"So what else is new?" Trevor retorted with no trace of humor. He threw a bulky ski sweater into the bag before zipping it closed and eyeing his uneasy companion. "You always think I'm making mistakes."

"You're a gambler," Everett pointed out with a frown. "Gambling and politics don't mix."

"I can't argue with that." Trevor reached for his jacket and tried to change the course of the conversation. "I thought you were downstairs going over political strategy or something of the sort."

Everett avoided the trap and concentrated on the subject at hand. "We're not talking about some obscure issue here," Everett reminded the lean, angry man staring at him from across the room. "Your entire political future is on the line—everything you've worked for. The way I see it, this is too big a risk to take."

Trevor's square jaw tightened and the thin lines around his eyes became more distinct as his gaze hardened. "The way *I* see it, I don't have much of a choice." The small red scar on his cheek seemed to emphasize his words.

"You're not thinking clearly."

"What's that supposed to mean?" Trevor demanded. He paced restlessly in the confining room before looking pointedly at his watch. Through the window, he could see gray storm clouds gathering, their somber reflection darkening the clear waters of the Willamette River. Raindrops fell against the window, blurring his view.

Everett shifted uncomfortably in his chair and pushed his stocky fingers through his thinning hair. "Ever since the accident you've been obsessed with Stephens Timber."

"It began before the accident."

"Okay, ever since those phony charges last August, then."

Trevor turned to face the short man seated near a small table. "The charge was bribery," Trevor stated, his lips thinning.

"I know. But the important thing is that it was dropped." Everett looked as exasperated as he felt. "Admit it, Trevor, that is what all this—" his upturned palm rotated to indicate the packed bag "—is all about, isn't it?"

"Part of it," Trevor allowed with a grimace. "The bribery was just the latest of Lazarus's tricks. You seem to have conveniently forgotten that Lazarus Stephens was involved with my father's disappearance."

"Ten years ago. Idle speculation. No proof. Look, Trevor, you can't become obsessed with that all over again." Trevor's cold blue eyes didn't waver. Everett pressed his point home. "You can't fight a corporation the size of Stephens Timber, for God's sake! It employs over three thousand people in Oregon alone and Claud Stephens knows just whose palm he has to grease to get what he wants."

"But Claud only works for the company. He doesn't own it, does he?"

Everett changed his tactics when he noticed the dangerous glitter in Trevor's eyes. If there was anything Trevor Daniels enjoyed, it was a challenge.

"Look, Daniels, you've come too far too fast to throw it all away now. Forget what happened in the past, forget the accident, and the bribery scandal last summer, and, for God's sake, leave Stephens Timber alone!" Everett's expression was pleading. "Concentrate on the election in November."

"It's not that easy," Trevor admitted, rubbing his hand over the irritating pain in his abdomen.

"Rise above it."

Trevor's muscles flexed. "That's a little too much to ask, don't you think?"

Everett rolled his eyes upward and let out a frustrated sigh. "What I think is that you should quit brooding about false bribery charges and the accident," Everett explained with a lift of his shoulders. "Besides which, we have to make up for lost time. The days you spent in the hospital are gone; you missed a couple of very important meetings."

"They can be rescheduled," Trevor thought aloud. "Right now I have other things on my mind."

"You should be concentrating on the opposition."

"I am."

"Stephens Timber," Everett guessed, shaking his balding head despondently. "You're going to have to ease up on them."

"And play into Claud's greedy hands? No way."

"If you want to win the election—"

Trevor stopped dead in his tracks and wheeled around to confront his friend. Anger flared in his eyes. "I'm not even sure about that anymore. I had a lot of time to think while I was lying in that hospital. I'm not really sure that being a United States senator is all that it's cracked up to be. It certainly can't be worth the price."

"You're tired—"

"You bet I am!"

Everett held up his soft palms as if to ward off a blow, hoping that the gesture would calm Trevor. It didn't. Trevor had good reason to be upset, but Everett had hoped that the politician in Trevor Daniels would overcome the anger. "You've got to think about your career, Trevor, and you can't afford to take any time off right now. Think of all the hard work you've put into this campaign before you go mouthing off to the press about all of this nonsense concerning the accident. The last thing we need right now is another scandal!"

"Is that all you ever think about?"

"It's what you pay me to think about," Everett reminded his employer before draining the remainder of his warm drink. "My only concern is to get you into that vacant senatorial seat this fall."

"Even if it kills me?" Trevor asked with a sarcastic frown.

"Don't be ridiculous—"

"Then don't ridicule me!"

Everett's light eyes were steady when they clashed with Trevor's angry blue gaze. "I'm the guy who takes care of your security, remember? If I thought, I mean really thought that someone was out to get you, then I'd be the first one to suggest that you pull out of the race. But face it, if someone wanted to nail you, they would have done it before now. And, believe me, it wouldn't be some two-bit job on your car. Even the police didn't buy that one. For Christ's sake, don't turn paranoid on me now!" Everett muttered.

The words sunk into Trevor's weary mind. He let out his breath and his broad shoulders sagged. "Maybe you're right," he conceded, though his voice still sounded skeptical.

"Of course I am."

A crooked smile tugged at the hard corners of Trevor's

rigid mouth. "I can think of a few times when you've been wrong."

"All in the past," Everett assured him with a knowing grin. "I don't claim to be infallible . . . just the nearest thing to it." The rotund campaign manager walked across the room and poured three stiff fingers of bourbon from a bottle sitting on the bar in the corner of the room. "Here, have a drink," he offered. "We both could use one."

After Trevor took the glass and swallowed some of the bourbon, Everett continued with his never-ending advice. "Now, whatever you do, try to forget about the accident and the scandal. Avoid the press at all costs until some of the noise dies down.

"Don't go spouting off about your car being sabotaged or you'll end up on the front page of the *Morning Surveyor* all over again. The last time was bad enough. Publicity from that rag, we don't need." Everett took a calming sip of liquor. He was somewhat satisfied that he had finally gotten through to Trevor, though it had taken a hell of a lot of talking. Trevor Daniels had a good chance of winning the primary in May, not to mention the election in November, if he didn't blow it by letting his hot temper control him. It was Everett's job to protect and mollify the would-be senator. That task might prove difficult if Trevor was hell-bent on seeing Ashley Stephens again.

Trevor set his empty glass on the bureau. He had tossed the campaign manager's words over in his mind, but despite Everett's warnings, the gleam of determination resurfaced in Trevor's hard gaze. Trevor wasn't the kind of man to take things lying down, and never had been. His roguish charm and country-boy smile had won him many votes in the past, but it was his fierce determination that had brought him to the forefront of the political race for senator. Everett Woodward knew it as well as anyone. No amount of logic or smooth talk from Everett would change Trevor's mind once it was set.

"I want you to cancel all of my appointments for the next couple of days," Trevor said.

Everett sighed audibly. "Why?"

"I'm taking a little time off."

"Now?" Everett rose from the chair and eyed his employer suspiciously. "But you can't, Trevor. Not now. It's just not possible."

"Anything's possible. You're the one who gave me that advice when I first considered running."

"Exactly why you can't take a vacation now. Your schedule's a mess as it is. All that time you were recuperating—"

"From the accident," Trevor interjected. Everett opened his mouth to argue, but thought better of it. He knew just how far to push Trevor Daniels, and when to stop. "Think of my leave of absence as following doctor's orders for rest, if it will make you feel better," Trevor suggested.

"Is that what you want me to tell the press?"

The skin tightened over Trevor's cheekbones. "I don't give a damn what you tell them. Say whatever you want."

"You're not being very reasonable about this," Everett cautioned.

"That's because I don't feel very reasonable at the moment." Trevor hoisted the canvas bag off the bed and slung his jacket over his shoulder before turning toward the door.

"So, where are you going?"

"Away . . . alone."

"Alone?" Trevor's remark sounded dangerous to Everett

and very much like the lie it was. Everett hesitated only slightly before playing his trump card. "I just hope you use your head, Daniels. And I hope that you're not going out on some personal vendetta against Stephens Timber Corporation. That wouldn't be wise—politically or personally."

Trevor's hand paused over the doorknob. He turned to face his concerned friend. "What's that supposed to mean?"

"It means that Ashley Stephens can't help you now," Everett said kindly. He noticed the stiffening of Trevor's spine and the sudden chilling of his gaze.

"Her name isn't Stephens anymore," Trevor stated. The tanned skin strained over Trevor's rugged features.

"But you and I both know that she and Richard Jennings were divorced several years ago. We also know that she owns the majority interest in Stephens Timber. Claud could be replaced in a minute, if Ashley decided to let him go."

The curse on Trevor's tongue was restrained. "You've done your homework," he observed, his voice cold.

Everett rubbed the tension from the back of his neck. "You pay me for that, too. Look, Trevor, I don't want to step out of line. What you do with your personal life is your business. I'm only worried when it begins to affect your career."

"So what are you suggesting?"

Genuine concern registered in the younger man's gaze. "Just be careful. Don't do anything, or get involved with anyone if you think there's a chance you might regret it later."

Trevor's voice was calm. "I'm not about to forget what's important in my life, if that's what you mean."

"The right woman sometimes can change a man's way of thinking."

Trevor frowned and turned the doorknob. "Then we really don't have much of a problem, do we? I think that you and I both agree that Ashley Jennings is definitely not 'the right woman.'"

With his final angry statement, Trevor jerked open the door and left his campaign manager to contemplate the half-empty bottle of bourbon.

Chapter Three

Ashley squinted into the darkness, watching warily as the snow piled around the edges of her windshield wipers. The mountain storm had come without warning and caught her off guard.

She had come to her father's Cascade Mountain retreat seeking solace. More than anything right now, she needed time alone to think things out. Now that her teaching obligations at the college had been fulfilled, she would be able to devote all of her energy to the timber company.

For the past week she had been in Portland, trying to sort through the books of Stephens Timber Corporation. As each day had passed it had become increasingly clear that Ashley couldn't trust her cousin Claud as far as she could throw him. There was little doubt in her mind that she would have to give him his walking papers as soon as she returned to Portland.

Armed with her briefcase full of financial reports concerning the operation of the vast timber empire, Ashley had spent the last two nights at the cabin poring over the accountant's figures concerning profit and loss, assets and liabilities and projected timber sales for the next two years.

Earlier in the afternoon she had pushed the neat computer printouts aside and decided to make a quick trip into Bend to replenish her dwindling grocery supply. On the way back to the cabin, the wind had picked up and within minutes powdery snow was falling from the heavens in a near-blizzard. The main highway was still clear, but the side roads, which already had an accumulation of snow, were quickly becoming impassable.

Her fingers tightened around the steering wheel and her thoughts wandered precariously to Trevor. In the short time since his accident, it seemed that there was no escaping him.

His engaging, slightly off-center smile had been photographed repeatedly and his rugged face had become incredibly newsworthy. Even last summer's scandal concerning alleged bribery charges hadn't tarnished his reputation; he was still considered by the local papers to have a lead in the primary election. Right now, Trevor Daniels was Oregon's favorite son, or soon would be, if the latest polls proved accurate.

According to Claud, Trevor's senatorial bid was sure to be a disaster for the company. Ashley disagreed. Trevor Daniels was too shrewd a politician to let personal rivalry interfere with his campaign. Besides which, Ashley was convinced that she couldn't trust Claud or his motives. What she had once considered a slight grudge against her because of Lazarus's will, Ashley now realized was a very deep flaw in Claud's character. For a fleeting moment she wondered if Trevor's accusations, which she had previously considered unlikely and vindictive, might be true.

Shifting gears as the Jeep started to climb the rugged terrain, Ashley thought about the events leading up to Trevor's sudden prominence and fame. Senator Higgins's fatal heart attack had left a vacant seat in Washington, D.C., and public opinion seemed to think that Trevor would be elected to fill the void.

Well, at least he got what he wanted, Ashley chided herself, feeling a trace of the old bitterness return. *That's a lot more than you can say for yourself.*

The tires slid on the snow-packed mountain road before holding the vehicle steady on the slippery gravel. "Just a little farther," Ashley coaxed.

Slowly she turned the steering wheel toward the narrow lane angling up the steep hillside. She frowned as she noticed ruts in the newly fallen snow. There were only two other pieces of property bordering hers and the mountain retreats that occupied those adjacent parcels were used for summer homes. Or at least they had been.

But this was her first visit to the cabin in several years. Perhaps the neighboring houses were being used over the Christmas holidays. She found the thought that she wasn't completely alone in the remote section of the mountains comforting. Though she had come seeking solitude, she now appreciated the knowledge that there was someone nearby in case the storm became more violent.

Once again Ashley's thoughts turned to Trevor and his recent accident. Though it had occurred only a week ago, she still couldn't forget about it and found herself wondering how he was doing. Her telephone calls to the hospital had never been returned and when she had tried to see him again, she had been thwarted by a determined security guard. Ashley got the message: Trevor didn't want to see her.

She couldn't blame him. For all practical purposes, she owned Stephens Timber Corporation, a corporation that in the past had represented everything in the timber industry Trevor opposed. Though she was forcing changes within the company it would still be a long time before some of the old techniques could be abandoned for safer, more environmentally sound modes of timber harvest.

"You're a fool," she admonished, and caught her lower lip with her teeth. She tried to concentrate while crossing the remaining distance to the cabin, but couldn't help hoping that Trevor had recovered from the injuries he'd sustained in the accident. How had the accident affected his career—*his damned career?* Were his eyes still as incredibly blue and erotic as they once had been?

"Damn it, Ashley," she swore, her knuckles whitening over the steering wheel, "why can't you forget that man? He never loved you—he just used you. . . ."

The pain in his side hadn't subsided. With each passing minute it throbbed more sharply, growing until a dull headache pounded mercilessly behind his eyes. Trevor had overexerted himself and he was paying dearly for it. The long drive had fatigued him and set his nerves on edge. Just the thought of seeing Ashley again disturbed him more than he would like to admit.

After fumbling in the pocket of his jeans he extracted a small vial of pills. He was chilled to the bone and the raw ache under his shirt throbbed mercilessly. Disgusted with himself and seeing the prescribed medication as a sign of weakness, he dropped the small brown bottle on the table and ignored it.

"Damn it!" Trevor cursed to himself as he reached for his neglected glass of Scotch. The liquor was warm and did little to relieve the dull ache in his abdomen.

Though his muscles were cramped from the cold, he could feel the warm trickle of sweat running down the back of his neck. He absently rubbed his forehead and wondered how much longer he would have to wait for Ashley to return. Leaning back in the chair, he closed his eyes and listened to the sounds of the night. Presently, the liquor started to take effect. The ache in his head was beginning to subside and the razor-sharp edge of his mind dulled slightly, sacrificed for the freedom from pain. He sat rigidly in the leather chair, his wet jeans clinging stiffly to his legs, while he sipped the remains of his distasteful drink.

The rumble of an approaching vehicle's engine caught his attention. Headlights flashed against the far wall, illuminating the rustic room. It was a place Trevor remembered well, a room where he had spent many lazy afternoons in years past. It was the very spot where he had first felt Ashley's trembling surrender. It had been early spring. They had run into the cabin to escape the sudden shower. He could still smell the fresh, damp scent of her black hair, taste the raindrops that had run down her cheeks. It seemed like a lifetime ago. How long had it been? Seven years? Eight? His mind was too cloudy to recall and it really didn't matter. He didn't give a damn about Ashley . . . at least not anymore.

The engine was killed and a car door slammed. Trevor had to force himself to remain patient. All of his senses were alert, his raw nerves stretched paper-thin. It had taken the better part of three days to track Ashley down and when he had finally found her, he had been pleased in a perverse sort of way. He found it ironic that Ashley had chosen to return to the cabin. It seemed to justify his reason for being here.

The key turned in the lock. Trevor heard the sound of cold metal resisting intrusion. Though he sat in another room, he could clearly see the entrance of the cabin from his vantage point in the darkness.

As the door was pushed open, Trevor narrowed his eyes. It was too dark to see clearly, but Trevor quickly determined that the small form brushing snow off her jacket and stamping her boots on the hall carpet was Ashley. As he watched her voyeuristically, the sour taste of deception rose in his throat.

He had hoped that he would feel loathing when he saw her again, but the contempt he had cultivated had refused to grow. His fingers tensed around the arm of the chair when her gaze swept past the door of the den. She pulled off her stocking cap and let her long, dark hair tumble free. Trevor's lips compressed into an unforgiving line of disgust; she was more beautiful than he had remembered.

Ashley hesitated a moment, thinking that the cabin felt different somehow, and then with a frown shrugged off the disturbing feeling and set the bag of groceries on an antique sideboard while she removed her boots and jacket. After hanging the ski jacket on the curved arm of the hall tree, she picked up the groceries, walked into the kitchen and put on a pot of tea as she replenished her cupboards.

The teapot had just begun to whistle when an unexpected noise made her heart miss a beat. "Ashley." The sound of her name made her gasp. It came from a male voice that was darkly familiar. She rotated quickly to confront the intruder.

The man was standing in the doorway to the den. "Oh my God," Ashley whispered, barely believing the apparition. Her eyes were captured in the shadowy depths of his blue gaze.

"Ashley," he repeated slowly, as if he knew how much of a shock he had imposed upon her. His voice caught on her name and it carried her backward to a past in which she had shared her life, her love with him. "I didn't mean to frighten you," he said softly.

Her throat was suddenly desert-dry, and she felt the sting of wistful tears burn against her eyelids. Her step forward was hesitant, as if she expected him to vanish as quickly as he had appeared. "What are you doing here? How did you get in?" Her voice was a muted whisper and her sea-green eyes were filled with a thousand questions spanning eight years.

"I hope I didn't startle you," he stated. "I . . . wanted to make sure that you were alone."

Though her smile was fragile, her round eyes never wavered. "Why are you here, Trevor?" she asked, finding her voice. "Why now?" All of Claud's warnings caused a painful wrenching of her heart.

The small light of defiance in her gaze bothered him. He felt the need to apologize but ignored it. He had planned this night for nearly two weeks and had never once considered that he might feel compelled to explain himself to her. His lips thinned as he reminded himself that she was the one who had to account for what was happening to him. His blue eyes held her transfixed.

"I got your message at the hospital."

"But you didn't call."

"I wanted to see you in person—"

"I came by the hospital."

"—alone."

Ashley's heart missed a beat but she forced herself to appear calm. She couldn't—wouldn't—let Trevor use her again. If he was here, it was for a reason, and she couldn't delude herself into thinking that it was just to be with her once more.

Trevor frowned at his own admission. "I thought it would be better for everyone concerned if we talked in private." He seemed sincere. But then, he had once before. She felt the old bitterness return.

"Are you sure that would be wise, Senator? What if your constituents found out that you were talking to the owner of Stephens Timber Corporation? Wouldn't that ruin your credibility?"

For a breathless instant anger sparked in his eyes. "We can start this by going for each other's throats, Ashley, but I don't think that would accomplish much, do you?"

"I suppose not." She walked past him and flipped the switch on a brass table lamp. The room was instantly illuminated in a bath of dim light. Ashley's smile trembled as she looked at him. Trevor appeared to have aged five years in the past month. Yet he was still the most intriguing man she had ever met. His cold blue eyes were just as enigmatic as she remembered.

It took a few moments for the shock of seeing him again to wear off. "I'm having a little trouble under-

standing why you're here," she stated, still trying to hold
on to her shattered poise. It was obvious that he had been
sitting in the leather chair near the fire. Ashley took a seat
on the edge of an overstuffed couch and tucked one foot
beneath her. The fabric of her jeans stretched over her
leg muscles, and Trevor was forced to shift his gaze back
to the concerned expression on her elegant face.

It was still unlined, a perfect oval of alabaster skin with
large, even features, lofty cheekbones and a sparkle of
innocence that danced in her eyes when she laughed.
Tonight her eyes were sober and suspicious. Her skin was
flushed slightly from the cold, and her dark, finely arched
brows drew downward in concentration as she tried to
understand the man who was silently regarding her.

"Okay, Trevor, I'm sitting down and I think I'm about
as calm as I'm going to get," she said.

"Good." His gaze was stony and cold.

Ashley had always had a powerful effect on him in the
past and time hadn't made Trevor immune to the seductive curve of her chin or the trace of sadness in her wistful
smile. Trevor had to force himself to remember the reason
for coming to the lonely cabin in the remote stretch of
mountains. It would be damnably easy to forget the rest
of the world tonight. All too easily Ashley could entrance
him and he would fall victim to the subtle allure of her
slow smile.

Ashley shook her dark curls, as if to clear her mind.
Dear God, what was Trevor doing here? "This is quite a
shock, you know. I thought that . . ."

"You thought that I was recuperating from an accident."

"Yes."

"I was," he admitted in a rough whisper. Though he sat

away from the light, Ashley could see his sharply defined features. His strong face no longer held the warmth she remembered, and deep lines of worry webbed from the corners of his eyes.

"And now that you feel up to it, you decided to break into my cabin. Right? That's against the law, Senator."

"I've been charged with worse." There was a viciousness in his words that she didn't understand until she remembered the bribery charges. She studied his face. His chin was still bold and square, but his cheeks had hollowed, probably because of the accident. A tiny scar, still an angry red line, cut across his jaw. Beneath his eyes were dark shadows, evidence of too many sleepless nights. When he stared at her she saw no trace of emotion on the rugged contours of his face, but she read something in the chill of his gaze. He looked haunted. "Trevor . . . what's going on?"

"I want to know just how desperate Stephens Timber is to get me out of the senatorial race."

"*I* have nothing against your politics, you know that."

A disdainful black brow cocked. "What I know is that for all practical purposes, you own Stephens Timber, right?"

The brutal glare in his eyes forced the truth from her lips. "Except for a few shares—"

"But your cousin, Claud, he's the general manager—the guy who's responsible for the day-to-day operations?"

"Claud reports to me. Look, Trevor, I don't know what you're getting at, and I really don't see that I'm obligated to tell you anything. Just what the devil is going on?" Her mysterious green eyes pleaded with him.

Light from the antique lamp diffused into the far

corners of the room, making the shadows dangerously intimate. Scarlet embers smoldered in the fire, just as they did on the first night she and Trevor had made love. Time might have hurried past them, but Ashley knew she would never love another man with the reckless, unbound passion she had felt for Trevor.

Trevor's eyes darkened, as if his thoughts had taken the same precarious path as hers. Passion flickered in their midnight depths before he jerked his gaze away from her to study the fire. It was as if, in that one hesitant moment, he had inadvertently divulged too much of himself to her.

Ashley reached over and brushed the back of his hand with hers. With a jolt, his head snapped backward and his eyes drove into hers. Gone was any trace of desire. In its stead lurked cruel suspicion, lingering just below the surface of his gaze, silently accusing her of a crime she couldn't begin to comprehend.

She withdrew her hand. Her fingers trembled as she pushed her hair out of her eyes. Dread crawled up her spine. "This has something to do with your accident, doesn't it?"

"I'm not sure it was an accident."

Ashley was stunned. Perhaps she hadn't heard him correctly. "But the papers said—"

"I know what they said. I know what the police report said. But I'm not convinced."

"Wait a minute." She closed her eyes in order to clear her mind. There had been too many emotional shocks tonight and her tangled feelings were interfering with her logic. Stretching her fingers outward in a supplicating gesture, she begged for his patience. The rumors of foul play entered her mind and she shuddered. "Let's start over. . . ."

His frown became a poignant smile. "A little late for that, wouldn't you say?" The sarcasm in his words sliced into her heart.

She bit back the hot retort forming on her tongue. She folded her hands over one knee and forced herself to remain as calm as possible. "I think it's about time you leveled with me. You owe me that much."

"I owe you nothing."

Her frayed nerves got the better of her and her thin patience snapped. "That's where you're wrong, Trevor," she contradicted. "First, you broke into my place after trudging God only knows how long in the snow just to hide your truck. Next, you sat in the dark in order to scare the living daylights out of me, which, by the way, you did. Then, you end up making vague accusations and ridiculous insinuations that don't mean a damned thing to me! I keep getting the impression that you're waiting for me to say something or fall into some kind of trap, but I can't for the life of me figure out what it is! What happened to you, Trevor? Just what the hell happened to you and what's all this nonsense about your accident—"

"I've told you before, I don't think it was an accident."

She lifted her arm as if to ward off another verbal assault. "Yeah, I know," she mumbled while placing her hand on the arm of the chair and pushing herself out of it. She stretched before bending over and examining the contents of the basket of wood sitting near the fireplace. She needed an excuse for time to gather her scattered thoughts.

Tossing a large piece of oak onto the coals, Ashley slid a secretive glance in Trevor's direction. The crackle of flames shattered the silence as the fire began to consume the new log. Returning her gaze to her task, Ashley spread her palms open to the warmth of the flames and didn't bother to turn her head or look at Trevor when she spoke. With practiced calm she asked, "I've known you for a long time, haven't I?"

"Eight years," he supplied, eyeing her backside as she knelt before the ravenous flames. He couldn't help but consider her supple curves. Her jeans were stretched tightly over her buttocks, leaving little room for his imagination. For a fleeting moment he wondered if her skin was still as soft as it once had been.

"Eight years, that's right," she agreed. "In those eight years I've called you a lot of things." His dark brows raised inquisitively when she paused. "But I've never accused you of being a lunatic." She dusted her hands on her jeans and smiled to herself as she stood. She was content to run her fingers over the rough wood of the oak mantel as she continued. "So you see, you're going to have a difficult time convincing me that you drove over a thirty-foot embankment intentionally."

"Of course not."

The first cold feelings of doubt had already taken hold of her. What was it Claud had said? That Trevor was still convinced that Stephens Timber had something to do with his father's disappearance?

He studied her quietly, watching the gentle curve of her neck as she laid her head against the mantel. Her ebony hair brushed against her white skin when she pushed it over her shoulder. Her round eyes were filled with concern and worry for him.

When Trevor rose from the chair too quickly, a dizzying sensation swept over him in a sickening wave. The pain in his side was once again beginning to throb. Grimacing against the dull ache, he made his way over to the fireplace and propped his shoulder against the warm stones. He pressed his hand against his abdomen until the ache subsided.

Holding her transfixed with his sober gaze, he spoke. When he did, the skin tightened over the rugged planes of his face and his eyes glinted with renewed determination. "Look, Ashley. I didn't intend to lose control of the car, you know that as well as I do."

Ashley's heart was thudding with dread. In her anxiety, she ran her fingers through the thick strands of her blue-black hair. Letting her forehead drop to her palm, she gently massaged her temple. Her voice was ragged, barely a whisper. "Then what you're suggesting is that someone tried to kill you."

"Not just someone, Ashley." His eyes drove into hers. "I think Claud hired someone to tamper with my car." Trevor's hand reached out and took hold of her wrist.

Ashley's breath caught in her throat. "That's preposterous!"

"I don't think so," he retorted. She tried to pull away from him, but he wouldn't release her arm. Dark blue eyes, the color of midnight, impaled her. "I think you'd better tell me everything you know about your cousin."

"This is insane," she managed to say, though her throat was constricting her breath. "I'm the first one to admit that Claud isn't a saint, but you can't go around accusing him of trying to kill you, for God's sake."

"Not until I have proof."

"Which you don't?"

"Not yet."

"Then how can you even suggest that he's involved?"

"Gut feeling."

"That won't hold up in court, Senator. But you know that, don't you? Or at least you should since you're a lawyer."

"Ashley, look, I know that I'm right."

She read the determination in his angry blue gaze. "And you want me to help you prove that Claud was trying to kill you, right? Trevor, you've got to be joking."

"I'm dead serious. I know that Claud and your father paid that mill owner in Molalla to file those bribery charges!"

"How?" Her green eyes sparked with indignant fury. "How do you know that? Did the man tell you?" Her lips turned downward in repressed rage and she pulled her hand free of his grasp.

"The police were convinced that the charges were false. They dropped the case."

"But what proof do you have that my father was behind it?"

"That mill, which had been on the verge of bankruptcy, was suddenly operational again."

"Circumstantial evidence, counselor." She waved her hand frantically in the air. "And even if your suspicions are right, who are you to say that my father was behind it?"

"I checked. Who do you think supplies that mill with rough timber?"

"I couldn't hazard a guess," she lied, knowing what he was insinuating. Her heart was like a trip-hammer in her rib cage.

"Then you're not doing your job, Ashley. The primary customer for Watkins Mill in Molalla is Stephens Timber." Trevor began to pace the floor in long, agitated strides.

"I don't understand you, Trevor," Ashley said, her voice beginning to tremble. "My father and Claud both warned me that you had some sort of personal vendetta against the timber company but I never believed them—"

"Until now?"

She nodded her head. Hot tears of frustration burned in her eyes as she stared at the only man whom she had ever loved. "Is it because of me?"

His pacing halted. He stood with his back to her and she could see the muscles of his shoulders tensing beneath the soft cotton fabric of his shirt. "No, Ashley, this started long before I knew you—"

"Because of your father's disappearance."

He turned on his heel and when he looked at her his eyes were filled with the torture he had suffered for nearly ten years. He didn't need to answer.

"Then Claud was right. You have a grudge." She closed her eyes against the truth. "You really don't think much of me, do you?"

"It's your family I wonder about."

"To the point that you would go out of your way to prove them guilty of anything." She shook her head in confusion and light from the fire caught in the ebony strands of her hair. "I own the company now. You know that I wouldn't be involved in anything illegal—"

"And I also know that you weren't in control of the corporation when my father disappeared, or when those phony charges were filed, or when my car was sabotaged."

"If it was."

"I have a mechanic who will back me up."

She ran her fingers nervously through her hair, but her

eyes never left his. "Why did you come here, Trevor? What is it exactly that you expect of me?"

His blue eyes never left her face and he pinched his lower lip between his thumb and forefinger pensively. "I want you to go through all of the company records and look for anything that might prove my theories."

"Wait a minute—you want my help in proving that Stephens Timber and my family were involved in something illegal?" She was incredulous.

His voice was low and steady. It sent a shiver as cold as the black night down her spine. "What I want from you, Ashley, is the truth."

Ashley's mouth was suddenly desert-dry. Her voice was barely a whisper. "And when I go through all the company records and I find nothing, what then?"

"All I want is the truth."

She weighed the alternatives in her mind as she reached her decision. "Okay, Trevor, I'll look through everything. But I want something in return."

"I wouldn't expect anything else from Lazarus Stephens's daughter."

"When I check all the records and clear my father's name, I expect you to make a public statement." His dark brows rose inquisitively. "A statement that ends once and for all the bitterness between our two families and a statement that absolves my father of all the charges you've attributed to him."

Trevor considered her request. "How do I know that you'll be honest with me?"

Her chin inched upward defiantly. "I guess you'll just have to trust me," she murmured. "I realize that might be difficult for you, but I don't see that you have much of a choice."

His eyes darkened. "I'll need proof, Ashley. I'll give you my public announcement, if you can prove to me that your family hasn't been involved in the accident, the bribery or my father's disappearance."

Her confidence wavered. "I'll let you know."

Trevor reached for his coat and Ashley's heart dropped. He had reappeared so suddenly in her life; she couldn't let go of him—not yet. There were so many memories they had shared, so much time that had separated them. Desperately she clung to the thread of hope that he still cared for her. "You can't leave," she whispered, her heart in her throat. He paused, one arm thrust into the suede jacket.

"Why not?"

"The storm—it's nearly a blizzard."

His eyes darkened ominously. "What are you suggesting, Ms Jennings? That I spend the night, here, alone with you?"

Chapter Four

Eight years seemed to roll backward as she stared into Trevor's smoldering blue eyes. His gaze touched the most feminine part of her soul and made her voice husky.

"You can't leave in this storm," Ashley repeated. "You'll have to wait until it dies down."

His eyes darted to the frosted windowpanes before returning to search her worried face. "That might not be until morning." Trevor slowly advanced upon her, his eyes lingering thoughtfully on the concerned knit of her brow. His voice was dangerously low. "Do you really think it would be wise for me to stay?" he asked as he reached her. Slowly, his fingers traced the elegant curve of her jaw.

He noticed the hesitation in her sensual sea-green eyes. "I don't think you have much of a choice."

Trevor's hands stopped their loving exploration and his gaze hardened. "That's where you're wrong, Ms. Jennings." He shoved his arms into the sleeves of his jacket and flashed a smile as bitterly cold as the night. "All I need from you is a lift to the Lamberts'."

Her brows quirked. "You're staying at the Lambert place?"

"That's right."

She stepped away from him and eyed him suspiciously. "Just how long have you been planning this?" she asked, tilting her palm upward and making a sweeping gesture to include everything that had transpired within the walls of the intimate room.

"Since my car went out of control and rolled down a thirty-foot embankment."

Her spine stiffened slightly. "You really believe that Claud was behind the accident, don't you?"

"If I didn't, I wouldn't be here." Eyes as cold as glass pierced hers. His voice was devoid of emotion and Ashley realized with a welling sense of disappointment how little he cared for her.

She shook her head and sighed. "I can't believe that anyone, not even Claud, would want you dead."

"I don't think he wanted to kill me, just shake me up a little. Scare me. And that, dear lady, he accomplished."

"But why?" Before he could answer she held up her hand and chewed on her lower lip. "Because of the election. You think that he's so paranoid you might win, that he set up the accident to warn you in hope that you might back out, right?"

"That's the way I have it figured."

Ashley managed a humorless smile. "I think you've been reading too many spy stories lately, Senator. Your entire theory reads like some cheap James Bond rip-off."

"Maybe that's because you can't see the truth when it stares you in the face, Ashley," he suggested with a frown. Deep furrows lined his forehead and surrounded the tense corners of his mouth. "But then you never have been able to sort fact from fiction where your family is concerned.

You probably still don't believe that Stephens Timber was responsible for the ecological disaster near Springfield."

"My father denied it," Ashley whispered.

"But you know better, don't you? Your father's company was spraying with a dangerous pesticide, Ashley. Probably because Lazarus recommended it. It was effective and cheap."

"No one knew it was dangerous—"

Trevor's eyes glittered ominously. "There had already been cases linking that pesticide with health hazards. The FDA was in the process of banning it. But your father didn't listen and the people living near the area that was being sprayed paid for it, didn't they?"

"It was never proven—"

"That's a cop-out, Ashley and you know it. Maybe you just preferred to hide your head in the sand. You didn't have to look into the eyes of the people when they found out that they were dying. The effects of the spray sometimes take months to show up, but when they do, the result is the same—a slow and painful death."

"No one knows if the pesticide was the cause."

"Yet. Researchers are still working on it." The skin stretched tightly over Trevor's harsh features as he remembered the day he had to revise Dennis Lange's will. Dennis was only thirty-three when he had come to Trevor's office, and mentioned that he had some of the symptoms of the pesticide poisoning. Dennis had died six months later, leaving a young widow and three-year-old daughter. Trevor had vowed on his friend's grave that if he ever was in a position of power, he would fight against the indiscriminate use of chemicals on the environment.

"Your father knew about the hazards, it was just more convenient to ignore them."

Masking the fact that his words had wounded her heart, Ashley turned, walked out of the room, grabbed her jacket and reached into a downy pocket for the keys to the Jeep. She had already pulled on her boots, zipped the ski jacket to her neck and wound her hair into her stocking cap by the time Trevor joined her in the small foyer. "Let's go," she whispered while purposely avoiding the silent questions in his bold eyes.

The Lambert cabin was only a little over a mile up the hill, but the drive took nearly ten minutes because of the snow that had drifted over the seldom-used road. The storm wasn't nearly as fierce as it had been, but large flakes still drifted leisurely to the ground and danced in the bright beams of the headlights.

Though it was nearly nine o'clock, it seemed like daylight. The pristine drifts of snow, settled carelessly against the trunks of graceful Ponderosa pines, gave the night a blue-gray illumination. Clumps of pine needles protruded proudly from their winter cloak of white and the shadowy mountains blended into the dark sky.

Ashley had to wipe the windshield with a cloth as condensation collected on the cold glass. The Jeep hit a patch of ice. One tire spun wildly, causing the vehicle to slide on the slippery terrain and roughly tossing the passengers against the dash. Trevor winced in pain when his shoulder was thrust against the door.

"Are you all right?" Ashley asked, when the wheels of

the Jeep were securely gripping the gravel once again. Her elegant face was pinched with concern.

"Just great," Trevor replied sarcastically. "Thanks to your cousin Claud."

Ashley pursed her lips together angrily and the remainder of the trip was made in mutual silence.

Lights were glowing in the paned windows of the Lambert cabin. Trevor's pickup was parked near the garage. Nearly three inches of snow had piled on the hood and roof of the truck.

Ashley stopped the Jeep and pulled on the emergency brake, but let the engine idle. She turned to face Trevor and found that he was staring thoughtfully at her. His eyes were deep blue and sensual. They seemed to caress her face.

"You could come in," he invited, tugging gently on her stocking cap and allowing her hair to fall in wisping black curls around her face. Her breath caught in her throat at the intimacy of the gesture.

"I . . . I don't think so," she whispered, shaking her head and avoiding his probing stare. "It would be best, for both of us, if I left."

When his fingers softly touched her temple, they trembled. Ashley closed her eyes and moved her head away from his persuasive touch. "You'll be okay, won't you . . . by yourself?" she asked, thinking of his injury. In the close quarters of the Jeep, it was difficult not to feel the urgency of his touch.

"I'll manage," he said, his voice tight.

"You're sure?"

"I'm used to doing things on my own, Ashley," he reminded her. "I can take care of myself."

"And that's why you spent a week in the hospital."

His jaw clenched furiously as he reached for the handle of the door. "You can blame Claud for that one."

Ashley's hand, which had still clung to the steering wheel, reached out to clutch his arm. "Let's not argue," she implored. "It's time to stop this fighting before it gets to the point where it can't be stopped."

For a breathless instant, there was silence. Snowflakes gathered on the windshield, providing a protective curtain from the rest of the world. His eyes searched the innocent wisdom in her gaze.

"Why did I ever let you go?" he asked himself, his blue eyes filled with dark self-mockery.

She swallowed against the dryness in her throat as, slowly, he lowered his head and his lips brushed tenderly against hers. How long had she waited for this moment? She sighed and one hand slid beneath his jacket to touch him gently on the neck. Old emotions, long dormant, began to assail the most intimate parts of her. His kiss was flavored with the hint of Scotch and reminded her of a time, somewhere in the distant past of her carefree youth, when they had made love in a fragrant field of clover.

"I've missed you," he whispered as he reluctantly pulled his lips from hers. "Dear God, Ashley, I've missed you." His strong arms held her close to him and he buried his face in the thick ebony strands of her hair. "Stay with me."

A sob, filled with the raw ache of eight forgotten years, broke from her lips. The warmth and protection of his embrace was all she had ever wanted. She leaned her forehead against his neck and she closed her eyes against the feelings ripping her apart. She had vowed never to let this man touch her again and yet she couldn't let go.

She could hear the sound of his heartbeat, feel the warmth of his breath as it whispered in her hair. Her heart wrenched painfully as she remembered how brutally he had thrust her out of his life and she knew that she could never trust him again.

"I . . . I have to go," she stated, her voice quaking with the small lie. She couldn't allow her vulnerability for Trevor to overcome her common sense.

"Why?"

"I have things I've got to accomplish."

"Such as?"

"Such as start looking through the company books. At your request."

Gently he released her. His lips were pulled into a thoughtful line of disbelief. "That's just an excuse, Ashley. You're afraid of me, aren't you?"

She let out a ragged breath. "No, Trevor, I'm not afraid of you, as a man or as a senator. But I am afraid of what becoming involved with you might mean."

"I don't understand."

She avoided his gaze and stared out the partially covered windshield. "I've worked a long time to become an independent woman. All my life I've had some man telling me what to do. First Dad, then you and finally Richard."

At the mention of her ex-husband's name, Trevor's muscles tightened. "I don't want to get involved with a man for a while," she murmured. "Not until I'm certain that I can stand on my own two feet."

"Haven't you been doing that?"

She nodded. "For several years. But now I have to prove myself—to myself."

"With the timber company," he guessed. "The last thing I would have expected from you, Ashley, is that you would turn into a latent feminist." He raked frustrated fingers through his chestnut-colored hair. "I thought you liked living in the lap of luxury."

She turned her mysterious eyes back on him. "There are a lot of things you don't know about me," Ashley suggested, smiling wistfully. "Maybe someday we'll talk about them. But . . . right now, I need time, Trevor. Time to think about you and me, about what we meant to each other and about everything that has happened between your family and mine."

He frowned, his dark brows blunted in vexation, but he seemed to accept what she said. "This is your decision, Ashley," Trevor reminded her. Then, with more dexterity than she thought him capable of, he opened the door of the Jeep, climbed out of the vehicle and walked, head bent, toward the front door. As he opened the door to the rustic Lambert home, he turned toward her. Ashley imagined that he was inviting her inside. She swallowed against the ache in her throat at the sight of him standing in the snow.

Somehow Ashley managed a weak wave before she put the Jeep in reverse, released the brake and headed back to her cabin. The picture of Trevor standing on the small porch in the darkness, with snowflakes clinging to his wavy chestnut hair, stayed with her on the short trip home.

Once back in her own cabin, she brushed the snow off

her shoulders, hung the jacket on the hall tree and hurried into the den. After checking her watch and contemplating the wisdom of her actions, she dialed the number of John Ellis, accountant for Stephens Timber Corporation.

The young accountant answered on the third ring. "John, this is Ashley. I know it's late, but I need a favor."

"Anything," was the congenial reply.

"Can you send me a copy of all transactions that have occurred at the company for the last eight months?"

There was a weighty pause on the other end of the line. "What do you mean by 'all the transactions'?"

"I mean everything—general ledger, checkbook, computer entries, expenses, payroll, the works."

"That's a lot of information . . . I suppose you want to audit the books of every branch—"

"I do. But let's start with Portland."

"You're joking," he said tonelessly while contemplating the magnitude of the task.

"No. Sorry, John, but I'm dead serious."

"Great. I figured as much." Ashley could almost hear the wheels turning in the young accountant's head. Despite his grumbling, John loved to scour the books. "And I suppose you want it tonight?"

"That would be nice, but I'll settle for tomorrow."

"Tomorrow!" John's anxious voice indicated that he thought she had just asked for the moon.

"Look, I realize that everything won't be available, but just start sending things to the Bend office through the computer. I'll pick up the first set of figures around three in the afternoon and then I'll get anything else on Thursday."

"You make it sound so easy—"

"I knew I could count on you. Thanks."

"Don't thank me yet. You might be asking the impossible."

"Don't I always?"

There was an amused chuckle on the other end of the line. "Yep. I suppose you do."

"Then you're going to love this. I'd like all the records for each branch available next week when I'm back in Portland."

"Is that all?" he asked sarcastically.

"Just one more thing. I want you to keep this confidential. Don't tell anyone at the office what I'm doing. Not even Claud."

There was silence on the other end for a moment. "You think someone's embezzling, don't you?" the accountant thought aloud.

"I hope not," Ashley murmured fervently. "God, I hope not." She replaced the receiver carefully and a small shiver of dread ran down her spine. What had she gotten herself into? If she found nothing in the books, Trevor still wouldn't be convinced that she was telling the truth. And, if she did discover that someone in the company was skimming money from the corporation to sabotage Trevor's campaign, she would only prove that all of the rumors that had circulated about Stephens Timber were true. Either way, it was a no-win situation.

Ashley opened her eyes against an intruding beam of sunlight, which was flooding the room in the soft silvery hues of winter. The sheets on the small bed were ice cold.

Ashley hurriedly reached for her velour robe lying at the foot of the bed. As quickly as her cold fingers could accomplish the task, she pulled the soft blue garment over her shivering body.

Tying the belt under her breasts, she raced down the steps leading from the loft and quickly restarted the fire in the den. Then, intent on putting on a hot pot of coffee and rebuilding the fire in the wood stove, she hurried into the kitchen. She was rubbing her forearms briskly as she entered the kitchen but she stopped dead in her tracks when she viewed the littered kitchen table.

Strewn carelessly over the smooth maple surface were dozens of pieces of paper. Computer printouts, general correspondence and financial statements were piled on the table without any trace of organization.

Ashley pulled an exaggerated frown at the documents as she walked over to the stove and lit the fire. So much for Trevor's theory. Nothing in the documents even remotely hinted at foul play. She had been awake until nearly two in the morning poring over the documents she had brought with her from Portland. True, she had just barely scratched the surface of the company records, but she felt an incredible sense of relief that all the books for the last month seemed in perfect order. "Put that in your mouth and chew on it a while, Senator," she whispered vindictively to herself. Then, without warning, a distant memory of Trevor, which she had locked away in a dark corner of her mind, came vividly back to her. His thick brown hair was rumpled, his muscled torso naked and bronze against pale wintergreen sheets, and as he had reached for her, his sleepy blue eyes had sparked with rekindled passion. . . .

Stop it, Ashley! she demanded. *It's over. When are you going to accept the fact that he never loved you?* But the thought of last night and his tender embrace nagged at her and contradicted her angry words. Last night, she had felt his need, witnessed his restraint and known that he still cared for her, if only just a little.

Forcing herself to ignore the traitorous yearnings which had begun to flow within her veins just at the thought of his kiss, Ashley went through the motions of brewing coffee. She couldn't afford to feel anything for Trevor— not now, not ever. The pain of the past had left her too vulnerable and scarred and she had vowed never to be trapped by his erotic eyes again.

When the kitchen began to warm up and the coffee was perking, Ashley straightened the corporate reports and put them into her briefcase before she went back to the loft, discarded her robe and headed for a hot shower. The warm water was invigorating as it splashed against her skin and hair. Softly, she began to hum.

By the time she had towel-dried and slipped into a clean pair of jeans and sweater, she could smell the inviting aroma of coffee wafting through the small cabin. Without bothering to put on her shoes, Ashley made her way down the stairs and padded over the scattered throw rugs and oak floors to the kitchen.

"Good morning," Trevor remarked as she raced through the open archway separating the den from the kitchen. Ashley's heart jumped to her throat.

She hesitated slightly at the shock of seeing him again. In the daylight he seemed more real than he had in the shadowy night. His eyes were as clear and blue as the mountain sky and the enigmatic smile that had trapped her in the past was neatly in place. Her heart hammered excitedly for a moment, but then reality returned to her. Indignant fire sizzled in her sea-green eyes. "Don't you know how to knock, for God's sake? Or do you just get a kick out of breaking in and scaring the living daylights out of me?"

His easy smile was self-assured and his blue eyes twinkled in amusement as he took a sip of his coffee.

"Help yourself," she mocked with a severe frown.

"Still have a sweet disposition in the morning, I see," he remarked before lifting his cup. "Join me?"

"Don't you have anything better to do than a bad impression of a cat burglar?"

He raised his hands in protest. "I haven't stolen a thing—"

"Yet." She took a chair opposite him at the table and accepted the coffee he had already poured for her. It was laced with sugar and cream. Just the way she liked it. "I drink it black—"

"Since when?"

"Since I got a little older and have to watch my weight."

Again his blue eyes sparked with humor. He cocked his head in the direction of her cup. "Go ahead," he suggested, "indulge yourself. Sin a little."

Her dark brows raised fractionally but she managed a smile.

"By the way, I did knock," Trevor announced, "but no one answered."

"I must have been—"

"In the shower," Trevor finished for her. Ashley nodded and smiled into her cup. "When you didn't answer, I got worried. After I came into the cabin, I realized you were in the bathroom, but it didn't seem to make much sense to go back outside and wait in the cold while you took your sweet time upstairs. I think we know each other well enough not to worry about formalities."

She was forced to smile, but the familiar caress of his eyes encouraged her to shift her gaze out the window to stare at the soft accumulation of snow. "How did you get in?"

He reached into his pocket, withdrew a dull piece of metal, and tossed it onto the table.

Ashley's heart missed a beat as she turned her attention to the object and touched the cold metal. "The key— how?" she began to ask, but her voice caught and faded. She had given the key to Trevor eight years ago, during Indian summer when they had met in secret tryst at the cabin. Tears, unwanted and filled with silent agony, stung the backs of her eyelids. Silently she dropped the key back onto the table.

"I never threw it away," he said solemnly. There was a wistful sadness in his gaze.

"You kept it all these years?" Her voice had grown husky.

He nodded and frowned thoughtfully into the black depths of his coffee.

The telephone rang shrilly and disrupted the intimate atmosphere which had surrounded them. Ashley was glad for an excuse to leave the table and avoid the unasked questions in Trevor's bold eyes.

"Hello?" she called into the receiver as she brushed the hot tears aside.

"Ashley. It's John."

Ashley managed a smile at the familiar voice. "Good morning."

"If you say so," he replied. "Look, I've got a start on the Portland records and I'll send them to Bend. I called Eileen Hanna at the Bend office so she'll be expecting them. She didn't ask any questions when I said they were just some financial projections that you asked for."

"Good."

"However, she might get a little suspicious when she sees the volume of paper involved," John warned.

"Don't worry about it. I'm sure Eileen won't question anything that I want." Eileen was one of the few employees in the vast timber empire who didn't begrudge Ashley her inheritance. The quiet, fiftyish woman was a feminist to the end and perceived that any advance of women in the timber industry was a major step in the right direction.

"I'm still working on the rest of it. I'm afraid it will take a couple of weeks to pull all the records together."

"That's fine. I'm not as concerned with how long it takes as much as I am that we do a thorough job." When she replaced the receiver, she found that Trevor had entered the room and was leaning against the arch separating the kitchen from the den. He studied her lazily, sipping his coffee.

The thought that he was listening in on her telephone conversation with John made her bristle. "Are you trying to add eavesdropping to your skills of crime, Senator?" she asked scathingly. Her ragged emotions took hold of her in an uncharacteristic burst of anger. "First we have breaking and entering and now we can add eavesdropping.

If you don't watch out, I might be inclined to believe that last summer's bribery charge wasn't phony after all."

The gentle smile that had curved his lips disappeared, replaced by a grim line of determination. The glint in his steely blue eyes became deadly and his jaw was tight with the restraint he placed upon himself.

"I came over here this morning because I thought that we could settle a few things between us," he stated flatly. "But obviously that's impossible."

Regret washed over her. "Look, I didn't mean—"

"It doesn't matter." He set his cup on the bookcase and stared at her with condemning eyes. "You never have trusted me and I doubt that you ever will. All your well-rehearsed speeches about being your own woman are a lot of garbage, Ashley. What it all boils down to is that you're afraid of men and me. You can't let yourself feel anymore."

His vehement words hit her like a blast of arctic air, chilling the kind feelings she had felt for him. She ignored the tears pooling in her eyes and leveled her disdainful sea-green gaze in his direction. "I was talking to John Ellis, the accountant for the timber company. He's doing some work for me—work that I requested because of you. In a couple of hours I can pick up the reports in Bend."

His smile was forced and cynical. "Good. Then maybe you can find out just how misplaced your loyalties have been." He walked to the door and put his hand on the knob. "Call me when you find out whom Claud paid to do his dirty work!"

"If I do—"

Every muscle in his body tensed and his hand whitened

over the doorknob. "Just remember that we have a deal, lady. I expect you to hold up your end."

A gust of cold air filled the room as he opened the door. He walked out and slammed the wooden door behind him. The tears that had been pooling in Ashley's eyes began to flow. "Damn you, Trevor Daniels," she whispered, her small fists clenching. "Why can't I just forget you?"

Managing to pull herself together, she walked across the room and picked up Trevor's empty cup from the shelf on which he had placed it. She started into the kitchen, but stopped, her green eyes focused on the table. There, shining dully against the polished maple, was Trevor's key to the cabin.

Chapter Five

The office in Bend wasn't particularly large, but it was run efficiently due to Eileen Hanna's sharp eyes and knack for organization. When Ashley entered the airy offices located on Wall Street, Eileen looked up from her desk and smiled broadly.

"I've been expecting you," the plump, red-haired woman exclaimed as she led Ashley into a private office.

"It's good to see you again," Ashley replied with a good-natured smile. "If all the offices of Stephens Timber were run this efficiently, I'd be out of a job."

"Nonsense!" Eileen replied, but warmed under the compliment. She unlocked a closet, withdrew a neat stack of computer printouts and handed them to Ashley. "John said you wanted to go over some projection figures. Looks like he got a little carried away."

"I told him to send me anything that might be pertinent," Ashley said, eyeing the reams of paper. "I guess he took me literally."

"He's an accountant, what do you expect?"

Ashley laughed. "What I expect is more printouts."

"You're not serious." Eileen withdrew a cigarette from her purse and tapped it on the corner of the desk.

"John said that he might be sending a few more things to me later today or tomorrow. I'll pick them up on Thursday."

"Maybe you should bring a semi," Eileen suggested as she lit her cigarette and blew a thin stream of smoke toward the ceiling.

"I'll keep that in mind." Ashley hoisted the neatly bound papers under her arm and smiled fondly at the industrious woman.

"Next time you're here, I'll buy you lunch."

"It's a date, but I'll buy," Ashley promised as she walked out of the room and winked broadly. "It's time I got some use out of my expense account." When Ashley left the building, she could still hear Eileen chuckling.

It had been difficult to keep thoughts of Trevor from interfering with her work. The harsh words of their final argument kept flitting through her mind. She had been unnecessarily cruel because of her conflicting emotions and now she regretted the fact that she had blown up at him. It had crossed her mind to call the Lambert house and apologize to Trevor, but she had discarded the idea for now. She wanted to review all the information she had received from John Ellis before talking with Trevor again. Besides, she figured she and Trevor each needed a little time to cool off.

During the following two days, Ashley studied every computer printout that John had sent. She wasn't happy with herself until she had looked over each entry and sifted through the documents with a fine-tooth comb. By the end of the second evening, Ashley had barely made a dent in the volumes of information sitting on the edge of the desk in the den. Her eyes were burning and her muscles ached from her cramped position of leaning over the desk.

The grandfather's clock had just struck eight when Ashley heard the rumble of an engine nearing the cabin. A pleased feeling of exhilaration raced through her body. Waiting, she removed her reading glasses and tapped nervous fingernails on the edge of the desk. The engine was cut and footsteps approached the cabin. Within seconds there was a loud knock.

With a satisfied smile, Ashley answered the door. Trevor stood on the porch wearing his enigmatic smile and tight, worn jeans. Snowflakes had collected in his dark hair and began to melt and catch the reflection of the interior lights. He was carrying a large package under his arms.

"If it isn't Senator Daniels?" Ashley teased.

"Not yet, it isn't," he replied. "Ask me again in November."

"Come in," Ashley requested, standing aside. She viewed him from beneath the sweep of dark lashes, and her green eyes gleamed wickedly. "Isn't it nice to have an invitation for once?"

His broad shoulders slumped, but his dark eyes glittered. "Why do you purposely goad me?" he asked in exasperation. "I came here with a peace offering, but I can see you're not in the mood to settle our differences."

"I doubt that we can do that in one night—"

"You might be surprised," he ventured, his voice lowering suggestively.

Ashley's interest was piqued. She couldn't hide the

light of expectation in her round eyes. A pleased blush colored her cheeks. "Just what have you got in mind?"

"You'll see. . . ." Trevor brushed past her and went into the kitchen. Ashley followed in his wake, barely able to conceal her interest.

"What have you got . . ." Her words died in her throat as he took off his jacket and unwrapped the ungainly package. Stripping the white paper away, he exposed two large Dungeness crabs. With a frown of approval, he placed the orange shellfish in the sink. "Where did you get those?" Ashley asked as she eyed the crabs speculatively.

"Newport."

"You drove clear to the coast and back?"

"It's only a few hours—don't you remember?"

She swallowed against the lump in her throat. "Of course I remember," she whispered hoarsely before turning away from him to hide the tears that were gathering in her eyes. The last time she had been with him, they had met in secret rendezvous near Neskowin on the rugged Oregon coast. All night long they had watched the stormy sea batter the rocky shoreline from the window of the small beach house. After dining on fresh crab and wine, Trevor had made erotic and endless love to her until the dawn had come and torn them apart.

"Come on, Ashley," he persisted, walking over to her and wrapping his arms around her waist. "Lighten up. Let's just try to forget the bad times and concentrate on the good."

"That might be easier said than done," she murmured.

He pressed a soft kiss into her blue-black hair. "Not if you try. Besides, it's Christmas Eve."

"I know." She had expected to spend the holiday alone for the first time in years and had tried to ignore the loneliness she felt. Now Trevor was with her and her spirits lifted.

"Then let's have a truce—in honor of the holiday."

"Okay, Senator," she said bravely, despite the churning emotions battling in her throat. "I'll give it a shot." Blocking out the storm of feeling raging within her, Ashley forced all of her attention on the simple tasks of heating French bread, tossing together a green salad and pouring the wine while Trevor cleaned and cracked the crabs. They worked in silence and Ashley was caught in memories of the past.

The light meal was enjoyable. Side by side, they sat by the fire in the den and laughed about the good times they had shared. Trevor was as charming as he had ever been and Ashley knew that if she let herself, she could fall hopelessly in love with him all over again. The rich sound of his laughter, the merry twinkle in his bright blue eyes and the sensual feel of his fingers when he would lightly touch her shoulder reminded her of the happiest time in her life—when she had been desperately in love with him. Even without all of the traditional trimmings, the evening became the warmest and happiest Christmas Eve she could remember. Relaxing with Trevor was perfect and natural.

Several hours had passed before Trevor cocked his head in the direction of the desk. "You've been looking over the records of Stephens Timber," he deduced.

"That's right. But I'm afraid you'll be disappointed. So far, everything looks fine. Nothing to prove that anyone in the family is the criminal you suspect."

"You're sure?" She felt him stiffen. He was sitting behind her on the floor, his strong arms folded securely over her shoulders. She was leaning against him as she stared into the glowing red embers of the fire.

She shook her head and her hair brushed against his chest. "l've barely started. Those reports are just for the last few months. I looked them over quickly and they seemed okay. I couldn't see anything glaringly obvious."

"Claud doesn't make glaring mistakes," Trevor stated. All traces of humor had disappeared from his voice.

"I know, I know. I've started going through the pages again. This time I'm studying each entry individually, but it's going to take weeks."

"Ashley." His fingers pressed urgently against her shoulders and dug into the soft muscles of her upper arm. "I don't have much time."

"Then I'm going to have to recruit help, Senator," she decided with a sigh. "I have other things I have to do. I can't spend the next two months sequestered with computer printouts just to uphold your good name."

"Or yours." He reminded her. "Just make sure your recruit is someone you can trust."

"Of course."

"This is important. Anyone who helps you can't tip Claud off. Can you be sure that the people working for you are loyal to you and not your cousin?"

Ashley didn't hesitate. "There are a few. Give me a break, Trevor. We employ over—"

"That doesn't matter. It's not quantity, but quality that counts."

"I can handle it."

"I hope so," he whispered, touching his lips to her hair. "Sometimes I question your judgment."

"That's the problem, isn't it? You always have."

The air was thick with unspoken memories. Silence weighed heavily on Ashley's slim shoulders as she stared into the bloodred coals of the fire. "I don't know you anymore, Trevor. Not at all," she said in a quiet moment of complete honesty. "And what I remember . . . what happened between us, turned out very badly." She turned her head and her green eyes looked directly into his.

"A man can change . . ." he ventured.

"And so can a woman."

His eyes searched the soft contours of her face before she turned away from him to concentrate on the slowly dying fire. "What if I said that I wish I had it all to do over again?" His fingers touched the round of her shoulders and lingered in the black silk of her hair.

The old ache burned savagely in her heart. "I'd say I don't believe you—no matter how much I'd like to. I'm not bitter, Trevor; just wiser than I was. What happened between us was your doing and nothing you can say will alter the past." She felt the warmth of his fingers in her hair and knew that she had to pull away from him and break the seductive spell he was weaving. She couldn't let herself forget the past and the pain. Struggling against reawakened love, she managed to stand and step away from the power of Trevor's touch.

Her voice was firm. " I think it would be better to forget what happened eight years ago and concentrate on what's happening now. For instance, the reason you're here and what you really want from me."

The grandfather's clock in the entry hall ticked off the silent seconds. A chill as cold as a North Pacific gale made Ashley shiver with dread and she rubbed her hands over her arms.

"I thought we could spend some time together. It's Christmas." Trevor's eyes never left her face. He watched even the most subtle of her reactions; the nervous manner in which she clutched the gold chain encircling her throat, and the movement of her tongue as she wet her lips. Desperately she wanted to believe him.

"And you need me to check into the company records to condemn my own family. Isn't that what this is all about? Isn't that the only reason you're here? Aren't you just trying to clear all the dirt surrounding the Daniels family and push it onto the name of Lazarus Stephens in order that you can get elected? That is the most important thing isn't it? Your career."

"And what's important to you, Ashley?" Trevor asked quietly. His face had saddened. "Eight years ago all you wanted to do was settle down, get married, have children. Now you're talking about women's rights and finding yourself! What the hell's that supposed to mean?" His blue eyes were blazing. "And what about your husband— how does he feel about all this new way of thinking? Or is he the reason you've become so liberated?"

Ashley's eyes snapped with indignation. "Richard and I were divorced four years ago."

"I know that."

"Then why do you continue to refer to him as my husband?"

"Because he was!"

"And that still bothers you," she said, understanding a little of his pain.

"Shouldn't it?" His cold blue eyes narrowed and he lifted himself from the floor, trying to relieve the tired muscles supporting his back.

"You were the one who couldn't make a commitment," she reminded him, hoping to hide the trace of wistful regret in her voice.

Trevor's fist opened and closed against his jeans, as if he were physically attempting to regain control of his temper. "Don't twist the truth," he warned. "I was willing to do just about anything to keep you—"

"Except marry me."

"Ha!" The sound of his humorless laughter was as bitter as the night. " How many times did I ask you to marry me? Or have you conveniently forgotten about them?" His voice was low, the sound dangerous. There was a kinetic energy in the air, ready to explode with the repressed passion of the heated argument.

Ashley's dignity wavered for an instant. "That's right, Trevor. You did ask me to marry you, several times." She waved the back of her slim hand in the air as if the number were insignificant. "But asking isn't the same as doing. I was tired of being engaged and tired of having an affair. I wanted to be your wife!"

"Correction," he interjected cruelly, his dark blue eyes burning with accusations. "You wanted to be anyone's wife. Even if it meant running back to the man your father had chosen for you."

"I loved you. . . ." She sighed, tears pooling in her eyes with the painful admission. "Trevor, I loved you so much."

"Until you realized that I wasn't going to become a millionaire overnight. The daughter of Lazarus Stephens wasn't able to live without the comforts of wealth. You couldn't wait for me, could you?"

"Now who's twisting the truth?" she charged.

"Damn it, Ashley, this isn't getting us anywhere." His fist crashed into the warm rocks of the fireplace and then he swore, wincing against a sudden, blinding stab of pain.

Ashley's anger fled and was replaced by concern. "Are you all right?"

"I'm fine."

"Trevor." She touched his arm. For a moment her fingers brushed his wrist and his blue eyes sought hers, unspoken questions in their stormy depths. Her throat tightened. He rubbed his forehead before letting his head fall backward to stare at the open rafters supporting the roof. "Dear God, Ashley, I wish I understood you."

His plea sounded earnest. A lump formed in her throat when she considered what she might have shared with Trevor. Had she waited, as he had asked, would all of the happiness of their youth have blossomed into a deep, selfless love? Could they have shared their lives? Would she have eventually borne his children, comforted him when he needed her, shared his deepest agony?

As if he had read her mind, he asked the one question he had been avoiding for three days. "Why did you come here, to the cabin?"

She withdrew her hand and tears filled her eyes. "There were a lot of reasons—I needed a rest, there was work I could do here, I wanted to get out of the office, but there was something else," she admitted with a wry frown. "I came here because of you." Sea-green eyes met his. "It seemed that every time I turned around, I was reminded of you. Just a few weeks after Senator Higgins's death, your name became a household word. Then there were the bribery charges—the newspapers . . . television . . . you were everywhere.

"When Dad died, all I heard about was what damage you would do if you were elected. Now, just lately, your accident hit the front page. I couldn't get away from you." Her voice softened. "I thought that if I came here for a couple of weeks, I could think things out, sort out my feelings."

"And have you?"

Her smile was frail and filled with self-mockery. "I thought I had." Her lips pursed into a thoughtful pout. "Now I'm not so sure." Emotions she had thought long dead were reawakening. She couldn't help but remember the feel of his hands against her skin, or the way his eyes darkened in passion when she smiled suggestively.

The rustic room seemed to shrink and become more intimate. Ashley had to concentrate to keep her thoughts from wandering dangerously to a distant past.

He stared down at her, attempting to look past the innocent allure in her eyes. She had always been a puzzle to him, enigmatic and beguiling; the only woman he had ever let touch his soul. He had vowed never to make that mistake again, and he had been able to keep that silent promise to himself until tonight, when he gazed into the intelligent complexity of her eyes. At this moment he wanted her more desperately than he had ever wanted anything in his life. "Do you want me to stay?"

She didn't avoid his penetrating gaze. "Yes. I've missed

you, Trevor." Giving up all the thin pretenses, she faced what she had tried to deny for eight solitary years. "I've missed you so badly."

He forced himself to look past the tears welling in her eyes. "Not badly enough to come back."

"I couldn't." She shook her head and fought the tears. "I think you understand that my pride wouldn't allow it."

"I've never been able to understand anything about you."

Standing, she faced him. "Only because you never really tried."

Slowly his strong arms encircled her waist and pulled her body gently to his. There was a restraint in his touch and torment in his gaze.

"I must be out of my mind," he muttered to himself as his head lowered and his lips brushed hers. The pressure of the kiss increased. Ashley sighed through parted lips at the power of his arms and the warmth of his mouth covering hers. The faint taste of wine passed from his lips to hers and the familiar taste brought back memories as bittersweet as the past they had shared together.

Her knees seemed to melt with the warm persuasion of his embrace. She touched him lightly on the shoulders and could feel the tightening of lean, corded muscles beneath her fingertips.

His tongue rimmed her lips before slipping between her teeth to explore the secrets of her mouth. It touched her familiarly, sliding seductively against the polish of her teeth.

Trembling with a wave of passion, her fingers dug into the firm flesh of his shoulders. The forgotten ache of womanly need uncoiled wantonly within her, forcing her blood to race wildly through her veins and pound in her ears. Her breathing became rapid and shallow. With each flickering touch of his supple tongue against hers, her desire for him increased and the uncontrollable yearning became more heated; a throbbing distraction demanding release.

He lifted his head from hers, but continued to press her body against his, letting her feel the taut rigidity of each of his muscles straining against his clothing. "I want you," he whispered hoarsely against her hair. It was a statement as honest as the cold mountain night. "I want you more than I've ever wanted a woman."

She swallowed against the dryness that had settled in her throat. "And I want you," she murmured.

His penetrating eyes studied the mystery of her. "With you it's more than passion or lust. It always has been."

Her heart nearly missed a beat. If only she could believe that he loved her . . . just a little. "You've always had a way with words, Trevor. That's why you've done so well in politics, I suppose."

"Are you accusing me of distorting the truth?" His voice was thick and slightly mocking. A hint of laughter danced in his eyes. Ashley was captivated by his smile—the slightly off-center grin she had grown to love that summer eight years before.

"Stretching the truth," she corrected.

"In order to seduce you?"

"To get your way."

"If I'd had my way with you, things would be a lot different between us." His fingers wrapped possessively over her wrist. "Do you have any idea what you do to me?"

"I just want . . . to be with you," she whispered, rising onto her toes and kissing his cheek. Softly she outlined the shape of his brows with the tip of her finger. Everything she did seemed so natural, just as it had in the past.

Trevor groaned with the frustration tormenting him. He noticed the innocence in her clear green eyes and the heat burning in his loins began to ache. "Ashley," he ground out, "I don't want you to do anything you might regret."

"I won't."

He clenched his teeth together and forcefully willed his passion aside. "What I'm trying to say is that you don't have to feel obligated to me."

"I don't, Trevor," she replied, showing just the hint of a dimple. "Not anymore."

Her hand pressed against his cheek and he could stand the bittersweet torment no longer. With a sensual movement, he turned his head and touched the tip of his tongue to her palm, letting the moist heat from his body flow into hers.

"Trevor . . ." she moaned, her voice fading into the night. "Oh, Trevor." She shuddered with the pain of ragged emotions, the same feelings she had been denying for eight agonizing years. His tongue created a moist path between her fingers and she felt as if her entire body were ignited by his warm touch. Her throat became dry, her voice a breathless whisper. "I've always loved you," she vowed.

"I want to know that you're mine," he said, steeling himself against the desire running rampant in his veins and the passion dominating his mind.

"I always have been."

"Ashley, don't. Don't lie to me. Not now."

"I'm not—"

"Prove it."

"If only I could," she wished.

"Let me make love to you." It was a simple request. His

dark blue eyes bored into her, exposing the depths of his torment. Her feelings for him were dangerous. They entrapped her in the same words of love that had betrayed her in the past. His offer was tempting, yet she hesitated, afraid of losing herself to him as she had once before.

"There's nothing I want more," she admitted.

"But you're afraid."

"There's no future for us. . . ." Her dark brows had pulled into a worried frown. With all of her heart she wanted to lie beside Trevor, to find the exhilaration once again of becoming one with him. But the old fears resurfaced.

"Shhh. Don't think about tomorrow." His fingers caught in the thick strands of her blue-black hair, pulling her head to his. For a delicious moment, his lips brushed over hers, lingering just a fraction of a second. "Let me love you, sweet lady," he whispered.

Her response was to let go of the fear and the pain of the past. Her surrender was complete. "Please," she murmured. Reaching upward she twined her fingers in his hair and turned her lips upward to accept the warm invitation of his mouth.

"It's been so long," he groaned as his lips pressed against hers and conveyed to her his overwhelming masculinity.

Her heart thudded irregularly with the urgency of his kiss. Desire, hot and fluid, crept up her veins as she felt his tongue meet hers. Without breaking the heated kiss, he shifted and lifted her off the floor to cradle her against his chest. Trevor began to carry her up the stairs to the loft.

"I can walk," she protested, thinking of his recent injury.

"Not a chance," he replied. "You might change your mind."

"Never." Tears of happiness welled in her eyes as she looked up at the angular face of the man she loved.

When he reached the top of the stairs, Trevor didn't hesitate. He strode across the small loft and dropped Ashley onto the bed, before lying beside her. The room was shadowed, but in the pale illumination from the skylight, Ashley could make out the masculine angles of his face.

She felt the touch of his hand as he caressed her cheek and she read the desire smoldering in the depths of his eyes. His fingers slid seductively down her throat to linger at the neckline of her sweater.

Closing her eyes, she leaned against him and let out a shuddering sigh when his fingers dipped below the ribbing at her neck to tentatively touch the swell of her breast. Her hands worked at the buttons of his shirt, letting it fall open to expose his solidly muscled chest. The bandage, a swath of white against his dark skin, reminded Ashley of the reasons he had come to the cabin, the reasons he was here with her now. Her fingers gently outlined the white gauze.

Slowly he lifted the sweater over her head. Shivering slightly when the cool air touched her skin, she was only aware that she wanted Trevor as desperately as she ever had. She needed him now, tonight. She was destined to lie in the shelter of his arms, feel the strength of his body straining against hers. And there would be no regrets. Tonight she belonged to Trevor alone.

He watched her silently, his warm hands touching her cool skin. She swallowed against the arid feeling in the back of her mouth when his hand cupped her breast. The ache within her burned more savagely. When his head lowered and he touched the flimsy fabric of her bra with his lips, she thought she would die in the sweet agony ripping through her. Her breasts pushed against the thin barrier of lace and silk as his tongue wet the sheer fabric and the cool night air caressed her skin. He groaned as his mouth captured the hidden nipple straining against the taut lace.

Ashley clutched his head against her, exhilarating in the torment of his lovemaking. Tears ran down her cheeks as he unclasped her bra and her breasts were unbound. His fingers moved in slow rhythmic circles over one nipple while his tongue rimmed the other.

"Oh, God, Trevor," she pleaded. "Make love to me, please make love to me."

His hands found the waistband of her jeans, and his fingers dipped deliciously close to her skin. She was unaware of the precise moment when he removed the rest of her clothes as well as his own. She was only conscious of the sweet torment heating within her, a wild tempest of passion only he could calm.

When at last he moved over her, she was rewarded by the feel of his firm muscles pressed urgently over her body. His bare legs, soft with dark hair, entwined with hers. His hands touched her rib cage as if he were sculpting her, and his lips, hard with passion and warm with desire, molded over hers. "Love me, Trevor," she cried, unashamed of her tears.

"I always have. . . ." He lifted his head and gazed into

her soft green eyes. Her dark hair was spread over the white pillow. He knew now what he had always suspected: Ashley Stephens was the most incredibly beautiful and intelligent woman he had ever met.

Burying his head in the soft curve of her neck, he claimed her in a sensuously slow union of his flesh with hers. The warmth within her began slowly to uncoil as he found that part of her he had discovered sometime in a stormy past. He tasted the salty tears of happiness that ran down her cheeks; he felt the heated moment of her submission and stiffened when her fingernails dug into the muscles of his back.

Ashley whispered his name into the night when the final moment of surrender brought them together and bridged the black abyss of eight lost years.

As his body fell against hers, he held her as if he expected her to vanish. The corded muscles of his arms offered the gentle assurance that he did love her and always had. If only Ashley could believe him. If only she could think that Trevor would never leave.

Chapter Six

Sunlight was streaming through the windows when Ashley opened her eyes on Christmas morning. She snuggled deep beneath the colorful patchwork quilt and felt the warmth of Trevor's body against her own. He made a low sound in the back of his throat and the arm draped possessively across her abdomen tightened before his even breathing resumed.

Ashley watched his dark profile against the stark white sheets. In slumber, some of the harshness had disappeared from his features; the tension that had been with him the last few days had faded with the night. The lines around his eyes had softened and the pinched corners of his mouth were relaxed. His hair fell over his eyebrows. Ashley lovingly brushed it out of his face while she pushed herself up on one elbow and stared down at the only man she had ever loved. *Why, Trevor,* she thought sadly, *why can't we live like this forever? Why do we continually do battle with each other?*

The quilt covering Trevor had slipped downward, exposing his chest to the cold morning air. Ashley's eyes followed the rippling lines of his muscular body to rest on the white gauze wrapped tightly over his torso. Gingerly she touched the bandage, frowning thoughtfully. Was it possible that Claud could have been responsible for Trevor's accident? It seemed unlikely, and yet Ashley knew that Claud could be cruel and ruthless if he felt cornered or threatened. And Claud had mentioned to Ashley that he considered Trevor's senatorial bid a direct threat to Stephens Timber. To what lengths would her bitter cousin go?

Her touch disturbed him. Trevor opened a sleepy blue eye and smiled when he saw that Ashley was already awake.

"You're a sight for sore eyes," he murmured. The hand that had been curved over the bend in her waist moved seductively upward until his thumb rubbed against her rib. "God, I could get used to this." He stretched before sitting next to her and looking into the incredible allure of her eyes. "Merry Christmas, Ashley," he whispered before bringing his face next to hers and pressing anxious lips to her mouth.

Slowly, he pushed her back against the mattress and let his weight fall carefully over her. Her breasts flattened with the welcome burden of him and slowly she slid her fingers up the solid muscles of his arms to rest on his shoulders.

When he raised his head, there was a trace of sadness in his gaze. "You don't know how long I've waited to wake up with you beside me," he admitted. A wistful look stole over her refined features. Trevor traced the disbelieving arch of her brow.

Ashley felt as if her heart had swollen in her throat. "You only had to ask," she whispered.

Something dangerous flickered in his gaze. "You were married," he reminded her.

"That was a long time ago."

Trevor lay over her, his supple body imprisoning hers against the bed. She didn't move or attempt to escape from the gentle bonds of his muscles flexed possessively over hers. As she gazed into his knowing blue eyes, Ashley realized that she could never love another man. Her marriage to Richard had been a mistake from the start and it was over before it had ever begun.

"I should never have let you go," Trevor whispered into the thick ebony silk of her hair. His body began to move rhythmically over hers, enticing the most delicious responses. Her heartbeat thudded irregularly in her chest. "I should have chased you down and forced you to marry me."

"You wouldn't have had to force me, Trevor. That was the one thing in the world I wanted."

"And the only thing that Lazarus Stephens's money couldn't buy."

She let out a ragged sigh and looked beyond him to the exposed rafters of the ceiling. Her breathing was becoming shallow and rapid. "Must we always argue?"

"I can think of better things to do . . ."

Her fingers tangled in his hair. " So can I."

Trevor lowered his head, his lips claiming hers in a kiss filled with passion and despair. His hands rubbed against her skin, softly caressing her body and making her blood warm as it ran through her veins.

The magic of his touch evoked the most primitive of responses within her. Liquid heat circulated and swirled upward through her body as she felt the firm muscles of his chest brush erotically across her breasts, teasing the dark nipples to expectant peaks aching with desire.

His lips touched and teased her, inflaming the wanton fires of passion to surge through her veins until she began to move beneath him. Her hands strayed downward, touching the rippling muscles of his back and outlining each tense sinew with her fingertips.

Trevor closed his eyes and groaned in helpless surrender. His hands began to knead her breasts and his knees impatiently parted her legs, testing her willingness by rubbing himself gently against her abdomen.

A soft gasp escaped from her throat, and when he lowered his head to capture her parted lips with his, Ashley thought she would die with wanting him. His tongue explored and plundered the sweet delights of her mouth while he gripped her shoulders firmly with his hands and entered the dark warmth of her womanhood.

Ashley's mind was swirling with erotic images. Her fingers dug into his back as she felt the womanly pressure within her build. Slowly, as if enjoying the torture of denial, he pushed closer to her, touching her most intimate core, closing the space that held her away from him and savoring the sweet agony of her cry.

"Please," she whispered throatily, her glazed eyes looking into his. Her throat was dry, the words a strain. "Take me, Trevor," she begged.

The light of satisfaction glimmered in his eyes as he began to thrust against her. He watched in fascination while she responded in kind, holding on to him in desperate need, as if she expected him to disappear into the cool morning air.

Sweat beaded on his brow and glistened against his

naked skin as he restrained himself, waiting until he felt the warmth of her explode in a liquid burst of satiation. Then he, too, let go and felt the sudden rush of blinding fire as he sealed their union of flesh and mind and fell heavily against her with a moan of triumphant release.

"I love you, Ashley," he claimed. "God forgive me, but I've always loved you. Even when you were married to another man."

The lump in Ashley's throat expanded with his words. "Shhh, Trevor—not now." Lovingly, her fingers touched his hair, smoothing the wavy chestnut strands away from his face. His words touched the deepest, most precarious part of her heart and she couldn't allow herself the luxury of believing them. Not now. Not ever.

She had felt the pain of his betrayal once before and had sworn never to live the life of a fool again. It would be too easy to believe him—to trust her heart—to let the pain recapture her in its bittersweet claws.

After a few moments of reflective silence, Ashley attempted to lighten the mood in the cold cabin. "How about breakfast in bed?" she asked.

Trevor smiled knowingly and ran a sensuous finger down the length of her body. "I'm afraid I wouldn't be able to concentrate on food."

She laughed and shook her hair out of her eyes. "Well, I could. I'm hungry enough to eat a horse. Come on." Slapping him playfully on his rump, she hopped out of the bed, grabbed her robe and slipped it on. "I'll make breakfast while you get the fire going in the den."

"And then you'll serve me in bed?"

Ashley was halfway to the bathroom by the time his words hit her. When she turned to look over her shoulder and cast him an intentionally provocative glance, she found him leaning on one elbow, his blue eyes following her every move.

"You are talking about breakfast, aren't you, Senator?"

"Among other things . . ."

"Um-hmm. I think we'd better eat in the kitchen. It might be safer."

"Spoilsport."

"Look who's talking. You're the one with the important project, or have you forgotten?"

"It's Christmas!"

Ashley smiled despite herself. "That it is. Merry Christmas, darling." She winked at him seductively, turned on her heel and made a big show of going into the bathroom to change. She half expected him to follow her and was more than slightly disappointed when he didn't.

After she had showered and changed, she walked through the loft again and noted that he was still in bed, but far from sleeping.

"Come here," he commanded when she breezed past the four-poster. His delft-blue eyes were smoldering with passion.

"Not on your life," she teased, but when he reached out and took hold of her wrist, she was forced to spin around and face the determined set of his jaw. Her wet hair dangled in glistening ebony ringlets around her flushed face as he roughly pulled her down on the bed.

"You're no gentleman, Senator Daniels," she laughed as she fell against him.

"And you love it." His fingers toyed with the buttons of her sweater. "Someone should teach you a lesson, you know."

"And you're applying for the job?" Her eyebrows rose a skeptical fraction.

"I've got it." One of the pearllike fasteners near her neck was loosened, exposing just a hint of white skin at her shoulder. Her green eyes danced in mock dismay as she clutched at her throat. The love she had harbored for eight long years was unhidden in the even features of her face.

There was something captivating about Trevor's slightly off-center smile, something inviting and dangerous in his midnight-blue eyes. When he leaned over to kiss her shoulder, Ashley shuddered with anticipation.

He buried his face in her neck and drank in the sweet scent of her clean, damp hair. It held the faint fragrance of wildflowers, just as he remembered it. They had been alone in the cabin, and the dewy drops of summer rain had clung to her hair.

"I've never wanted a woman the way I want you," he admitted, touching her throat with his lips.

A thousand emotions made Ashley shiver as he pressed himself against her. She felt the ache of desire begin to flood her veins when he lay atop her and pressed the length of his naked body over hers. Even through her slacks and sweater she could feel the heat of his passion pressed urgently against her skin.

"Forget breakfast," he suggested, running his tongue against her ear. "I have a better idea. . . ."

Without regret, Ashley wound her arms around his neck and brought his head against hers, eager to let the happiness linger and feel the warmth of his lips dispel the chill in hers.

* * *

As she poured water for coffee, Ashley could hear Trevor grumbling about the things he had to put up with. She smiled to herself when she remembered her hasty escape from the bed. After making glorious love while the late morning sun infiltrated the room through the skylight, she had dozed quietly in the shelter of Trevor's arms. Then, when she could tell that he wasn't expecting her to leave, she had bolted from the bed, snatched up her clothes from where they had been carelessly tossed and raced down the stairs to the kitchen.

He had sworn roundly, which had only caused her to laugh at his frustration. It felt so right, so natural being alone with him. It was almost as if what had separated them in the past was beginning to disappear.

While Trevor attended to the fire in the den, Ashley started preparing what she could for a festive brunch. The cupboards were pretty bare, but she prided herself on the end result of broiled grapefruit, blueberry muffins, sausage and poached eggs.

"Not too bad for a novice," she decided as she dusted her hands on the apron she had tied over her clothes.

Trevor must have heard her. "It's Christmas, you know. I'm expecting baked ham, cinnamon rolls, eggs Benedict. . . ." He poked his head into the kitchen.

"Keep it up, Senator, and you'll be lucky if you get cornflakes."

He studied the floor for a minute before his eyes came back to rest on her. "It wouldn't matter what we ate, you know."

She returned his grin. "I suppose not. But since I put out the effort, I expect you to do the meal justice."

They ate in the kitchen and Trevor, for all his protests

earlier, ate with relish. A surprised glint surfaced in his blue eyes. "I didn't think Lazarus Stephens's daughter knew how to boil water, let alone cook."

"I'm learning," she joked, before adding more seriously, "There are a lot of things you don't know about me, Trevor. I've grown up in the last eight years." He lifted his dark brows appreciatively, as if in mute agreement, and took a long swallow of his coffee.

The intimate conversation made Ashley bold. "So why haven't you ever married?" she asked before her courage escaped her.

He set his cup down and stared out the window for what seemed an eternity. "I'd like to give you the old cliche about never finding the right woman," he replied, rubbing his chin in the process and continuing to stare at the frosty panes. "But then, we both know it would be a lie."

Ashley stared at him, her breath caught in her throat. She shook her head sadly. "I just told you that I've grown up. I'm not as naive as I was, Trevor, nor as—"

"Trusting?"

"That, too, I suppose. I'd like to think that you and I were just star-crossed lovers and that our time hadn't come yet. Now that we've found each other again, everything will be fine." She ran one finger around the rim of her cup and stared at the murky coffee. Her voice had grown hoarse. "But that's not the way it is. You're not Prince Charming, and I'm certainly no Sleeping Beauty, waiting for a man to change my life." Her sea-green eyes held his calmly. "Too much has happened between us. And," she added pointedly, "it's my guess that the reason you haven't married is that you haven't found the perfect mate."

"Is there such a thing?"

"I doubt it." She shook her head. "You want too much in a wife, Trevor. A strong woman, who will support you and your damned career. A woman who will do what you want without question, but still has a mind of her own. A woman who will give up everything to be at your side— if and when you want her. And a woman who will wait with the home fires burning until you decide to come home. That's too much to expect from anyone."

"Including you."

She smiled sadly. "Especially me."

"And what do you want in a husband?"

Love, she thought to herself, but couldn't force the word from her lips. Instead, her lips puckered into a secretive frown and she started picking up the dishes. "I don't want a husband," she replied.

"You did once. Very badly, as I recall."

"That was a long time ago."

He scowled darkly and his fingers drummed angrily on the table. "And you managed to get yourself one, didn't you?"

"It didn't last."

"Why not?"

She shrugged her shoulders to indicate that it really didn't matter, but Trevor's fingers gripped her forearm and restricted her movements. "Richard and I weren't suited—"

"That's a lie! The man was hand-picked by your father."

"Maybe that was the problem." She looked pointedly at her wrist and the tanned fingers restraining it.

With obvious reluctance Trevor let go of her arm. "This isn't getting us anywhere," he muttered, pushing back his chair before fiercely striding out of the room. Ashley heard his footsteps echo in the hall before the front door of the cabin opened, only to slam shut with a resounding thud that rattled the timbers of the rustic mountain retreat.

Knowing that it would be best to let him cool off, Ashley finished clearing the table and set the dishes in the sink to soak before grabbing her jacket from the hall tree, slipping on her boots and going outside.

Trevor's footprints left deep impressions in the snow. She followed the powdery prints and forced her hands deep into her pockets. She loved Trevor with a passion that was achingly evident every time she was near him, and yet, try as she would, she could find no way of resolving those problems that held them apart.

When she found Trevor he was standing near the edge of a sharp ravine, his back to her. He was staring past the snow-covered abyss to the majestic peaks beyond. The sky was a brilliant blue and the snow-laden mountains stood proudly in the distance, their treeless upper slopes reflecting the icy radiance of the winter sun's rays.

Trevor hadn't heard her approach and when Ashley put a reproachful hand against his sleeve, he stiffened. "I didn't mean to pick a fight, you know," she whispered, her breath misting in the cold mountain air.

His smile was cynical, and a muscle worked beneath his clean-shaven jaw. "Seems like you and I can't avoid arguing."

"It's hard to clear the air."

"Especially when so many lies cloud it." He thrust his fists deep into his pockets and leaned against the denuded white trunk of a birch tree. Thoughtfully he pursed his lips and his dark brows drew together in careful consideration over intense blue eyes.

"I never have lied to you," she replied.

He looked as if he didn't believe her. "But your family. First Lazarus, now Claud—"

"My family would never have come between us," she replied, "if you weren't so hell-bent to ruin Stephens Timber Corporation."

A sound of disgust formed in his throat. His eyes had turned as frosty as the winter day. "You can't convince me that Claud isn't out to get me."

"I know. I've tried."

"He's out to ruin me politically, Ashley."

"I think you're jumping to conclusions."

"The right ones. Claud is scared spitless that if I win I'll be able to lobby for wilderness protection and some-how cut off his supply of timber. Your father was op-posed to any new wilderness protection acts. He didn't give a damn about the environment, and it seems as if Claud was tutored well."

"But Claud doesn't own the company."

"No, he just runs it. And he won't rest until he's ruined me politically."

"That's ridiculous!" Ashley retorted. She brushed the snow from a boulder and sat on it, holding her knees with her arms and huddling for warmth. Try as she might, she couldn't believe that Claud would be so murderous. It was true that Trevor's campaign included a firm stand on wilderness protection, which, in the past, Stephens Timber had vehemently opposed. The issue was a delicate one, pitting the economy against the environment. In lean times, when unemployment was high, jobs and the timber industry won over the environment. But right now, unemployment was down and public sentiment seemed to support Trevor's position.

"Senator Higgins was an efficient lobbyist for the timber industry," Trevor said. His broad shoulders slumped as if he were bone-tired.

"And you won't be?"

"Right. Higgins was in your father's pocket and I suspect that Claud is hoping that another candidate will fill Higgins's shoes." Trevor's voice was without inflection, but his face was a study in grim resolve. "He can look somewhere else because it sure as hell won't be me."

Ashley smiled bitterly. "I don't see where you get off acting so sanctimonious. Your family is still a very viable force in the timber industry."

"But my brother keeps his nose clean."

"What's that supposed to mean?" Ashley demanded.

"Just that Jeremy has managed to follow pretty closely in my father's footsteps. Daniels Logging Company has always worked within the law."

"And my father didn't? Is that what you're implying?"

"I'm just stating the facts," he replied coldly. "Jeremy has seen to it that Daniels Logging has been ahead of its time. We've never clear-cut, always participated in reforestation, even before it was fashionable, and always left a buffer zone near streams, to protect the rivers." Trevor's square jaw hardened. "And to my knowledge, the use of pesticides by Daniels Logging has been kept to a minimum, in order to protect the public."

Ashley's elegant brows raised scathingly. "You've implied some pretty heavy charges, Senator."

"I've always called 'em as I see 'em."

"Or so your campaign manager would like the public to think."

Trevor scowled angrily, but didn't offer a rebuttal. He noticed the bluish tint to Ashley's lips and reluctantly he stood. After brushing the wet snow from his jeans, he said, "I think we'd better go back inside before you freeze to death."

"'Are you worried about me—or the scandal my demise would cause?"

Trevor's admonishing stare was stern. "I wish for once, just once, you'd give me a break."

"That works two ways, you know."

They walked back to the cabin in silence, each wrapped in secret thoughts of the past that linked them, bound them together, and always kept them at sword's length from each other.

In some respects, Trevor was right, Ashley decided. Daniels Logging had always had an untarnished reputation for working with the government, its employees and the environmentalists, instead of opposing them. While Stephens Timber was forever being gossiped about for being ruthless and unsympathetic to both employees and the public, Daniels Logging was considered a cornerstone of Oregon industry.

Ashley gritted her teeth in determination. All that was about to change. Then both Trevor Daniels and Claud Stephens would understand what it meant to deal with her. She intended to make Stephens Timber a model company, come hell or high water.

Ashley's thoughts were grim, but she had trouble believing that Claud would actually try to force Trevor out of the campaign, either by the phony bribery charges or this last, unbelievable mishap with Trevor's car. Claud was too much of a coward to do anything so bold. It wasn't his style to take unnecessary risks. And none of the records indicated foul play, at least she hadn't found anything out of the ordinary.

Ashley breathed a silent prayer begging that her instincts about her cousin were right.

Once back in the cabin, she managed to steer the conversation in any direction but on Trevor's career or the past. Trevor seemed to be taking pains to avoid another argument as well. The afternoon faded slowly into nightfall.

It wasn't a traditional Christmas by any standards. No candles, roast goose, lighted tree or carolers gave the holy day the special traditions Ashley had observed in the past. However, being alone in the mountains, wrapped in the strong arms of the one man who had ever meant anything to her, made this Christmas more special and intimate than any she could remember celebrating. What better way to observe the holiday than to share it with the man she loved with all her heart?

That night, lying in the security of Trevor's embrace, listening to the regular beating of his heart as he slept, Ashley cried soft tears of quiet happiness and whispered a silent prayer of gratitude for the special moments she had shared with him.

The cabin was illuminated only by the glowing, blood-red embers of the fire and the pale moonglow reflecting on the soft blanket of snow outdoors. The paned windows were frosted from the cold and the only sound breaking the stillness of the night was the occasional hiss of the fire as it encountered pitch.

Ashley closed her eyes and tried not to think that this night might be the last she would ever spend with him.

The sharp ring of the telephone brought Ashley out of a deep and trouble-free sleep. Trevor groaned, shifted on the bed and then continued to snore peacefully without even opening an eye. The last few weeks had exhausted him.

Carefully, so as not to disturb him, Ashley slipped from beneath the covers, grabbed her robe and hurried down the stairs to answer the phone in the kitchen. As she picked up the receiver, she pushed the tangled strands of her hair out of her eyes.

"Hello?"

"Ashley!"

With a sinking sensation, Ashley recognized the smug male voice of her cousin. "Good morning, Claud," she replied quietly, careful not to awaken Trevor. After sneaking a careful glance up the stairs, she walked to the far side of the small room, stretching the telephone cord its full length.

"What's going on?" Claud demanded after a few strangling moments of silence.

"What's going on?" she repeated casually, though her heart had seemed to miss a beat. She knew in an instant that Claud was on to her plan to help Trevor. "What do you mean?"

"Knock it off, Ashley. I know that you've been checking up on me."

Ashley's nerves were stretched to the breaking point.

She had to support herself by leaning a slim and sagging shoulder against the wall. Somehow, despite the dread constricting her throat, she managed to keep her voice steady.

"Of course I have. You've known that all along. That's why I quit my job. I decided that Stephens Timber needed me."

"So why are all the reports being sent to the Bend office?" Claud asked in a voice filled with gruff indignation. "It looks to me like you're doing a major audit of the books."

"I told you I wanted to check all of the records," she replied evenly.

"There's more to it than that," Claud accused. Ashley could almost hear the wheels turning in his mind.

"Just a simple, all-encompassing audit."

"We have accountants to do that."

"I prefer to look over everything myself."

"You can stop whitewashing, Ashley. I know you're up to something. I just want to know what it is."

"Nothing all that mysterious, Claud. I just want to personally examine the books."

"In Bend? Over Christmas? Give me a break, for Christ's sake. You're supposed to be on a vacation."

"I am."

"With the company records?" He was clearly dubious.

"Right."

"You sure know how to have a good time," he mocked, openly challenging her.

Ashley smiled grimly to herself. "I'm not the kind of person to shirk my responsibilities, Claud. You may as well face that fact right now. Either you can work with me or against me, but we both know who makes the ultimate decisions regarding the company."

"And you just love to rub my nose in it, don't you?" Claud said disgustedly.

"Only when I'm forced to." She let out a weary sigh of frustration and tried to assuage her cousin's growing suspicions. "Look, Claud, what I'm doing is merely routine. Now that my job with the college is over, I think I should spend as much time as possible acquainting myself with the company books. Otherwise I won't be all that effective, will I?

"I intend to be more than just a figurehead with this corporation. It's my duty to learn everything there is to know about Stephens Timber."

"So you called John Ellis? Why didn't you get in touch with me?"

Nervously she twisted the phone cord, but she forced her voice to remain determined. "I did. Remember? You were the one who balked at sending me the information I needed."

"So you went behind my back."

"I did what I had to do."

Claud was still angry, but his suspicions seemed to be placated, at least for the moment. "So when will you be in Portland?" he asked, changing the subject.

"Soon. I don't have a precise date, but sometime before the first of the year." Ashley wanted to end the conversation as quickly as possible, before Trevor woke up. "I've got things to do right now, but I'll talk to you when I'm back in town. I'm sure you'll be interested to know how the books look."

"I already do," Claud muttered before hanging up.

When Ashley replaced the receiver, she let out a long sigh of relief and turned toward the stairs. She found herself face-to-face with Trevor. His expression was murderous.

"So someone at Stephens Timber tipped Claud off," he charged.

Ashley stood her ground, refusing to back down to the anger in the set of his jaw. "Claud's suspicious, if that's what you mean."

"What I mean, dear lady," Trevor spat out, "is that no one in that damned timber company of yours can keep his mouth shut." A deadly gleam of anger sparked in his eyes. "Or else you were just stringing me along all the time. This entire meeting was just a charade."

"I didn't come knocking on your door," Ashley pointed out, her eyes widening in disbelief.

"But you didn't exactly fight me off, did you?" he threw back at her, his angry glare burning through to her soul.

A small part of Ashley wanted to wither and die. Could this be the same man she loved with all of her heart? Did he really believe that she had sold him out? The fists rammed against his hips and the tense muscles straining beneath his shirt indicated that he was barely holding on to his temper, as if he really thought she had betrayed him.

"I wanted to be with you, Trevor."

"Why?" he demanded, taking a step nearer to her and gripping her shoulders with his tense fingers. "Why? So that you could get close to me? Are you just like the rest of your family, Ashley? Would you do anything to protect your name?" he asked, his words slicing through her heart as easily as a razor.

"Of course not!"

"No?" Disbelief contorted his rugged features. His eyes narrowed in unspoken accusation. "You didn't believe a word I said, did you? And you had no intention of holding up your end of the bargain."

"You know better than that," she insisted, her words trembling as they passed her lips. Dread slowly inched up her spine.

"What I know is that you used me, lady. You slept with me just so you could get close—see how I planned my campaign—so that you could protect your timber empire."

Ashley was too numb to speak. The fingers pushing into her flesh were painful, but not nearly as agonizing as the words coming from Trevor's lips.

"You missed your calling, lady," he stated. "You should have been an actress. That performance you gave me last night was damned near convincing!"

Without thinking, she raised her hand as if to slap him, but the fingers tightening on her shoulders prevented the blow from landing.

"You bastard," she hissed, tears beginning to run down her face.

"Like I said before—I call 'em as I see 'em."

"Then you're a blind man!" She pulled herself free of his grasp, lifting her head above the treachery of his insults. "You never could believe that all I ever wanted was you. You never could trust me and you never will."

A muscle worked at the corner of his jaw. For a moment the anger on his face was replaced by raw and naked pain. But just as quickly as it had appeared, his misery was hidden and Trevor's blue eyes became as cold as the midnight sun.

"Just remember that you and I have a bargain, lady. I expect you to keep your end."

She took in a shuddering breath. "And if I don't? What will you do, Trevor?"

"I swear to you that I'll destroy Stephens Timber Corporation and drag your family's name through the mud until it will never come clean."

"So much for the image of the kind and just politician," she threw back at him. "You'd better watch out, Senator, that gilded reputation you work so hard to keep in the public view might just become tarnished."

"I don't give a damn about my reputation, Ashley, and you know it."

"What I know is that nothing matters to you—nothing other than your damned career. That's all it's ever been with you, Trevor." His head snapped upward, as if she'd struck him. "I was foolish enough to think that you cared for me once," she continued, unable to stop the words from tumbling from her lips. "But now I'm a little older and wiser."

He looked as if he was about to protest. His broad shoulders sagged and he shook his head, as if he couldn't stand to hear another word. "If only you knew," he whispered.

"I'll keep up my end of the bargain," she stated wearily, "just to prove you wrong."

He managed a bitter smile before he turned toward the door. She stood in the hallway, unable to move, her arms cradled protectively over her breasts, and watched in miserable silence as Trevor slowly pulled on his boots, buttoned his jacket and placed an unsteady hand on the door.

"Good-bye, Ashley," he whispered, casting one last glance over his shoulder in her direction.

She couldn't even murmur his name. Her throat was hot and swollen with the grief of losing him again. In an instant he was gone, leaving her cold and bereft, just as he had done nearly eight years ago. . . .

She slumped to the floor totally alone and surveyed the cabin with new eyes. Was this the place, the very spot, where her love for Trevor had begun?

The tears ran down her face in earnest as she remembered the first time she had ever laid eyes upon the ruggedly handsome face of Trevor Daniels.

Chapter Seven

Eight years ago, at the age of twenty-four, Ashley had been aware of the vicious rivalry between Stephens Timber and Daniels Logging. The rumors surrounding her father and some of his business practices couldn't be completely ignored, although Ashley chalked most of the gossip up to envy. Lazarus Stephens was a man of wealth and power. That was enough to start the eager fires of gossip running wild throughout the Oregon timber industry.

After she had graduated from a university in Paris, Ashley had taken a job with her father's company. In the year since she had started with the firm, she had held several positions; it had been apparent from the start that Lazarus was grooming his only child for the presidency of Stephens Timber, if—and when—he decided to retire. Ashley had been only too willing to follow in her father's footsteps. The only person who'd seemed to mind at all was her cousin Claud, who had been with Stephens Timber for several years and was jealous of his younger cousin.

Though she didn't like to admit it, Ashley realized that she had been spoiled beyond reproach by her overly indulgent father. Lazarus had lavished Ashley with anything she wanted after her mother's death. Expensive schooling abroad, flashy European sports cars, exotic vacations anywhere in the world; nothing had been too good for Lazarus's only child.

The end result was that Ashley had grown up pampered and expected to be treated like a princess. In a word, she was spoiled. And at twenty-four, it had begun to bother her. Her conscience had begun to twinge, if only slightly.

On her first vacation since starting to work with the company, Ashley decided to cancel her planned Mediterranean cruise, and instead, she spent her free time at her father's rustic cabin in the Cascade Mountains not far from Bend. For the first time in her life, Ashley began to recognize that the world didn't revolve around her or Stephens Timber. The glamorous life she had heretofore led began to lose its luster and appeal.

Even the image of her father was beginning to dim. She told herself that she had overheard too many idle tongues wagging, but she couldn't shake the feeling that something wasn't quite right with all of Lazarus's business dealings. Though she was loath to admit it, Ashley was beginning to wonder about the truth in the rumor surrounding Robert Daniels's disappearance. It was one subject her father avoided like the plague. He would never discuss anything to do with Robert Daniels or what had come between Lazarus and the man who had once been his business partner. Not even with Ashley. At the mention of Robert Daniels's name, Lazarus would visibly pale and then gruffly dismiss the subject. For the past year, ever since she had left the security of school abroad, Lazarus's animosity toward Robert Daniels had begun to make

Ashley uneasy. She needed time to think things out and reevaluate her pampered life. And so, at the first opportunity, Ashley took off for the mountains.

The solitude of the rustic retreat made her depend solely upon herself for the first time in her life. The cabin hadn't been used since the summer before and smelled musty. As soon as she had changed into faded jeans, Ashley opened the windows, aired the rooms, washed the linen and scrubbed floors feverishly. No job was too difficult. She stacked wood in the garage and washed windows inside and out. At night her muscles ached, but she fell into a restless sleep with a feeling of vast accomplishment.

For the first week, she spent all of her time at the cabin either cleaning, experimenting in the rustic kitchen, reading or riding the horses that her father kept on the place. Zach Lambert usually took care of the two geldings, but while Ashley was staying at the cabin, she looked after the horses, much to Zach's obvious disapproval.

It was the second weekend since she had come to the mountains when the trouble began. Zach's daughter, Sara, who had been a childhood friend of Ashley's, insisted that Ashley come to a party Sara was hostessing for some of her friends from college. Ashley wasn't in the mood for a party and didn't want to attend, but found the prospect of spending another afternoon by herself just as dull. Besides, Ashley rationalized, there wasn't a polite way of declining. The Lambert place was just up the lane, and both Sara and her parents knew that Ashley was alone. There was no choice but to attend the party and hope for the best.

Ashley walked into the Lambert cabin knowing she had made a big mistake. The only person she recognized was Sara, and as hostess, Sara was dashing in and out, from one knot of jeans-clad guests to another. She smiled and waved to Ashley before hurrying into the kitchen to replenish a tray of hors d'oeuvres.

Ashley wandered through the modern cedar cabin and captured the attention of more than one pair of appreciative male eyes. In her backless apricot sundress, with her long black hair flowing loosely past her shoulders, she looked the part of a rich man's daughter.

Her green eyes moved over the other guests with cool disinterest, the smile on her face well practiced but vague. She wondered why she had accepted the invitation to the party at all and hoped she could find a viable excuse to leave the festivities early and return to the solitude of her father's cabin. She needed time alone to think about her life, her father and the business.

She accepted a glass of wine before edging toward the sliding glass door leading to the back of the cabin. Feeling the need to escape from the laughter and thick cigarette smoke, Ashley slipped out of the cabin and away from the crowd.

When she stepped onto the deck, a tall, broadshouldered man approached her. He was older than she, but probably not yet thirty. His face was handsome, if somewhat angular, and his eyes were the deepest shade of blue she had ever seen.

He studied her intently, not bothering to hide his interest. Ashley experienced the disturbing feeling that she should recognize him. There was something familiar about him that made her uneasy.

The set of his mouth was slightly cynical for so young a man, and a few soft lines etched his forehead, giving him a wiser, more worldly appearance than could be expected for a man his age. His thick hair ruffled slightly in the wind and Ashley noticed that the chestnut color was streaked with gold—as if this man spent many hours in the sun.

Probably a cowboy, she thought to herself, glancing at his worn jeans and boots.

He stopped a few feet from her and leaned against the railing of the deck, supporting himself with his elbows as he stared brazenly at her.

"Is there something I can do for you?" she asked, tossing her wavy black hair behind her shoulders.

His thoughtful eyes narrowed. "Do I know you?"

"There's an original line," she retorted.

"It's not a line."

"Then, I doubt it." Ashley was sure that she would remember such a proud, defiant face.

A glimmer of recognition flashed in his eyes. "You're Ashley Stephens," he stated, as if the name meant something to him.

"And you're . . ." She lifted her dark brows expressively, begging his indulgence.

"Trevor Daniels."

Ashley's smile fell from her face. The name hit her like a ton of bricks. She was standing face-to-face with Robert Daniels's son. Though she had never met him, she had seen pictures that had been taken years ago. All the whispered innuendos she had heard about her father flitted through her mind. She swallowed back the sickening feeling rising from her stomach.

"I think it's about time we got to know each other,"

Trevor stated, his calm belied by an angry muscle working overtime near the back of his jaw.

"Why?"

"Because we have so much in common, you and I."

She looked disdainfully up at him. "I doubt that."

"Sure we do. Let's start with our fathers. Weren't they in business together once?"

"If you'll excuse me," Ashley whispered, taking a step away from this formidable man.

"I don't think so." A hand, large, powerful and surprisingly warm, reached out and took hold of her arm, spinning her back to face him. "I want to talk to you."

"About what?"

His face drew into a vindictive scowl. "Let's start with what you know about my father."

Other guests had joined them on the deck and were showing more than casual interest in the confrontation between Trevor Daniels and the attractive, raven-haired woman. Ashley's gaze flickered to the unfamiliar faces before returning to Robert Daniels's angry son. "I don't know anything about him," she whispered.

"But your father does."

Her eyes turned frigid. "I'm not interested in causing a scene, Mr. Daniels."

"I'll bet not."

"Then maybe we could drop this discussion."

"Not on your life."

"I have no idea what my father does or doesn't know about your family."

"Tell me about it."

Once again she glanced at the interested eyes trained

upon her. "Not here!" She jerked her arm away from his grasp with as much pride as she could muster.

"Where then?"

He crossed his arms over his chest and eyed her speculatively. That intense, midnight-blue gaze started at her feet and inched up her body, appraising her. By the time his eyes had returned to hers, Ashley felt the stain of unwanted embarrassment burn her cheeks. "Let's talk about this in private."

"Anywhere you suggest," he agreed with a sarcastic curve of his sensual lips.

She had to think quickly. Guests had crowded the small Lambert cabin. Ashley was sure that there was no privacy anywhere in the house. "My father has a cabin . . . not far from here. After the party . . ."

"Now!"

She was about to protest but the hardening of his jaw convinced her that he meant business. After hasty apologies given to a slightly confused Sara, Ashley left the Lambert cabin with Trevor Daniels, his boots crunching ominously on the gravel, striding behind her.

Without an invitation, or so much as a look in her direction, Trevor got into the passenger seat of her sporty Mercedes convertible and for the first time in her life, Ashley was embarrassed by the ostentatious display of wealth.

The short drive was accomplished in stilted silence. Only the dull whine of the engine and the tires spinning on loose gravel disturbed the quiet of the mountains.

Ashley roared to a stop near the garage, pulled on the emergency brake and shut off the engine. "We can talk here," she suggested, but Trevor was already getting out of the car.

Damn the man! He intended to go inside. Just the thought of being alone with him made Ashley's pulse quicken. She chalked it up to the fact that he was Robert Daniels's son. That alone made her nervous.

Her hands were shaking when she unlocked the door, opened it and silently invited him inside.

Once in the den, Trevor looked at the less-than-opulent surroundings with a cynical arch of his brow. "Spending a quiet vacation in the mountains?" he mocked, his skeptical gaze taking in the interior before returning to her.

"I was."

"A change of pace from your usual style," he observed as he walked across the rustic room and stood near the window, pretending interest in the view of the craggy slopes of Mount Washington. He placed a boot on a footstool and leaned on one elbow as he studied the view. His jeans stretched tightly over his hips and thighs and Ashley had to look away from the erotic pose. Was it intentional? For a moment she wondered if he intended to seduce her, but pushed the rash thought aside. He seemed like a rational man, not one who might seek revenge against her father by compromising her.

But if he did, how would she react? The thought quickened her heartbeat. Trevor turned to look at her and Ashley realized he expected her to reply to his comment.

"How would you know what my usual style is?" she asked, her throat uncommonly dry.

Trevor grinned cryptically before moving away from the window and settling into one of the worn leather chairs near the empty fireplace. "There's a lot I know about you," he admitted, watching the slightly confused knit of her brow. "I know that you studied art in Marseilles before switching majors and universities, that you prefer BMWs to Chevys, that you would rather shop in San Francisco than L.A., and that you don't, for the most part, spend time alone in the Cascades."

Ashley listened to his observations with her breath catching in her throat. Either he was incredibly lucky at first impressions or he had spent a lot of time studying her. It occurred to her that their meeting at the Lamberts' wasn't by chance.

She gambled. "So why did you come looking for me?"

He didn't deny it. "I wanted your help."

She was wary. Her elegant brow puckered suspiciously. "But why?"

"I want to find out what happened to my father."

"I have no idea where he is," she replied honestly.

He thought for a minute, but seemed to believe her. His broad shoulders slumped slightly and he changed the subject, convinced that he would get no further with Lazarus Stephens's stubborn child. "So what are you doing up here, anyway?" Once again his merciless eyes traveled over the interior of the room, lingering for just a moment on the book Ashley had been reading. He picked it up and frowned. It was written in French. *"Les Miserables."* He looked at her sharply. "What're you trying to do—see how the other half lives?"

"Improve my mind," was her pert retort. Suddenly she wanted him out of the cabin and out of her life. There was something enigmatic and dangerous about him, something that touched her and wouldn't let go. . . .

"Why did you come here?" he demanded, blue eyes seeking hers.

"I needed a vacation."

"You work for your father."

"That's right." How much did he know about her? Why did he care?

Trevor glanced from her to the loft, and back again. His fingers were tight with tension when he pushed them through the coarse strands of his hair. "It just doesn't fit," he muttered.

"What doesn't?"

"You . . . this . . ." He held up the book, making a sweeping gesture to include everything in the cabin. Finally, somewhat defeated, he returned his gaze to her. "You're not exactly what I expected."

"Sorry to disappoint you," she replied, noticing the hardening of his angular jaw. "Maybe you should have done your homework a little better."

He slowly rose from the chair and walked back to the middle of the room where she was standing. "I hate to admit it, lady," he whispered, "but you haven't disappointed me at all." He reached out. The tips of his fingers trailed the length of her bare arm, sending chills of anticipation through her veins, before lingering at her wrist.

"I haven't been much help to you."

"Yet." He stepped closer, and his gentle fingers didn't release her wrist. He tugged on her arm, bringing her body next to his. Ashley knew that he was about to kiss her and that it was madness, but the thrill of it all—the excitement of his touch—made it difficult to resist.

For a heart-stopping moment, she felt his hesitation, as

if he, too, was unsure. "This can't happen," he whispered just before his lips pressed urgently against hers.

Ashley closed her eyes and swallowed against the persuasive warmth his kiss inspired. His fingers caught in the strands of her hair, holding her close, brushing against the exposed muscles of her back, begging for more intimacy. She felt her body, as if ripe with need, respond to him.

His fingers splayed against her naked back, forcing her closer to him. The gentle pressure of his chest crushing against her breasts created a savage fire that burned bright in the deepest part of her.

Her breasts ached for his touch and when an exploratory hand cupped the restrained fullness, she lifted her arms upward and wound them around his neck, thus offering more of herself to him. *This is crazy*, her mind screamed from somewhere in the dim reaches of her rational thoughts, but she couldn't stop the torrid fires beginning to consume her.

His head lowered and his lips nuzzled the exposed length of her throat, leaving in their wake a dewy path of desire. He kissed the hollow of her throat, his lips hovering over the sensitive pulse in soft warm breaths. Ashley responded, her heartbeat quickening convulsively.

Slowly, he pressed on her shoulders, forcing her to kneel with him. Then, when she was positioned to his liking, he lifted his head from her neck and gazed steadily into her eyes, watching her reaction as he leisurely slipped the thin strap of her halter dress over her left shoulder. She shuddered in anticipation, but continued to hold his gaze.

The dress fell open and one breast spilled out of the soft apricot fabric. Ashley felt an embarrassed blush rise upward through her body as Trevor gazed at her, his blue eyes fierce with desire. Tenderly his fingers came forward and traced the straining dark peak.

Ashley inhaled deeply, closing her eyes against the warm sensations swirling within her. How could one man make her feel as if she would do anything he commanded? She told herself that she was being reckless, playing with fire, but she didn't care. All she could think about was wanting hlm, a wild lust that was traveling in wicked circles within her body, aching for release.

"I've wanted you for a long time," he admitted, his voice rough. He was half lying now, and the warmth of his breath fanned her breast.

"You . . . you don't even know me."

"That's where you're wrong, sweet lady. I've known you for so long, so very long."

"Just because I'm Lazarus Stephens's daughter."

His blue eyes were wicked when he looked up at her. "Just because you're Lazarus Stephens's beautiful daughter." Gingerly, his lips closed over the rosy tip of her breast. The denial that had been forming on her lips was never spoken. She could think of nothing other than letting him touch her, assuaging the bittersweet ache that was beginning to throb within her.

His tongue teased her gently and she moaned for more of the savage pleasure. Her fingers twined in his hair, forcing him closer. He took more of her into the warm cavern of his mouth. One hand splayed against her naked back, while the other softly kneaded her breast as he suckled and drew out the sweetness she offered.

Slowly, his lips moved from the naked breast to the delicious mound covered in soft apricot fabric. The nipple was taut and straining against the dress and Trevor placed his mouth over the covered tip, suckling and wetting the fabric with his mouth.

Ashley's head was spinning crazily and she knew that if she didn't stop his masterful lovemaking now, she wouldn't be able to break the magical spell of love he was weaving.

"Touch me," he whispered as he lifted his head and wound his fingers in the ebony silk of her tangled hair and tugged on it, forcing her head backward so that he could nuzzle her exposed throat. Gently he guided her hand to the evidence of his desire.

Ashley let her fingers linger slightly on his straining jeans. The low moan from the back of his throat convinced her that he wanted her as much as she wanted him.

"Oh, God," she whispered. Slowly, she withdrew her hand. " I . . . I can't." Tears of frustration stung her eyes.

"Shhh . . . Ashley," he said. He kissed her eyelids and tasted the salt of her tears. "Just let me love you."

"I don't know you, Trevor," she said, trying desperately to rise above the lustful urges of her body. Never before had she been so tempted by a man, so ravaged by desire. Never had the ache within her throbbed for a release only he could offer.

"You will," he promised, gently rising on one elbow. His eyes took in the tangled disarray of her blue-black hair, the mystic allure of her green eyes and the swelling invitation of her firm breasts. "I've waited a long time for you," he vowed, as one long finger traced the column of her throat, past the hill of her naked breast, to probe beneath the apricot dress draped over her waist. "I can wait a few more days."

"And what makes you think that I'll agree?"

He smiled despite the strangling ache in his loins. "Bcause you want me as badly as I want you."

"You're so damned sure of yourself, aren't you?" she asked, her breath still ragged.

"When I have to be." His finger traced the definition of her lowest rib. "You and I have so much in common, you see."

"So you think it's fate. Right?"

"Most definitely not."

"What then?"

His eyes drove into hers as if he were searching for the darkest part of her soul. "It's a case of a man being obsessed with a woman."

She laughed at the absurdity of the situation, holding the bodice of her dress over her breast. "Obsession? You can't be serious!"

His eyes darkened dangerously. "Just wait and see how serious I am." With that, he hoisted himself from the floor and offered a hand to Ashley, who accepted his help.

When she straightened and managed to slip her shoulder strap back into place, he took hold of her arms and roughly pulled her against him. His lips moved suggestively over hers. "I'll see you tomorrow."

Her breath caught in her throat. "I have plans," she offered lamely.

"Cancel them." With his final words, he left her and walked out of the door.

"Bastard," she muttered under her breath, determined never to see him again.

* * *

Ashley spent a sleepless night dreaming of making wild and wanton love to Trevor and in the morning she admonished herself for her immature lust. She told herself that some of the fascination she felt was because he was the adversary—the one thing in life she had to deny herself.

"He'll use you," she warned herself whenever she caught herself thinking about him that morning, but she couldn't help but look out the window in anticipation whenever she heard a vehicle rumble down the lane.

At ten o'clock there was a knock on the door. Ashley's heart was racing when she answered it and discovered Trevor, his cynical smile in place, standing on the small porch.

"I thought you were going to be busy today," he mocked. His blue eyes twinkled devilishly as they raked possessively over her body.

The anger she wanted to feel refused to surface. "It wasn't anything important." She moved out of the doorway, allowing him to enter. "I thought you might like to go on a picnic."

"That's not exactly what I had in mind—"

"I'll bet not. But I've already saddled the horses and thrown together a lunch," she replied, trying to overlook the hint of seduction in his intense gaze. "It'll be fun."

"Promise?"

"Guaranteed."

He smiled before laughinig out loud. "You're full of surprises, aren't you?" he asked with a pleased expression softening his face. "The daughter of Lazarus Stephens saddling horses and making sandwiches—it just doesn't fit."

"Maybe what doesn't fit is your stereotype of spoiled little rich girls who refuse to get their hands dirty."

"Maybe." He shrugged his shoulders and followed her into the kitchen. Ashley pulled a bottle of wine out of the refrigerator and shoved it into the already bulging leather bag, which was slung over the back of one of the kitchen chairs.

Trevor watched her pack. "Saddlebags?"

"How else are we going to carry all this food? What did you expect? A picnic basket?"

"I suppose."

Ashley smiled to herself. "Then I guess my first impression of you was wrong."

"Oh?"

"You're not a cowboy?"

"Far from it." Trevor chuckled to himself at the thought. "I'm working at a law firm in Bend for the summer."

"A lawyer?"

"Not yet. But soon, I hope."

"You're still in school?"

"Willamette University," he replied, taking the bulging leather pouch and slinging it over his shoulder. "I hope to take the bar exam in January."

"And what then, counselor?" she teased, her green eyes dancing merrily. Strange as it seemed, she hadn't felt this happy in years. She was comfortable with this man; the fact that he was her father's rival's son added just a little bit of daring to the relationship.

He hesitated for a moment, sizing her up, and decided there was no reason to hide the truth. "Politics."

There was something in the way he said the word that gave Ashley pause. "Whatever for?"

He grinned cryptically. "To change things, of course."

He held the back door for her and then waited somewhat impatiently while she locked it.

They walked together down the short path that led to the stables. Diablo and Gustave were tied to the fence and nickered softly when Ashley approached.

"Looks like rain," Trevor remarked, eyeing the cloudy sky.

"You're not going to weasel out of this," Ashley stated. "I worked all morning planning this thing, and we're going on a picnic come hell or high water."

"Whatever you say, ma'am," he drawled with a bad western affectation.

"You do know how to ride?"

Trevor positioned the saddlebag on Diablo's broad, black back. "A little." Diablo stamped a dark hoof and tossed his head, jingling the bridle in contempt.

"It's all right." Ashley soothed the agitated horse with a soft pat on the neck before taking the reins of the smaller horse and swinging into the saddle.

They rode together in silence, Ashley leading the way on Gustave, a fiery bay quarter horse who had the bad habit of shying away from any noise. "Don't be such a scaredy-cat," Ashley admonished as she rubbed Gustave's thick neck.

The dusty path led uphill through sagebrush and pine trees. After traveling for three miles, they reached the spot Ashley remembered from her childhood. It was a barren ridge with an enthralling view of the snow-covered Cascades.

When she stopped, Trevor pulled up next to her and cast an approving eye at the view. "Worth the ride," he muttered as he studied the mountainous horizon. The blue sky had filled with gray clouds that gathered around the highest peaks. "Could be in for some rain," he reminded her.

"Then we'd better eat now," Ashley stated as she swung out of the saddle. "I'm starved."

While Ashley spread a blanket and arranged the food, Trevor tethered the horses. Ashley smiled as she watched him work. "Not bad for a tenderfoot," she teased.

Trevor smiled and took a seat next to her on the blanket.

The first drops of rain started to fall just as Ashley poured the wine. As quickly as possible, they drank the wine and feasted on cold chicken, cheese, grapes and French bread. Even with the threat of rain, the meal was perfect. Ashley, as she laughed at Trevor's witticisms, wondered vaguely if she was falling in love.

Because the storm looked as if it would worsen, Trevor repacked the saddlebags and they started back to the cabin much earlier than Ashley had planned. She had envisioned a warm, lazy afternoon with Trevor, learning more about him.

The summer shower began in earnest about halfway back to the cabin and Ashley was forced to urge Gustave into a trot. Once back on familiar soil, the quarter horse sprinted for the barn with Diablo on his tail.

Ashley was breathless by the time they were back in the stables and her long black hair was tangled from the fast ride.

Trevor unsaddled and cooled the horses while Ashley returned to the cabin, started a fire and unpacked the saddlebags. The wind picked up and the sky grew overcast, darkening the interior of the cabin. Rain pelted against the windows.

The fire had just caught and Ashley was sitting on the hearth attempting to brush the knots from her hair, when Trevor came back into the cabin. Raindrops lingered in his dark hair and reflected the warmth of the crackling flames. The interior of the cabin was filled with the scent of burning wood and hot coffee.

"I . . . I made some coffee," Ashley stated, straightening and setting the brush aside.

Trevor walked across the short distance separating them and his magnetic blue eyes never released hers. Ashley's pulse quickened at the nearness of him. When his cold lips pressed hungrily against hers, she knew that she would never find the strength to deny him again. His strong, muscular body was tense. She could feel his want in his restraint.

His tongue tested and probed and her lips parted willingly for him. She would offer everything to this exciting, mysterious man, hoping that he would care for her . . . if only a little.

A rush of liquid heat began to build within her, sending pulsating messages throughout her body. She couldn't think or move when his warm, persuasive lips lingered on her neck and nibbled at the sensitive skin near her ear.

"Tell me you want me," he whispered, his demand gentle.

"You know—"

"Say it!"

"I want you," she admitted hoarsely.

"Why?"

"I don't know—"

"Why, damn it!" He gave her shoulders a shake and forced her to look in his eyes. "Tell me it's not just a game with you. That you're interested in more than a quick one-night stand with the son of Robert Daniels."

The words stung, but she bravely returned his gaze. "Oh, Trevor, it's not because you're a Daniels," she whispered. "I know that I want you and not just for the rest of the afternoon."

His relief seemed genuine and the lines of frustration marring his brow relaxed as his lips found hers in a kiss that was as tender as it was urgent.

His fingers slowly unbuttoned her blouse and he paused only to kiss her downy white skin when the fabric began to gap. Her breasts strained against the wet cotton and tingled in swollen anticipation when his tongue probed near the lace edging of her flimsy bra.

"No more excuses," he whispered against the ripeness of her aching nipples.

Ashley swallowed against the dryness settling in her throat. "I only want to be with you," she murmured, sucking in her breath as he unhooked the front clasp of her bra and pushed both it and her blouse over her shoulders to be discarded in a wrinkled heap on the floor. Then, gently, using his weight, he forced her to the floor and let his hands run in sensual circles over her smooth, white skin. Though the ache in his loins burned uncomfortably, he forced himself to go slowly, to give as much pleasure as he would extract from the voluptuous daughter of Lazarus Stephens.

She was lying next to him, and her damp, black hair fell over the white mounds of her delicious breasts, brushing over the taut, protruding nipples when she moved her head.

Slowly he descended, and when his mouth covered one

rosy point, she moaned in pleasure, running her fingers through the thick, damp strands of his hair. Never had she felt such ecstasy and torment. Without considering her actions, she began to unbutton his shirt, forcing it off his shoulders and letting her fingers run over the tight muscles, the mat of curly black hair and the hard male nipples. His breathing became as ragged as her own and Ashley knew that there was no going back. Tonight she would give herself willingly, gloriously to this man. The fiery union of their bodies would be equaled only by the blending of their souls.

When his fingers toyed with the waistband of her jeans she didn't resist. She belonged to Trevor and she felt an overwhelming sense of relief when his strong hands forced the denim fabric to slide easily over her hips, down her legs and past her ankles to find the same fate as her crumpled blouse.

His fingers lingered on her legs and the warmth within her grew. His eyes held hers as he slowly unzipped his jeans and kicked them off. She saw the reflection of the fire in the passion of his gaze. They were naked together, one man and one woman, high in the privacy of the proud Cascades. The smell of coffee and pitchy wood mingled with the scents of rainwater and sweat to blend together in a sensual aroma.

When he came to her, it was the most natural act she had ever experienced. Slowly he lowered his body over hers, positioning himself so that he could read the expression on her face, withholding the urge to take her in a quick eruption of desire.

At first he had planned to bed her quickly and forget her, but he knew now that he was forever lost to her. He wanted Ashley to feel the exquisite pleasure of their mating.

His face was tight, the lines of strain evident when his head lowered and his lips touched hers at the very moment that she felt his desire touch her soul.

"Trevor," she moaned in resplendent agony as he slowly moved within her. "Please . . . please . . ." Her words were fuel to the fire of his white-hot desire. The rhythm quickened until, at last, he could hold back no longer. With a rush of unbound passion, he let go, and Ashley felt the shudder of his release as he collapsed upon her. His weight was a welcome burden. She wrapped her arms around his torso and closed her eyes against the tears of joy threatening to overtake her.

Was it love she felt for this man or merely lust?

The affair had run a torrid course through the rest of the summer. Whenever Ashley would get the chance, she would leave the Willamette Valley and meet Trevor in a private tryst of love in the Cascades: After that first moment of triumph and uncertainty, Ashley knew that she loved Trevor Daniels, not because his father was a rival to Stephens Timber Corporation, but because he was the most exciting and wonderful man she had ever met.

It was a glorious summer filled with dreams and promises, laughter and love. For the first time in her life, Ashley learned how to care for someone other than herself. It felt wonderful. She wanted to shout her love for Trevor from the mountaintops.

Somehow—Ashley suspected that Claud was the

source—Lazarus found out that she was having an affair with Trevor. Her father was livid.

"How could you do this to me?" he had raged. Seated at the scarred wooden desk in his den, he seemed suddenly old.

"It just happened, Dad," she had tried to explain.

"Just happened! Don't tell me you're that naïve, for God's sake! All that schooling in France—didn't you learn a damned thing! I'll bet Daniels planned this affair all along."

"That's preposterous," Ashley replied indignantly, but a niggling doubt entered her mind. Hadn't Trevor as much as admitted that he had been looking for her, that he had wanted her for years? Was their affair just a way to seek revenge against her father?

"You're so blinded by love that you can't see the truth when it stares you in the face," Lazarus charged, his complexion turning scarlet. His hands raised into the air in a gesture of defeat and supplication for divine intervention. "That son of Robert Daniels is just using you as a weapon against me! He's obviously trying to dig up some dirt on our family and find some way—no matter how obscure— to blame me for his father's disappearance!"

"This has nothing to do with Robert Daniels," Ashley insisted, but she couldn't forget her first heated conversation with Trevor at Sara Lambert's party.

"The hell it doesn't!" Lazarus's fist crashed onto the desk, rattling the drawers.

"Dad, I love him!" Ashley cried.

"Oh, for crying out loud!" Lazarus braced himself against the desk in his office. His eyes slid from Ashley to the view of the Portland city lights before returning, condemningly, to his only child. "Can't you see that he's using you? If that bastard can't find a way to ruin my reputation, he'll settle for you and yours. He knows that by seducing you, he's wounding me." He ran agitated fingers through his thinning hair and his large shoulders slumped in defeat.

Though Ashley's heart went out to him, she couldn't deny the love she felt for Trevor. "You'd better get used to this, Dad," Ashley warned rebelliously, though her faith in Trevor was beginning to waver.

"And why's that?"

"Because I'm going to marry him."

"Out of the question!" Lazarus's watery blue eyes flamed in indignation. "The man isn't even your social equal, for Christ's sake!" He tapped his fingers restlessly on the desk. "If I were you, I wouldn't get my hopes up. Trevor Daniels has no intention of marrying you. To him, you're nothing more than a quick affair. Take my advice and get rid of him. If you want to get married, why not someone with a little class, like Richard Jennings?"

Ashley stormed out of her father's estate, intent on proving him wrong. Trevor was waiting for her at Neskowin on the coast and she was sure, with just the right amount of persuasion, she could coax him into marrying her now, before he finished law school.

She was sadly mistaken.

The weekend at the beach was wonderful and she kept the fight with her father a secret. They spent the days walking on the rain-drenched sand, and during the nights they lay together, sipping imported wine, warming their feet on the bricks of the fireplace and staring out at the black waves crashing furiously in the winter's storm before making incredible love and promising their lives to each other.

It was heavenly and it ended.

When Ashley finally explained that she wanted to get married right away, Trevor was adamant. He wanted to finish law school and establish his career before taking on the added responsibilities of a family.

"Then what am I supposed to do, sit around and wait while you decide whether you want to run for the presidency?" she replied caustically, the pain of his rejection cutting her to the bone.

His features hardened at the mention of his politics. "Of course not—"

"Then you still want me to wait for you."

"Only a few years."

"A few years." It sounded like the end of the world. All of her fears and her father's prophecies were coming true. For the first time in three months, Ashley doubted Trevor's love.

"Look, Ashley," he whispered, gently running his fingers through the silken strands of her hair. "I love you—I'm just asking you to be patient."

"Patience isn't my long suit."

"It's not forever."

"You're sure about that?"

"Of course." His eyes were clear blue and honest. For a moment she was tempted to believe him.

"Then what about the reason you got to know me in the first place—to try to get me to admit that my family was involved in your father's disappearance. The reason you took the time to get to know me at all was just so that you could get some information from me, information to discredit my father."

"That's not the only reason."

Ashley could tell that he was lying through his straight white teeth. The veiled hatred in his eyes at the mention of Lazarus convinced her that the love she thought they had been sharing was all based on a lie.

"I think it's over for us," she stated, tears stinging her eyes.

"Only if you want it to be."

"There's no other way," she murmured, slowly gathering her things and throwing them into her suitcase. Silently, she prayed that he would back down and apologize, that he would beg her to stay. But it didn't happen.

She left the cottage in the middle of the storm, regretting that she had ever laid eyes on Trevor Daniels.

Chapter Eight

The thoughts of the past took their toll on Ashley and she had to remind herself that what had happened didn't matter. She and Trevor had a bargain and she was going to do her damnedest to prove that all of his accusations about her father, Claud and the timber company were unjust. If he had given her nothing else, Trevor had granted her the chance to clear her family's name. For that much, she supposed bitterly, she should be grateful.

She placed her hands on the floor and straightened from the position she had assumed when Trevor had left her. The cabin was cold. She managed to light a fire in the wood stove in the kitchen to give her a little heat as she packed her things and secured the cabin against the winter weather. She worked without really thinking about what she was doing. Her thoughts, still filled with pain, continued to revolve around the past.

Disgusted with herself for being so maudlin, she walked to the window and looked out at the snow-covered ground. Winter birds, dark against the backdrop of white snow, flitted through the pine needles, chirping out lonely cries as they landed on the ground and foraged in the powdery snow.

"You really can't blame Trevor," she whispered to herself as she saw a bird find the seeds she had placed on the deck. Ashley's breath condensed on the window, clouding the clear panes. "You only got what was coming to you."

Most of the agony she had endured was her own fault. If she had just forgotten Trevor, as she had promised herself that stormy night in Neskowin, the following events never would have occurred. But as it was, blinded by fury and disgrace, Ashley had stormed out of the beach cottage and had returned to Portland.

In the following few weeks after the breakup with Trevor, Ashley had resumed working for her father and had secretly hoped that she might be pregnant. She wanted desperately to have Trevor's baby, a lasting memory of the love affair that wasn't quite strong enough to survive. At the time, she had been sure that a child, Trevor's child, was all she needed to heal the pain.

It hadn't happened. Ashley cried bitter tears of anguish when her monthly cycle resumed and all her hopes of bearing Trevor's child were destroyed. Her dreams of the future had been shattered as easily as if they had been delicate sea shells crushed by the tireless anger of the sea.

Ashley had married Richard out of spite. Richard Jennings was the man she had been dating before she met Trevor. Richard worked for Stephens Timber and was the only son of rich, socialite parents. It hadn't taken long for him to propose to the beautiful and headstrong daughter of Lazarus Stephens.

For her part, though at the time she had suspected that she might be deluding herself, Ashley had hoped that another man would replace Trevor. It didn't take her long to realize that she had been wrong.

The marriage had been a mistake for both Richard and herself. Richard had expected a doting wife interested only in supporting him in his engineering career, but Ashley had shown more interest in the timber business than in homemaking.

It wasn't all Richard's fault that the marriage had failed, Ashley decided with a grimace. Though Ashley had hoped to purge herself of Trevor, and though she had tried to be everything Richard wanted, she had failed miserably. Even Lazarus hadn't gotten the satisfaction of the grand-child he had expected from the short-lived union.

A divorce was inevitable. Lazarus Stephens went to his grave an unhappy, selfish man who never had suspected that his daughter was incapable of providing an heir to the Stephens Timber fortune.

Perhaps it didn't matter, Ashley thought as she walked up the stairs to the loft and opened her suitcase. When she and Richard had divorced, she had lost all interest in owning any part of the vast timber empire. If she had learned anything from her brief but passionate affair with Trevor, it was how to be her own person and still care for other people. Trevor had helped her mature. By leaving her, he had forced her to rely on herself and become self-sufficient.

Maybe that was why her marriage had failed; she'd been too strong, while Richard was weak. It hadn't been Richard's obvious affairs that had finally gotten to her; it had been his lack of character and strength.

What's the point of dredging it up all over again? she asked herself as she folded her clothes and placed them in the open suitcase on the bed. The sheets were still rumpled in disturbing evidence of her recent lovemaking with Trevor. She swallowed the urge to cry and hastily straightened the bedclothes.

Working swiftly, she managed to clean the cabin, pack her bags and bundle up all the reports from the Bend office. As she took out the garbage she noticed an empty champagne bottle and remembered how she had shared a glass of the sparkling wine with Trevor in front of the fire the night before. It seemed like weeks ago, when it had only been hours. Could so much have happened in so short a time?

When she finally had packed everything into her Jeep, she returned to make sure the fire was no longer smoldering and to cast one last, searching glance around the interior of the rustic home. Her heart ached painfully. She wondered if Trevor was still at the Lambert cabin just a few minutes away. She pushed the nagging question aside and frowned. She couldn't run to him—not yet. Until she had cleared her father's name, she had nothing to offer Trevor.

"That's life," she muttered to herself, climbing into the Jeep. "Merry Christmas, Ashley," she chided with a self-effacing frown. She turned the key in the ignition and the trustworthy engine sparked to life: Ashley drove away from the snow-covered cabin without once looking back.

It had grown dark by the time Ashley made it back to the Willamette Valley. The blackened skies were moist and the city streets of Portland were slick with rain. Most of the large homes in the West Hills were illuminated with colorful Christmas lights that twinkled in the gathering darkness and were reflected in the raindrops collecting on the Jeep's windshield before the wipers slapped them aside.

Her father's home was a huge, Tudor structure with seven bedrooms and five baths. Why he had ever purchased so large an estate was beyond Ashley, as Lazarus had never remarried and had no children other than herself. Most of the bedrooms had never been occupied. It seemed an incredible waste.

As Ashley turned up the cedar-lined drive, she noticed that the interior lights of the house were glowing warmly.

Ashley smiled to herself, knowing that Mrs. Deveraux, a fussy French lady who had been Lazarus's housekeeper ever since Enora's death and was still in charge of the house and grounds, must have guessed that Ashley would return tonight.

"Wouldn't you know," Ashley said to herself, pleased that Mrs. Deveraux had thought about her. The kindly old woman still treated her like a child. Tonight it would be appreciated. What Ashley needed right now was a warm meal and a hot bath. Once refreshed, she was sure that she could tackle the mountain of computer printouts once again.

No one answered her call when she entered. Ashley left her bags at the foot of the grand, oiled-oak staircase and walked into the kitchen, where she found a note from Mrs. Deveraux tacked to the refrigerater door. The message was simple: Mrs. Deveraux had gone out to the movies, would be back around ten and had left a crock of soup in the refrigerater. Also, as a postscript, there was a message from John Ellis, the accountant for

Stephens Timber, requesting that Ashley call him the minute she was back in town.

The note made Ashley uneasy. There was no telling what Claud had done after calling Ashley this morning. She couldn't help but wonder if her cousin had pumped John for information after getting no satisfaction from her.

After heating the homemade chowder in the microwave, Ashley dialed John's number at home and let the soup cool.

"Hello?"

"John? This is Ashley."

There was a sigh of relief on the other end of the connection. "Are you back in town?" John's voice sounded anxious, almost fearful.

"Just got in."

"At your father's house?"

" Yes. Why—"

"Good! I'll be there in about half an hour."

"Slow down," Ashley demanded, unnerved by the calm man's uncharacteristic impatience. Her palms were beginning to sweat. There was something about the conversation that made her more than slightly uneasy. "What's going on?"

"I'll talk to you when I get there." With that, he hung up the phone and Ashley was left to consider the unusual conversation.

"What the devil?" she wondered, as she sat down at the kitchen table. Her mind was racing when she tested the soup with the tip of her tongue, decided it was the right temperature and began eating the delicious meal of hot chowder and warm biscuits.

Had John discovered something out of the ordinary in

the financial reports? What was it that made him sound so worried and concerned? It was almost as if he were frightened of something . . . or someone.

"You're beginning to sound as paranoid as Trevor," she admonished herself, smiling slightly at the rugged image her willing mind conjured.

Ashley finished her soup and placed the bowl in the dishwasher just as the doorbell rang. She walked to the front door, opened it and ushered in a very agitated John Ellis.

"What's going on?" she asked as he shed his coat and tossed it carelessly over a bent arm of the wooden hall tree near the door.

"That's what I want to know."

They walked into the formal living room and John stalked from one end of the elegantly furnished room to the other.

"Did you find something suspicious in the books?" Ashley asked, her throat beginning to constrict. Something was wrong—very wrong. John was usually a calm individual known for his attention to detail and sound judgment.

Tonight his face was flushed and his eyes darted nervously from Ashley to the door, the window and back to Ashley again. Several times he rotated his head, as if to relieve the tension in his neck.

"I don't know—" He held his hands, palms up, in her direction. He seemed genuinely confused.

"Take your time," Ashley insisted. "Have a seat and let me get you a cup of coffee, or brandy?"

"Anything." He looked as if he didn't care one way or the other. He was restless and uneasy.

She combined the two drinks and gave him a black cup of coffee laced with brandy. He took the mug, drank a long swallow, and then settled back in one of the stiff chairs near the windows.

Ashley took a seat on the corner of the couch and sipped her coffee. "Okay, so tell me what's happening?"

"I don't know, but I don't like it. Claud is suspicious."

"About the reports I requested to be sent to Bend?" Ashley guessed, knowing the calculating nature of her cousin. It was too bad Claud was so well qualified for his job; his sharp mind and legal background made him indispensable.

"Right. For the last few days he's been questioning me—make that grilling me."

Ashley nodded. Her features showed none of her inner distress. "What'd you tell him?"

John rolled his myopic eyes toward the ceiling. "Nothing, I think. He asked why there were so many printouts and I said that you wanted to go over the books and get a feel for running the company. Claud told me that you could never possibly need that much paper, and I told him that I was just sending you what you requested. He didn't like it much, especially when I said that I would do the same thing, if I had inherited a company the size of Stephens Timber and it had been several years since I'd actually worked in the business."

Ashley let out a long, ragged breath. "Did Claud buy your story?"

Shrugging his shoulders, John shook his head. "Who

knows? I told him that I was working on this special audit with you and Claud told me that I was to report directly to him. If there were any discrepancies in the books, he wanted to know about them—pronto."

Ashley frowned and tossed her hair over her shoulder as she rubbed her chin. "Did you—report to him?"

John seemed genuinely disappointed. "Of course not."

"Good." The tension in Ashley's muscles relaxed slightly. "So what did you find?"

"Most everything is pretty cut-and-dried," he replied, smiling at his own unintentional pun.

"Except?"

"Except for a couple of things." John drained his cup, reached for his briefcase and snapped it open. He handed a few crisp sheets of paper to Ashley. They were copies of invoices to the Watkins Mill in Molalla.

Ashley's heart nearly stopped beating when she saw the price Claud had charged for the timber and the date on the invoice. "This . . . this happened last June?" she asked, her throat constricting. The transaction occurred only a few weeks before the bribery charges were made against Trevor.

"Right. And the price of the timber is way off— ridiculously low. At first I thought it had to be a computer error. We were selling rough timber at three times that much."

"But you changed your mind?" Ashley prodded, barely daring to breathe. Something in John's mannerisms told her to brace herself.

John adjusted his glasses and scowled. "Yes. It just didn't make any sense to me."

"But now it does?" Ashley was almost afraid to ask.

"No. I know how it happened, I just don't understand why."

"What do you mean?"

He seemed to hesitate before he reached into his briefcase and extracted some gray photocopies of invoices, which he handed to Ashley. "I did some more checking. Claud was the one who gave the mill the price break, but he had your father's approval."

Ashley let out a shuddering sigh. "You're sure about that?"

"Got the memo right here." He handed the next incriminating piece of paper to her. Ashley accepted it with trembling fingers.

"Dear Lord," she whispered as she recognized her father's bold scrawl.

"What's this all about?" John asked.

"I'm not really sure," she replied. "But I'm afraid it means trouble—big trouble."

"I thought so." The young accountant rose and paced around the room. "I'm not too crazy about being in the middle of this," John admitted, "whatever the hell it is." He regarded his employer intently. "I thought at first that this might just be a power struggle between you and Claud. But there's more to it than that, isn't there?"

"I think so."

"Does any part of it have to do with Trevor Daniels?" The question sent a cold shock wave through Ashley.

"Why would you think that?"

"I just put two and two together." John's mouth slanted into a sarcastic grin. "That's my job."

"And did you end up getting four?"

"I think so." John held up one finger. "Claud's been

furious ever since you took over." Another finger was raised. "You ask me for all of these reports. The only discrepancy concerns the Watkins Mill. Beau Watkins, the owner, was the one who was involved in that bribery mess with Daniels last summer, wasn't he?"

Silently, Ashley nodded.

"Right." He held up a third finger. "Claud's been storming around the office ranting about Daniels's bid for the Senate. It's really a sore spot with him. Therefore—"

"You deduced that Trevor was involved."

"Bingo." The fourth finger straightened.

Ashley couldn't lie. She was asking too much of John to expect him to follow her blindly. "Trevor's convinced that there are shady dealings within the company."

"That's hardly today's news."

"I know." Ashley sighed. "But he thinks that Claud would go to any lengths to ruin his chances in the senatorial race."

"What lengths?" John's expression was grim.

Ashley shrugged indifferently, though the skin was stretched tightly over her cheekbones and her stomach was knotting painfully. "Bribery, sabotage . . ."

"Attempted murder?"

"He implied as much," Ashley admitted.

John ran unsteady hands over his chin. "I can't believe that Claud would be involved in anything like that."

"Not only Claud, but my father as well."

"No way!" But the pale accountant didn't seem convinced.

"I have to prove that they're innocent."

John looked at the incriminating memo and invoices. "I only hope we can."

"If we can't, then we'll have to face up to the problem, won't we?" Ashley asked the stricken young man.

"Nothing else to do."

"Good. Then we're both of the same opinion." She strode across the room and stared out at the black drizzly night. The city lights of downtown Portland twinkled in the distance. "What I want you to do is request a leave of absence. Use any excuse you want to, maybe a medical reason, too much stress on the job, that sort of thing. Then you can come here and work. You'll be paid just the same, and you can work without Claud staring over your shoulder."

"Just in case we find something incriminating."

"Exactly."

John took in a deep breath before cracking a nervous smile. "All right," he agreed.

Ashley smiled. "You don't have to do this, you know."

"Why not? Because it might get dangerous?"

She sobered. "I don't think so. At least I hope not. If I really thought there were any danger involved, I wouldn't ask you to be a part of this. It's just that there aren't many people I can trust at the company."

"I know. And I like being one of the few."

"I do appreciate it, John."

The accountant smiled. "Then keep it in mind the next time I'm up for a raise."

Ashley laughed. "It's a deal."

John gathered his coat and briefcase and left a few minutes later.

A thousand questions filled Ashley's mind. Was Claud involved in a plan, as Trevor had claimed, to keep him out of the primary in May? And what about the accident and bribery charges? Could Claud or Lazarus have been part of such a deadly scheme?

Ashley picked up her suitcases and began to trudge up the stairs. What about the disappearance of Robert Daniels? All these years Trevor had maintained that Lazarus had been involved in a plot which had led to Robert's . . . Ashley shuddered. If Robert Daniels wasn't dead, why had he abandoned his family? And where was he now?

"I'm too tired to think about any of this," she told herself as she reached the upper floor, deposited her bags in her room and went into the adjoining bath. She turned on the water to the sunken tub and began removing her clothes.

Could all of the wicked rumors be true? Had she hidden her head in the sand to avoid facing the truth about her father? She stared at her image in the mirror. She was a mature woman today, worldly wise, slightly cynical, and she wasn't afraid to face up to the truth. She only wished that she had been wiser when she was younger and hadn't been so blindly trusting of her father or Trevor.

After peeling off her clothes and pinning her hair loosely on her head, she settled into the hot tub and moaned as the water covered her body. "Dear Lord, what a mess," she whispered to herself. Closing her eyes, she wondered vaguely where Trevor was, and with whom.

Trevor paced between the cedar walls of the Lambert cabin like a caged animal. He alternately stared out the window and glanced at the telephone. The argument with Ashley this morning had been a mistake and all day long he had half expected Ashley to call or drive over seeking amends.

Maybe that was asking too much of her. If he knew anything about that woman it was that she had inherited her father's stubborn pride.

His hands clenched and relaxed at his sides as he swore, walked across the room and picked up the telephone. He dialed the number of Ashley's cabin angrily and waited with impatience as the flat rings indicated that Ashley wasn't there.

"Answer it," he ground out, desperation taking hold of him. All day he had tried to convince himself that what he had overheard this morning had been innocent. If Ashley had wanted to deceive him, she wouldn't have taken the chance to speak with Claud.

But Claud had called her.

"You're making a mountain out of a molehill," he told himself as he replaced the receiver and took a long drink from his warm bourbon.

Then why had she left? It wasn't like Ashley to run away. She'd only done it once before and that was because he had asked her to wait for him. That time she had run to another man and married him. His fingers clenched around the short glass and the cold taste of deception rose in his throat.

He finished his drink and set the empty glass on the table. His lips had tightened over his teeth when he dialed the phone again. This time there was an answer.

"Hello?"

"I'm on my way back to the valley."

"About time," Everett replied. "You missed a couple

of Christmas parties that could have been feathers in your cap."

"Give the governor my regrets."

"Already done." There was a slight hesitation in Everett's voice. "Did you accomplish what you set out to?"

Trevor's smile was grim and filled with self-mockery. "No."

The statement should have put Everett's worried mind at ease. It didn't. The campaign manager came directly to the point. "So what are you going to do about Stephens Timber?"

"I'm not sure."

"And Ashley?"

"I wish I knew."

"I hope you come up with some better answers before you start campaigning in earnest, my friend."

"I will."

"Then you didn't find anything out about your accident or the bribery charges?"

"No—not yet."

The reply sounded ominous to Everett. "Then, forget them. At least for now."

"A little difficult to do," Trevor stated, rubbing the bandage over his abdomen with his free hand.

"Concentrate on the election."

"I am."

"Good." Everett let out a relieved sigh.

"You worry too much."

"With you, it's a full-time job. When will you be back?"

Trevor's eyes narrowed as he stared out the window at the darkness. "Tonight."

"Call me when you get in. I'll meet you at the house."

"See you then." Trevor hung up feeling suddenly very old and incredibly tired. He raked his fingers through his coarse hair and sat on the edge of a recliner positioned near the windows. What if Ashley was coming back to the cabin? What if she had only gone out for the day— shopping, or to clear her head. What if she was, now, at this very moment, returning?

"You're a fool," he muttered under his breath, "a damned fool!" Once again he reached for the phone.

Everything was going as planned. John Ellis had requested a three-week medical leave, which Ashley had granted. Claud had muttered unhappily when he heard that the head of the accounting department was taking an unscheduled leave of absence, but hadn't made too big a deal about it.

"Why now?" Claud had grumbled.

"Because he's ill—stomach problems. Probably too much stress on the job," Ashley had answered with a patient smile, though her throat constricted with the lie.

"Lousy timing, if you ask me," Claud had pointed out. "Year-end is always a bitch for the accounting department. Ellis couldn't have picked a worse time if he'd tried."

"Give the man a break, for crying out loud. He'll be back soon. I'm sure that the rest of the staff is perfectly capable of pulling his weight, at least for a couple of weeks."

Claud had glared unhappily at Ashley for a few uncomfortable minutes. Then, with a sound of disgust, he had snapped open the morning edition of his favorite financial journal and turned his attention back to an article dealing with mining rights.

Ashley, displaying professional aplomb despite the fact that her knees were shaking, turned on an elevated heel and walked briskly out of Claud's office. Deception had always been difficult for her, even with her slightly under-handed cousin. It had been difficult hiding the fact that John Ellis was working at her house in the West Hills. So far, no one knew that he was there other than Ashley, John's wife and Mrs. Deveraux, who were all sworn to secrecy.

This cloak-and-dagger business will be my undoing, she thought ruefully as she entered her own suite of offices. *I'm just not cut out to be a spy.*

She sat down wearily in the chair her father had occu-pied for so many years, closed her eyes and rubbed her forehead. The nagging headache behind her eyelids began to throb.

In the last week, neither she nor John had found any other incriminating evidence against either Claud or Lazarus. Even if her father had been involved with Beau Watkins of the Watkins Lumber Mill in Molalla, that didn't nec-essarily mean that he instigated the bribery charges. So far, the evidence was only circumstantial at best.

But the invoices represented the first set of concrete facts indicating that Trevor's charges against her family might be more than the idle speculation of a wronged son.

Thoughts of Trevor, his eyes narrowed suspiciously and his chin set in ruthless determination, invaded her mind. His charges against her father and Claud couldn't be ignored. What about the spraying of the pesticide near Springfield? Did Lazarus understand the health hazards involved and then just go ahead with the spraying, neglecting the welfare of the public? Ashley couldn't find it in her heart to believe that her father would do anything so cruel. Though not a particularly warm individual, her father had taken care of her when Enora, Ashley's mother, had died.

Ashley didn't hear Claud open the door. She was so wrapped up in her own morbid thoughts that Claud had advanced upon the desk before she realized he was in the room.

He slapped a magazine down on the polished walnut desk. The glossy periodical was open to the current events section. Accompanying a short article on politics in Oregon was a snapshot of Trevor. Ashley's heart nearly skipped a beat as she looked at Trevor's intense expression and the glitter of determination in his eyes, The bold letters of the headline were a question: TREVOR DANIELS, OREGON'S NEXT SENATOR?

"We've got to stop this before it turns into popular opinion," Claud stated. One of his short fingers poked at the snapshot of Trevor.

"Stop what?"

"Daniels, for God's sake." Claud dropped into a chair near the desk. His dark eyes were clouded in disgust. "Read the article. The reporter acts as if Daniels is a shoo-in in the primary!"

"The latest polls show that—"

"The hell with the polls. It's the election that counts."

"And you're afraid that Trevor will win."

Claud let out an angry gust of air. "Damn right. If he does, we may as well close down."

Ashley's arched brows pulled together as she studied her cousin. Her heart was pounding warily in her chest. "Why?"

"He's out to crucify us."

"By us, do you mean you and me, or the company?"

"Same thing."

Ashley gathered her courage and met her cousin's furious glare. "Why does Trevor Daniels threaten you?"

Claud looked at her as if she were insane. "You still don't understand, do you?"

"Understand what?"

"The man's sworn that he'll get us one way or the other. He still blames your father and the timber company for the fact that his old man ran off with another woman—or whatever. Not only that, he thinks that someone here was involved in the bribery charges leveled against him last summer."

Ashley held her breath, watching, waiting, while Claud confided in her. Claud paused, rose from the chair and, after ramming his hands into his pockets, walked over to the window.

"Were we?" she asked softly.

Claud braced himself on the window ledge and smiled cynically. "Of course not, Ash! What would be the point?"

"To discredit a political adversary—"

"Bah!"

"You just stated that we had to do something about him."

"We do." Claud's fingers drummed nervously on the window sill. "But something legal."

"Such as?" Ashley held her chin in her hand and her wide sea-green eyes noted all of Claud's aggravated movements.

"Back the other candidate."

"Orson?"

"Right. Bill Orson is Trevor's biggest competition in

the primary. He was also pretty tight with your dad. He's the logical choice." Claud frowned thoughtfully.

"I'm not sure—"

"Look, Ashley, we're running out of time. Daniels is beginning to get a lot of press." He pointed a condemning finger toward the magazine. "National publicity. We've got to do what we can to protect our interests."

"Don't you think you're jumping off the deep end?" Ashley asked. "We're only talking about the primary and it's still several months away. Even if Trevor wins in May, he'll still face the other party's candidate in November."

"If he gets the chance."

"Which you want to thwart."

Claud pulled at the edge of his mustache. "That's putting it a little bluntly, but sure, let's call a spade a spade. If Daniels somehow managed to get himself elected, it would be a disaster!"

"His own family is in the logging business," Ashley replied. "Don't you think you're overreacting?"

A cruel smile touched Claud's thin lips. "What I think is that you're still carrying a torch for that bastard! God, Ashley, when will you ever grow up? He used you!"

Ashley crossed her arms over her chest. "And I think you're boxing with shadows."

Claud laughed out loud. "You still think you have a chance with him, don't you?" Ashley had to bite back the hot retort forming on her tongue. Angering Claud any further wouldn't accomplish anything. "Well, I'm inclined to agree. I wouldn't be a bit surprised if Trevor came sniffing around you, at least until after the election. That way he could stop the opposition before it began. All the easier for him."

Ashley swallowed back her indignation. "If you think you can get me to go along with whatever it is you want by insulting me, Claud, you're wrong."

Claud shrugged his bulky shoulders. "I wouldn't want to do that, cousin dear. After all, you're my boss."

"And that still sticks in your craw."

"A little." Claud frowned to himself. "But what concerns me more is the upcoming primary. You may as well reconcile yourself to the fact that we've got to do all we can to stop Daniels before all hell breaks loose."

With his final words, Claud walked past the desk, took one last look at the magazine article and left the office.

"You're wrong," Ashley whispered as the door closed behind her cousin, but his accusations had hit their mark. Had Trevor pretended interest in her just to get what he wanted from her?

The long nights of lovemaking came to her mind and Ashley remembered the honesty in Trevor's clear blue eyes. "If anyone's being deceptive," she thought aloud, "I'm willing to bet it's you, dear cousin," she mimicked. "And I'm not about to back a bastard like Bill Orson!"

Finding new resolve, she reached for the phone, intent on calling John Ellis. The sooner she found answers to Trevor's questions, the better.

Chapter Nine

"That's it," John announced, his weary voice filled with relief.

"You're sure?" Ashley couldn't believe that the task that had seemed so monumental a few weeks ago was now finished.

"There's nothing else." John's expression was one of certainty. Other than the incriminating invoices and memo from Lazarus, John had found nothing to substantiate Trevor's accusations against Stephens Timber.

Ashley should have been jubilant, but she wasn't. "You've checked through everything?" Her fingers tapped nervously against her chin as she sat in the chair facing the desk. John was sitting behind mounds of computer printouts, each carefully labeled and banded together on the top of Lazarus's desk in the den of the stately old manor.

"I've gone over every piece of paper you've brought me." John leaned back in the chair and propped his boots on the desk in a gesture of satisfaction. He stretched and even from where she was sitting, Ashley could hear his vertebrae crack. How many hours had the poor accountant sat at her father's desk, poring over black-and-white figures?

Ashley tried to accept John's audit as final, but during the last couple of weeks with Claud at the office, she had begun to doubt her earlier convictions about her family's innocence. Working with Claud on a daily basis had forced her to face up to the fact that the man had no sense of moral responsibility. Dollars and cents were his only motivation.

Abruptly she got out of her chair and paced anxiously between the desk and the window. The city lights of Portland winked seductively in the clear, black night.

"I thought you would be relieved," John remarked.

"I am—sort of."

"But?"

"These reports are all recent—all in the last six months."

"What're you getting at?"

She stopped near the window and stared at the cloudless night. "I want to clear the family name once and for all. There are a couple of things I want to check out, but it will have to be done at the office. If I take home the reports I need, Claud will become suspicious."

"Why?"

"Because they're old. Some of the documents won't even be on the computer," she thought aloud, her eyes piercing the blackness of the still night.

"What will you be looking for?"

Ashley smiled cryptically and faced him. "I don't know. I won't until I see it. But I want to check the records about the time of the Springfield spraying." She saw the look of protest in the accountant's eyes and she continued.

"I want to see the books from day one—when Dad started the company—"

"Because of Robert Daniels's disappearance?"

Ashley let out a long sigh. "Right."

"I don't think you'll find anything," John offered, hoping to give some comfort to her worried mind.

"Let's just pray that you're right."

Later, after John had left for home, Ashley sat in her father's desk chair, worrying about the future. Several times she considered calling Trevor and once she had even gone so far as to reach for the phone. But she hadn't. Her pride forbade it. She sighed and let her hand fall to her side.

Ashley felt that she couldn't go to Trevor until she was certain of all the facts. The small piece of evidence against Claud and Lazarus would only add fuel to Trevor's inquisitive nature and Ashley wanted to be prepared with all the answers to his accusations before she saw him again.

If she saw him again. The argument between them was still unresolved and Ashley doubted if there would ever be a time when they could feel the freedom and love they had shared while alone in the mountains. *It was all just a lie*, she tried to convince herself, but the memory of Trevor's intense blue eyes, filled with honesty and raw passion, still touched a very vital part of her. She found herself hoping that he still cared, if only a little.

For the last two weeks, each time she had picked up a newspaper, Trevor's face had been plastered all over it. Claud was no longer worried about Trevor's bid for the Senate, he was downright furious that the polls showed Trevor Daniels leading the race.

Just the previous week Ashley had walked into Claud's office and overheard the tail end of a telephone conversation.

"I don't care what we have to do," Claud had stated emphatically, his lips white with rage, just as Ashley had walked into the room, "we can't let that son of a bitch win!"

Ashley had known instinctively that Claud was referring to Trevor, but she pretended that she hadn't understood the conversation.

Claud had glanced in her direction, paled slightly and then changed the course of the discussion, as if he were talking to an advertising executive about a future ad campaign.

Ashley's step faltered slightly and her heart filled with dread, but she didn't call Claud on the lie, knowing that it would be better for everyone concerned if Claud didn't think she was suspicious of him.

At that point, she had become convinced that Trevor's accusations about her family weren't completely idle speculation on his part. The look of pure hatred and ruthlessness that had crossed Claud's face while he was on the phone had been blood-chilling.

Just a few more weeks, she had thought to herself. *Just until John and I have all the evidence available. Then, when I know what really happened in the past, I'll confront Claud and give him his walking papers.* No matter how valuable he was to the timber company, Ashley knew that Claud was power-hungry and dangerous. Just like her father.

* * *

In the days that followed, John had returned to the office and when Claud would go out for an afternoon, John and Ashley would go over the old records of the timber company. There never seemed to be enough time to sort through all the handwritten documents, but at least Ashley felt certain that Claud wasn't suspicious, not yet anyway.

Ashley's industrious work at the office seemed to convince Claud that she was interested only in the timber company. If he had any earlier thoughts about her relationship with Trevor, he didn't voice them.

Even though she ached to see Trevor, she had made a point of avoiding him for two reasons. The first was that she couldn't face him without being certain of the facts. The argument with him still cut her to the bone and she knew that she could never confront him until she had uncovered all of the truth and had solid facts to present to him.

The other reason was Claud. If anyone saw Ashley with Trevor, or overheard a telephone conversation between them and reported it to Claud, the results would be disastrous. For, as each day passed, Ashley was beginning to believe that Claud might have been involved in the planning of Trevor's accident. But she didn't have any proof. Not yet. She was working on gut instinct alone and that wouldn't hold up in court, which was exactly where she supposed her snaky cousin would wind up facing criminal charges.

Claud had business in Seattle. For the first time since Ashley had returned from the mountain cabin and her tryst with Trevor, Claud had been called out of town. Ashley, as president of the timber company, insisted that he go; the matter in Seattle was pressing and Claud's legal expertise was desperately needed. Or at least she managed to convince Claud that his business acumen was without compare. Though his ego was stroked, he boarded the plane to Seattle reluctantly, casting Ashley a final glance that made her shiver with inward dread.

Once back in the office, she forgot Claud's cruel, cautionary stare. For the first time in several weeks, Ashley felt free. There were things she had to accomplish, one of which was to contact Trevor. Her heart raced at the thought and she wondered what kind of a reception she would receive.

He didn't answer when she tried contacting him at home, and when she called his campaign headquarters an efficient but cold voice told her that Mr. Daniels would get back to her. Ashley waited impatiently all afternoon, busying herself in the office, studying the old ledgers for the company, but Trevor didn't return her call.

At seven o'clock, she went home, helpless to shake the uneasiness beginning to settle on her shoulders. She told herself that he was busy, and for him not to call her wasn't out of the ordinary. Maybe he wanted to wait until he was sure that she was alone. Perhaps he would call tonight.

Frustrated from waiting, Ashley changed her clothes and tried, once again, to reach Trevor at home. There was still no answer and her nerves were frayed as she tried the campaign headquarters. The phone was answered by a recording machine, which played a message about the hours of business.

Ashley slammed the receiver back into the cradle and

stalked downstairs. Was Trevor purposely avoiding her? It wasn't unlikely considering the circumstances, except that he had been so damned interested in the records of the timber company. Maybe that was because his accident had been so recent, and now, nearly six weeks later, his attention was focused on the future rather than the past.

A past which included Ashley, and a future which couldn't.

As outspoken as he had been against the Stephens Timber Corporation, Trevor couldn't risk a clandestine relationship with Ashley even if he wanted to, which Ashley seriously doubted.

"Hard day at the office?" Mrs. Deveraux asked when Ashley finally went downstairs and into the kitchen. The housekeeper had prepared Ashley her favorite dinner of pot roast and potatoes. The table was set for one.

"A little rough," Ashley admitted.

The lady with the perfectly coiled white hair pursed her thin lips together thoughtfully as she placed the steaming serving bowls onto the table. "You don't have to go around killing yourself, you know."

"Pardon me?" Ashley was taken aback. Mrs. Deveraux had never made personal comments to her, not since she had moved out of the house at eighteen.

"Just because your father left you the company, doesn't mean that you have to run it."

"But I enjoy it—"

"Bah! It doesn't take a genius to see that you're miserable. How much weight have you lost since you moved back here?"

"Only about five pounds." Ashley set a platter of beef onto the table.

"And on my cooking!"

"I haven't been particularly hungry," Ashley said with a shrug.

"Why?"

"I don't know, no appetite, I guess."

"Hmph! It's the timber company," Mrs. Deveraux pointed out. "It killed your father and it's doing the same with you. Either that, or you're pining for some man you left back at the college."

Ashley felt an uncomfortable lump form in her throat. Because Mrs. Deveraux was the only mother Ashley had known since she was in her early teens, the kindly old woman had a way of making Ashley feel like a contrite child. "I wasn't seeing anyone there."

"Well, sit . . . sit." Francine pointed a plump finger toward the table.

"You're not eating?"

A twinkle lighted the elderly woman's blue eyes. "Not tonight. I'm going out."

"With George again?" Ashley accused and clucked her tongue. "Another hot date? My, my, this is getting serious."

Mrs. Deveraux chuckled but the smile curving her lips at the mention of her beau quickly faded. "You should be the one going out. You're young and single."

"Divorced."

"Makes no difference. So am I."

Ashley forced a grin she didn't feel. "When I find the right man—"

"Well, you certainly won't find him here." The doorbell chimed and Francine Deveraux smiled. " You're too young and pretty to be losing weight over that damned company. Sell it to your cousin, he would like to own it. Then you'll be a wealthy lady without all these worries."

"And afterward what would I do?"

"Marry a duke, an earl. . . ."

A senator, Ashley thought wistfully to herself.

The doorbell chimed again.

"I must go. You think about what I've said."

"I will. And you have a wonderful time."

"Okay. End of lecture." Mrs. Deveraux kissed Ashley lightly on the cheek and hurried out of the kitchen. As Ashley pierced a piece of the roast with her fork, she heard the door open and the sound of laughter as Mrs. Deveraux greeted George. Within a minute, the door was closed and the great house seemed incredibly empty.

"If only everything were so simple," she said to herself, forcing the delicious food down her throat. Try as she would, she couldn't eat half of what Mrs. Deveraux had served.

With a groan, she got up from the table and tossed the remains of her dinner down the garbage disposal. "What a waste," she muttered before cleaning the dishes and trudging upstairs.

After a leisurely bath, she settled into bed and turned on the television for background noise as she sifted through the pages of a glossy magazine. When the local news came on, Ashley set the magazine aside and turned her attention to the smartly dressed anchorwoman who smiled into the camera.

"Rumor has it that one of the candidates for the senatorial seat vacated by Senator Higgins may be out of the race," the dark-haired woman stated evenly. Every muscle in Ashley's body tensed. "Trevor Daniels, a popular, pro-environmentalist candidate and lawyer originally from the Springfield area who later practiced law in Portland, will neither confirm nor deny the rumor that he is considering dropping out of the race."

"No!" Ashley screamed, bolting upright in the bed.

"Mr. Daniels was leading in the most current polls," the anchorwoman was stating, "and so his alleged withdrawal from the race before the May primary comes as somewhat of a shock to the community and the state."

Footage of Trevor, taken very recently at a campaign rally at Oregon State University, showed him talking with the students in the quad under threatening skies. The would-be senator was smiling broadly and shaking hands, looking for the life of him as if he were born to be a politician. Trevor's chestnut hair ruffled in the breeze and his face was robust-looking and healthy.

Ashley's heart contracted at the sight of him and she noticed more than she was supposed to see. There was something different about him; a foreign wariness in his eyes, and a slight droop to the broad shoulders supporting the casual tweed jacket. Tanned skin stretched tautly across his high cheekbones and the set of his thrusting jaw somehow lacked conviction. What Ashley noticed were the slightest nuances, which had apparently eluded the press.

"Dear God, what happened?" she whispered while the anchorwoman listed Trevor's accomplishments and the pitfalls of his campaign.

". . . not only was Mr. Daniels able to fend off false charges of bribery, which occurred last summer, but just recently he sustained an injury in a single-car accident that nearly took his life. . . ." The anchorwoman continued, giving a little background on Trevor's life, including the fact that his father had disappeared ten years ago and though his brother, Jeremy, ran the family business of Daniels Logging Company, Trevor had been known for his tough stands on fair timber-cutting practices and wilderness preservation.

"Again," the woman was saying, "we can neither confirm nor deny this rumor, but if anything further develops on the story, we'll report it to you later in the program. Mr. Daniels is scheduled to speak at a rally in Pioneer Square tomorrow at noon. Perhaps we'll all know more at that time."

When the news turned away from the May primary, Ashley snapped off the set and fell back against the pillows while uttering a tremulous sigh. *Why would Trevor be planning to drop out of the race?* All of his life he had had political aspirations, and he was currently leading Bill Orson in the polls for the primary. Pulling out now just didn't make a lot of sense.

Just then Claud's words of a few days earlier rang in her ears. "We can't let that son of a bitch win!" he had stated to an unknown caller. Could Claud be somehow responsible for the rumor? And was it even true? KPSC wasn't a station to report sensational rumors just to gain viewer attention. Most of the stories reported by the Portland station were purely factual, very seldom conjecture. And yet, the rumor was unconfirmed.

Though it was nearly eleven, Ashley reached for the bedside phone and with quaking fingers punched out the number of Trevor's home. There was still no answer in the grand house on the Willamette, and Ashley wondered if Trevor had moved. He'd never felt completely comfortable in his father's stately home. The vestiges of wealth were too harsh a reminder of the price his father had paid to make Daniels Logging Company successful.

With a sigh, Ashley hung up the phone and settled into the pillows, hoping for sleep. If nothing else, she would be at Pioneer Square the next afternoon to see Trevor, if only from a distance. It seemed like years since she had set eyes on him.

Fortunately Claud was still out of town, so there would be no one looking over her shoulder. *Tomorrow,* she promised herself, come hell or high water, she would find Trevor. Maybe, just maybe, she would force a confrontation with him.

Pioneer Square was a mass of cold, disenchanted citizens. People from all walks of life milled around the red brick amphitheater with frowns. Elderly couples rubbed their hands together for warmth as they stood next to men and women dressed smartly for work in the business offices flanking the city block designated for the square. Gaudily costumed young people with punk hairdos and glittery clothes were joined by a disenchanted group of street people. Joggers paused on their daily run through the city streets on the way to Waterfront Park and young mothers pushing strollers braved the cold February air to hear Trevor Daniels speak.

Ashley stood on the edge of the crowd, her stomach tied in knots. Pieces of angry conversation filtered to her ears.

"You really don't think he'll show?" a jeans-clad student with a scruffy beard asked his friend.

"Nah—politicians, they're all alike—say one thing and do another."

"This guy—he's supposed to be different."

"Sure, he is. Then why isn't he here?"

"Beats me."

"They're all alike, I tell you. They just want you to think that they're something special." The shorter of the two paused to cup his fingers around the end of a cigarette before lighting it. He blew out an angry stream of smoke as he shook his blond head. "I'll tell ya one thing, I'm not votin' for this clown, Daniels. Hell, he can't even show up for his own goddamn rally."

"Maybe his plane was delayed—"

"His plane? Gimme a break. He's supposed to be in town."

"Okay, okay, so the guy's a jerk. Who're you gonna vote for? Orson? That son of a bitch would sell his own mother's soul if there was a dime in it."

"God damn!" The short man ground out his cigarette and frowned. "I was hoping this guy would do something—"

"Meaningful?"

"Give me a break!" His gruff laughter drifted off as the two young men walked toward the podium.

Ashley's anxious eyes skimmed the crowd. Nowhere was there any trace of Trevor. The rally was supposed to begin at twelve and it was nearly twelve-fifteen. Worried lines creased Ashley's forehead as she blew on her cold hands. It was cold, but fortunately dry, and the wind blowing down the Columbia Gorge cut through her coat and chilled her bones.

"Come on, Trevor," she whispered, and her breath

misted in the clear air. "If you want to lose this election, you're certainly going about it the right way."

Finally there was a flurry of activity near the podium. Ashley's anxious eyes were riveted to the small stage that had been prepared for the event. The crowd murmured gratefully as a small, round man stepped up to the microphone.

It had been many years since Ashley had seen Everett Woodward, but she recognized Trevor's campaign manager, whose high-pitched voice was echoing in the square. He introduced himself to Trevor's restless public and then politely explained that Trevor had been detained in Salem and that the rally would be rescheduled for another, undisclosed date.

No one was pleased at the news. While some of the would-be Daniels supporters began to disband, a group of hecklers standing near Ashley began to taunt Everett.

"So where is he?" one demanded gruffly. "I don't buy your story that he's in Salem. He was supposed to be here today."

"Yeah, right. And what's all the rumors about him pulling out of the race? What happened? Did he get caught with his hand in the till or something?"

Everett, in his seemingly unflappable manner, ignored the jibes, but his brow was puckered with worry.

The hecklers continued their conversation in private. "If you ask me, Daniels was probably caught with his pants down—in bed with somebody's wife."

"Oh yeah?" The other youth chuckled obscenely and Ashley started to walk away. She was concerned about Trevor, and wasn't interested in any gossip about him.

"Sure, why not? The way I hear it, he was involved with a daughter of some hotshot timber guy—a rival or something—and she was married to someone else."

"Hey, I've got new respect for this guy . . . tell me about it. . . ."

A protest leaped to Ashley's tongue when she realized the hecklers were discussing her. She had to physically restrain herself from causing a scene and telling the two men that her love affair, that beautiful and fleeting part of her life, had been long over before she married Richard. An unwanted blush flooded her neck and her steps faltered slightly, but she clamped her teeth together, lowered her head against the wind and walked resolutely toward the object of her quest: Trevor's campaign manager.

Everett noticed her approach and a flicker of recognition registered on his placid face. The corners of his mouth twitched downward.

When she was close enough to be heard, Ashley didn't mince words. "I want to talk to Trevor."

Everett smiled coldly. "You and the rest of the voters in this state."

"It's important. I telephoned the campaign headquarters yesterday and a receptionist promised to have Trevor return the call."

"Which he didn't?"

"Right."

Everett was about to make a hasty retort, but changed his mind.

"I don't think he got the message," Ashley informed the round campaign manager.

"Or maybe you didn't. Did it ever cross your mind that maybe Trevor didn't want to talk to you?"

The muscles in Ashley's back stiffened and for a moment she considered letting the subject drop. But too much was at stake. In the past few weeks she had learned that her love for Trevor would never die and that at least some of the pain in the past was her fault for not trusting him. It was imperative that she see Trevor again. With newfound strength she swallowed her pride.

"Which is it?" she demanded, her muscles rigid. She braced herself for the rejection she was sure would follow. "You're his campaign manager, and from what I understand, very good at what you do. Certainly Trevor would confide in you, let you know if he didn't want to see me again."

Everett considered the woman standing before him. The pride and determination in the lift of her chin were compelling. Ashley Stephens Jennings was a far cry from the spoiled timber brat she had once been.

He fingered the handle of his umbrella and his gaze left her to study the architecture of the buildings surrounding the square. "I think it would be best if you forgot about Trevor Daniels," he ventured. "It would be political dynamite if the press found out that you were seeing him again."

"That's ducking the issue, Everett. Has Trevor told you that he doesn't want to see me?"

Everett gazed into the quiet fury of her blue-green eyes. There was a new dignity and spirit in her stare. He found it impossible to lie to her. "Right now, Trevor isn't really sure what he wants," the campaign manager admitted.

"Including his ambitions for the Senate?"

The portly man's eyes glittered dangerously. He knew he'd given too much away to the becoming daughter of Lazarus Stephens. "Leave him alone, Ashley," he warned. "Before Trevor saw you again, he knew what he wanted. And now . . . oh, hell!" A fleshy fist balled in frustration.

"And now what?" Ashley whispered, her throat constricting.

Everett laughed feebly. "I guess you and your father got what you wanted all along," he said in disgust. "Single-handedly you seem to have convinced the best goddamn man in Oregon to back down from his one shot at making it. Do you know what you've done? Have you any idea what you alone have cost this state?" His face reddened with conviction and his hands gestured helplessly in the air. "He would have been good, Ashley, damned good."

With his angry remark, he turned toward his car, and then cast another warning over his shoulder. "Give up, Ashley, you've gotten what you wanted. It's over for him. Now, for God's sake, leave the poor bastard alone!"

After grinding out his final, gut-wrenching advice, Everett slipped into the dark interior of a waiting cab. The battered car roared to life, melding into the traffic heading east toward the Willamette River.

Ashley was left standing alone in the wintry air. She felt more naked and raw than she had since the last time she had seen Trevor walk out the door of the mountain cabin. Shivering from the frigid wind, she wrapped her arms under her breasts.

An ache, deep and throbbing, cut through her heart and pounded in her pulse. "Dear Lord , Trevor," she whispered, "what happened to us?" She looked up at the cold gray sky and tears gathered in the corners of her eyes. How had she been so blind for so long? Why had she let other people, other things, unnecessary obstacles separate her from him? Was it pride, or was it fear of the truth that had kept her from facing the fact that she loved him more desperately than any sane woman should love a man?

Her fingers were clenched tightly around her abdomen when she heard her name.

"Ms Jennings?"

Unaware that anyone had been watching her, Ashley whirled and faced a young man, no more than twenty-five, who was staring intently at her. His clean features gave no hint of what he wanted.

"Pardon me?" she whispered, carefully disguising the huskiness in her throat with poise.

"You are Ashley Jennings, aren't you—Ashley Stephens Jennings?"

"Yes." She was instantly wary. The last twenty-four hours had been a roller coaster of conflicts and emotions and something in this man's studious gaze warned her to tread carefully.

The young man flashed a triumphant smile. "I thought so. Elwin Douglass." He stretched out his hand and reluctantly Ashley accepted his larger palm in her icy fingers.

"Is there something I can do for you?"

"I hope so. I'm a free-lance reporter." Ashley's heart froze in her throat. "I'm doing a series of articles about the politicians in the primary . . . and, well, I'm starting with Trevor Daniels."

"Mr. Daniels wasn't here today," Ashley replied, sensing that she didn't want to become embroiled with this young man. "You should be talking to him and I have to get back to work—"

"I'll walk with you. This won't take long," he reassured her. "You're in charge of Stephens Timber, aren't you?" He was writing in a notebook, glancing at her and refusing to be put off.

"Yes. I'm the president. Several people help me handle the management. I couldn't do it alone." Involuntarily she thought of Claud and cold dread stiffened her spine.

A traffic signal on Fifth made her pause. Douglass grabbed the opportunity. "I know. But your company, at least in the past, has been very vocal in condemning environmental candidates such as Daniels."

The signal changed and Ashley stepped off the red-brick curb and onto the wet pavement. "Look, Mr. Douglass. I really don't want to give an impromptu interview right now. Perhaps if you called the office, we could arrange a time that would be convenient for both of us."

The bold reporter refused to take the hint. "Well, there's just a couple of questions."

"Really, I don't think—"

"You're Lazarus Stephens's daughter, right?"

"Of course, but—"

"His only child, the one who got involved with Trevor Daniels several years ago."

"If you'll excuse me," Ashley stated, increasing the length of her stride. The offices of Stephens Timber Corporation were now in view. Ashley was never more glad to see the renovated turn-of-the-century hotel sitting proudly on Front Avenue.

"Wait a minute. What do you know about this rumor that Daniels is withdrawing from the race?"

That's an easy one, and safe, too, Ashley thought to herself. "Absolutely nothing," she answered honestly. Her smile was well practiced and cool. "Now, seriously, if you'd like to continue this interview, at another time, just give the office a call." She fished in her purse, found a business card and extended it to him. "Right now I have work to do."

Grudgingly Elwin Douglass accepted the small white card and slipped it into his wallet.

Ashley pushed open the wide glass door of the building and effectively ended the interview. Her chin was held proudly, her strides determined. Despite the warnings from Everett Woodward, and the unspoken insinuations from the reporter, she knew that she had to see Trevor again.

Tonight.

Chapter Ten

Twilight had fallen by the time Ashley arrived at Trevor's stately home. Despite the gathering darkness, Ashley could see that the grand two-story structure hadn't changed much in the past eight years. Built of cedar timbers and bluestone, the English manor stood proudly on the banks of the silvery Willamette River.

Sharp gables angled against the steep roofline, and ancient fir trees guarded the estate. Leaded windows winked in the harsh glare of security lights, which illuminated the rambling structure and cast ghostly shadows over the dormers.

Gathering her purse and her composure, Ashley got out of her car and walked up the rough stone path to the front door. Though she had entered that door dozens of times in the past, her heart began to thud anxiously as she ascended the steps of the stone porch and braced herself for Trevor's inevitable rejection.

Everett's warning echoed dully in her mind—*Leave the poor bastard alone.* What did that mean? It was more than a threat; the campaign manager's words sounded like a plea, as if Everett was attempting to protect Trevor.

The thought sent cold desperation racing through Ashley's bloodstream. Why did Trevor need protecting? He had always been a strong, proud man, capable of taking care of himself and finding a way of getting what he wanted in life. He had always stood alone, fighting whatever battles he had to without anyone's help.

Unable to dispel the overwhelming sense of dread settling upon her, she rang the doorbell and waited impatiently. The melodic chimes sounded through the solid wood door, but there was no evidence of life from within the huge house. Fear for the man she loved took a stranglehold on her throat.

The scent of burning wood drifted in the air, indicating that a fire was burning in one of the massive fireplaces within the manor.

She stood alone on the porch and the only sound that interrupted the stillness of the night was her own irregular breathing. Nervously, she stretched upward on the toes of her shoes and peered into the closest window. The room into which she was looking was dark, but there were soft lights glowing in the far doorway, as if illumination from another room was filtering down the corridor. Apparently whoever it was within the manor preferred his privacy.

After a few quiet minutes of indecision, Ashley tossed her hair over her shoulders and rapped sharply on the dark wood door. She had come to see Trevor and she was bound and determined to find him, even if it took her all night. Whoever was in the house would just damned well have to get off his duff and answer the door. After eight years, she was sick and tired of waiting.

Her heart was beating wildly when she heard footsteps approaching the door.

It opened with a moan and she found herself staring

into the anxious blue eyes of the man she loved with all her heart. He looked older than she remembered; his hair was unkempt, his eyes dull. *He looks as if he's been to hell and back,* she thought to herself. He was a far cry from the strong, unbeaten man with the flash of determination in his eyes that she remembered so well. Her heart twisted in silent agony for him and the pain he bore.

"Ashley?" Trevor asked, leaning between the door and the frame, as if he were too tired to stand unaided. The scent of Scotch lingered in the air.

His voice was surprisingly indecisive and the thrusting determination of his jaw was undermined by the painful questions clouding his eyes. A stubble of beard darkened his chin and his skin was stretched tightly over gaunt facial features. His clothes consisted of worn jeans and an unbuttoned flannel shirt, which was faded and rumpled, with the sleeves rolled over his elbows as if he hadn't wasted the time or the effort to change in several days. When he looked into her eyes, the rigid lines near his mouth softened slightly and the tension in his shoulder muscles slackened.

"Ashley . . . dear God, woman, is it really you?"

She hesitated. Nothing could have prepared her for the tired and broken man she was facing. A faint smile touched the corners of his mouth, but even that seemed an effort. Tears of misunderstanding filled her eyes.

"Oh, Trevor, what's happened to you?" she whispered, her voice catching in the dark night.

"Nothing that matters. At least not now." He closed his eyes as if to push aside the demons playing with his mind. "I've missed you, lady," he admitted roughly, and he opened the door a little wider.

It was all the encouragement she needed. With a

strangling sob, she ran to him and wrapped her arms securely around his neck to hold on to him in quiet desperation. All the old barriers that had held them apart for so many years semed to crumble and fall. His arms held her securely, crushing her body with the power of his, as if he, too, were afraid that she was only a figment of his imagination and would vanish into the night as quickly as she had appeared.

Silvery tears streamed down her face and she drank in the familiar scent of him, all male and warm. There was the lingering trace of Scotch on his breath. When he pressed his lips to hers, she felt as if she would melt into the polished oak floors of the grand entry hall.

"I thought I'd lost you," he rasped, and for the first time Ashley noticed the tears gathering in his eyes. Never before had she seen Trevor cry and there was something endearing in the knowledge that this proud man cared enough to let her see his weakness.

"Shhh . . . I'm here now. That's all that matters," she murmured, smoothing the disheveled chestnut hair from his eyes and kissing his tear-stained cheeks.

"I won't let you leave me again," he vowed, recovering his composure and kicking the door closed with his foot.

"If I remember correctly, Senator, it was you who left me."

"Not eight years ago, lady. That's when I made my mistake with you. I should never have let you walk out of my life."

"And I shouldn't have walked—"

"Amen."

With a quick movement, he bent and slipped one arm

under the crook of her knees, lifting her lithely off her feet.

"What are you doing?" she murmured into his neck as he started to carry her to the back of the house.

"What I should have done a long time ago," he returned. "I'm going to make love to you until you promise that you'll stay with me forever." His words pierced her heart like silver needles, reminding her of a past that held them together only to push them apart. "I've made more than my share of mistakes in my life, but not tonight. I've waited too long for you to show up on my doorstep."

"And what if I hadn't? How long would you have waited?" The warmth of his body seemed to flow into hers, and his rock-hard muscles rippled slightly when he walked. Despite the unspoken questions lingering between them, Ashley felt her body responding to Trevor's captive embrace and the sparks of possession in his eyes.

"I don't know," he replied darkly.

"You could have called."

Shame tightened his jaw. "I was afraid."

"Of me?"

He let out a disgusted sigh. "For you. Whatever it was that I was up against, I didn't want you involved."

"But you asked me to check the company records—"

He placed a silencing finger to her lips. "After our argument, I realized that it had been a mistake to ask you for your help in the first place and then, later . . ."

"Wait a minute—slow down. What the devil are you talking about?" she asked, her arms still encircling his neck. When she pulled her head away from his shoulder in order to study the anxious lines of his face, she could read nothing but worry in his gaze.

Trevor noticed the confusion in the mysterious sea-green depths of her eyes as he carried her into the den. He shook his head as if to knock out the cobwebs that had gathered in his mind from too many nights without sleep and too many bottles of alcohol to deaden his nerves.

"Not now," he whispered as he placed her on the plushly carpeted floor before the fire. Passion darkened his eyes as he brushed a strand of dark hair from her face and gazed down upon her. His finger traced the length of her jaw, pausing slightly at the pout on her lips. "Tonight you and I are going to forget about all the craziness between our families, all the lies, and all the betrayals. Tonight, we're going to concentrate on each other, just as if the slate were clean."

Her fingers grabbed hold of his wrist, effectively halting the assault on her senses from the sensual touch of his hands. Her words came out in a ragged whisper. "You act as if you expected me to show up here tonight."

His shoulders drooped from an invisible burden and he looked away from the elegant contours of her face to stare into the fire. Drawing his bent legs to his chest, he placed his folded arms over his knees and stared at the scarlet embers of the dying fire. "I didn't think I'd ever see you again," he admitted reluctantly. "I thought you were lost to me forever."

"But why?"

"I almost lost you once before when you married another man."

Ashley felt the burn of her betrayal in her chest. "You know that was a mistake, I told you so. Even Richard would admit it." She touched Trevor gently on his arm, forcing him to turn and face her again. "Don't you know I've never loved another man, not with the passion I've felt with you? I only married Richard because I didn't think you wanted me, and I'll never make that mistake again. It wasn't fair to anyone. Not you, or Richard, or myself. In the past eight years I've learned a lot; one thing is that if you find something you want, I mean really want, you've got to hold on and never let go. I learned that from you, Trevor. That and so much more."

Trevor buried his face in his hands. "I hope you know that I would never do anything to hurt you," he said.

"I do." She didn't question him for a moment. She had come to him and found him raw and naked and vulnerable. For the first time in her life she knew that he cared, that he had always cared as much as he could allow himself.

"And the last thing I would want would be for you to be subjected to any kind of danger."

"Of course—Trevor, why are you talking like this?"

He turned to study her worried expression. Her fingers on his forearm moved slowly, soothingly against his skin. He swallowed against the uncomfortable lump which had formed in his throat and made speech impossible. "I love you," he admitted, his eyes boring into hers.

The movement against his arm stopped abruptly and a sad smile touched the corners of Ashley's mouth. How many years had she waited to hear just those words?

Trevor took her small fingers in his and touched each one to his lips. The moist warmth of his tongue as it slid seductively against her skin forced a tremor of longing to shake her body.

Blue eyes held her fast as his hands pushed her coat off her shoulder before straying to the top button of her blouse.

"I'm not going to let you go," he promised as the first pearl fastener slid through sea-blue silk. "I'm going to keep you here, protect you, and you'll never be able to get away from me again." Another button was soon freed of its bond by the warm insistence of his finger.

Ashley's breathing was rapid, coming in short little gasps, and her heartbeat thundered in her ears. Her breasts rose and fell as his hand slid lower, to the third button. "I've never wanted to get away from you, Trevor," she rasped when her blouse parted and the firelight displayed the French lace of the camisole covering her breasts. His hands touched the silken fabric, and Ashley's fingers wrapped around his wrist to forestall the attack on her senses. There were things she needed to know. Questions that had no answers.

"Why didn't you call or come to me?" She looked up at the strained angles of the face, shadowed now in the fire's glow. There was a weariness about him and the smile he rained on her was bitter, filled with agonized defeat.

"It's better this way. I couldn't take a chance of placing you in danger."

Regardless of the passion smoldering in his midnight-blue gaze, the set of his jaw was grim and rigid. His shirt hung open and as he leaned over her, she noticed that the muscles of his chest were tense and strained. There was no bandage to swath his abdomen, but a jagged red scar sliced across the tanned skin, reminding her of the reason he had sought her out in the lonely mountains.

Lightly, her fingers traced the scar. Trevor sucked in his breath and closed his eyes, as if in pain.

"What's with all this talk about danger?"

He paused a long moment and stared down at the vulnerable and beautiful woman lying on the carpet. Her mysterious eyes were heavy with seduction and the fine lace of her camisole couldn't hide the twin points of her nipples straining against the flimsy cloth. "There's nothing to worry about now," he whispered, lowering his head to the inviting cleft between her breasts. "I'll take care of you. . . ."

She felt the heat of his tongue slide against the lacy fabric as a slumbering desire began to awaken within her. She was lost in her love for this man. Seeing some of his pain and worry only intensified her yearning to be a part of him and his life.

His fingers twined in the ebony strands of her hair. He whispered words of love against the sensitive shell of her ear before his lips pressed against hers with the fire of too many nights of lonely restraint.

Passion parted her lips and she eagerly accepted the touch of his tongue against hers. Her hands pushed his shirt off his shoulders, lingering over the smooth, hard muscles of his upper arms as the cotton garment slid silently to the floor.

"Make love to me," he murmured when her hands touched his belt and hesitated at the buckle. He rubbed against her, making her achingly aware of the urgency of his desire stretching the faded denim of his jeans.

She moaned in response and slowly removed his pants, letting her fingers slide in a familiar caress down the length of his lean thighs and calves. The corded muscles tensed at her gentle touch, and when her fingers slid against the tender arch of his foot, he began to shake from the restraint he placed upon himself.

Passion glazed his eyes. When at last he was freed of his clothing, he stretched out beside her and gently pushed a satiny strap off her shoulder. The result was that one of her breasts was bared to him. He studied the delicious, ripe mound, before cupping its swollen weight with his palm.

"I love you," he whispered again, lowering his head and taking the taut nipple into his mouth. His tongue circled the straining dark peak, moistening and teasing the ripe bud until Ashley moaned in bittersweet ecstasy.

At last he placed his lips around her breast and began to suckle, drawing out the sweetness within her until she thought she would go mad with desire. She cradled his head in her hands, holding him closer, wishing that she could offer more to him than just her body.

When Trevor finally lifted his head to gaze into her eyes, Ashley's heart felt like a bird trapped in a gilded cage as it fluttered wildly against the prison of her ribs. The shadowed corners of the room seemed distant. All she could see were the bold features of Trevor's face as he slowly lifted her camisole over her head.

After discarding the unwanted garment, his fingers trailed slowly up her stockinged legs.

"Trevor . . . please," she murmured tremulously before feeling him pulling her skirt and underthings down her hips. Soon she was lying naked with him.

Perspiration dampened his torso and gleamed like oil in the fire glow. He kissed her softly on the lips and rubbed his body against hers, all the while watching for the subtle changes in her expression.

"I want you," she whispered to the unspoken questions in his knowing eyes.

"That's not enough."

She swallowed the hot lump in her throat, understanding the words he yearned to hear. A coaxing hand rubbed against her breast in gentle circles, breaking her concentration and causing the liquid fire within her to pulse through her veins.

She was incapable of thinking of anything but this man lying atop her, teasing her gently by rubbing his rigid length over the soft slopes of her body.

"I love you, Trevor," she said again, her heartbeat echoing in the dark room. "I always have."

A sheen of perspiration covered her body and trickled between her breasts. Slowly, Trevor's head lowered to catch the salty droplet with his tongue. "And I love you, Ashley. . . ." His head lifted and his eyes held hers with all the passion of eight lost years. "I never stopped."

With his traitorous admission, he closed his eyes and gently forced her knees apart, surrendering at last to the fire in his loins and the seduction in Ashley's sea-green eyes. He entered her slowly, but with a determined thrust that claimed her as his own. For too many years he had ached for another man's woman, and in the rush of heat building within him, he attempted to expunge forever the mark of Richard Jennings from Ashley's soul. She was his woman now and forever. If he'd learned anything in the past few weeks it was that nothing else in life was worth a damn.

Trevor's torment was evident in the strain on his face

and the unleashed power of his lovemaking. Never had their coupling been more bittersweet than now, and Ashley gave herself to the authority of his touch. The sweet fury within her began to rage, hotter and hotter, demanding release until, at last, she convulsed in a passion born of years of denial.

"Trevor," she cried as she felt his answering shudder, and his weight fell against her. Tears glistened in her eyes and when his breathing slowed, he rolled off her before tenderly cradling her head against his shoulder.

"Nothing will ever come between us again," he vowed, his voice rough with emotion and his breath ruffling her hair.

"How can you be so certain?"

"Because for the first time in weeks, I feel like the master of my own destiny." Softly he kissed the tears from her eyes and fought against his own. "You and I, lady, we're going to get through this and we're going to get through it together."

"If only I could believe—"

"Believe."

She wrapped her arms securely around the man she loved, to drown in the scents mingling in the room— the smell of burning wood, the gentle tang of sweat and the muskiness of stale Scotch.

Tenderly he smoothed her hair away from her face. "I was afraid that you would never come here," he stated, blue eyes regarding her solemnly.

"But I called—"

"And no one answered."

"I left word at the campaign headquarters. The receptionist said you'd call me back."

Trevor stiffened beside her. "When?"

"Yesterday afternoon."

His shoulders relaxed slightly. "I've avoided that place," he admitted, "and I didn't answer the phone when I was here."

"But why?" She touched his shoulder lightly. "What's going on with you? The rumor's out that you're pulling out of the race."

"Is that why you came here tonight?" he demanded, his eyes instantly glittering with smoky blue fire.

"No. But it made me realize I had to see you again . . . touch you. There are things we need to discuss."

Trevor managed a beguiling smile. "We will, after I fix you something to eat."

"I'm not hungry," she began to protest.

"Come on, indulge me, I'm starving."

"What you're doing is avoiding the issue."

"In the manner of a true politician." He stood up and pulled on his jeans before tossing her clothes to her. "If you want to talk, you'd better get dressed. Otherwise, I won't be liable for what happens." His eyes slid seductively down her body and lingered at the swell of her breasts. "You're too damned beautiful for my own good."

Ashley smiled wryly as she stepped into her skirt and slid the camisole over her head. While adjusting the zipper of the slim skirt, she caught Trevor staring at her. He was leaning against the fireplace and his arms were crossed over his chest as he watched her work with the obstinate zipper.

"A lot of help you are," she muttered.

"If I come over there and touch you, you can bet that I would be pulling down instead of up."

Her head snapped upward. "You were the one who wanted me to get dressed."

"You got it all wrong, lady."

"Don't I always?"

He shook his head and laughed. "You wanted to talk and I told you that would be impossible, unless you had some clothes on. Otherwise, I might get distracted."

"Promises, promises," she teased just as the zipper locked into place.

Trevor's eyes flashed ominously. "I'm not through with you yet, you know. And every time you tease me, I'll extract my own kind of punishment on you later."

"Sure of yourself, aren't you?" Ashley cocked her head to the side and her dark hair framed her face in soft curls.

Trevor shrugged, refusing to be baited by her coy mood, though he wondered to himself how one woman could tear his guts out with a coquettish toss of her head. "With you, I'm never sure of anything."

Ashley sobered instantly. Trevor took her hand and led her to the kitchen near the back of the house.

"I don't think there's much here . . ." he said, beginning to scrounge through the contents of the refrigerator.

"Doesn't matter. I'm not the one who's starved," she pointed out, staring unabashedly at the way his jeans strained over his buttocks as he leaned into the refrigerator.

"Hmph . . . Here we go. How about an omelet?"

"Anything—would you like me to cook?"

"Not on your life." Then, when he looked up, he smiled disarmingly. "It might be safer if you did."

Ashley was glad for an excuse to keep busy. While whipping the eggs and grating the cheese, she could feel

Trevor's eyes on her and for the first time in weeks she was completely relaxed, as if she had come home from a long and tedious journey.

They ate the meal in silence, and Ashley savored each sweet second she shared with Trevor.

"So tell me," she insisted, clearing the plates from the small table in the windowed alcove just off the kitchen, "what's with all this talk about your withdrawal from the race?"

"So far that's what it is: just talk."

"Where there's smoke, there's fire," she observed.

"You should know all about that."

She felt the muscles of her back stiffen, but when her eyes met his, she knew that the old animosity had mellowed and that Trevor hadn't meant to bring up his accusations against her father.

"That reminds me," she said, wiping her hands on a dish towel near the stove. "I have something for you."

His gaze sharpened. "You found some proof?"

"I wish I knew what it was," she admitted. "It's in my purse . . . in the den."

Once back in the cozy study, Trevor stoked the fire, while Ashley turned on a table lamp and extracted the documents condemning her father and cousin.

When the fire was blazing to his satisfaction, Trevor dusted his hands on his jeans and approached Ashley. She started to hand him the documents, but Trevor shook his head. "I don't want to know what you found, if it's something that will hurt you or your family."

Ashley's eyes narrowed a fraction. "I don't understand. You asked me, no, demanded is a better word, that I look for evidence against my family. For the last six weeks I've worked my fingers to the bone. Now you don't want it?"

"What I don't want is to hurt you—not anymore. If there is something in those pages—" he pointed to the papers she was clutching "—that would be better off hidden, then I think you should burn them. Right now."

He was offering her a way out, a lifeline for her father's reputation, but she couldn't accept it. If she and Trevor had any chance at happiness, it was by destroying all the myths of the past and laying to rest the lies.

Any future they might share would have to be founded on truth.

"Here." She put the papers in his hands. "Let's start over—a clean slate. Remember?"

He took the pages from her trembling fingers and sat on the hearth near the fire. "I'll be damned. . . ."

"It's what you wanted, isn't it? Proof that my father and Claud were behind the bribery charges."

His broad shoulders sagged. "Was there anything else?"

"Not that I could find," she said roughly. "John Ellis and I worked day and night with all the company records. Sure, we could have overlooked something, I suppose, but I doubt it. There was nothing I could find around the date of your accident that would lead me to believe that Claud had any part in it. As for your father's disappearance . . ." Trevor's eyes sharpened and he watched her face. "I checked, everything I could think of, as far as ten years back." She shook her head and the firelight caught in her raven-black hair.

"I suppose that may be one mystery that's never solved," Trevor thought aloud. He rubbed the tension from the back of his neck and wondered, for the thousandth time, what had happened to his father. "Now it's my turn to be honest," he stated.

Ashley's heart chilled. Had he been using her? Were all his words of love only to extract what he wanted from her? She couldn't believe it, and yet her heart was filled with dread. "About what?"

"I had a meeting with Claud."

His words settled like lead on the room. "You what?"

"I instigated a private confrontation with Claud—just yesterday. That's why I didn't show up at Pioneer Square. I was in Seattle."

"But Everett said you were in Salem."

"That's where he thought I was. If I had told him that I was flying to Seattle to have it out with Claud Stephens, Everett would have hijacked the plane."

"So what happened?" Ashley asked, almost afraid to hear.

"Claud was his usual friendly self," Trevor replied cynically.

"I'll bet." Claud's words again rang in her ears: *We can't let that son of a bitch win.*

"He wanted, make that insisted, that I pull out of the senatorial race. There had already been some rumors to that effect and Claud wanted to substantiate them."

"But that's ridiculous."

"Precisely what I told your cousin."

"And?"

Trevor rubbed his chin and looked intently at Ashley. "When I refused, Claud got a little nasty. He told me that if I didn't withdraw, he would see to it that not only was my name dragged through the mud, but yours as well. He thought the public would want to be reminded of our past association, and he insinuated that he thought it would make good copy for the local papers, including the *Morning Surveyor*."

Ashley sagged into a recliner by the window. How far would her cousin go to get what he wanted? Her throat was desert-dry, her knees weak, but her conviction strong. "You can't be bullied by Claud's threats."

"Not as long as I know that you're with me—on my side."

Ashley fought against her tears. "I always have been," she murmured.

He looked as if a terrible weight had been lifted from his shoulders. "Now that you're safe, nothing else matters."

"Except your career."

"Damn my career."

"Trevor, you've worked too long and hard to give up now. It's all within your grasp. Everything you've wanted."

His blue eyes darkened savagely. "What I want, dear lady, is right here."

"Meaning what?"

"You never have understood, have you? I'm asking you to marry me, Ashley, and I'm not about to take no for an answer."

"Are you serious?" Desperately Ashley wanted to believe him, and yet, the entire night seemed like part of a dream.

"I've never been more serious about anything in my life. Will you marry me?" He strode across the room and pulled her out of the chair, forcing her to meet the sincerity of his gaze.

Tears pooled in her eyes and she managed a weak

smile. "Of course I'll marry you, Senator. I just wonder why it took eight years for you to come to your senses?"

"Because I've been a fool, Ashley. A goddamned, self-righteous, egotistical fool."

"Join the club."

Trevor laughed aloud before scooping her off her feet and carrying her through the darkened house and up the stairs to his bedroom.

Chapter Eleven

When Ashley awoke the next morning, Trevor was already out of bed. She stretched in the cool sheets and smiled as she remembered making love to Trevor long into the night. They had spent the dark hours passionately entwined in each other's arms, with the only interruption being one telephone call that Trevor had received in the early hours of the morning.

"I thought you weren't taking any calls," Ashley had grumbled groggily when she glanced at the digital display of the clock on the nightstand. The luminous numbers had indicated that it was nearly two in the morning.

"I'm not," had been Trevor's cryptic reply. "Only those that come in on my private line, like this one. Then I know it's important." She felt as if he were holding back something from her but she was too tired to care. After his brief explanation, he had reached for the phone and taken the call, which had been lengthy and very one-sided.

Ashley hadn't been able to decipher Trevor's end of the conversation, and she had been too sleepy to concentrate. Before Trevor had finished talking, she had curled up around him and drifted off to sleep, warm and content as he stroked her hair with one hand while holding the telephone with the other. She had felt the coiled tension in his rigid muscles and had wondered vaguely if there was something seriously the matter, but she had fallen back into a dreamless sleep without any answers to her questions.

This morning the entire incident loomed before her and bothered her a little, but she shoved her worried thoughts aside.

"Your imagination is working overtime again," she chastised herself with a self-mocking smile.

After taking a quick shower, she put her clothes on and brushed her hair before walking down the curved oak staircase to the main floor of the house. The warm morning smells of hot coffee and burning wood greeted her. Ashley was smiling when she breezed into the kitchen looking for Trevor.

The room was empty. There were signs that Trevor had been there; the coffee had finished dripping through the coffeemaker into the clear glass pot, and the morning newspaper had been brought into the house and torn apart. Several sections were still lying haphazardly on the table near the bay window. Ashley scanned the headlines and noticed that the front page of the paper was missing.

It was then she heard the low, angry rumble of Trevor's voice coming from the direction of the den. With quickening steps, Ashley followed the sound. What could have happened? The sketchy memory of the late-night telephone call entered her mind and her heart began to race.

Trevor sounded furious. His rage shook the stately timbers of the old house. "This is the last straw," he vowed and swore descriptively.

When she approached the door of the study, she paused, not wanting to eavesdrop on a private conversation.

"I want to know who in the hell is responsible," Trevor nearly shouted into the receiver and then waited impatiently for the person on the other end of the phone to respond. "Well it's a hell of a way to run a campaign, if you ask me. . . . What? Yeah, I'm not going anywhere." He looked pointedly at his watch. "See ya then."

Ashley noticed the lines of strain in the rigid set of his jaw and she remembered his look just the night before when he had seemed so beaten. Her mouth went dry when she realized that he hadn't been honest with her. There was still a secret gnawing at his insides and she knew instinctively that it had something to do with her. He looked as if he were a man possessed.

When he slammed the receiver down, his mouth was drawn into a thin, determined line. Rubbing the tension from the back of his neck and shoulders, he closed his eyes and stretched. "Damn!" he muttered, thinking he was alone.

"What happened?" Ashley asked. His eyes flew open and he turned his head in her direction.

"What hasn't?" His fingers rubbed anxiously against the heel of his hands. "Looks like Claud beat me to the punch."

"What do you mean?"

Trevor cocked his head in the direction of the front page of the newspaper, which was lying near the phone on his desk. "See for yourself," he invited with a dark scowl.

Ashley crossed the room, reached for the paper and as her eyes scanned the headlines her stomach began to knot painfully. "Oh, my God," she whispered when she found the article about Trevor. The by-line indicated that the story had been written by Elwin Douglass, the young reporter who had accosted her at Pioneer Square just the previous afternoon. Ashley felt her knees beginning to buckle and she had to lean against the bookcase for support.

The article was a scandalous piece of yellow journalism about Trevor and his affair with the daughter of Lazarus Stephens, who was currently president of Stephens Timber Corporation. Slanted in such a manner as to present the worst possible image of Trevor, the story, which had fragmented pieces of the truth woven into a blanket of lies, suggested that Ashley and Trevor had been lovers for the past eight years, even during her brief marriage to Richard Jennings.

Ashley swallowed against the nausea rising in her throat. There were enough facts within the text of the article to make the report appear well researched. It would be blindingly obvious to any reader that someone close to the story had been interviewed.

The premise of the article was that since Trevor was so close to his own family's business, as well as entrapped in a relationship with Ashley Stephens Jennings, of Stephens Timber, he couldn't possibly support a campaign of wilderness protection and environmentalism with any modicum of sincerity in his bid for the Senate.

The truth of the matter is, the article concluded, *that our would-be senator spends more time with people closely associated with business and industry than with the environmentalists who support him. Trevor Daniels*

*seems to be able to speak out of both sides of his mouth
with great ease and little conscience.*

Ashley's face had drained of color and she was trembling by the time she finished reading the condemning article. "This is all a lie," she said, shaking the crumpled paper in the air indignantly.

"You can thank dear cousin Claud for that," Trevor replied, pacing the floor.

"Dear God, I'm so sorry," Ashley whispered, lowering her head into her palm.

"For what? Being related to that bastard? You didn't have much choice in the matter."

"No, you don't understand. I don't think Claud was behind this. Yesterday, at Pioneer Square—I had gone there to look for you, and when you didn't show up, I approached Everett. . . ."

Trevor's head snapped up to look in her direction and his dark gaze hardened. "Go on," he suggested. A cold feeling of dread was beginning to steal over him. What was Ashley admitting?

She lifted her palms in a supplicating gesture before letting them fall to her sides in defeat. "When Everett left, I began to walk back to the office and this guy, Douglass, started walking with me and began asking questions. You know: Wasn't I Ashley Jennings? Didn't I know Trevor Daniels? Was it true that I was president of Stephens Timber? That sort of thing."

"And you talked to him?" The gleam in Trevor's eye was deadly.

"No! At least I tried not to. But he wouldn't stop walking with me . . . kept requesting an interview." She shook her head at her own folly. "I refused, of course, only answering his questions as briefly and politely as possible. I guess I didn't want to look like a snob. Anyway, he kept asking about an interview and I told him to talk to the office and make an appointment." She shrugged her slim shoulders. "It was stupid of me."

Trevor squeezed his eyes shut tightly and rubbed his temples. "So how did this guy know you would be there?"

"He couldn't have. I didn't tell anyone."

"Not even Claud?"

"He was out of town, remember, in Seattle talking to you."

"But he must have known. Somehow. Someone at the office must have told him."

"I don't think so. I wouldn't have gone to the rally if I thought he would find out about it."

"So you don't trust him either?" Trevor cocked a questioning black brow in her direction. A guarded secret lurked in his dark gaze.

"Of course not, at least not since we found the evidence against him. And one day I walked into his office and overheard him telling someone that . . . well, I don't know for sure if he meant you, he never said your name, but he said, 'We can't let that son of a bitch win. . . .' When he saw me he pretended that the conversation was about an ad campaign, but—"

"You didn't believe him?"

"No."

"Unless I miss my guess, Claud's behind all this." The doorbell rang and Trevor frowned. "That must be Everett. Watch out, he's fit to be tied."

"Aren't you going to answer it?"

Trevor shook his head. "He has a key. He just rings the bell to warn me—"

"Why?"

A sly smile slanted across Trevor's handsome face and he trailed a familiar finger along the curve of her jaw. "Just in case I'm in bed with a beautiful woman."

"Give me a break."

"I'll give you more than that." His dark eyes penetrated the sadness in her gaze. "Buck up," he suggested, squeezing her shoulders fondly. She felt the strength and determination of his character in his touch. "We'll rise above all this political dirt."

"I don't see how." As far as Ashley was concerned, everything she'd hoped for, especially a future with Trevor, was slipping away from her. "Maybe you should tell me everything. Trevor, I know that something's bothering you—"

Everett Woodward stormed into the den in a rage. His face was puckered into a belligerent scowl that darkened when he saw Ashley. He tossed his briefcase and a copy of the *Morning Surveyor* onto the couch before glaring pointedly at Trevor.

"Well, that's it—the ball game," Everett announced without the civility of a greeting. "All that work and effort right down the proverbial drain."

"Don't you think you're overreacting?" Trevor interposed with a bitter smile.

"Overreacting? *Overreacting!*" Everett retorted, his round face going beet red. "For God's sake, man, your career is on the line here, and you have the audacity to suggest that I'm—"

"Jumping off the deep end."

Everett let out a long, bewildered breath. "What're you doing here?" he asked Ashley when he turned his attention away from Trevor and trained his furious light eyes on her. "Was this Claud's idea, too?"

"That's enough, Everett," Trevor warned. "Ashley's staying here." There was a fierceness in Trevor's voice that made Ashley shudder. His fingers, which had touched her lightly on the shoulder, gripped her more savagely, as if in proof of his possession.

"You're joking!"

"Not at all. We're going to get married as soon as possible."

"Not on your life! You can't; not now! The press will have a field day with the both of you," Everett exclaimed, stunned, his eyes widening behind thick glasses. He took hold of Trevor's sleeve and looked into the candidate's eyes. "Not now, Trevor. You can't associate with Ashley or anyone else at Stephens Timber without looking like a hypocrite. You've already lost points in the most recent polls. All those rumors about withdrawing from the race really hurt you, and now this." He pointed an outraged, shaking finger at the condemning newspaper on the couch. "The last thing you can do right now is announce an engagement to the president of Stephens Timber, for Christ's sake!"

"I said we're going to get married."

Everett was thinking fast when he turned pleading eyes upon Ashley. "Can't you talk some sense into him? What would waiting another year hurt? The campaign would be over—he'd be comfortable in Washington. You could get married then."

"Forget it, Everett. I've made my decision." Trevor's voice was firm; his determination was registered in the tight muscles surrounding his mouth.

"Oh, Lord," Everett said with a sigh. He sunk into the soft cushions of the couch before swearing roundly. "I need a drink."

"It's only ten in the morning—"

"Make it a double."

Trevor smiled at the campaign manager's pale complexion. "How about champagne? To celebrate?"

"Scotch."

Trevor laughed aloud and poured the portly man a stiff drink. Everett accepted it gratefully, took a long swallow and sighed audibly. "I don't suppose you'll name your first child after me, will you?" He raised his sheepish eyes in Ashley's direction.

"We'll see," she said with a smile, relieved that the tense confrontation had abated.

"You're serious about this, aren't you?" Everett asked Trevor.

Trevor cast a meaningful smile at Ashley. "More serious than I've ever been in my life."

"Even if it means losing the election?"

"No matter what."

Again Everett let out a defeated sigh. "Well, just for the record, I think this is political suicide. You're going to alienate every voter in this state. And if you think today's article was bad, just you wait. The press will cut you to ribbons and make today's story seem like a piece of cake.

"Just for once, it would be nice if you would do things the conventional way." He looked at Trevor's thick, unruly hair, the faded jeans and the cotton shirt with the rolled-up sleeves. "But then you never do, do you?"

Trevor crossed his arms over his chest and frowned at his campaign manager and friend. "Do you want to resign?"

Everett weighed the decision. "No. At least not yet, unless you'd rather have someone else."

"Don't be ridiculous." Trevor forced a smile that was as charming as it was self-effacing. "Who else would put up with me?"

"No one in his right mind."

"Good." Trevor clasped Everett's hand. "Then everything's settled."

"I wouldn't say that." Everett wiped the accumulation of sweat that beaded his balding head. "Oh, hell. Let's go over campaign strategy, what little there is left of it."

The two men discussed politics on the leather couch in the study while Ashley poured them each a cup of coffee. After she had placed the cups on the scarred oak table, Trevor took hold of her wrist and forced her to sit next to him before asking her opinion on several issues.

Never one to withhold her opinions, Ashley pointed out what she considered flaws in the campaign, and even Everett had to grudgingly agree with some of her opinions. More than once, out of the corner of her eye, she caught Everett silently nodding encouragement to her, while she explained her feelings regarding Trevor's campaign and the issues.

Trevor smiled at her continually and attacked Everett's

arguments calmly. He explained that he wasn't against the timber industry as a whole. How could he be? Daniels Logging Company was a part of his heritage. He only objected to some of the shady business practices of a few of the companies, a prime example being Stephens Timber.

"I still think you should wait to announce your engagement," Everett offered, a hopeful light showing in his eyes. "At least until after the primary. Once you're the party's candidate—"

"No dice."

"But with this article and all, it might look as if you're buckling under to bad press."

"I don't care how it looks."

"All right, all right," the campaign manager said in utter defeat. "Have it your way—you always do anyway." He snapped his briefcase closed and sighed. The round man left the house shaking his balding head.

"Maybe you should listen to him," Ashley suggested, once Everett had driven away and Trevor had closed the door to take her into his arms.

"Why start now?"

"I'm serious—"

"So am I." They were standing in the foyer of the large house. Thin shafts of wintry sunlight pierced through the long windows on either side of the door. The strong arms around her tightened.

"Look, lady, you're not weaseling out of this marriage no matter how hard you try."

"But your career—"

"Can go to hell if it means I have to knuckle under to the Claud Stephenses of the world. I'm sick and tired of worrying about how anything I do will reflect on my political image. I like to think that I learn from my mistakes, and I'm not about to repeat them. You're going to be my wife come hell or high water!"

"As if I don't have any say in the matter."

"You said plenty last night," he reminded her, kissing her tenderly on the lips. A warm rush of desire began to flow through her.

Ashley smiled and shook her head. Being in Trevor's arms made concentration on anything but his exciting touch impossible. "So what are we going to do about Claud?"

The smile that spread slowly across Trevor's face was positively sinful. He reached behind her and grabbed two coats from the curved spokes of the brass hall tree. After helping her with her down-filled garment, he slid his arms into a denim jacket.

"I doubt that we'll have to worry about Claud much longer," Trevor stated cryptically as he led her out of the front door and draped his arm over her shoulders.

"What have you done?"

"Something I should have done about six months ago. I hired a private investigator." They walked along a brick path leading around the great house toward the river. "He's been on the case for about a month, I guess."

"And that's who you were talking to last night," Ashley suddenly realized. Perhaps now he would explain everything and drive away the lingering doubts in her mind.

"Right." Trevor winked broadly. "With what this guy has found out on his own and the evidence you and John Ellis supplied, I think we'll have enough proof of Claud's illegal activities to lock him up for a while."

"If he doesn't get to you first."

"I'm not too worried about that." Taking her chilled hand in his, he led her to the banks of the silvery Willamette. The wind on the water was brisk, causing whitecaps to swell on the swiftly flowing current. Trevor leaned against the trunk of a barren maple tree and placed his arms securely around her waist. She leaned against him, feeling the warmth of his body surrounding hers while the chill winter wind blew against her face.

"This isn't going to be easy for you, you know," he suggested. "Claud will make it rough. How will you feel if you have to testify against him?"

She shrugged her shoulders. "I don't know. I guess I'll have to wait and see how involved he is."

"Oh, he's involved all right. Right up to his scrawny mustache."

Ashley closed her eyes and fought against any feelings of sympathy she might harbor for her cousin. "You know there's no love lost between us. I swear that he wanted to kill me when he found out that Dad hadn't disinherited me as the rest of the family had thought. I was hoping that he would learn to live with the fact that I own the majority of shares of the corporation, but . . ." She sighed and shrugged her slim shoulders. "I doubt if he'll ever really accept that I'm his boss. It's hard for him, but that's no excuse for what he's put you through. I just kept him on the payroll because the company needed his expertise and because I wasn't sure that he had done everything you thought. . . . Now I know differently."

She felt the strain in Trevor's body and his arms circled her as if to protect her from all the evil and injustice in the world. Once again she had the feeling that there was something bothering him, a secret he was afraid to divulge.

His cold lips brushed against the crook of her neck. "I think that you should leave," he cautioned.

The words hit her with the force of an arctic gale. Hadn't he just insisted that she marry him? "Leave—to go where?"

"Maybe you should go out of town, just for a couple of days. Until I get some things ironed out."

"But why?"

"Because the press is going to be all over me. And you. Everett wasn't kidding when he said that they'll put us through hell once they find out that we're going to get married. And when the story about Claud breaks—I doubt if either of us will have a minute's peace." He let out a weary gust of breath that misted in the frigid morning air. "As a matter of fact, I'll bet we get more than our share of visitors this afternoon. Everett said that several reporters had already tried to contact me at campaign headquarters. It's just a matter of time before they show up here."

"That may be true, but I'm not leaving," Ashley decided with a proud toss of her head.

"Haven't you listened to a word I've said?" Was there a thread of desperation in his words?

"And that's why I'm staying." She turned to face him and held his square jaw between her hands. "I'm tired of running from everything, including the truth. If I'm going to marry you, and you can be sure that I am, then I'd better get used to the occupational hazards of being a senator's wife."

"If I win."

"*When* you win."

A slow-spreading smile creeped over Trevor's handsome features and the sun seemed to radiate from the midnight blue of his eyes. "You're an incredible woman," he whispered, his throat feeling uncomfortably swollen. "And I don't want to do anything that would put you in jeopardy. I can't lose you, not again."

"You won't. Hey, I've seen my share of bad press," Ashley stated, thinking of all of the gossip surrounding her father and the family business, "and I think I can handle whatever they dish out."

"I can't talk you into leaving, just for a couple of days?"

"It would be a waste of your breath and my time."

"So you intend to stay."

"Forever," she said with a sigh as his arms crushed her against him.

Trevor pressed his lips against her black hair. "You may as well know that I'm not into long engagements."

"Neither am I." She clung to him and listened to the steady, comforting beat of his heart, knowing she could face anything the future had to offer, as long as she was with the man she loved.

"Then, next month. Or sooner."

She smiled against the coarse denim of his jacket. "We have plenty of time," she whispered as tears of happiness pooled in her eyes.

Two hours later, after breakfast, the first reporter called. Trevor took the call, declined an interview, referred the reporter to Everett Woodward and slammed down the receiver.

"Well, it's started," he said, his piercing blue eyes holding her gaze. "If you want out, you better make a hasty exit."

"Not on your life."

Quickly she called Mrs. Deveraux to explain the situation, in case any reporters started looking for her. The fussy old woman burst into tears of happiness when Ashley mentioned that she and Trevor were going to be married.

"And here I was worried about you," Francine exclaimed, clucking her tongue. "I should have guessed that you never got over that man."

"It's not quite like it appears in the papers," Ashley stated, hoping to start rectifying the damage to her reputation that the *Morning Surveyor* had wrought.

"Of course it isn't. Who would believe a story like that?" Francine asked indignantly.

"No one, I hope. Look, I'll come back to the house later in the day and pick up a few of my things."

"Good. Then you can tell me all about it. Oh, I almost forgot," the housekeeper stated as an afterthought. "Your cousin has been calling this morning—"

"Claud?" Ashley asked, and Trevor, overhearing the name, whirled to face her. Every muscle on his face was pulled taut.

"He needs to talk to you."

"Isn't he still in Seattle?"

"Oh, no. He got back into town sometime last night, I think." Ashley was sure that Claud wasn't due back into town until the day after next, and from the deadly look in Trevor's eyes she felt instant dread.

"Did you tell him where I was?"

"Oh, no. I explained that you had gone shopping for the day and that I would give you his message."

"How did he take the news?"

"As usual. Not well."

"So things are normal," Ashley thought aloud, though the darkness in Trevor's eyes warned her that just the opposite was true. "I'll see you later."

After Ashley hung up, Trevor switched on the answering machine and began to pace from room to room like a caged animal, alternately surveying the telephone as if in indecision and then looking carefully out the windows to the long, asphalt drive.

"I take it that Claud's back in town," Trevor said, his hands pushing impatiently through his coarse hair.

"He's looking for me."

Trevor stopped midstride. "Damn! I knew I couldn't trust that bastard!"

Ashley put a hand on Trevor's forearm and found the muscles rigid. "What's going on?"

The telephone rang and the recorder automatically took the call. "You know, it wouldn't surprise me to find out that Claud called all the papers in town," Trevor remarked with an undertone of vengeance.

"You can't blame him for everything," Ashley replied with a frown.

Trevor took her hand and led her to the couch in the study. "I think it's about time you knew what we're up against," he said with obvious regret. "Pete Young, the private investigator I hired, looked into several things: the accident with my car, the bribery charges and—"

"Your father's disappearance," Ashley guessed with a shudder.

"Right. Now that the press is involved, it could get very unpleasant."

She smiled despite the dread inching up her spine. "I

know." Settling into the corner cushions, Ashiey tucked her feet beneath her and stared up at Trevor as he paced the floor.

"When I talked to Pete last night, he was sure that he had enough evidence to prove that Claud had paid to have my car tampered with. He found someone at the garage where my car was serviced who was willing to talk, for a small fee."

"So Claud paid off a mechanic to tamper with your car." Ashley felt sick inside, as if a part of her were slowly dying. She had thought her cousin capable of deceit, and bribery perhaps, but something this cold-blooded and cruel was beyond those bounds. "Dear God," she whispered, turning cold inside.

The corners around Trevor's mouth pulled downward. "According to Everett, Pete also thinks that Claud planted the story in the paper."

"But the reporter talked to me," Ashley offered tonelessly. Why was she even trying to defend her cousin?

"Because somehow he knew that you would be there, or maybe it was just a lucky guess on his part. It doesn't matter. I'll bet that Claud was involved."

Ashley lowered her forehead into her hands and gave in to the tears threatening her eyes. "I really didn't think it would all come down to this," she whispered. All the lies about her family and her father were really true.

Trevor sat on the couch beside her and kissed away the lines etching her smooth brow. "We can handle it if we just stick together."

"I thought you wanted me to leave."

He took her hand and his eyes narrowed in concern.

"I never want you to leave, but I think that it might be safer for you."

"Safer?" Her face suddenly lost all expression as the meaning of his words became clear and rang dully in her weary mind. "There's something you haven't been telling me, isn't there? A reason why you want me to go. Ever since I got here last night, I've had the feeling that there was something bothering you, as if there is some kind of danger lurking around every corner. It's more than concern about your reputation or even losing the senatorial race, isn't it?

"Trevor, what's going on? And don't give me any double talk about reporters and mudslinging." Her face was grave. "I want the truth. All of it. And I want it now."

Trevor let out a weary sigh and touched her cheek tenderly before lowering his eyes.

"What did Claud say, Trevor? When I came here last night you said something to the effect that you never thought you'd see me again. At the time, I thought you were talking about the scandal, but it's more than that, isn't it?" She noticed him wince and pale and a wave of understanding washed over her in cold rushes of the truth. Everything, all of Trevor's actions, were beginning to make sense. "Oh my God . . . Claud threatened you, didn't he? *And . . . the price was my life!*"

Chapter Twelve

Trevor closed his eyes against the cold truth. His lips whitened and he swallowed back the savage rage that had been with him for the better part of two days.

"Yes," he ground out, as if the admission itself were tearing him into small pieces, making him impotent against the injustice of the world. "Claud told me point-blank that if I didn't get out of the race, you would get hurt."

"But he only meant that he would ruin my reputation," Ashley protested weakly.

Trevor's eyes glittered dangerously. "He meant that and more. He'd feed you to the wolves if it would save his skin."

"But surely you couldn't believe—"

"What I couldn't do was take a chance with your life. I know how ruthless your cousin can be. He nearly killed me by having my car tampered with, and I'll lay you odds that he was involved in my father's disappearance."

"But he was only twenty-two."

"And a very ruthless, determined man. He learned his lessons from the master well."

"Meaning my father." Ashley slumped against the cushions of the couch, wishing there was some way to end the pain, the agony, the bitterness and hatred between the families of Stephens and Daniels.

"Are you beginning to understand what we're facing?" he asked. "That's why I think you should go away. Just until Claud is safely behind bars and the press has cooled off a little."

Ashley shook her head. "It won't matter. If I did leave, the minute I'd get back to Portland, someone would hear about it and the reporters would start to track me down. That's how it works. If I left we'd only be putting off the inevitable. As for Claud, I'm not afraid of him. I told you before that violence isn't his style. If there's dirty work to be done, he'd hire someone else to do it, and I can't really believe that he's desperate enough to harm me.

"I'm staying and we're going to fight this thing together," she finished determinedly. A small, proud smile touched Trevor's lips. Having made her decision, she straightened, slipped on her shoes and stood.

Trevor was still considering the options. She noticed that the wariness hadn't left his eyes. "Then you're staying here, with me. That way, I'll know you're safe."

"I can't just sit around here like some fearful hostage. I've got a job—"

"With Claud."

"That will be rectified very shortly."

"Then stay with me for a couple of days—"

"Just that long?"

Trevor smiled despite his fears. "You're welcome

forever, you know that. As far as going to work, forget it. You'd be too vulnerable."

"I can't—"

"Let that accountant take care of things."

"For how long?"

"As long as it takes for the private investigator to put the pieces together and convince the police that Claud's dangerous."

"Oh, Trevor, you're jumping at shadows. Claud would never hurt me."

"That's a chance I'm not willing to take."

Seeing that there was no way she could convince him otherwise, she gave in. "In that case, I'd better dash home and pack a few things."

"I think it would be safer if you stayed here."

Ashley smiled indulgently. "I've lived in these clothes for two days. I need to change into something more practical than heels, a silk blouse and a skirt. I feel positively grody."

Trevor's eyes slid down her body. "You look great."

"But I feel sticky. Now, nothing you have here is going to fit, so I'd better go home and pack a few things. I'll be perfectly safe. Mrs. Deveraux is home; I just called her a few minutes ago."

"I don't know—"

"Give me a break, Trevor."

"All right. I'll come with you," he said finally, reaching for his wallet and stuffing it into his back pocket.

"I thought you had to stay here and wait for Everett's call."

"The recorder will take the message. Or, he'll call back."

"But—"

"You're stuck with me, okay? I've worried enough

about you and I'm not about to let you out of my sight, not until I'm satisfied that you're not in any danger."

"Worrywart."

Trevor helped her with her coat and his fingers lingered on the back of her neck. "It's just that I can't take any chances," he said roughly, his voice catching on the words. "You're the most important thing in my life." Gently he touched her shoulders, forcing her to turn and face him. "Nothing else matters—my career, this house—" he gestured widely to encompass all of the estate "—nothing. Unless you're with me."

"But for so many years—"

"I was alone. I lived, Ashley, and I thought I could bury myself in my work. I guess I was somewhat satisfied. But then in December, when I saw you again, I knew that I'd been living a lie and that I could never go back to that empty life again."

"But you didn't call, or write. I didn't hear anything from you."

"Because I knew that it would be no good until we settled what had happened in the past. And that included the truth about your family as well as mine."

Just as Trevor reached for the handle of the door, Ashley heard a car roar down the driveway.

"Damn," Trevor muttered. "Too late. Some reporter must have gotten tired of leaving a message with the recorder." His blue eyes pierced into hers. "Are you ready for this?"

Ashley braced herself and her fingers twined in the strength of his. "As ready as I'll ever be."

The doorbell rang impatiently several times and then a fist pounded furiously on the door.

"Not the most patient guy around," Trevor mumbled. "I've got a bad feeling about this."

He jerked open the door and Claud rushed into the foyer, his face ashen, his eyes dark with accusations when they rested on Ashley.

"Wait a minute," Trevor said, placing his body between that of Ashley and her cousin. "What're you doing here?"

"We had a deal," Claud spat out. Then he straightened, regained a small portion of his dignity and let his cold eyes rest on Ashley. "I thought I'd find you here."

"What do you want, Claud?"

"Call him off!" her cousin blurted furiously.

"Who? What?"

"Him!" Claud pointed an accusatory finger in Trevor's direction and it shook with the rage enveloping him. "That bastard's been hounding me for the last month."

"I think you should calm down—"

"And *I* think you should leave, while you still can." Trevor's eyes snapped.

Claud stopped abruptly. "What's that supposed to mean?"

"Just that we're on to you, Stephens."

Visibly paling, Claud turned to Ashley. "He's been telling you all sorts of lies, I suppose."

Ashley held out her palm, hoping to diffuse the uncomfortable tension. She never really had been afraid of her cousin and she couldn't really fear him now. Despite Trevor's accusations, Claud was too much of a coward to try to do her physical harm. "Why don't we all go into the living room and I'll make some coffee. We can discuss whatever it is we need to, once everyone has calmed down."

"I don't know. . . ." Trevor said, his eyes calculating as he studied his opponent.

"I don't want any coffee—"

"Something stronger?" Ashley asked, watching Claud walk agitatedly back and forth in the foyer. She started toward the living room and Claud followed.

"I need to talk to you alone."

"Not on your life," Trevor boomed, falling into step with Ashley. "I'm not about to forget what you said a couple of days ago, something to the effect that Ashley was expendable and you were willing to do the expending."

"He's lying, Ash! I swear—"

"Don't waste your breath," Trevor suggested, and the look of steely determination in his eyes coupled with his tightly clenched fists convinced Claud to keep quiet.

Claud sank into one of the stiff royal blue chairs near the bay window and had to hold on to his knee to keep it from shaking. "There's been some guy following me, Ashley," he said, avoiding the deadly look on Trevor's face and concentrating on his cousin. "I don't know who or why, but I think that it's someone looking for information about the company. You know, there's kidnappings all the time—families with money."

"Don't flatter yourself," Trevor said with a cynical smile growing from one side of his face to the other. He sat next to Ashley on the couch, one arm curved protectively over her shoulders, the other at his side. He looked coolly disinterested, almost bored with the conversation, but he was tense, all of his muscles coiled. Ashley could feel it. If he had to, Trevor was ready to spring on Claud.

"I think someone might try to kidnap me, for God's sake!"

"Why? Who would pay the ransom?" Trevor demanded, his lips curling bitterly.

"Ashley, please. Can I talk to you alone?" Claud was beginning to sweat. Tiny droplets formed on his forehead and there was a note of desperation in his voice.

"Forget it."

"I can speak for myself," Ashley intervened, but Trevor would hear none of it. He leaned forward, pushing his body closer and more threateningly toward Claud.

"While we're on the subject of kidnappings, why don't we discuss what happened to my father," Trevor suggested, his voice low and demanding. "I have an idea that you know just what went on ten years ago."

Claud lost all his color. His bravado was dismantled and he suddenly looked like a very small and frightened man. Nervously, he toyed with his mustache.

Movement caught Trevor's eye and he looked from the scared face of Ashley's cousin through the window behind Claud. "It looks as if we have more company—"

"What?" Claud's gaze moved to the long drive and he saw the police car driving toward the house. "Oh my God . . ." Turning frantic eyes on Ashley, he whispered, "You can't let this happen. Daniels is trying to frame me for something that I had no part in. Ashley—for God's sake, you're my cousin, can't you help me?"

Ashley's throat was dry. No matter how miserable Claud was, he was still her own flesh and blood. The doorbell rang impatiently just as she answered. "I'll call Nick Simpson."

"Jesus Christ, Ash, I need more than an attorney!"

"Then I suggest you start talking, and fast," Trevor insisted, "if you want to save your miserable hide." Trevor was convinced that Claud wouldn't do anything harmful to the one person he felt would save him. "Stay where you are," he warned as he left to answer the door.

Claud nearly leaped across the living room, so that he was close to Ashley. "I need to get out of here. I just want a little time, show me the back way out—"

"You can't escape like they do on TV, Claud. This isn't 'Magnum, P. I.'"

"But I haven't done anything—"

His words were cut off by the entrance of two policemen.

"Claud Stephens?" the taller of the two asked.

Claud made one more appealing look in Ashley's direction before straightening and finally finding his voice. "Yes?"

As Ashley sat in stunned disbelief, the officer read Claud his rights and escorted him outside to the waiting police car. For several minutes she sat on the couch, trying to quell the storm of emotions raging within her.

"Was that really necessary?" she asked, her eyes searching the harsh angles of Trevor's face once he returned to the living room.

"I wish it weren't," he admitted, "but whether you believe it or not, Claud can be dangerous." He noticed that Ashley had paled. She was still wearing her coat, but looked as if she were cold and dead inside.

"I don't think we should go anywhere, not for a while." He came back to the couch and wrapped comforting arms around her. "Come on," he said, squeezing her tightly, "I'll get you a drink."

"I . . . I don't think I want one."

"It's been a rough couple of days, and it's bound to get worse," he cajoled.

"Then I think I'd better keep my wits about me." She ran her anxious fingers through her blue-black hair. "And there's no reason to put off going back to the house, now that the police have Claud." She forced her uneasiness aside and tried to concentrate on Trevor and her love for him. Regardless of anything that might come between them in the future, she felt secure in his love.

"I don't think it would be wise—"

Ashley placed a steady finger to his lips. "Shhh. If I'm going to be your wife, Senator, I'd better learn to cope with crises, wouldn't you say?"

"It's going to get worse before it gets better."

"But that's what it's all about, isn't it—for better or for worse?"

"You are incredible," he said with a seductive smile.

She slapped him on the thigh and stood up, filled with renewed conviction. "Let's get a move on. I wouldn't want to miss the reporters when they get here."

Trevor groaned, but got off of the couch. "Anything you say." He laughed and kissed her lightly on the forehead.

When they returned to Trevor's home, after having tea and a lengthy discussion with Mrs. Deveraux, Trevor checked the messages on the tape recorder. As he had suspected, several reporters had called requesting interviews.

There was also a terse message from Everett to call him immediately.

Trevor dialed Everett's number and smiled wickedly as the agitated campaign manager answered.

"I thought you were going to wait for my call," Everett complained. Trevor could picture steam coming out of the campaign manager's ears.

"I had other things on my mind. . . ." Trevor's eyes slid appreciatively up Ashley's body. Dressed in jeans and a red sweater, with her black hair looped into a loose braid wound at the base of her neck, she looked comfortable and at home in Trevor's huge house.

"I'll bet," Everett replied. "Now that you and Ashley are together, you'll never be able to keep your mind on the campaign."

"That would be a shame," Trevor murmured irreverently as his eyes followed Ashley up the polished wooden stairs. She was carrying two suitcases, oblivious to his stare or the fact that her jeans were stretched provocatively over her behind as she mounted each step.

"Listen, there are a couple of things you really should know," Everett commanded. "And they have to do with Ashley and Stephens Timber."

The low tone of Everett's voice and the mention of Ashley's name captured Trevor's attention. "I'm listening."

"You'd better brace yourself," Everett warned. "Claud Stephens has started to talk. . . ."

Ashley felt his eyes on her back as she unfolded the last blouse and hung it in the closet. She whirled to face

Trevor, a sly smile perched on her lips. "What took you so long?" she asked, but the wicked grin fell from her face when she saw Trevor's expression. He was leaning against the doorframe, watching her silently and fighting the overwhelming urge to break down. "What happened?" She was beside him in an instant, placing her warm hands against his face. He managed a bitter smile filled with grief.

"The case against Claud looks pretty solid," Trevor said at length, while gazing into the misty depths of her sea-green eyes. "The private investigator I hired called Everett when he couldn't reach me."

"And?"

"Claud's having a rough time. He can't seem to make up his mind whether he needs an attorney or should plea-bargain on his own. I think he opted for the lawyer."

"I hope so," Ashley said fervently. "Claud's used to doing things his own way, and since he's a lawyer I was afraid he would try to defend himself."

"He's smarter than that." Trevor entered the room and sat down on the edge of the bed. His shoulders sagged and he forced tense fingers through his unruly chestnut hair.

"What else?" Ashley asked as she sat next to him. She felt her throat constrict with dread. Something horrible had happened to Trevor. *What?*

Trevor's midnight-blue eyes pierced into hers and his arms wrapped around her as if in support. "Claud's desperately trying to clear his own name, you realize."

"And?"

"And he's saying that Lazarus is the one who instigated the bribery charges against me last summer as well as having kidnapped my father ten years ago."

Ashley felt as if a hot knife had been driven into her heart. She slumped for a minute, but Trevor's strong arms gripped her. "It's not unexpected," she said, her voice failing her. "It's just that I hoped and prayed that Dad wasn't involved." She let out a long breath of air and realized that she had to know everything before she could start her life with Trevor.

"What happened?"

"Claud's saying that my father had gained information proving that Lazarus had used the harmful pesticide near Springfield—the one that's subsequently been linked to the deaths."

"I remember." Ashley fought against the sick feeling deep within her. Dennis Lange had been a friend of Trevor's and had died because of her father's neglect. His was just one of several families who had been inadvertently poisoned by the spraying.

"Claud seems to think that Lazarus knew what the impact of the spraying would be and the hazards it would impose on the residents as well as the environment. Lazarus panicked when he found out that my father was meeting with the lobbyist in Washington, and after the meeting, he coerced him into his car. They drove to your father's cabin—"

"No!" Not the place where she and Trevor had made love. "Not the cabin."

Trevor's hold on her shoulders increased. "Lazarus tried to buy my father's silence, and an argument ensued. Dad tried to escape from the cabin and he fell down an embankment, probably breaking his neck. Lazarus was afraid that he would be up on kidnapping, bribery and probably negligent homicide charges, so he buried my father somewhere on his land in the Cascades."

"Oh dear God," Ashley murmured, seeing the bitterness in Trevor's features. "Trevor . . . I'm so sorry, so sorry," she murmured, releasing the hot tears that had burned behind her eyelids and letting them trickle slowly down her face.

"It's not your fault—"

"But I never believed—I couldn't face it."

Gathering strength from the warmth of her body, Trevor let out a long, trembling sigh. "I knew Dad was dead, you know. I just kept hoping that I'd been wrong, that someday he'd show up again. But deep in my heart, I knew."

The news was too distressing for Ashley. She extricated herself from Trevor's embrace, walked across the room and stared out the window to the clear, ever-changing waters of the Willamette River.

"I knew that my father wasn't a warm person. And I might have even gone so far as to say that he was unthinking and therefore unkind. But I never thought of him as cruel or ruthless." She shook her head and let the tears of pain slide down her cheeks. "There's not much I can do except make a settlement with those poor victims in Springfield. It won't bring back the dead, but maybe it will help their children." Her shoulders stiffened with newfound pride. "And I'll make sure that Stephens Timber Corporation complies with every government and environmental standard as long as I'm involved," she promised.

When she walked back toward the bed, Trevor was staring at her, admiring her strength. He captured her wrist and pulled her down on the bed with him before offering kisses born of sorrow and grief.

"Don't ever leave me," he begged.

"Never . . . oh, darling." She kissed him with all the fervor her torn emotions could provide. "It's all behind us now."

The telephone rang and Trevor eyed it with disgust. "Go away," he muttered.

"It's the private line. You'd better answer it."

"It could be more bad news."

She smiled through the sheen of her tears. "Then we'll face it together." Hastily brushing her tears aside, she curled against him, feeling more loved and protected than ever.

He frowned and answered the intrusive instrument. "You and that damned recording machine!" Everett blasted. "I hate talking to those things. I just thought I'd better warn you, the press has gotten hold of Claud's story."

"I expected as much."

"Bill Orson is in a near-panic. You know he was pretty tight with Claud and the rest of the timber industry. Orson has already begun amending his stand on the environment and it looks to me that despite everything, you still have a good chance of winning the election. Orson's been in too tight with Claud Stephens to come out clean on this one."

"Good."

There was a stilted silence in the conversation. "You're still in the running, aren't you?" Everett asked.

"I'll let you know tomorrow . . . or maybe next week," Trevor replied, looking meaningfully at Ashley. "Right now I'm busy, Everett."

"What the devil?"

"How would you like to be best man at my wedding?"

"Today?"

Trevor laughed aloud. "Very soon, Everett, very soon." With his final words, he dropped the phone and took Ashley into his arms.

"Everett's not going to appreciate being treated like that," she teased.

"I don't give a damn what Everett appreciates." Slowly he removed the pins holding her hair at the nape of her neck. "Right now there's only one person I intend to satisfy."

"Your constituents wouldn't like to hear that kind of talk, Senator," she quipped.

"Oh, I don't know . . . I think it would improve my image if I were to become a happily married man."

"So this is just for the sake of the voters?"

"One in particular—she's very independent, you see." He unclasped the top button of her blouse. "But that may change once she's saddled with a husband and a family."

"A child?" Ashley asked, her breathing becoming irregular.

"Or two . . . or three!" As he counted, he undid the buttons of her blouse and kissed the white skin at the base of her throat. Ashley's heart began to swell in her chest at the thought of becoming Trevor's wife and bearing his children.

"You're very persuasive, you know," she whispered.

"Years of practice, darling."

She smiled up at the man she loved. "Do you think this

will ever work for us?" she asked. " There's been so much keeping us apart."

"All in the past," he assured her. "I told you I was never going to let go of you again, and I meant it." He touched the soft slope of her cheek. "Believe me when I tell you that I love you."

"Oh, I do, Trevor," she said with a sigh. She wound her arms around his neck, never to let go.